Earls Trip

JENNY HOLIDAY

KENSINGTON
PUBLISHING CORP.

www.kensingtonbooks.com

ISBN: 978-1-4967-4508-8 (ebook)

ISBN: 978-1-4967-4507-1

First Kensington Trade Paperback Printing: May 2024

10 9 8 7 6 5 4 3 2 1

Printed in the United States of America

For Josie
Lord help the mister who comes between me and my sister

Roy: "Who the fuck are the Diamond Dogs?"

Ted: "It's just a group of people who care, Roy. Not unlike folks at a hip-hop concert whose hands are not in the air."

—*Ted Lasso*

1

The Boys Are Back in Town

What happens on Earls Trip, stays on Earls Trip.

Usually.

In 1821, on the eighth annual Earls Trip, things took a bit of a turn.

When Archibald Fielding-Burton, the Earl of Harcourt, arrived at Number Seven Park Lane to collect his friend, Simon Courteney, the Earl of Marsden, Marsden was waiting in front of his town house.

"Hullo," Archie said, hopping out of the coach. "Ready?"

"He's been ready since seven this morning," said Mr. Janes, Simon's valet, who was stationed at attention behind his master.

"Of course he has." Archie shot an affectionate look at Simon, then a placating one at the long-suffering Janes. "Has he also been standing here since seven this morning?" Archie took the valet's sniff as affirmation. "Poor Janes. Marsden, you ought to wait inside like a properly bred person."

"Well, remember," Simon said mildly, "I'm *barely* a properly bred person."

Archie chuckled as small muscles in Janes's jaw visibly tightened. "Mr. Janes, what will you do with yourself for a fortnight without your wayward earl and his wretched wardrobe to wrangle?"

"I look fine," Simon said, and a muscle in Janes's jaw twitched.

Strictly speaking, it was true. There was nothing wrong with Simon's current ensemble or any other in his wardrobe. It was more that he tended toward the bland in all matters material, be they sartorial, culinary, or bodily. He always had. Today he was wearing a pair of buff breeches and a brown coat cut in a style that had been the height of fashion five Seasons ago when he'd ascended the earldom, and his hair . . . Well, his hair was best not discussed. Archie himself was no dandy, but he tried to keep up appearances.

As Janes supervised the loading of a small trunk into the coach, Archie picked up a valise resting on the bottom step of Simon's house—and nearly tore his arm off. "Oof. What's in here? Bricks?"

"Books." Simon climbed into the coach.

"Ah, yes." Archie was flooded with affection for his friend. Simon was so very much himself. He used to try to smuggle books out of the Winchester College library on term breaks. He was still doing it, apparently.

"Where's Effie?" Simon asked when Archie joined him inside. "I'd've thought you'd have collected him first, as his house is between mine and yours. Now you'll have to backtrack."

Simon disliked inefficiency, but perhaps not as much as he appreciated a logical argument, so Archie made one: "Yes, but unlike you, he won't be ready. He may not even remember that we're to make the trip at all. Either way, he almost certainly won't have done his packing. I'd rather go out of my way and have some company for the extraction process, since it's likely to be laborious."

"A fair point." Simon heaved an enormous sigh and slumped back against the squabs.

Archie examined his friend, cataloging the darker-than-usual circles under his eyes and the paler-than-usual cast of his skin. "All right, then?"

"Yes, yes, but I am sorely in need of respite. I've been run off my feet of late. I've been—" He cut himself off. "It is of no mind."

Archie smiled. He understood perfectly what Simon meant, because he understood Simon perfectly. The uneasy earl tended to reside in the caverns of his mind and had to be wrenched out of them periodically by his friends, which was a process he both abhorred and relished. It was as if something inside him knew he needed the respite he'd referenced, but something *else* inside him resisted. He was a man at war with himself. He always had been, and it had only gotten worse since he'd unexpectedly inherited the earldom.

Janes popped his head into the coach and closed his fingers around a stack of newspapers resting on Simon's lap. "Shall I take these, my lord?"

Simon's hands flew to the opposite edge of the papers, and a polite tug-of-war ensued.

"It's no use, Mr. Janes," Archie said. "He shall have to be weaned slowly from them, like a man from the poppy."

"Thank you, Janes. That will, uh, be all," Simon said in the voice he used when he was trying to project authority in the domestic sphere, over the staff who would always think of him as the painfully shy, seldom-seen third son of their late lord. Archie had told Simon a hundred times to use his Parliament voice at home, but somehow Simon didn't, or couldn't, and he ended up sounding like a boy playing at manhood.

Janes shot a dismayed look at Archie.

"Worry not, Mr. Janes. I shall keep his lordship in line at the posting inns, and once in Cumbria, we shall be completely alone." Archie couldn't wait. Town made him jumpy and irritable. His lungs were crying out for fresh air, his trigger finger was itching for a good hunt, and, not to put too fine a point on it, his soul was in need of a prolonged dose of exposure to his best mates.

Speaking of. One down; time to collect Effie. He rapped on the ceiling, and the coach rumbled off.

"Shall we wager on how long it will take to wrest Effie from his papers?" Archie asked a while later, as they turned onto Berkeley Square. "Or his paints. Or merely the dark depths of his imaginings?" He chuckled. "Surely there will be some manner of wresting required, is my point, and shall we lay a wager on it?"

"I'd have to be bound for Bedlam to take that wager." Simon bent his head to join Archie in peering out the window at Number Twenty. "God's teeth! Who's died?"

"I don't know!" Archie exclaimed, alarmed. The steps of the town house were strewn with straw and the door bedecked with the black ribbons of mourning.

"You don't think . . . ?" Simon's voice reflected the horror that had taken root in Archie's gut.

"*No,*" Archie said, though he was all too aware that wishing something weren't true had no bearing on whether it actually was. "We'd have heard if the earl died," Archie said to himself as much as to Simon. Effie would have come to them straight away.

It occurred to Archie, though, that someday, the old earl *was* going to die, and his son, Edward Astley, Viscount Featherfinch, would inherit the earldom. It also occurred to Archie that no one, least of all Effie himself, was prepared for that day. As they approached the door, Archie, trying to regain some equilibrium, said, "I wager it takes us seventy minutes to extract him."

"Considering that he planned this year's trip," Simon said, "I'm going to give him the benefit of the doubt and say three-quarters of an hour."

"We shall see. Loser sits backward on the journey."

"If there's even going to be a journey," Simon said as the straw crunched beneath their feet. "*Someone* has clearly died, and we can't go without Effie."

"Indeed." Well, they could. But they wouldn't. "Then we're here to pay our respects, I suppose. Still, I maintain he would have told us if something terribly dire had happened." Although Effie did tend to live in his head. Not in the same manner Simon did. Simon lived inside his Parliamentary arguments; Effie lived inside his daydreams. Whereas Simon could usually be counted on to remember to do things like eat and bathe—he saw them as necessary annoyances—often Effie could not.

Archie's knock was answered by a footman he did not recognize. The man was not wearing a mourning armband and greeted them as if nothing were amiss.

"We're here for Featherfinch," Simon said.

"I'm afraid the viscount is not at home to visitors at the moment."

"He's at home to us." Archie started for the stairs. "He's expecting us." Or, rather, he *should* be.

"I *beg* your pardon!" the footman called after them.

The housekeeper appeared, no doubt drawn by the commotion. Archie paused in his ascent. "Ah. Mrs. Moyer. We're here to collect Featherfinch for our trip."

"Your trip?" she echoed blankly before recovering herself and curtsying to them. "My lords." That caused the footman to stand straighter.

"Our trip to Cumbria?" Archie tried, though he knew full well what had happened here. Effie hadn't told any of the household staff, never mind any of his family, about his travel plans.

Mrs. Moyer wrinkled her brow and said, predictably, "I'm afraid I don't know anything about such a trip, my lord."

"The trip we take every year the second fortnight in September?" Honestly. Was Effie's dreaminess like the plague, capable of infecting the rest of the household?

At least Archie was going to win the wager.

"Mrs. Moyer, a good morning to you." Simon, able to sense Archie's rising frustration, spoke soothingly to the housekeeper. "May I ask who has passed?"

Mrs. Moyer tilted her head to one side, as if she were searching for words but coming up short. "Perhaps you ought to ask Lord Featherfinch about that."

"Are the earl and countess well?" Simon pressed.

"Oh yes, quite. They're at Highworth," she said, naming the family's Cornish estate.

"Let's go." Archie mounted the stairs and made for Effie's room, trusting Simon would follow and reflecting on what a poor job the staff was doing keeping people from Effie if they had, in fact, been instructed that he was not at home to visitors.

"Featherfinch!" Simon called as Archie knocked.

Archie, not waiting for a response, pushed open the door. "Unless someone very important has died, you had better be at the ready, or I shall—"

Edward Astley, Viscount Featherfinch and heir to the Earl of Stonely, was not at the ready.

He was also not dressed.

He was seated at his desk, naked as the day he was born, his long hair wild and tangled. "I *told* you," he said without turning from where he was madly scribbling with an overlong quill, "I *don't want* anything to eat."

When he received no answer, he turned. An expression of annoyance quickly gave way to one of astonishment as his dark eyebrows climbed his forehead. Next up in the parade of mental attitudes was delight. "Hello! Wait until you lot hear my newest sonnet. It's only half done, but I am so very pleased with it."

He started to stand, and Archie turned away, as did Simon. "For God's sake, cover yourself, man."

"Oh, yes." Some rustling and muttering followed. "All right."

Simon turned to find Effie wearing a dressing gown. Made of pale-pink silk and trimmed with lace at the elbows, it was entirely too small for the towering Effie. The hem came to his knees, and his upper arms strained against the confines of the sleeves. His dark hair hanging loose around his shoulders, together with the pallor of his face against the pink, added an almost otherworldly note to his otherwise comical appearance.

"What in God's name are you wearing?" Simon asked.

Effie looked down at himself as if he did not know the answer to that question. "Oh. Yes. I had a most unfortunate encounter with some hogweed about a fortnight ago." He winced. "I developed the most spectacular rash, mostly on my arse. You should have seen it."

"I thank Heaven I did not," Simon said drily. "I want to ask how your arse came into contact with hogweed, yet I don't."

"Better not to know," Archie agreed.

"I was painting deep in the woods at Highworth, and it was unreasonably hot," Effie began, apparently intent on relating the fate of his arse. "And I was very much alone." He cocked his head. "A silver lining: I have now learned how to identify hogweed, and I shan't be making that mistake again. As to my present attire, when I got back to the house, I was in terrible pain. The only place I could find a modicum of comfort was the bath, but one cannot live in the bath, though I made a good run at it. Sarah lent me this bloody wonderful thing, and when my rash had healed and I was preparing to head back to Town, I nicked it. You've never felt anything so wonderful as silk against your bare skin."

"Won't Sarah miss it?" Simon asked, focusing on an inconsequential logistical detail, as was his habit.

"I sincerely doubt it. She has dozens more where this came from."

It was true. Effie's sister was very likely responsible for a good portion of her modiste's annual revenue.

"I tell you, it is a magical garment. I attribute my success with this poem"—Effie gestured with an ink-stained hand at his desk, which was covered with parchment—"to the comfort and freedom it has afforded me." He tilted his head. "Well, I attribute my success to this garment and to having outfitted the house for mourning."

"Yes, who died?" Archie inquired.

"Sally," Effie said quietly.

On the one hand, this was a great relief, for Sally was—had been—Effie's parrot. On the other, she had been a beloved companion of many years, and to the sensitive Effie, full mourning protocol would not seem unreasonable.

"Oh no, I'm terribly sorry," Simon said.

"As am I," Archie said. "Sally was a good bird."

That was a lie. Sally had never shut up, and she'd never had a kind word to say about anyone. Archie wasn't going to miss her at all.

"It's all right," Effie said stoically. "She was very old, and her death was quick. She was standing on her perch one day last week, squawking happily between bites of beetroot, which was her favorite treat, when she was suddenly transported by some sort of fit. She fell to the ground, spasmed, and went still." He lowered his voice. "We were in the music room. You should have seen the picture she made against the Axminster carpet. Her vibrant green and yellow feathers, lifeless, against the pinks and reds of the carpet. An almost obscene riot of color, and yet . . . Death comes for us all, does it not? Even the most beautiful among us?" He shook his head. "You *really* should have seen it."

Archie *could* see it. He could see it because Effie could see it. That was Effie's gift, seeing beauty, or noticing it, when others didn't. Even when, perhaps especially when, that beauty was overlain by something less pretty.

"I had the house outfitted for mourning, and I came in here and thought about what a good death she'd had. I thought about those colors, and about the black ribbons outside. And I wrote this." He gestured back to the desk. "I don't like to boast, but I'm *terribly* pleased with it." Effie's poems, as much as he seemed drawn to creating them, generally caused him a great deal of pain, so this was an unusual sentiment.

"Capital." Simon pulled out his pocket watch, no doubt concerned about the wager. "Perhaps you can read it to us in the coach."

"The coach?" Effie echoed blankly.

"We're going to Cumbria?" Simon prompted.

Effie looked startled, then delighted. "Oh! Is that today?"

"It is indeed," Archie said, taking in the clothing-strewn bedchamber. When not naked—or wearing his sister's dressing gown—Effie was a clotheshorse. He was quite the opposite of Simon in that way. Yet nearly all his clothing was black. Archie had once wondered aloud why a person who always wore the same color needed so many *different* items of clothing in that color. He had received in return an impassioned lecture on cut, seasonality, and fashion. Shot silk, for example, was better suited for a ballroom than, say, sarsenet, as it reflected the light in a way that was both pleasing and mysterious.

What Archie did not see among all the clothing was a trunk or bag of any sort. Indeed, the disarray in the room seemed of the general variety, not the sort that might result from packing for a trip. Archie tamped down a smile; he was going to win the wager.

"Oh good! Sit down!" Effie cried, carelessly shoving a pile of garments and papers off his bed. "Shall I call for tea while I pack? Or perhaps something stronger?"

"No," Simon said brusquely. "We're in a hurry. Make haste."

"On the contrary," Archie said soothingly to Effie, who had begun imposing a sort of order on the chaos. He glanced at the ormolu clock on Effie's mantel—and smiled to see the ornate gilded timepiece bedecked with dried roses. "Take your time. You wouldn't want to forget anything, and I, for one, could do with a nip of brandy."

Despite his efforts to stall, Archie lost the wager. Effie packed with uncharacteristic expeditiousness, and the three friends climbed into the coach thirty minutes later. Archie took the rear-facing seat, accepting Simon's triumphant jeer with good humor.

Archie didn't mind losing. He enjoyed gambling. And riding and boxing and all manner of gentlemanly pursuits. He loved to be active, and he loved to compete. But he had never been overly concerned with *winning*. This indifference used to drive his father to distraction. But for Archie, the appeal of any pursuit was the experience of it rather than the outcome. Hunting, arguably the greatest of his passions, was about the actual hunt, not the kill. The clean air scouring his nostrils, the focus that always came with physical exertion, the strategy developed among friends with whom he was sharing the day.

Well, no, in the case of hunting, it *was* also about the outcome: dinner never tasted so good as when one shot it oneself.

But the larger point stood: Archie enjoyed games and contests, but he was not elementally competitive. So he was quite happy for Simon to win their wager, though he played his role and scowled and grumbled over the loss. Truth be told, he was pleased Simon had won, because it meant they'd gotten underway sooner rather than later. There was nothing like an Earls Trip. These two weeks in September were his favorite of the year.

"We wagered on how long it would take to extract you, you know," Simon said to Effie.

"Did you? Who won?"

"I did," Simon said with an air of what looked from the outside like haughtiness but Effie and Archie knew was merely Simon's innate seriousness. He had an earnest nature that was often tinged with worry. Most people didn't realize that.

"Well, good," Effie declared. "Archie wins entirely too much. Always has. Remember that archery competition in fifth form?"

Simon snorted. "As if I could forget it. I thought I'd starve to death waiting for it to be over."

"And then the rain began," Effie remarked wryly.

The boys were referring to the annual archery contest at school. Perhaps Archie needed to revise his previous thought that he wasn't naturally competitive. He wasn't naturally competitive with his *friends*. But put him in an archery contest where everyone had been eliminated but him and his fifteen-year-old arch-nemesis, the bully Nigel Nettlefell, and he would shoot arrow after arrow into the night, in the middle of a rainstorm, until his arms shook. He would do it again today, had he the chance, purely for the satisfaction of beating that miserable little toad.

"I think," Archie said, "that I win exactly the right amount. Which is to say frequently." His friends jeered good-naturedly, and he doubled down. "I do attempt to lose every now and again, mind you, to keep from smothering your spirits." The pair of them made various noises of disgust. "It must be very trying to always be coming up short around me, so I try to keep myself humble," he added with an air of exaggerated martyrdom.

Simon sniffed and opened one of his newspapers, which caused Effie to pull out a leatherbound journal. Effie looked like a raven, dark and regal, and Simon like a dunnock, unassuming and brown. Archie tamped down a smile. His air of martyrdom had been just that—an air. In truth, Archie loved his friends in spite of their quirks—*because* of their quirks—with a depth of feeling that was perhaps unseemly for a grown man. But he didn't care overmuch about seemliness. A man needed friends in this world, and he had the best of them.

Mind you, he didn't go around *saying* any of that. Some sentiments did not lend themselves to earnest declarations.

He allowed Effie and Simon to get lost in their individual pursuits as the cobblestones of Mayfair gave way to the dirt road out of Town. The toast would happen later. He reached for his valise, intending to extract his beads to pass the time, but was greeted by the unwelcome sight of a ragged counterpane. "*Bollocks.*"

Curious how something could be so familiar yet so unwelcome. Familiar because the bed covering used to be his. He knew the soft silk of the front and the scratchy linen of the back. His fingers used to trace the elaborate pattern of stitching that was meant to keep the wool batting the thing was stuffed with in place while Mother read to him at night. The batting was long since gone, and the silk had faded from its original blue to a drab gray.

Unwelcome because they would have to double back now. At least Mother was in London.

Still, what a stroke of bad luck. "Damn it all to hell."

"Whatever's the matter, Archie?" Effie asked, peering over the edge of his journal.

He held up the coverlet.

"What in the devil is that?"

"It's my mother's . . ." How to explain? The boys knew about his mother, but the day-to-day details, the grind that was the caretaking endeavor, was not something with which he burdened them. It was not something he knew how to explain. He would try, though. "This is what remains of the counterpane from my bed when I was a boy. When I was seven, we got a dog named Baron. He was my father's dog—he was a birder—but much to Father's annoyance, Baron attached himself to me."

"Your father, the earl, named his dog Baron?" Simon asked.

"He did indeed."

Simon snorted, and Effie said, "Of course he did."

"Well, at least we *knew* Baron would never live up to Father's standards," Archie said. He'd been aiming for a breezy delivery but to his dismay, the declaration had come out sounding more bothered than he would have liked. "When I was away at school, Baron would drag this counterpane around. He missed me, and I suppose it smelled like me. Mother was always taking it from him and putting it back in my bedchamber. It became somewhat of a jest between us." And, he supposed, a jest between Mother and Baron when Archie was at school. He smiled, thinking about how each time he'd come home, there would be another tear or stain on the coverlet. Mother would pretend to be irritated and threaten to replace the counterpane, which she always said wasn't suited for the man Archie was becoming. But she never did.

"Somehow, as her mind has . . . become clouded, Mother has become fixated on the bloody thing." Archie paused. "I am understating the matter. I am not sure Mother and Miss Brown can weather the fortnight ahead without this rag. Mother has grown inordinately attached to it. It brings her comfort. Calms her when she has episodes." It was to her as his string of beads was to him. Miss Brown, Mother's companion, had given them to him—she had initially given them to Mother, having fashioned them after some ancient Greek contraption she'd read about. They were akin to the rosaries of the Catholics, though they carried no religious meaning: they were intended merely to occupy the hands and soothe the mind. They hadn't worked with Mother, but they had worked on him. They gave him something to do with his hands, focused his mind. The difference was he could do without the beads if he had to.

"How did it get in your bag?" Simon asked.

"I've no idea. Probably Mother put it there herself. No one else in the household would have. Even the staff in Town know how important the blasted thing is."

"Even if the dowager has become reliant on the counterpane and has taken ownership of it, perhaps some part of her mind still connects it with you," Simon said. "If she knew you were setting off on a journey, perhaps she thought you ought to take it."

Archie paused. It would be easy enough to agree with that assessment, but these were the people to whom he did not lie. "That would be a sound theory if Mother knew who I was."

"Oh, Archie," Effie said. "Is she that much worse, then?"

"Yes," Archie said tersely. "She no longer recognizes me at all." There had been days, as recently as six months ago, where he would join her in her breakfast room, and she would say, "Good morning, Archibald dearest," as if nothing were amiss. Those days had become fewer and farther between until there were none left. He thought of it like watching a boat disappear over the horizon: it would bob in the waves and come in and out of view before it was well and truly gone. And even then, you kept staring, long after you knew it was futile.

"I'm so sorry," Effie said with real dismay in his tone.

"Likewise," Simon said. "What a bloody terrible business."

"It's all right." It made it easier, in a way, to love her, than had been the case in recent years, when he'd still been trying to hold her to the standards to which he thought a mother ought to adhere. He hadn't understood then that her behavior wasn't personal.

Though he did wonder if one could reasonably love someone who had lost her mind. Was there any of *her* left to love? What happened when one's mother walked the earth in corporeal form yet existed only as a memory?

Goodness. This was too much philosophy for Archie, who had

never been a scholar. What happened was that it felt bloody awful. He knew that much.

"Well, we shall just have to turn back, then," Effie said.

"I'm afraid we will, though I do recognize how absurd it is to do so over a tattered piece of fabric." Archie sighed. "It will add two hours to our trip."

"Yes," Simon said, "but think how quickly Effie got ready. It all comes out in the wash."

"Thank you," Archie said quietly. "And I'm sorry."

The boys waved away his apologies, and soon enough they were headed back the way they'd come.

"Would you like to come in?" Archie said when they came to a stop in front of the house on Hanover Square. He didn't want them to, but he felt he ought to ask.

"Yes," Effie said vehemently. "It's long past time I paid my respects to your mother."

"She's unlikely to recognize you." Archie and Simon and Effie didn't interact with each other's families overmuch, mostly because their families were, frankly, tommyrot. But not Mother; she was the exception. Or she had been.

"All the better," Simon said as he climbed out of the coach. "That way she won't remember the time we showed up for dinner at this very house utterly foxed."

Effie groaned and held his head. "We were so jug-bitten. If she does remember me, I shall make my apologies again for that appalling lapse."

Archie winced at the memory. "I don't know that I've ever seen her so angry." Father yes, but not Mother. She had been angry on account of the fact that she'd also had other guests at the table. It had struck Archie as a fair sort of anger. Mother had only ever gotten angry at Archie over behaviors, things he could control. She never scorned him for the way he *was*.

"And I should enjoy seeing Miss Brown," Simon said. When Archie looked at him, perplexed, for he couldn't remember Simon and Miss Brown ever meeting, Simon added, a touch defensively, "You probably have not noticed that Miss Brown is very well read."

Apparently, he had not. He had been too busy noticing that Miss Brown was his and Mother's savior, their angel of mercy. "All right, here we go."

The house was, as he'd feared, in a minor uproar. Archie's letting himself in attracted a harried footman. "My lord." He skidded to a halt in front of them. "We did not expect to see you back so soon."

"Angus." Archie held out the counterpane. "I didn't expect to be back, but I realized this had sneaked its way into my things."

Angus's shoulders visibly relaxed. "Very good. I'll summon Miss Brown."

"No need. I'll say hello—and goodbye again—to Mother. Featherfinch and Marsden would like to greet her. I assume she and Miss Brown are in the music room?"

"They are, my lord."

Miss Brown would be trying to engage Mother in some singing. Strangely, although Mother had forgotten so many people and events, she remembered the words to every song she'd ever learned.

All seemed calm when they entered to find Mother and Miss Brown sitting side by side at the pianoforte. Miss Brown turned at the sound of their arrival, and Archie held up the counterpane. Miss Brown had a similar reaction to Angus, sighing in obvious relief and shooting Archie a grateful smile. She laid her hand on Mother's arm. "Look who is here, my lady, and what he has brought."

Mother turned. If Archie was harboring hope that there might be a flicker of recognition in her eyes, he was, as ever, disappointed. He pasted on a smile and forged ahead, as he always did. "Hello, Mother. This made its way into my bag, and I thought you would want it."

He approached slowly, holding out the counterpane, which

she took from him easily. "And I've brought Lords Featherfinch and Marsden. You remember? My friends Edward—Effie—and Simon from school?"

Of course she did not remember. He wasn't even sure why he kept trying, except he didn't know how to conduct himself around her other than the way he always had. To accept the shortcomings of her mind as she always had those of his.

The boys murmured gentle greetings, but they seemed to agitate Mother. "Are you friends of Charles's?" she asked, naming Archie's late father. "Mother insists I cannot accept his suit." She shot a disdainful look at Miss Brown before returning her attention to the boys. "Please tell Charlie . . ." She giggled. "I beg your pardon, please tell Lord Harcourt that I shall be at the park this afternoon."

"I am not a friend of Charles," Simon said gently. "I am a friend of your son, Archie."

"Who?" A look of bewilderment washed over Mother's face. She was going to start crying. "I think I'm confused," she whispered before the tears began to fall. Even though this was a familiar pattern, it never failed to make Archie's chest feel heavy. It was the same feeling he always used to get at school, when confronted with an essay he could not write. It was a feeling of powerlessness, as if he were drowning in his own pathetic helplessness. But back then, he'd been able to dissolve the lump in his chest, to take the reins of his own life again, by going outside. By riding or fencing or engaging in an activity that absorbed all his senses. That didn't work with Mother.

Miss Brown murmured words of comfort, and Archie took Mother's hand. That sometimes seemed to soothe her, even when she didn't know who he was.

This was not one of those times. His presence only seemed to upset her further, and she snatched her hand from his.

Ah, bollocks. He hated leaving like this. Miss Brown, who no doubt knew that, said, "Thank you for bringing the counterpane back, my lord. Your mother was bereft, earlier, to discover it missing." She smiled brightly. "Enjoy your holiday." She was dismissing him, telling him it was all right to go.

Still, he hesitated. It had very likely been a mistake to install Mother and Miss Brown in London for the duration of this year's Earls Trip. His reasoning had been that Mother's London doctor had suggested a new course of treatment that would take a week. Still, he should have arranged that to happen at a time he could be on hand. Mother should be at Mollybrook while he was away, where she was comfortable and could walk in the gardens. He turned to Miss Brown, "I think we ought to return—"

"The doctor is coming in an hour," Miss Brown said, firmly but not unkindly. Mother's companion, though not yet thirty, reminded him sometimes of a wise, time-seasoned governess. "Your mother should rest before he gets here."

Still, he was torn.

"My lord," she said, getting up and going so far as to actually shoo him and his friends toward the door. "Go. Enjoy yourselves."

"But—"

"You will recall that I took four weeks of holiday this past summer." He did recall, and they had missed her dearly. "We can spare you for a fortnight. You're no use to anyone without some rest and reinvigoration."

Mother was still agitated. Effie walked back to her and said, "Miss Emma, I don't think Harcourt had planned on the park this afternoon, but if he knows *you're* to be there, I wager he'll change his mind."

Mother stopped crying. "Oh, do you think so?"

"I do," Effie said warmly.

"Well, that's all right, then," Mother said almost shyly. Though Archie had seen her in this state many a time, it was still unsettling. The Mother he remembered had never been shy, around Father or anyone. That was part of why he loved her so.

"I too think he will be there," said Miss Brown, resuming her shooing motion. "How will he be able to resist such a diamond of the first water?"

Mother smiled, Archie whispered his fervent thanks to Miss Brown, and he and the boys beat a retreat.

No one spoke until they were back in the coach.

"She is lost in the past," Archie murmured, once they were underway. "Although that is stating the obvious, isn't it?" He was always a trifle embarrassed when outsiders witnessed Mother having an episode, and his mind was beginning down that familiar path of chagrin, but he reminded himself that Effie and Simon were not outsiders.

"I am sorry," Simon said quietly, "that we didn't realize how bad things had gotten."

"Will they manage without you, Archie?" Effie asked. "Because we can just as easily spend the fortnight in Town."

"They will manage fine," Archie said, and it was the lowering truth. "Mother won't miss me." He waved away the murmurs of sympathy that statement drew forth. "Miss Brown will miss me, but only because we spell each other off during the day. It's gotten so Mother requires constant companionship. She's begun to wander off. And she'll tip over candles, forget to eat, that sort of thing. A nurse sleeps with her, but I prefer, during the day, not to relegate her care to servants. Not that ours aren't good and loyal. I just . . ."

"She's your mother," Effie said, as if that explained everything. Perhaps it did.

"I know it won't be easy," Simon said, "but can you try to put her out of your mind? I rather think Miss Brown was correct. I believe you are in need of respite."

Archie was so much in need of respite that the kind words of his friends were making tears gather in the corners of his eyes. He nodded and took out his beads. The boys correctly interpreted the gesture as a signal that he wanted not to talk anymore just now. Effie opened his journal and Simon his newspaper, and silence settled as they rumbled out of Town for the second time.

2

The Girls Enter the Chat

By the time they reached Hampstead Heath, which Archie deemed a suitable landmark for the official opening of Earls Trip 1821, he had recovered himself. On the way out of Town on an Earls Trip, he generally looked for a marker to signify that they were well and truly out of London, with its too-close buildings and too-close people. He liked to observe a ceremonial passing from Town to country, from responsibility to respite, and this year the marking of such felt particularly hard-won.

He cleared his throat. "If I may have your attention?"

"Oh, I'm meant to be the one doing this, aren't I?" Effie said as he lowered his diary. It was true that they traded hosting duties among them, and that this was Effie's year. In practice that meant that Effie had chosen the castle in Cumbria awaiting them on the other end of their journey and thought no further about anything.

"It's quite all right," Archie said. He enjoyed this part. The jesting formality of "the rules" always amused him, but this year in particular it was a welcome ritual, and he was glad to be the one performing it. He needed to feel useful. He uncorked a bottle of brandy, passed out glasses, and carefully splashed a bit of the ruby liquid into each, which was as much as he dared given the lumbering of the coach.

When he lifted his glass, the others followed suit.

"Gentlemen. Welcome to Earls Trip. Allow me to remind you

of the rules. Perhaps this year you numbskulls will actually get them through your heads. Number one: every time Marsden says the word 'Parliament,' he must down a dram of whisky. Number two: Featherfinch is strictly prohibited from writing poems, unless they are naughty ones. And should you be harboring any concerns that I fancy myself above the law, we come round to number three: Harcourt is not permitted to shoot anything. Alas."

Harcourt is not permitted to shoot anything that you know about, he amended silently, thinking fondly of the fowling piece he had hidden in his trunk.

"The rules established," he continued, "I'm so very glad to—"

A surge of sentiment rose through Archie's chest and lodged in his windpipe, preventing him from finishing his sentence. It ought to have been mortifying, but no one seemed to notice. Effie merely said, "I am, too," and Simon said, "Likewise."

They knew Archie's true feelings without him needing to put them to words. He cleared his throat and in so doing dissolved the lump caught there. He raised his brandy. "And, finally, the most important rule of Earls Trip—"

The coach lurched to a stop, and though Archie had taken care not to overfill their glasses, all were upended. Effie cursed the sight of the ruby stain sullying his cravat, which was a snow-white beacon against his otherwise black attire, whereas Simon merely blotted a spot that was invisible against his dark brown coat.

Simon peered out the window. "What is it, I wonder?"

"Do you think it's highwaymen?" Effie asked with entirely too much excitement in his tone, his cravat forgotten.

"'Tis a rider, my lord," their driver called. "He's hailing us."

"Dear Lord, *is* it a highwayman?" Simon asked.

"I don't believe highwaymen generally warn their marks ahead of time," Archie said, opening the door and alighting. Sure enough, a rider approached. Archie had the sense he knew the man but couldn't place him.

"My lord." The man bowed his head. "I bear a message from Sir Albert Morgan."

Ah, yes. Archie recognized the liveried messenger as a servant from the household of Sir Albert. The Morgans had a house in Chiddington near Mollybrook, Archie's family's estate in western Kent. These days the Morgans spent most of their time in London, so Archie, who spent most of *his* time at Mollybrook, never saw them anymore. But Sir Albert and Archie's late father, the former earl, had been fast friends, and for many years when Archie was young, the two families had moved in the same circles in local society. Well, *most* of the Morgans had moved in those society circles. One of them had been too . . . untamed for that. He quirked a grin, remembering his old friend.

In fact, curiosity about her—in addition to embarrassment over the piss-poor job he'd done keeping up with what had once been his father's closest friendship—had prompted Archie to call on Sir Albert that very morning, but the man had been out. To Archie's discredit, he had not seen the Morgans in any meaningful fashion for years, and he had recently learned that Sir Albert was quite ill with the gout. Archie himself had never been particularly close to Sir Albert, or, to be honest, particularly fond of him, but that didn't excuse his having let so much time go by without calling on him. They were geographically mismatched these days, but that was no excuse. Could he have not have called on them once when he was in town for a crucial vote in Lords?

"Is everything all right?" he asked, unable to imagine why Sir Albert would send a rider after him.

The rider handed him a letter. "Sir Albert bade me try to overtake you."

With a rising tide of unease in his belly, Archie broke Sir Albert's green wax seal.

My dear boy,

You can't imagine the relief—the hope—that seized me when I returned home to find your note. That you should be not only in Town, but Cumbria-bound! It seemed positively providential.

I shall get straight to the point, for I know I can trust you to be discreet. Olive has run off with a man named Theodore Bull. Mr. Bull was recently betrothed to Clementine, and all of us, including Clementine, were shaken to our cores this morning to discover a note from Olive proclaiming that she and Mr. Bull were Scotland-bound.

Dear God. Archie had to look away from the parchment for a moment to gather himself, to give his stomach time to reintegrate into the rest of his corporeal form. Olive Morgan was like a sister to him. Clementine Morgan was . . . Clementine. He felt anew the chagrin of having let his connection with the family grow stale.

"What is it?" Effie asked urgently. He and Simon had disembarked the coach.

Archie waved a hand dismissively and returned to his letter.

Mr. Bull is a writer, a philosopher with what might charitably be called modern views. To put it less charitably, and more plainly, he is odious. Smug and self-impressed and in possession of extreme views he is determined to foist upon everyone else. After an initial vogue for the man among certain members of the Upper Ten Thousand, today he is hardly received. Clementine was entranced by his work and professed not to care when he fell out of fashion. When he asked for her hand, I swallowed my distaste and gave my assent. You will perhaps recall how despite one's best attempts, Clementine will do what Clementine will do.

Archie chuckled despite the gravity of the situation. He certainly did recall that.

And not to put too fine a point on it, but I'd begun to give up hope of Clementine's making a match. She does not possess any of the traits quality gentlemen seek in a wife.

Archie didn't know that he'd go that far. Clementine Morgan had a true spirit of adventure and kindness in spades, at least she had when they were young. Though given what he knew of London society, he supposed such qualities may not be those sought by the average gentleman in want of a wife. Still, she had remarkably pretty hair.

He returned to the letter.

They announced their engagement, and I thought all was well. The banns were called, but the very same day, Clementine informed me of her desire to cry off the match. I put it down to a case of nerves. I assumed it would pass and was attempting to smooth things over, as the die had been cast.

Then we awakened this morning to the shocking note from Olive. Clementine aside, Mr. Bull is an ill match for my Olive. No, he is a disastrous match. You know Olive: she is changeable and easily flattered. I fear she is making the gravest mistake of her life. Clementine I can trust to make a rational decision, to know what she is giving up in exchange for what she is getting. Olive . . . well, once again, you know Olive. I know you have not seen either girl these recent years, but since their mother's passing Olive has become even more . . . Olivelike.

Clementine and I found the note very early this morning, and I left the house to seek counsel from a trusted friend. When I returned, Clementine was gone. I fear she has run after them. What can the outcome be? She stops the marriage but the girls are stranded in Scotland? She does not stop the marriage? I fear the most likely result is one girl unhappily married, the other ruined.

On her deathbed, their dear departed mother made me promise I would see them both satisfactorily wed. I have made a complete hash of things. You have never known me to be overdramatic. Therefore know that when I say I am begging you to go after them, I am beseeching you with my whole heart.

*I've taken ill in recent months, and my girls are all I have left.
I'd been about to take to my own carriage in pursuit of them,
but travel is slow and painful on account of my condition. If
you ever held your father in any esteem, I implore you to do
this service for his dearest friend.*

   Please, Archibald: save my girls.

Archie had to take a step to right himself because for a moment
there, he'd been overcome. He should have been a better friend
to the Morgans, especially after the death of Mrs. Morgan. Yes,
Mother's situation made leaving Mollybrook difficult—as had just
been so exquisitely illustrated, Archie's being gone for the annual
Earls Trip required a heroic effort by Miss Brown. And yes, beyond that, Archie despised Town.

   And yes . . . Sir Albert was perhaps not Archie's favorite person
in the world. Even now, he could remember him chuckling with
Father over some perceived shortcoming or other of Archie's.

   But none of that was the fault of Olive and Clementine, both of
whom he liked very much. Could he not have made, say, one trip
a year to check in on the family? His scalp prickled with shame.

   "Whatever's the matter, Harcourt?" Simon asked.

   "You've gone altogether pale," Effie said.

   He handed over the letter, and after a minute, Effie said, "Well.
I think this year's Earls Trip is about to take a turn."

   It was indeed. Archie strode over to the servant. "Please advise
Sir Albert that I will take care of this matter. Tell him not to worry
and to stay where he is. It is all in hand, and I shall send word as
soon as I am able."

   The rider departed in a cloud of dust, and Archie's friends
drew near, the three of them forming a tight circle in the September sun.

   "Olive and Clementine Morgan are the daughters of Sir Albert,
who has a country house near Mollybrook," he said. "Clementine
and I . . ." How to explain what Clementine was to him?

   "Used to be fast friends," Effie supplied. "Yes, we know."

"You do?"

"You used to talk about her all the time at school. Afterward, too," Simon said. "Though not so much in recent years."

"You used to write to her," Effie said. "I seem to remember you trying to pay me to answer her letters for you."

"That's right." Archie had forgotten. "She used to write to me, and though I'd neither the patience nor the inclination for letter-writing, I couldn't bring myself to ignore her correspondence." He hadn't wanted to, really. Archie had never been any good at writing—letters, essays, any of it—but the arrival of a newsy letter from Clementine Morgan, reporting on the local flora and fauna, had always lifted his spirits for days.

He shook his head. Now was not the time to be lollygagging about in memories of yesteryear. "I must go in search of them. I am sorry. We'll have to detour to the nearest posting inn. I'll hire a horse, and you two can continue on to Cumbria." He sighed. "It seems fate is determined I shan't make this year's trip."

"Oh no, you don't," Simon said. "If you believe we won't be accompanying you, you're completely daft."

"Honestly." Effie sniffed. "You think we're simply going to abandon you? There's a wrong that needs righting here, and of course we're with you all the way."

"Besides," Simon said, "none of us has ever missed a trip. I say we institute a new rule whereby the trip bends to accommodate the travelers—*all* of the travelers. Perhaps next year we will holiday near Mollybrook so you may be close to your mother."

"Thank you." Archie was again overcome by his affection for his friends, for the unconditional, if unspoken, loyalty that bound them together. If only he had extended some of that same loyalty to the Morgans, perhaps they wouldn't be in this mess.

"I know of Theodore Bull," Simon said. "He's the author of a tract entitled *On the Moral Obligation of Not Eating Animals*."

"I beg your pardon?" Archie said.

"He's part of a fringe movement that holds to the precept that men should abstain from eating animal flesh for moral reasons."

"*Fascinating.*" Effie's brow furrowed. "The dilemma, however, is that animal flesh tastes good." The furrow deepened. "Do you think animals are aware of their own mortality? Do you think Sally knew she was going to die?"

"Mr. Bull was briefly popular in the drawing rooms of Mayfair," Simon went on, ignoring Effie. "He made a splash among the sort of hostess who fancies herself an arbiter of taste. You know the type: séances today, turnip gratin tomorrow. I believe, as Sir Albert wrote, that Mr. Bull has fallen out of fashion of late."

Archie was agog. He had never heard of this vegetable-championing bounder, though that wasn't saying much as he made no effort to keep up with society doings. It was all so incomprehensible, though, both the man's ideas and the fact that such a man had enchanted the fickle Olive Morgan in a way that she was ready to jump the anvil with him. And the self-contained, unflappable Clementine Morgan before that? The world had turned upside down.

He shook his head. Time for agog later; action was required at present. He conferred with his driver about the change in plans, and Simon and Effie climbed back into the coach. When he joined them, they'd repoured the brandy, and he was handed a glass.

"You weren't done with your speech," Simon said.

"Yes, you were just about to remind us of the most important rule of Earls Trip," Effie said with a twinkle in his eye. "It suddenly seems all the more relevant this year."

"Right." Once again, Archie and his friends lifted their glasses. "No poems, no Parliament, no hunting, and, finally, the most important rule of Earls Trip . . ."

They spoke in unison. "What happens on Earls Trip stays on Earls Trip."

3

Clem Shoots Her Shot

Two days later

Clementine could not wait to get out of these blasted trousers.

That part was a disappointment. In novels, when girls disguised themselves as boys, they always remarked on the freedom they found in the wearing of breeches. They could ride faster and scale fences more efficiently and undertake all manner of pursuit with greater ease.

They never talked about how terribly *uncomfortable* it was to wear breeches. Breeches cut into the flesh of one's midsection in a *most* unpleasant way. Perhaps if one was accustomed to wearing stays, this sort of pain was familiar. But when one was a country lass at heart and on the verge of spinsterhood—and may she soon return to that verge, where she belonged—one managed to avoid stays quite a lot of the time.

Thinking of all the instances recently when she had worn stays—when she'd worn them for *him*—made her blood boil. That blunderbuss. That knave. That— "Oh!"

The coach lurched to a stop, throwing her up against the passenger next to her, a Bible-clutching man who hadn't spoken a word since Chorley and smelled of cabbage and mildewing parchment. He turned to her, no doubt startled by some combination of her regrettably girlish exclamation and the regrettably girlish mound of bosom she had inadvertently brushed against his shoulder.

Clementine had learned a great deal about bosoms of late, during her conscription in London, her forced march through the Marriage Mart. She had learned that some women powdered theirs. Sometimes they even traced the veins there with blue paint, for reasons that entirely escaped her. Some inserted busks in their stays, stays apparently not being torturous enough on their own. Others even turned to wax and cotton in service of a mission of augmentation.

Everything Clementine had learned in this regard was about enhancement. The drawing of attention. She had not, alas, learned anything about the *deflecting* of attention from the often inconvenient mounds of flesh with which ladies were burdened. Today, to her dismay and despite her most ardent efforts in the art of concealment, her own rather ample bosom was *not staying where she put it.* Namely, beneath a long piece of muslin she'd wound around her torso before sneaking out of the house two days ago.

Two days or a lifetime, one or the other.

The cabbagey man narrowed his eyes at her. She lowered her voice, muttered a vague apology, and the moment the coachman opened the door and called, "Oi! Five minutes!" she was out, blinking into the bright sun.

The yard of the coaching inn was, as coaching inn yards were wont to be, unpleasantly populated with people chattering, ostlers changing horses, and trunks being heaved in and out of conveyances. But there was also the dirt beneath her feet and the sky above her head. She couldn't remove her boots and wiggle her toes in the mud like she wanted to, but she could imagine all the creepy-crawly friends below the surface, going about their days profoundly undisturbed by the machinations of the men above them. And she could tip her head back and narrow her eyes, not in suspicion like her erstwhile seatmate, but strategically, so as to block out the roof thatch of the inn and the chimneys rising from it, until all she could see was sky. The bolstering, beautiful blue of an English sky. The same one sheltering her home in the country.

She would soon be back at Hill House. She just had to rescue Olive first.

Olive.

Her heart squeezed. Clementine and Olive had never been particularly close. The same could be said for Clementine and all of her family. She loved them, but sometimes Clementine wondered if she belonged with them. Indeed, when she was young, she'd harbored a fancy that she was a changeling, that the fairies had come and taken her parents' true firstborn and left Clementine in her place. But as Clementine grew tall and strong and failed to sprout elven ears, she had to accept that she was, in fact, a true, if atypical, Morgan.

Clementine had different interests and priorities from the rest of her family—especially Olive. Olive was at home in a crowded ballroom, wearing the latest fashions and giggling with her friends over which gentlemen they hoped would ask them to dance. Clementine felt most herself in the forest. The stream. Under the starry heavens. She preferred thickets to tea, would sooner visit a meadow than a modiste. There was a devastating sort of beauty all around if one only paid attention to it, discernable in the tiniest details: the veins of a leaf just as it starts to turn color in the autumn; a ladybird perched on a rose, red against red except for its signature black spots; even the cold iridescence of a fish washed ashore and left to perish on the sand by a receding wave.

Most people didn't pay attention, though. Olive didn't pay attention.

Still, they were *sisters*. Motherless sisters. And soon the gout, or something else, would take Father, and they would be alone together.

All this to say that Olive had hurt Clementine so *very* much more than Theo had.

And a week ago, Clementine would have said that Theo had hurt her very much indeed, in both body and spirit.

But it did no good to dwell on any of it. The fact remained that Olive did not know what she'd gotten herself into, and she was in need of rescuing. So Clementine was going to rescue her. Because in her world, that was what people did for their sisters.

But as soon as that was done, Clementine was putting her foot down with Father. No more parties, no more balls, no more gentlemen. No more *London*. She would leave that to Olive and retreat to Hill House. She had been telling Father for years that she was not going to marry, and he had been ignoring her for just as long. If there was one upside to this dreadful business, it was that he might finally accept defeat.

It made her shudder to think how near she had come to making such a terrible mistake. All the heartsickness she felt now was worth that fate averted.

A hawk soared into view, and she gasped in delight and awe— and gratitude. Tears prickled her eyes, as they sometimes did when the world was being too much itself—too beautiful and terrible and capable of expressing a kind of steadfast rightness through its creatures and its colors.

An all-too-human muttering had her reluctantly transferring her attention from the tableau above to a pair of men standing at the foot of the coach. It was the driver and the cabbage man. The latter was no longer silent but looking at her and speaking a great deal indeed.

Clementine's three Seasons in London had not taught her much of use, but her childhood in the country had. She had spent enough time watching—deer bounding through the forest, a spider spinning a web in a hollow tree, the bowing of a willow in the wind as it bent to skim the surface of a pond—that she had learned to be sensitive to small shifts in the air. She had honed her instincts and learned to trust them.

She hitched her satchel up on one shoulder, picked up her skirts—and because she'd forgotten she wasn't wearing any, that amounted to picking up two handfuls of air—and ran.

Twenty minutes later, she crept back into the yard, hoping Mr. Cabbage had departed with the coach. She hadn't been planning on stopping here. Indeed, in her mind, she'd been going to take the London-to-Glasgow Mail coach all the way straight through to the end of the line. Forty-eight hours hadn't seemed an impossible stretch. Her favorite ramble through the woods at home took two hours, and forty-eight was only that twenty-four times over.

She had not accounted for the corporeal realities of cross-country travel by Mail coach. There was the hunger, of course. She had anticipated the fact of that, filling her pockets and her bag with apples and walnuts and bread, but not the degree. She should have brought more food. Worse, though, was the discomfort. Before this, the longest trip she had made was between her family's London home and Hill House in Kent—western Kent, not so terribly far from Town geographically, though in another sense, it was as far from London as the moon in the sky. And those journeys had always been undertaken in the family coach, which went more slowly than the Mail and therefore made for a much less rough-and-tumble experience. Here, by contrast, the hours and hours spent curled in on herself, the jostling, the lack of fresh air and light—well, it was grim.

So, part of her didn't mind the fact that, twice now, the need to maintain her subterfuge had forced her to take refuge inside a posting inn and to wait for the next Mail coach, which, here at the Blue Lion in Thorpesden at four o'clock in the afternoon, was going to mean staying the night. The delay was regrettable, but the image of a soft, clean bed made her near delirious with want.

If this were a novel, she would not have attempted to make the trip without pause. She would have stopped along the way, asking at posting inns if anyone had seen a pretty young auburn-haired woman accompanied by an uncommonly tall gentleman wearing boots made of cotton.

But in novels, she would not have been acquainted with the man in question. He would have been a mere villain who had absconded with her sister, not a man Clementine *knew*—in all the senses of the word, to her great regret. Novels also disregarded how very many Mail routes there were to Scotland, but that was not the primary point. Clementine, unlike so many hapless literary heroines, knew that Theo was bound not for the nearest border town with an anvil and an unscrupulous innkeeper, but for Glasgow. He had friends there. He had *acolytes* there. There he would be sheltered and cosseted and flattered, and no one would give Olive any thought beyond her supporting role in the life of Mr. Theodore Bull. Theo wanted Olive, therefore his friends would move mountains that he should have her.

If there was any good to come from Clementine's *knowing* of Mr. Theodore Bull, it was that she could use her knowledge—of his mind, his vanity, his habits, of *him*—to save her sister.

But since she was here, at the Blue Lion in Thorpesden, she might as well make like in novels and ask if anyone had seen Theo and Olive even if, *unlike* in novels, the answer would almost certainly be no.

She scanned the room. There was an innkeeper manning the bar she could interview, and she could get something to eat.

"Ye want *just* potatoes?" the innkeeper asked after she'd ordered.

"Yes, but only if they are not cooked in beef tallow. I'd prefer them boiled." The poor man was wearing such a look of befuddlement that she added, "Beef and its by-products do not agree with me." She patted her stomach and made a mournful face.

"Ah, well, if that's the case, this will see you in good stead." He set a pie on the battered oaken bar. "'Tis only lamb in this one."

She sighed and took a sip of her ale. Ale, it turned out, could be rather pleasant. Better anyway than the sickly sweet ratafia Theo had always pressed on her at parties. When the bartender turned away, she extracted a newspaper from her satchel, wrapped the pie in it, and deposited the whole package back in the bag. She would find a yard dog to give it to later.

"You made quick work of that, lad." The friendly innkeeper was back. "My missus's lamb pies are famous in these parts and for good reason, if I may say so." He positively beamed with pride. "I tell her the last thing I want to pass my lips in the final minute of my life is a bite of her lamb pie."

Clementine could not help but be touched by the man's praise of his wife. What must it be like to be married to a man who valued one's accomplishments enough to boast of them to strangers? Not that she was going to be married to any man ever—she had briefly entertained the notion, and look where it had gotten her. Still, if a lady *had* to be married, which she realized most ladies did—Clementine was unaccountably lucky not to number among them—it must be gratifying to be appreciated.

"Well, no, scratch that. The last thing I'd want to taste is a mouthful of her apple dumplins, if you get my meaning." The innkeeper winked in a way that suggested to Clementine that it wasn't a mixture of fruit and pastry he was talking about.

That was another thing about being a man: other men said the most *shocking* things to one as easily as if they were remarking upon the weather.

"Yes, quite." She picked up her ale and took a long drink in order to avoid having to say more. She was nearly done with the pint and feeling much less distressed about life in general when the innkeeper returned. "I say, sir, I'm looking for someone who may have been here ahead of me. An unusually tall man, and he'd've had a very pretty auburn-haired woman with him."

"Man wearing very strange boots?"

"Yes!"

"He's taken a private parlor."

"*Oh!*" Clementine was so shocked, she nearly fell off her stool. She righted herself and made a point to lower her voice. "He's here *now?*"

In novels, this sort of sleuthing would have yielded intelligence about which direction the fugitive lovers had gone and how long ago they had left, not that they were *under the same roof at that very moment.* But Clementine knew where Theo and Olive were going—Glasgow. And she had to admit that if she'd been any kind of detective, she would have been prepared for the possibility that the Mail coach would overtake Theo's landau.

"Yes, indeed." The innkeeper paused. "Bit of an odd one, he is."

"Yes. He's—" She considered telling him the truth. They were both "men," after all, and the easy confidences between men she had just been observing might allow her to say, "He is a beast who has run off with my sister." The innkeeper might bluster and express moral outrage and help her confront Theo. But what then? Backed into a corner, Theo would expose Clementine as a woman, and probably a woman passing herself off as a man was a greater scandal than a man running off with a girl to marry in Scotland against law, reason, good taste, morals, manners, and . . . She refocused her thoughts, which were going a little fuzzy, and concentrated on answering the innkeeper in a manner that would reveal neither her femaleness nor the true degree of her interest in the man with the unusual boots. "He's an old friend I'd heard might be passing this way." The floor lurched beneath Clementine's feet as she slid off the stool, and she set a hand on the bar to steady herself.

"Fortune smiles on you." The innkeeper pointed. "They're in the last parlor down that corridor."

"Have you a room for the night?" She hated to spend the money—the funds she'd stolen from Father's desk were dwindling—but she could hardly march into Theo's parlor without so much as a plan. She needed a moment to get her bearings.

There was a room to let, and when the innkeeper came back with a key, he was also carrying a plate of roast beef. "If you're going to see them, do me a good turn and take this with you."

"Oh, you must be mistaken. This must be for another party." Theo hadn't allowed the flesh of a dead animal to pass his lips for nigh on fourteen years.

"Nay, 'tis bound for your friends. They already finished a plate of beef and liked it so much they called for more. To my mind, my wife's roast beef isn't as good as . . ."

Anger drowned out the man's next ode to his wife's culinary skills and/or corporeal endowments. How *could* Theo? It was almost as bad as his having run off with her sister. But on the other hand, was she truly that surprised? Something Olive herself had said to Clementine during Clementine's first London Season came to mind: *Most people will show you who they are if you only watch closely enough.*

That observation had been creeping into Clementine's thoughts a great deal lately, but it had been making her uncomfortable enough that she'd shoved it down every time.

And look where they all were now.

Clementine made her way upstairs gingerly, holding her breath so as not to smell the meat she was carrying. Once inside her room, she crossed to the window, hurled both the beef and the lamb pie out of it, and smiled in grim satisfaction when a pack of skinny cats came running.

She had to steady herself on the windowsill as she straightened. The trip up the stairs had suggested to her that perhaps it had not been shock, or not *only* shock, that had made her unsteady at the bar. She feared the ale had a hand in her discombobulation. She ought to wait until the effects of the drink faded before going back downstairs, but she could not afford to. She had no idea if Theo was staying the night or if he planned to be off again after his *second helping of dead cow.*

Resolved, she upended her satchel on the bed. She pulled out a novel, some dried fruit, and a dress—though she had made her flight from London in men's clothing stolen from Father's wardrobe, she had packed a dress in the hopes that once she rescued Olive, she could give up her subterfuge. Beneath the dress, she found what she was looking for—yet another item nicked from Father.

The rage that flowed through her carried her over to a mirror mounted on the wall. She rewrapped her bosoms and buttoned her too-large coat over them, tucked some errant strands of hair into her hat, and slid the flintlock pistol into the back of her breeches.

So perhaps breeches were good for one thing.

She allowed the rage to continue to direct her actions. It carried her down the stairs, through the tap room, and along the corridor lined with private parlors. The door to the last stood partially open.

In novels, this would be the climax. The moment of dramatic tension. The standoff. In novels, this was where somebody would get shot.

It was much easier than that, almost laughably easy. Clementine was able to sidle up to the door and peek in. Olive, and Olive alone, was in her line of sight. Theo was talking. Well, Theo was always talking. But here, now, he was *orating*.

What had possessed her sister? Clementine had resigned herself to some of Theo's more distasteful traits, but Olive never resigned herself to anything unless she absolutely had to.

"So you see," Theo was saying, "on the Continent, there are other innovative thinkers, men on the vanguard of numerous movements. Having pondered it, I've decided a permanent move is in order."

"You never said anything about that!" Olive cried. "I never agreed to leave England permanently!"

That made Clementine wonder exactly what Olive *had* agreed to—and, once again and more to the point, *why*. Olive had entertained some flirtations last Season, her first, and, by her own account, enjoyed herself immensely—so much so that she'd declared herself disinclined to accept any suits until she'd had one more Season. Even had that not been the case, she could have had her pick of gentlemen who were much less . . . an acquired taste than Theo.

"I've decided we will find a warmer welcome for our ideas on the Continent," Theo said.

"You mean *your* ideas."

"All that I have is yours," Theo said smarmily, and didn't *that* sound familiar? "Just as all you have is mine." That part was less familiar, Theo not having been so bold as to state his philosophy so overtly to Clementine—at least until that last day.

Olive huffed an exasperated sigh that would seem more in keeping with not having received a coveted party invitation than the potential collapse of her elopement. Clementine supposed she should be relieved that Olive did not seem to bring out Theo's dark side.

"Don't sigh at me, Olive!" Theo shouted in concert with the sound of glass shattering. Clementine heard something unsettled beneath the surprise in her sister's answering shriek.

There was Theo's dark side. Clementine's pulse kicked up, and her senses sharpened, allowing her to shuck off the lingering effects of the ale. She was that hawk she had seen circling outside, homing in on her prey. She would be damned before Theodore Bull laid a hand on her sister. She laid *her* hand on the butt of her pistol and crept closer to the crack in the door.

Olive looked over, and Clementine saw real fear in her eyes. She hadn't seen Olive look like that since the day Mother died. The fear turned to shock as she registered Clementine's presence. Her eyebrows flew up. Only momentarily, though, before she composed herself and looked away. Then, while Clementine was trying to think what to do, Olive looked back at Clementine and ever so slightly shook her head before turning back to Theo and pasting on a smile. "Theo, darling." Olive spoke soothingly. "I'm sure you're right about all of this." She got up and disappeared from view, presumably going to Theo's side.

"I should think you would know by now, Olive, that I am possessed of higher-than-average intellect."

"Of course, my love. That is why I am here, is it not? You'll have to be patient with me. You know I've never been exposed to a man so positively *brimming* with ground-breaking ideas."

Clementine could almost see her sister's long eyelashes batting innocently, her mouth turned into a perfect pink pout of entreaty.

"Which is exactly why I am in need of a helpmeet," Theo said.

Clementine resisted snorting but only just.

"A true meeting of the minds," Theo went on, using *exactly* the phrase that had hooked Clementine.

"You're right, of course. You're right about everything," Olive purred in that voice everyone else heard as innocent but Clementine recognized as guileful. It was the same voice she used to shake loose extra pin money from Father. "Theo, darling, I need to use the necessary. I'll be back in a moment and we can talk some more about our initial Continental itinerary. I have a feeling the Romans might be open to some of your more interesting ideas, but of course you'll know best."

"Inquire after that plate of roast beef, won't you? It's been ages since I asked for it."

Clementine smiled, thinking of those skinny cats.

Olive appeared at the door. Clementine hadn't needed her weapon. She hadn't even needed to say anything. She merely had to stand there, take her sister's hand, and gesture for her to shut the parlor door behind her.

This novel was going to have a very anticlimactic ending indeed.

They didn't speak—or they didn't speak with words. Something passed between them, though, a kind of anguish and relief and, Clementine dared say, love. Whatever had happened here was Theo's fault. Or mostly Theo's fault.

Of course, he hadn't run away by himself.

Half Theo's fault?

They climbed the stairs to Clementine's room silently, and Olive burst into tears as soon as the door shut behind them.

"Come now," Clementine soothed, leading her sister to the bed. Olive had had the foresight to leave the parlor with her portmanteau, and she was holding it against her chest as if it were a shield. Clementine tugged it gently from her and encouraged her sister to sit on the bed. "It's over."

"It's not over!" Olive's voice was high and frightened, which unnerved Clementine. Olive's fear was in such contrast to her previous self-possession. "He's going to find me! He's going to find both of us!"

"I'm not going to let him do that." Clementine pulled out of the embrace and regarded her sister. Olive's eyes had turned into tiny blue waterfalls.

"I'm sorry," Olive said in a pitiful, small voice that was more alarming than the tears. That Theo had cowed her unflappable sister was, in this moment, the greatest of his many offenses.

"You are not the one at fault here," Clementine said, though the declaration sounded less than certain. She wasn't sure what her feelings about Olive were, truth be told. The sense of betrayal she'd been carrying around had faded somewhat now that she had her anguished sister in hand, but Clementine was still hurt. And bewildered. But Clementine of all people understood how flattering Theo could be. How he could see inside one's very soul, it felt like, find the holes one had thought were invisible to others, and start patching them, working so fast and so intently that it was only much later, when the patches dried and started crumbling that one realized he'd used only the thinnest and cheapest of plaster.

"It doesn't matter who's at fault," Olive said, her voice taking on a hard edge as she dried her tears. "There's no way out. If I don't go with him, he's going to ruin us. You don't know what you're up against."

Clementine laughed bitterly, pulled her pistol from her waistband, and said, "I assure you, I know exactly what I'm up against."

The next few seconds passed as if in a dream, one of those dreams where time gets muddled and things seem to happen both more quickly *and* more slowly than they ought. First, time moved too fast. Clementine heard Olive's name being shouted, then her own. She spared a moment to wonder how Theo knew she was here but concluded it didn't matter. What mattered was that Theo was *not* marrying her sister.

The door burst open. The gun was in her hands. A shot rang out. Her sister screamed.

Next, time slowed, nay, lurched to a stop, as abruptly as the coach in the yard had earlier. A man cursed. It was a familiar voice, but not that of Theodore Bull. It was a voice from her past, a voice that used to laughingly sing "Here we go round the mulberry bush" with her when they came upon such a shrub in their wanderings.

Her own voice was the next to ring out across the room. "Arch!"

"Clem."

"I shot you."

"You did indeed."

4

Go Ahead and Panic

The room erupted into a frenzy of feminine alarm as the Morgan sisters, after a beat of staring at Archie as if he were their own dead mother back from beyond the grave, started shrieking. They descended on him like a pair of vultures, and the relief that had slammed into him when he'd burst into the room and found them both well was replaced by annoyance. Ignoring them, he tore off his coat and cravat and yanked his shirt down from the collar to examine his wound, which felt like it was on fire. Using the cravat, he cleaned it sufficiently to confirm his sense that it wasn't a dire injury. It hurt like the devil, though.

"Hush!" he snapped as he put his shirt back to rights—the Morgans were still in an uproar—and he was downright shocked when it worked. He had to take a moment to adjust to the silence and to think about what came next. "We have your Mr. Bull in hand, and I daresay that with a bit of strategy we can get out of here undetected, but only if no one causes a scene."

"Who is 'we'?" Olive said at the same time that Clementine said, "But I shot you!"

And then Olive said, "That's true; she *did* shoot you" at the same time that Clementine said, "He's not *my* Mr. Bull."

"'Tis merely a flesh wound," Archie said, choosing to address first the unfortunate circumstance of Clementine having *shot him*.

He winced as he gestured behind him. "The ball, I believe, is lodged in the paneling of the corridor outside." Archie was an accomplished hunter now, but he hadn't always been, and as a boy, he'd hit enough trees in error to know the sound of lead embedding in wood. "It only grazed me." His shoulder hurt like the devil, but the wound was nowhere near mortal.

"She thought you were Mr. Bull," Olive said weakly.

"What in God's name are you *doing*, Clem?" he shouted, forgetting for a moment his own directive that they should keep their voices down. But for Heaven's sake, Clementine was disrobing.

"I am disrobing."

He rolled his eyes. "I can see that. In case you have failed to grasp what is happening, I am attempting to *salvage* your reputations, but you have discharged a weapon that has surely been heard by everyone downstairs, and—"

"I have several yards of muslin beneath this shirt that I was using to bind my . . . apple dumplins."

"Your *what?*"

"I'll thank you to turn your back for a moment, Arch."

"Don't call me that," he said automatically, but he turned as instructed, his face oddly hot.

"I say, Clementine," Olive said, "your disguise is ingenious. *I* recognized you, of course, but that's because I'm me and you're you. But if I remove that familiarity, you look remarkably like a boy."

"You may turn, Arch," Clementine said.

"*Don't* call me that," he said peevishly, though he turned back and registered that Clementine Morgan was wearing gentlemen's clothing. Plain buff knee breeches, scuffed but serviceable Hessians that appeared absurdly too large, and a wrinkled white shirt she was finishing buttoning back up.

She did not look like a boy whatsoever.

Clementine made a shooing motion at Olive, who said, "Oh, yes!" and hurried over to him with Clementine's muslin in her hand and said, "Archie, take off your shirt."

"I will do no such thing." There had been quite enough public disrobing for one day.

"If you want to escape without drawing attention to ourselves, we've got to stop that bleeding," Clementine said, looking reproachfully at him.

He followed her gaze to his arm and had to admit that his wound, while superficial, was doing a rather impressive job of bleeding through his shirt.

Archie sighed and shrugged out of the bloody sleeve. The muslin Olive wrapped around his arm was still warm. From Clementine's body, he supposed. It was damp, too. He eyed her. It was an unseasonably hot September. She must have been quite warm with her . . . self wrapped in so much fabric beneath a shirt, waistcoat, and coat. And now that she was no longer thusly wrapped, he was confronted by the fact that there was an awful lot of her . . . self there. More than he remembered noticing in the past, anyway. How . . . discomposing.

The sound of footsteps jolted him back to the task at hand. "*Clem*," he said urgently, "look at me." She did, and he noted, as he always had when they were young, that her eyes were the exact color of an old thruppence. He shook his head. That the color of her eyes was unchanged was unremarkable. "Someone is coming. Probably to investigate the noise from your having *shot me*." She winced. Good. She *should* wince. "If anyone knocks, Olive and I are going to hide behind this door. You open it and profess to have heard the gunshot but say you are certain it came from the floor below, from the other end of the building." He pointed. "Do you understand?"

She nodded, and though he feared she wouldn't be able to pull off the subterfuge, especially now that she had de-muslined her . . . self, he needn't have worried. A knock came, and she opened the door a few inches and conferred with the innkeeper in a voice Archie would have recognized as hers in the middle of a ballroom full of nattering masses, but he supposed she was doing a decent enough job lowering it that she sounded credibly mannish to a stranger.

When she shut the door again, he said, "That will buy us a little time, but we must make haste."

"What did you mean when you said you had Mr. Bull in hand?" Olive asked, tucking in the end of the muslin to secure the bandage she'd been fashioning around Archie's upper arm. "Where is he?" She tilted her head at him in the exact same way Clementine used to. "What are you even *doing* here, Archie?"

He started on her first question as he pulled on his coat. He'd merely been winged, but good God, the wound smarted. "I threatened Mr. Bull with a rifle—quietly, without *actually* shooting him." He looked pointedly at Clementine, and she winced again. *Good.* "He's currently outside, being held discreetly by two friends of mine."

"Oh, yes, it's September!" Clementine exclaimed, her serious demeanor undergoing a sudden reversal. "Are Lords Marsden and Featherfinch with you? How wonderful."

"You sound as if you're commenting on a musicale we all happen to find ourselves at and not the potential ruination of yourself and your sister." He turned to Olive to answer the latter of her questions. "I'm here because your father bade me come after you."

He watched both girls absorb the fact that he had been dispatched by Sir Albert. After a beat, they said in unison, "I can explain."

Clementine shifted her attention to her sister. "Don't you think you owe *me* an explanation as well?"

There had been a distinct note of . . . something in that question. Not quite anger, but certainly some sort of heightened sentiment. Was Clementine *hurt* by the loss of this Bull character? Had she not cried off her engagement to the man before he ran off with Olive?

Olive's expression was uncertain, as if she, too, were unsure of Clementine's state of mind. "Oh, Clemmie, I'm sorry. I—"

"There will be time for that later," Archie interrupted. "For now, we must get out of here before someone calls a magistrate. We'll make our way down the back stairs. The only question is what we should do with Mr. Bull. I'd like your thoughts on the matter before we make our escape."

"What do you mean what we should do with him?" Clementine asked warily.

Archie huffed a frustrated sigh. He had no doubt Clementine's flight after her sister had not included any plans for how to manage the aftermath of her wild scheme, should it actually prove successful—which, he had to admit, it had, at least insofar as she had managed to locate her sister and separate her from Mr. Bull. "I came here prepared to call out Mr. Bull and to marry one of you if need be, but I'd really rather not do either of those things if they can be avoided." Clementine's eyes widened in a fashion he would have found amusing had the circumstances been less dire. "Do you think if I extract a promise from him to leave England and to never speak to—or of—either of you again, that would be sufficient?"

"Yes!" Olive cried. "You can't die on our account, Archie!"

"I concur," Clementine said. "Please, no dying on our account. Or, nearly worse, please, no weddings." Her scrunched nose jolted him back in time. She used to pull *exactly* that face—she looked like she'd smelled something distasteful—when he'd bait her by claiming he could climb a tree faster than she could. Or when she wasn't convinced by one of his lies about why Mother hadn't been able to attend a dance at the Chiddington assembly rooms. "But how will you extract this promise?"

Instead of answering Clementine's question with words, he cracked his knuckles and shot her his own wide-eyed look. She would remember his many youthful pursuits. Archery. Slingshots. Hunting, his particular favorite.

"I see." Yes. She remembered. "Please try not to kill, maim, or otherwise disable Mr. Bull. He is a complete and utter knave, but I think it vastly preferable we not get caught up in a criminal investigation."

"He's bound for the Continent next week anyway," Olive said, "so I don't know that you need threaten him at all, Archie."

"I'll take that under advisement," Archie said mildly, but he was turning his mind to the grim task ahead. He hadn't been lying before: he did want to avoid murder. But perhaps only just. A man did not bring such harm, such potential ruin, down on not one, but two Morgan sisters and escape without consequences.

It was now time for Mr. Bull to face those consequences.

As Clementine finished changing into her wrinkled dress, she started to feel poorly. Her head ached something awful, her hands were shaking in a manner she wasn't entirely sure she could attribute to the ale she'd drunk, and something in her chest felt . . . not right.

"Perhaps I ought to change my bonnet?" Olive, who was studying her reflection in the mirror, asked. "If it's better for you to look like someone else, perhaps I should endeavor to alter my appearance as well? To look different from when I arrived?" They had decided that Clementine should transform herself back into a girl in order to lessen the likelihood that anyone would connect her boy incarnation with . . . whatever Archie was going to do to Theo. He was being maddeningly vague on that topic.

"A good idea," Archie said.

Clementine motioned toward Olive's portmanteau, though she felt as if she were watching her arm move under water. "If you've another bonnet in there, put it on and give me the one you're wearing."

She regarded the monstrosity Olive handed her, hoping her trouble focusing on it was due to *it* and not her. Like most of her sister's attire, the hat was a riot of overadornment. Pink feathers competed with a cascade of flowers fashioned from blue tulle. There was even a bird perched in the center of one of the flowers. Clementine found herself unaccountably irritated by the fact that it wasn't a specific sort of bird, but rather some overpriced milliner's idea of improving on what nature had already perfected. She grabbed it and pulled.

"What are you *doing*?" Olive cried.

"Making this bonnet less obtrusive." Clementine took a strange pleasure in freeing the bird from its bondage, and, in fact, the act grounded her, made her feel more herself. For good measure, she ripped the tulle off, too, ignoring her sister's wail of protest.

"*Enough*," Archie said, and Clementine couldn't begrudge him the annoyance in his tone. They really oughtn't to be bickering about hats at a time like this. "Follow me," he said, "and for God's sake, *be quiet*."

They encountered no one on their flight from the building. A cacophony of voices rose from the other end of the corridor below as they rounded the landing, no doubt thanks to Clementine's false account of the gunshot having come from there, but mercifully, their escape went unnoticed.

Outside, Archie's friend, Edward Astley, Viscount Featherfinch, was waiting for them in the muddy yard, looking like a Gothic hero from one of the novels Clementine secretly enjoyed. He and Archie undertook a kind of silent communication via raised eyebrows and nods as Archie handed off Clementine and Olive and turned on his heel.

"Where is he going?" she whispered as Lord Featherfinch hustled them over to a boy waiting with five horses. He didn't answer, but he didn't have to. She knew. Archie was off to "extract a promise" from Theo. Archibald Fielding-Burton, the Earl of Harcourt, could be very forceful in defense of his friends. She considered herself fortunate he apparently still counted her among them.

"Harcourt says you ladies are skilled riders?"

"We are," Olive was speaking to Lord Featherfinch but looking at Clementine. Her eyes narrowed as if she did not like what she saw. Clementine pressed her hands to her cheeks. They felt colder than they reasonably ought to given the heat of the afternoon.

"We were bound for Cumbria," Lord Featherfinch said. "We thought it best to leave the coach here and hire fresh horses to ride—it will be much faster and"—he looked in the direction Archie had gone—"given what is likely happening even now, we thought it best to prioritize expediency. Though it is a hard two hours' ride. We could stop somewhere along the way if need be, but given your precarious situation, we thought it better to go directly there, rather than to be seen at a nearby posting inn, if you ladies can manage the ride."

"Are you up to the task?" Olive asked Clementine.

"I'm a better rider than you," Clementine snapped, forgetting for a moment that she was meant to be reserving most of her ire for Theo. "Of course I'm up to the task."

In truth, though, she wasn't sure. Whatever had begun to afflict her upstairs was worsening. She felt increasingly light-headed, and her hands were shaking something awful.

"Clemmie," Olive said, and Clementine had to look around as her sister's voice suddenly seemed farther away, as if she were speaking from the far end of a long tunnel. She was surprised to see Lord Featherfinch in the process of handing Olive up onto one of the horses. "When did you last eat?"

"I . . ." Was that what this unsettling sensation was? Hunger?

Clementine's attention was drawn by the approach of Archie. It wasn't that he made any noise, but she somehow knew when he was near. She always had.

He and Simon Courteney, the Earl of Marsden, were striding purposefully toward them. The blood at Archie's shoulder was now showing through his coat, and she observed with dismay that he was also bleeding from a cut on his face. Lord Marsden was cradling one fist in the opposite palm, as if it pained him.

They had extracted their promise, and it had cost them.

Clementine *was* hungry, but she was also . . . overcome. By all she had lost—no, by what she had *given away*, she corrected herself ruthlessly, and she didn't just mean her maidenhood. She had surrendered that, but also her regard, her careful attention, her *loyalty*. She was overcome, too, by the nearness of the fate her sister had so narrowly escaped. And by the goodness of her old friend coming to her rescue.

Her knees started to wobble.

"She's going down!" she heard one of the men—not Archie—yell.

Strong arms caught her. She tilted her face to the sky. It was still there. Still blue. It would not be this blue in London. She needed to look her fill now.

"We'll have to double up on one of the horses." That *was* Archie speaking.

One of the other men said, "Hand her up here."

"I'll take her," Archie said gruffly.

"But your arm," the other not-Archie male voice protested.

"She's with me," Archie said in a tone that brooked no argument, and then she was floating, up, up, up toward the sky she so loved.

She cried out involuntarily when the floating stopped, but then those strong arms came around her again. A jostling started, but somehow its effect was buffeted by the arms. It felt more like rocking.

"I've got you, Clem," he whispered. "I've got you." And he did. She knew he did.

Two hours later, when Archie, his friends, and the Morgan sisters—one conscious, one not—turned up the drive to Quintrell Castle, horses and humans alike run through with exhaustion, Archie had just enough pretense of mind left to note that, normally, he would be rolling his eyes at the pile of limestone ahead of them. The ancient keep looked as though the removal of one stone would cause the whole structure to come crumbling down. As they drew closer, it became apparent that the more modern house—modern being a relative term, for he guessed the house was at least two hundred years old—attached to the fortification was not in much better condition. Its slate roof was missing quite a lot of pieces, and the tower nearest them appeared ready to collapse in on itself. The forest, which had been allowed to encroach onto the castle grounds, was poised to reclaim the property. One could almost imagine beleaguered Macbeth holed up in the castle as Birnham Wood encroached. They were very near Scotland, after all.

This was what happened when Effie was in charge of planning an Earls Trip. He got some fanciful notion in his head, and lo, they'd be off to some wildly impractical spot or other. This time, Effie had been offered the use of the property by an acquaintance of his, a fellow writer who was apparently not in residence this autumn.

"It's rumored to be haunted," Effie had said by way of explanation when pressed as to why they needed to undertake such a long journey when any of them could offer up a country house at a moment's notice. A *comfortable* country house. A house with an intact roof.

As they approached, their attention was drawn by the sudden, shrill cawing of a bird. Archie looked up to see a raven circling what he suspected had once been a guardhouse. It alit on a turret, and Effie exclaimed, "*Marvelous.*"

So, yes, under normal circumstances, Archie would be cursing the fact that they'd allowed Effie free rein with the holiday planning. But now, he was just so damned glad to have arrived somewhere—anywhere. His shoulder throbbed, and though Olive's hypothesis that Clementine's condition was due to hunger-induced light-headedness was likely correct, he was worried. He wanted to get some food into Clementine, check her for injuries—and, once he was assured she was all right, shout at her until his voice went hoarse.

They made their way past the ruined guardhouse and looked around for signs of life—a groom, perhaps? Anyone? Archie considered the notion that one benefit of this remote, run-down pile of stones might be that the arrival of three gentlemen and two unmarried women would not be quite the problem he had assumed. He'd begun to allow himself to hope, as he'd confronted Theodore Bull at the inn, that he *wouldn't* have to marry one of the Morgan sisters. But as they'd ridden away as if the devil himself was on their heels, it'd occurred to him that they weren't out of the woods. They would need a plausible explanation for the presence of unmarried women among their party when they arrived at Quintrell Castle. He'd been going to suggest he pose as Olive and Clementine's older brother. It wasn't that far from the truth, given how intertwined their childhoods had been.

But perhaps such subterfuge would not be necessary. Perhaps they *were* out of the woods.

Except, of course, for the whole forest-literally-encroaching-on the grounds bit.

"Let's walk the horses in and see if we can rouse anybody," Effie said.

"Dear God," Simon exhaled as they made their approach. Archie's sense that the forest had overtaken the grounds wasn't entirely true, or at least it wasn't true right here. They appeared to be in a large topiary garden. Except instead of the usual spheres and pyramids, or even swans and dragons, the entire park was populated by depictions of the male anatomy in its at-attention state. There must have been three dozen individual plants of different sizes, each painstakingly shaped into a prick and bollocks.

"Featherfinch!" Simon said censoriously, even as it was apparent he was trying not to laugh.

"Yes, well," Effie said brusquely, "Sir Lionel did say he was a hobbyist."

"A hobbyist of what sort?" Simon pressed. "Are we, in fact, talking about gardening, or something more . . . ?" He wagged his eyebrows and snickered.

"*Gentlemen.*" Archie, too, was suppressing laughter, and after the day's events, amusement felt like a balm. But there were ladies present, and one of them was conscious. He glanced at her. Olive Morgan *did* feel like a little sister to him, though he hadn't seen her in years, and it had been even longer since she'd been anything close to little. Still, he had the strongest impulse to put his hands over her eyes.

Which, of course, he could not do because his arms were full of her elder sister.

What a trip this was turning out to be.

"Yes, right." Effie dismounted, handed his reins to Simon, and made for what appeared to be the front door, though it was hard to tell as it was nearly covered over with vines.

"Remind me whose place this is?" Archie asked Simon. "Sir Lionel, he said? How did Featherfinch"—he reverted to Effie's title as that seemed to be what Simon was doing, probably on account of Olive's presence—"make the acquaintance of a Cumbrian baronet?"

"Sir Lionel Maundy. And he's not a baronet. The 'sir' is because he's a knight."

"Dare I ask what service to the Crown Sir Lionel performed?"

"Featherfinch said he is an essayist and an artist, though in what . . . medium I don't know." Simon looked around again in amusement. "What say you, Harcourt?"

The use of formal titles continued to feel strange. Especially Archie's own on Simon's lips. Here they were addressing each other by their proper titles instead of the given names and nicknames they'd been using since they were boys, yet they were in a positively lewd garden. The juxtaposition was amusing.

When Archie didn't answer, Simon continued. "Apparently Sir Lionel never married, which may explain the state of this place."

Archie rather thought it would take more than one generation of neglect to account for the state of the place, but he had more important concerns at the moment. He eyed Olive, fretting over what, if anything, to say about the garden. Thankfully, she seemed unruffled. She hardly seemed to notice the topiary at all as she turned a brow knit in concern toward Archie. "How fares my sister?"

The question sobered him. "She sleeps, but she is breathing and she is warm." But she needed to get off this horse. He eyed Effie, who was still pounding on the vine-choked door. Just as Archie began to fear the castle was as unoccupied as it looked and that they'd have to break in, the giant slab of wood swung open to reveal a stooped old man dressed in shirtsleeves. A conversation Archie couldn't hear ensued. Eventually, the man tottered out and announced in a thick Scottish brogue that he would see to the horses. It took some doing to get Clementine down, but eventually the lot of them limped inside, where they were welcomed by an ancient-looking woman who introduced herself—also in a brogue—as Mrs. MacPuddle.

Mrs. MacPuddle seemed not to have any idea who they were, but at the same time seemed perfectly satisfied with their explanation that the absent Sir Lionel was a friend of Lord Featherfinch's who had offered to lend the castle to the three lords for a fortnight. "Never tells me anything, the old jolterhead," she muttered under her breath, but to Archie's ears it was an affectionate sort of muttering.

After being made aware of Clementine's condition, Mrs. MacPuddle showed them directly to a bedchamber. Once again Archie was struck with the urge to laugh. The whole situation was so patently absurd, all of them crammed into this small room that looked as if it hadn't been occupied—or dusted—in a century. There was a great deal of to-ing and fro-ing as Effie and Simon, who'd been carrying Clementine between them since Archie's wounded arm had apparently turned to jelly, lowered their patient onto the bed. Eventually, Archie ordered the boys out, a feat he achieved only by promising that he would find them and allow them to tend to his shoulder as soon as he had Clementine settled. It was rather like having two overinvolved parents hovering.

Truth be told, he loved it.

"Hush," he said to Clementine, who had begun to protest. Leave it to Clementine to sleep through a punishing ride only to object the moment she was being installed in a comfortable bed. To the hovering Mrs. MacPuddle, he asked, "May I trouble you to have some food brought up? Something fortifying and easy to eat? Perhaps some cold meats?"

"I think some bread soaked in milk would be better," Olive said quickly, turning from where she was moistening a cloth from an ewer Mrs. MacPuddle had provided.

"Yes, thank you," Clementine whispered. She smiled weakly at Archie as he laid her back against the pillows. He all but sagged forward to join her, so relieved was he by that pathetic little smile.

"Are you all right?" he whispered back, though he had no idea why *he* was whispering. Or why the question had come out so tenderly, given that he was so *angry* with her. Or why his hand floated up to brush away a lock of hair that had fallen across her face.

Archie had no idea about anything, apparently. Only that the whispered nature of his question matched the wobbly feeling in his knees. The latter was making it difficult to imagine ever rising from Clementine's bedside, though he knew he was going to have to eventually, if only because the boys would come looking for him.

Clementine did not answer. They stared at each other for several seconds until Olive, bearing her cloth, inserted herself between them.

"You're fine, Clemmie," she said firmly. "Everyone's fine. We're all fine, and we'll talk tomorrow and sort ourselves out."

That seemed to be a dismissal. Archie rose from the bed.

"I am not injured," Clementine's voice rose in both pitch and volume as if to send her belated answer after Archie.

"Not injured" was not the same as "well," or even Olive's "fine," but Archie nodded and backed out of the room. Clementine's copper gaze held his the entire way out.

5

Unsteady as She Goes

The next morning, Archie was enjoying a cup of tea in the so-called breakfast room—which did not contain any breakfast despite Mrs. MacPuddle's assurances that she would manage to feed them for a fortnight—thinking about how Earls Trip was finally underway when Clementine marched in.

Gone was the whispering girl of last night. She had been replaced by a tall, assured, wild-haired woman who walked and spoke with confidence.

And, judging by the mud on her boots and the hem of her dress, she had already been outside, though it was not yet half seven. That part was familiar, too, and, more than anything else, an indication that she had not been elementally harmed by the events of yesterday.

"There are a few things we need to discuss," she said, sinking into a chair next to Archie before he could organize his limbs to stand in acknowledgment of her arrival. "First, I do not swoon."

"And a good morning to you, too," he remarked, trying not to be too obvious about letting his gaze roam her person, searching for any signs of lingering damage.

She was wearing a slate-blue day dress, which aside from the mud, was unremarkable. Her mahogany hair had been braided and the braids pinned up, but the whole thing was sloppily done.

Hanks of hair hung loose, and the still-pinned-up part was listing off to one side. Her cheeks were pink and her brown-copper eyes bright. She had a smattering of freckles across her cheeks and slightly-beaky nose. This was all familiar. The Clementine of his memory had often looked like this. Yet somehow, today, all these usual characteristics added up to something different.

He tried to think how long, exactly, it had been since he'd seen the Morgans. He'd attended Mrs. Morgan's funeral, of course, but the sisters had been veiled and surrounded by well-wishers. Beyond that, it had very likely been four, perhaps five years. He did some arithmetic: he was twenty-seven, which would make Clementine twenty-four. Suppose she had been nineteen the last time he saw her. How could the difference between nineteen and twenty-four be so great?

Yet it *was*. She was different.

Or perhaps, he thought with unease, she was the same, and *he* was different.

"I am not the sort of woman who swoons when confronted with unpleasantness," she declared. "I don't faint my way out of trying situations."

"I should think not. You're the sort of woman who shoots your way out of them."

Her posture softened. "I *am* sorry about that. How is your shoulder?" She leaned closer. "And your face?" She must have bathed, for whereas yesterday she had smelled . . . not bad exactly, but the way a person smelled after spending days on the Mail coach, today she smelled like . . . sugar and herbs. She smelled like Clementine.

And she had twigs in her hair, little ones that could only be seen from this close vantage point. He turned his head away to smile so she wouldn't see. A man shouldn't be seen to be too fond when discussing his own near murder. He composed himself before turning back and saying, gruffly, "I'm fine."

"Did you require a surgeon?"

"No. The injury looked worse than it was, bled more than was called for." Mrs. MacPuddle had interrupted the boys' ineffectual fussing over his wound last night and given him two stitches. It bothered him still, the sharp pain of yesterday having settled into a deep ache, but Clementine didn't need to know that.

"And this?"

She reached out as if to touch the scrape on his face, and he instinctively leaned back to dodge her hand, though he wasn't sure why. "Fine. Healing over already."

Now that he was calm and some time had passed, he could scarcely believe that he and Simon had . . . well, they'd ganged up on Theodore Bull. Archie was an avid boxer, sparring with a teacher in Sevenoaks, the town nearest Mollybrook of any size, as often as he could. And Heaven knew, he'd gotten into enough scuffles at school. But he'd never gotten into a proper, adult fight before. It was disconcerting. But it had worked: they'd gotten in several jabs before Mr. Bull surrendered. They'd frightened him enough, Archie dared say, that they could trust his promise to disappear. Simon had left him with a warning: "We know *everything*, and we shall make it public if we ever see or hear of your presence in England again." When Archie had questioned Simon about the threat, Simon had merely said, "Men like that always have secrets. I don't know what they are, but he doesn't know that."

So Archie supposed their fit of violence had worked. He eyed Clementine. He'd do it again if he had to, as uneasy as it made him.

"Well, good," Clementine said, "but I'm still sorry for shooting you, and for dragging you into this mess to begin with." She sighed. "Oh, Arch."

"Don't call me 'Arch.'"

"Why not?" she asked. "As diminutives go, 'Arch' is much more dignified than 'Archie.'"

"I don't like it," he said, though that wasn't precisely true. When Clementine called him "Arch," tossing the single syllable off as if it were her right, it made his insides feel wobbly, the same way his knees had yesternight at her bedside. Like a blancmange being transported too aggressively. Archie did not fancy being compared—even when he was the one doing the comparing—to a blancmange. "It doesn't suit me," he added peevishly.

"Well, you do it to me, too. You call me 'Clem.'"

"I do not," he said reflexively, though he wasn't sure why, as she was correct. He did call her "Clem." Or he used to. Yesterday aside, he hadn't had occasion to call her anything for several years.

"You do, though."

"Well, it isn't only my habit. Olive calls you 'Clem.'"

"She does not. She calls me 'Clemmie.' You're the only one who calls me 'Clem.'"

Was that true?

"I call you 'Arch' and you call me 'Clem,' but usually only when other people aren't around."

Was *that* true? He would certainly never have used her Christian name in company, nor she his, but when they'd been alone, or among immediate family, they'd never stood on ceremony. Archie called Olive by her Christian name, too, in private. But again, that was years ago now, and both sisters had since had their debuts. And he had been trying to remember to call Simon and Effie by their titles here. Although this remote pile of rocks could hardly be considered society.

He shook his head. They were getting lost in the weeds here; none of this mattered. "Are we going to talk about yesterday?"

"What about it?"

The part where your sister eloped with a knave to whom you'd previously been betrothed? The part where you disguised yourself— poorly—as a boy and took flight after them? Or perhaps the part where you shot me?

He didn't articulate any of that, though. Instead, he said, "You weren't surprised to see me at the inn." The fact of which had just occurred to him because he remembered that she'd called him "Arch" when he'd burst into her room.

"I suppose I wasn't. That's a bit odd, isn't it? But on the other hand, perhaps not. You always seemed to be there when I needed you." She huffed a resigned sigh. "I suppose I shall have to tell you everything from the beginning, but I'd rather wait for Olive to awaken, because *I* don't know the whole story. Perhaps between the three of us, we can put the pieces together."

Fair enough. "And I'd prefer to wait for Marsden and Feather-finch if it's all the same to you. They're my closest companions, they were there yesterday, and they can be trusted absolutely. If there's anything more to be done to secure a good outcome from this near disaster, they can be of use. Still, if you'd prefer not to involve them any further, I will of course keep your confidence."

"I am quite willing, if not pleased, to recount the entire unfor-tunate saga for the lot of you. So let's wait for them, and for Olive." He was about to agree when she added, "However, there are a few things we can and should discuss now, the first being that, as I said, what you witnessed from me yesterday was not a swoon despite how it may have looked. I had barely eaten for days, and I hadn't slept at all. It *wasn't* a swoon."

"Noted." He wasn't sure the distinction mattered—what was a swoon but a loss of consciousness?—but it seemed important to her to make one. He refrained from upbraiding her on the sub-stance of her assertion—the fact that she hadn't eaten or slept for days—reasoning that he would save that for the larger conclave. But honestly, if one was going to make an impulsive, hazardous journey of the sort she'd undertaken, the least one could do was provision oneself sufficiently.

She looked surprised by his lack of ire, and it took her a mo-ment to begin speaking again. "Secondly, I would like it stated for the record that I have no plans to marry. I am opposed, in the strongest possible terms, to the very concept. This whole mess with Mr. Bull resulted from an appalling lack of judgment, but I am returned to my senses. While I appreciate your loyalty to my family, I'm sure you are relieved by the fact that it hasn't resulted in an imperative to wed either Olive or me. Regardless of whatever my father has said on the matter, after three Seasons to acquaint myself with the . . . selection, I shan't be marrying anyone—not even to avoid ruination. I thought I ought to make that clear."

The *selection*. Archie stifled a chuckle. He was tempted to commiserate, to say that he understood what it was like to have an overbearing father who thought he knew best, but he was still peeved at her, so he settled once again for saying, "Noted." Again, she looked surprised that he wasn't going to fight her. "Is that all?"

"No. There's one more thing. I should like to stay here for the rest of your planned sojourn. With Olive, of course. I should prefer that we not go back to London at this time."

"Yes, fine."

"*Fine?*" Surprise transmuted into astonishment. Her eyes went so wide her eyebrows nearly disappeared into the unkempt hair slanted across her forehead.

"We are already late arriving because we detoured to go after you," he explained. "We've only ten days left of our holiday. If I took you back to London at a more humane pace than either of us took to get here, several more days would pass. There would then be no point in making my way back here."

And now that he was here, after the pair of false starts, he couldn't bear the idea of giving up his holiday. The boys had been right, as had Miss Brown. Archie *needed* this break.

"I shall write to your father straight away." Well, he would dictate a letter and Effie would write it. "I will tell him all is well and that I will deliver you and your sister home at the end of my holiday. Surely there can be no objection? He did trust me enough to send me after you." And more to the point, Sir Albert was many hundreds of miles away, so even if he did object, there wasn't much the old man could do about it.

"Mind you," Archie added, "I *would* have taken you back to Town if I'd had to, but it seems clear that no one in this odd house is in any position to harm your reputations or standings in society." Effie had had a chat with Mrs. MacPuddle, and besides her and the elderly man who'd seen to their horses last night, the only other people in residence were a kitchen maid, a housemaid, and the housemaid's four-year-old daughter. The housemaid was Mrs. MacPuddle's granddaughter, a girl of about twenty who'd been round to light the fires that morning. There'd been no mention of a husband to Mrs. MacPuddle's granddaughter. Archie didn't give a fig about any of it, except to the extent that perhaps people in glass houses, et cetera, et cetera. As a result, he felt quite confident that there was no harm—of either the literal or reputational variety—waiting to befall anyone at Quintrell Castle. Assuming, that was, that they could shield themselves from falling roof tiles and protect against invading armies disguised as trees. "So," he said in conclusion, "I'd just as soon not have my holiday ruined if it's all the same to you."

Clementine opened her mouth, closed it, and opened it again. Along with her still-wide eyes, it brought to mind a haddock. He tried not to laugh. Clementine Morgan loved all the creatures of field and stream, but he suspected even she would not take kindly to being compared to a fish so ill-featured as a haddock. He told himself to enjoy this moment of having struck Clementine dumb. It was the first time he could remember it happening, and it was entirely possible it would be the last.

"That would be quite satisfactory," she said once she'd regained the power of speech. "Father will not object. He knows you are like a brother to Olive and me."

"However, there is one condition: You and your sister will make yourselves scarce. Not scarce enough to get into any trouble, mind you, but scarce." As glad as he was that Clementine was safe, and as much as he vowed to renew his friendship with the Morgan family, that was not what this trip was about. "Do I make myself clear?"

"Quite."

"This trip is a sacred masculine tradition."

"I understand."

"I had a walk about the house this morning, mostly to make sure it is, in fact, structurally sound, but I observed that it is sizable enough that we can easily stay out of each other's way."

"Yes."

"I cannot stress this point firmly enough. I don't want you—"

"Arch!"

"What?"

"I am agreeing with you. I have done nothing but agree with you since you started talking! You won't even know Olive and I are here. I *promise.*"

Right. Well, then. He picked up his teacup. "Don't call me Arch."

After her petition to Archie had been so unexpectedly successful, Clementine's next order of business was to pay a visit to Olive's bedchamber. She found her sister, who had never been an early riser, still abed, snoring lightly as if she hadn't a care in the world. Clementine marched in, slammed the door behind her, and threw open the curtains to the misty morning.

"Get up," Clementine said curtly. She tried to summon some of yesterday's faith that her sister had not knowingly and callously betrayed her. But with a clear head and in the bright light of morning, it was harder to cling to that certitude. The fact remained that Olive had run off with Theo. *Olive had run off with Theo.* With the fear and panic of recent days having faded, what remained was anger, and while Clementine had a healthy supply of it for Theo, at the moment there was plenty left over for Olive: for stealing Clementine's erstwhile, good-for-nothing fiancé, for almost throwing away her youth and good name on such a man, for sending them on a wild-goose chase that could have ended very badly for both of them—and that *had* resulted in Archie's being injured.

"Clemmie?" Olive said sleepily as Clementine stood looking out the window. In novels, anger was often described as hot. Invigorating. A force that animated a person, making her impulsive and rash. *This* anger was like snow, white and cold and deadening.

Perhaps she ought to stop expecting life to be like novels.

"Clemmie, are you all right?" Olive asked. "I was so worried about you last night."

Slowly, Clementine turned and saw that her sister believed what she said—that she *had* been worried. Olive was, generally speaking, careless and selfish and impulsive. She thought nothing of manipulating people and situations to satisfy the most passing of whims. Olive never *intended* to hurt people with her behavior, but the fact remained that she *did*, because she didn't think about the *implications* of such behavior, beyond whether it would get her what she wanted.

But to be fair, Olive was also loyal to a fault. It was as if Olive had drawn a circle around herself, nay, *branded* a circle around herself, scorching a line in the earth with fire. The result was an unmovable enclosure, and if you were inside it, there was nothing Olive wouldn't do for you. Clementine had seen this pattern unfold dozens of times, had witnessed her sister give the cut to people whose only crime had been a slight, sometimes even an unintentional one, against one of Olive's friends.

Clementine and Olive had little in common and had never been close. There were five years between them, and though they'd shared a governess for a while, at some point a tutor had been brought in for Clementine, and later, when Olive's interests had bent more toward drawing and singing and painting, music and art masters had been brought in for her. The sisters were like stars that appeared close together in the sky, but in truth existed on different planes. Still, Clementine would have thought she'd be inside Olive's circle by virtue of blood if nothing else.

But why? Why would she think that? What was blood, really? Look at the brotherhood Archie had forged with his bosom friends.

"I am fine—physically," Clementine said slowly, turning her mind to her sister's question. "But for all you know, my heart is broken."

Olive tilted her head and said, "It isn't, though, is it?" She threw off the bedclothes and extended her arms, inviting Clementine to embrace her.

Clementine kept her arms by her side. The anger was still cold; it was making her brittle, disinclined to allow such a gesture of comfort.

Except it wasn't *only* anger. It was pride, the only defense she had here, outside of the circle. "Olive, everyone knows you're the prettier of us." Clementine's voice sounded as cold as her body felt. Her tone was dispassionate, as if she were commenting on, say, a piece of embroidery—and it was difficult to overstate how little she cared about embroidery.

Olive started to bluster over Clementine's remark. Clementine held up a hand. "You're clever, too, so don't pretend not to understand me. You're pretty, you sing like a lark, and you speak three languages. You embroider and play the pianoforte with great skill. And your father is a baronet." Olive's brow furrowed. Clementine would have to spell it out, which somehow made it all the more mortifying. "I have the same baronet father, of course, but I don't have those other qualities. I don't have your classic English beauty, your charm, or your mastery of the feminine pursuits. I know what people say about me, that I'm odd and wild and unbiddable and in possession of an ugly nose and that I ought to do a better job concealing my freckles if I want to catch a husband. You, on the other hand, could have any man alive. Why did you have to take the only one I'd ever wanted?"

She had tried to keep the hurt out of her voice, but was very much afraid she had not succeeded.

She saw understanding dawn as Olive climbed out of bed and came to stand in front of her. "But you didn't want him anymore, did you, Clemmie? That was exactly the point—and the problem." Pity flooded Olive's expression as she took Clementine's hand.

That could not be allowed to stand. Clementine snatched her hand away. "What do you mean? How do you know that?" How *could* she know? Clementine had spoken to Father about her change of heart regarding the engagement, but he had been attempting to convince her to stay the course. Whether he'd have been successful or not, he would *never* have breathed a word to Olive. Father believed his younger daughter to be more innocent than she was. He was forever trying to shield Olive from the machinations of men when really what he ought to be doing was shielding men from the machinations of Olive.

"Theo told me," Olive said calmly. "He told me you'd cried off, that he'd taken your maidenhood, and that he was going to tell everyone as much unless you changed your mind and agreed to marry him after all. He was preparing to blackmail you."

Clementine did not like to think of herself as a gasper. She was not the sort of lady who swooned *or* gasped. She had once stared down a wild boar, for Heaven's sake. But the gasp that ripped from her throat at Olive's matter-of-fact recitation of Theo's misdeeds was so theatrical as to be worthy of inclusion in a pantomime.

The last few days had proven very lowering indeed.

She had not thought Theo capable of such cruelty. But she had also not thought him capable of many other things she had gone on to witness him doing, including ordering not one but two plates of roast beef.

"So I suggested that *I* marry him instead, in exchange for his keeping quiet about you," Olive went on, summoning another gasp from Clementine. "I am not as witless as you think, Sister. One of us was as good as the other from his perspective, I reasoned. What Theo wanted was a generous dowry and to marry into a respectable family. He didn't actually care about *you*."

So Clementine had learned. She wanted it not to sting, but it did.

"Or me," Olive added, and that stung, too, but it was more akin to a bee sting, a galvanizing pinch that made Clementine angry. How *dare* Theo not care about Olive? Even though Clementine was angry at Olive.

This was all very confusing.

"But I *knew* he didn't care about me," Olive went on, "so I wasn't bothered by it."

"Then why would you offer to take my place?" Clementine asked. "Why would you sacrifice yourself for . . ." Oh. Oh no. "Olive, did you also . . . ?"

Why couldn't she finish a sentence? In addition to not gasping or swooning, Clementine did not dissemble.

"*No*," Olive said firmly, and in a way that suggested she'd heard the unarticulated part of Clementine's question. "No, I did not." She looked at Clementine with an expression that seemed to say, *Unlike you.*

Clementine's cheeks burned. Not with shame over what she had done exactly. Perhaps to her discredit, she had not seen any great moral problem with anticipating her marriage vows. Nay, her hot cheeks heralded shame over her spectacular lapse in judgment in choosing Theo to begin with. She shoved it down. Her humiliation was not the point here; getting to the bottom of Olive's extraordinary actions was.

The only explanation left was that Olive carried a genuine tendre for Theo. Olive did tend to do that. And Theo was a very good actor. Clementine sighed. "Had you fallen in love with him, Olive?"

"Good Heavens, *no!*" Olive made a face as if she'd drunk spoilt milk.

"If you didn't have warm feelings for him, and if you hadn't given him your maidenhood, why would you offer to take my place?" It couldn't have been purely to spare Clementine the humiliation of ruination. Clementine wasn't inside Olive's circle. *Was she?*

"I had my reasons," Olive said briskly, moving to look at herself in a small mirror mounted above the bureau. Like everything in the castle, it was timeworn. Olive had to contort herself to find an untarnished spot.

"That's all you're going to say?" That could not be the end of this conversation. Clementine hadn't learned anything—well, beyond the ultimately unsurprising fact that Theo had been intending to blackmail her into un-breaking their engagement.

"You needn't know everything about me, Clemmie, just like I needn't know everything about you."

While true, that declaration, and the blithe manner in which Olive tossed it off, caused a pang in Clementine's chest. A day ago, she would have agreed, would've had no wish to know the details of Olive's social scheming, and no desire to show Olive the contents of her own heart. Today, though, she wondered if she'd been too quick to declare their sisterly differences disqualifying.

"For example," Olive went on, "I don't need to know why you gave Theo your maidenhood." Clementine's face heated anew. "That's between the two people involved—and God, I suppose, if a person is inclined that way."

If a person is inclined that way? Goodness, was her sister secretly a heathen? What else didn't Clementine know about Olive?

Olive began pinching her cheeks to bring color into them, and all Clementine could do was stand there, agog. "But although I had my reasons," Olive continued, pressing her lips together in a fashion that called to mind a duck, "and although I'd made my peace with the trade-off I was planning to make, I will admit that I did not understand Theo's intentions for our life together until our journey was underway. So I do think the best possible outcome was achieved. Thanks to Archie, neither of us is ruined, and neither of us has to marry Theodore Bull." She finally stepped away from the mirror and turned and smiled cheerily at Clementine. "And now we can put this bit of unpleasantness behind us."

"But . . ." Clementine wasn't even sure what she was objecting to. She desperately wanted to know about this trade-off Olive had referenced. She wanted to know what *I had my reasons* meant. She wanted to know how Olive could be so calm. So cheerful. So not consumed by dread, or even any sense of mild unease, over what might have been. But she knew pressing would do no good; Olive could be endlessly stubborn when she had a mind to be. Regardless, Clementine was certainly in agreement that the absence of both ruination and husbands was a good outcome.

"But what?" Olive prompted.

"But you can't call him 'Archie' here," Clementine finished weakly, needing something to append to her aborted thought. "In company, he is Lord Harcourt."

"I *know* that, silly. You *just* said yourself that I was clever." A small smile suddenly appeared and was just as quickly extinguished.

"He said we may remain here, with him and his friends," Clementine explained. "Well, we may remain as long as we're not *with* them. If we agree to stay out of their way, he'll send word to Father that all is well, and we will return to Town with them at the conclusion of their holiday."

"Really?" Olive did a little twirl that made her look younger than her nineteen years, and Clementine's heart performed another confusing pang she did not know how to interpret. "Oh, goody!"

Clementine was a little surprised by Olive's enthusiasm. As much as Clementine preferred the country, Olive favored the city. "But he is entirely in earnest about us staying away from him. We mustn't be underfoot."

"Well, that is a pity. I would like very much to find out who Lord Featherfinch's tailor is. He certainly is a swell of the first stare, isn't he? He looks like the hero of a Gothic novel, like he's meant to be wandering around the heath suffering terrible pangs of unrequited longing."

Clementine had thought the same, but she was not about to admit to it. She tended to read such novels only when perched high in trees; she always took care that her drawing-room reading was more respectable. Though now that she thought of it, she wasn't sure why. She was profoundly uninterested in catching a man, and she was beginning to think that life was too short not to simply read what one wanted to read.

"But yes," Olive said solemnly, "I understand, and I shan't do anything to compromise our sojourn here, for in my estimation, we truly need it, the both of us."

"All right, then." What more was there to say? Apparently nothing, though Clementine could not shake the sense that they were slithering out of this near-disaster too easily.

"I say, are you sure you're all right, Clemmie?" Olive called after her as she turned to go.

Clementine considered the question. She did not know if she was all right. But if she wasn't, what *was* she? Not heartbroken over Theo. Not heartbroken over Olive either, as it turned out, since Olive had apparently been acting at least partially in Clementine's interest, if for reasons that remained mysterious and were probably at least somewhat self-serving.

She was no longer hungry anymore, either, as she'd visited the kitchen for some more milk and bread this morning and had drunk several cups of tea.

She should be feeling buoyed. She *should* be all right.

"You look a bit unsteady," Olive added.

Yes. That was a good word for it. She was unsteady. How could something so potentially life-changing, so frightening, end with such a whimper? She'd been primed for so many days to fight. And now, not only was there no need to, it appeared she was on holiday.

"I'm fine," Clementine lied.

And then she did what she always did when she was in any sort of discomposed state—she went outside.

6

Guess Who's (Not) Coming to Dinner

That afternoon, Clementine and Olive and Archie and his friends took a nuncheon, such as it was, on the terrace, such as it was.

Clementine had been worried about whether there would be anything for her to eat. The kitchen seemed well able to supply bread, but she was fairly certain neither Olive nor Archie would allow her to continue to subsist on bread alone. To her relief, Mrs. MacPuddle served baskets of grapes and peaches along with what she supposed were meant to be biscuits. A curious nuncheon indeed.

It was the biscuits that were the problem.

"My goodness," Lord Featherfinch said after an unsuccessful attempt to bite into one.

"Indeed," Archie said, making a face and setting his own gingerly back on his plate after a single bite. Clementine had done the same.

Lord Featherfinch regripped his small, hard puck and applied himself to the task anew. After several seconds of chewing, he asked, "Is that . . . anise?"

Clementine popped a grape into her mouth and surveyed the terrace. The setting for their repast wasn't much more functional than the biscuits, though it was pretty in a ramshackle sort of way. The stone wall between their party and the overgrown gardens beneath them—unlike the remarkable topiary out front that Clementine had discovered on her morning ramble, the back garden appeared not to have been tended in years—was crumbling.

The ground beneath them was in similar condition, as evidenced by the fact that Lord Marsden, who appeared, saying, "Forgive my tardiness; I lost track of time," tripped over an errant stone and stumbled his way to the table.

"Beware the biscuits," Lord Featherfinch said as Lord Marsden took his seat.

Olive said, "I've consulted with Mrs. MacPuddle and visited the kitchen, where there is but one maid. No cook. Apparently the master of the house does not keep one, not being 'of a mind to fuss over his food.'"

"Ah, yes, that does not surprise me," Lord Featherfinch said. "Sir Lionel lives a life of the mind." He looked around. "Which perhaps explains the . . . state of things."

"Where is Sir Lionel, anyway?" Lord Marsden asked. "He seems a rather eccentric sort."

"He is writing a collection of essays on solitude," Lord Featherfinch said, "so he has gone away to really immerse himself in the sensation."

"His giant, understaffed Cumbrian castle in which he lives alone not providing enough solitude for the task," Lord Marsden said wryly.

Lord Featherfinch shrugged. "He has removed to the Outer Hebrides."

"Mrs. MacPuddle advises that a cook might be borrowed from a nearby estate," Olive said. "If everyone is in agreement, I shall inquire this afternoon."

Clementine contemplated Olive, who had been daintily eating a grape as if this were a perfectly normal afternoon in perfectly normal company and not the day after she'd been rescued from a botched elopement with her sister's erstwhile betrothed.

Everyone was in enthusiastic agreement with Olive's plan, including Clementine, because this meant her sister would be able to explain Clementine's unique dietary requirements to the cook. Olive was always attuned to these sorts of domestic details. Clementine smiled gratefully at her sister before remembering that she was, well, not angry anymore, but . . . something.

Regardless, Olive really was going to make some man a marvelous wife someday. Clementine was thrilled that someone was not going to be Theo.

"Shall we reapply ourselves to these beastly biscuits?" Lord Featherfinch asked, and just as they were about to, a slate tile fell off the roof and landed on the stone floor a few yards from them.

"Goodness!" Olive exclaimed. "This is quite the house."

"It's haunted, supposedly," Lord Featherfinch said.

"Truly?" Olive turned, rapt.

"Yes, it underwent a siege during the Jacobite risings and is reportedly haunted by the ghost of a Highlander called Magnus MacCallum." Lord Featherfinch lowered his voice. "Did anyone hear or see anything unusual last night?"

"Aside from the topiary garden, you mean," Lord Marsden said drily, and Clementine had to stifle a laugh.

Lord Featherfinch leaned forward, as if he were about to impart a great secret. "I can't be sure, but I awakened suddenly from the midst of a dream well after midnight, and I could have sworn I heard bagpipes."

"But mightn't you actually have heard pipes?" Lord Marsden asked. "Real ones, I mean, not phantasmagoric ones? We *are* quite close to the Scottish border."

"Hmm," Lord Featherfinch said, and Clementine had the sense that he was disappointed by this application of logic. "I suppose we shall have to undertake a bit of ghost-hunting to be certain."

Olive made a delighted noise and Lord Marsden an exasperated one.

"I propose a walk down to the forest." Lord Featherfinch gestured to the encroaching wilds. "I understand that the path of the marauding MacCallum clan can still be seen, even all these centuries later. Supposedly, nothing grows over the route their invasion took."

Clementine had to admit that was a sight she would like to see, not because she believed the spirits of the long-dead MacCallums had salted the earth but because a stand of beech trees near Hill House had fallen subject some years ago to a rapid and terrible blight that had resulted in similar-sounding conditions.

Archie cleared his throat, drawing everyone's attention. He hadn't spoken yet, but Clementine had been acutely aware of him since she arrived at the table. He had a commanding presence she didn't remember from their youth. He'd always been tall, but he was leaner than he used to be, with prominent cheekbones and a fall of dark hair that made him seem very grown up and very polished. He had grown into his title. "Ghost-hunting is all fine and good for those so inclined, but we have matters to discuss first, do we not?" He looked at Clementine censoriously. "Now that we are all present, shall we get on with it?"

Yes. As much as Clementine wished the ghosts of the MacCallums would seize this moment to spirit her off, she owed these men an explanation. She took a fortifying breath. "I suppose I shall have to tell you all everything."

"I wish you would," Lord Featherfinch said. "I have a notion it's bound to be a most exciting tale."

"*I* have a notion that both you and your sister have been grossly mistreated," said Lord Marsden, his voice laden with kindness and affront in equal measure. "If you would care to tell us what happened, you can rest assured we will do what we can to assist."

"Indeed," Lord Featherfinch agreed. "I assure you that my interest, while perhaps not entirely selfless—I am a poet, after all, so human experience is my muse—is not salacious."

"Thank you," Clementine said, and she meant it. "And thank you for all you have already done for us."

"Yes, thank you," Olive said, reaching for Clementine's hand under the table.

Clementine let her keep it this time, allowed herself to be bolstered by the gentle pressure of her sister's hand. She thought of the woods she would escape to after this meal.

"I met Mr. Bull at a party given by some neighbors in London," she began slowly, thinking back to that unfortunate evening with the benefit of hindsight. "I was in my third London Season, which was for me three too many." She glanced at Archie, who was watching intently, though he remained silent. "Lord Harcourt will remember that I was never inclined toward Town, preferring to spend my time at my family's house outside Chiddington, near Mollybrook."

"Two of a kind you are that way," Lord Marsden said. "Harcourt's aversion to London is such that I hardly see him anymore."

"My father has been anxious that I marry," Clementine continued, "despite the fact that I realized early on in my first Season that I had no desire to do so. So we have been spending nearly all our time in Town, or in Bath, these recent years. Anywhere my father thinks I might catch a husband." She paused, trying to think how to put this. "I have not as yet found one I can abide."

"Ah," Lord Featherfinch said, "the men of the Upper Ten Thousand are rather a disappointment, are they not?"

Clementine wasn't sure if he was in jest. Regardless, she might as well tell them the unvarnished truth. "It's more that I discovered how constitutionally ill-suited I am to matrimony. Perhaps I started too late: my initial Season was delayed two years by my mother's lingering illness. It may be I was already too formed in my opinions by the time I debuted. Regardless, I have declared my fervent wish to remain unmarried. My father has nevertheless remained insistent, and so we have been at odds."

"It was our late mother's dearest wish that our father see us married," Olive explained. "And that wish runs counter to my sister's natural inclinations," she added diplomatically. Hmm. Perhaps Olive *had* been more observant these recent years than Clementine had given her credit for.

"To put it plainly," Clementine said, deciding to be direct, "I'm not a good prospect, and Father is growing desperate."

"Not a good prospect how?" Lord Marsden objected. "You seem a very capable sort to me."

"It's not every man who wants a wife who would run away alone to confront a criminal," Archie said drily.

"I am well aware that my interests and inclinations run counter to those of most well-bred young ladies." Clementine did not want to enter into a debate about her marriageability. To do so suggested she was entertaining the notion to begin with, which she most decidedly was not. She pushed on with the story. The sooner it was out, the sooner this would be over. Archie's friends were very kind, but she couldn't escape the feeling that she was on trial. "Mr. Bull is a proponent of what is deemed vegetarianism—the removal of animals from one's diet."

"So we have heard," Lord Featherfinch said.

"He's written a pamphlet. It was all the crack early last Season. I read it, and even though I now understand that Mr. Bull is the worst sort of hypocrite"—the image of that plate of roast beef still boiled her blood—"I was taken by his ideas. I've always been a friend to animals and have often wished I didn't have to eat them. His writing was the first time I'd seen anyone put words to the notion that perhaps I *didn't* have to. And not only that, but perhaps I *shouldn't*. Perhaps no one should."

She glanced at Archie, who had raised a single eyebrow—she'd forgotten that he could do that—before continuing. "Mr. Bull and I struck up a friendship, and before I knew it, he was . . ." She closed her eyes briefly. It was so lowering. "Well, he was flattering me, I suppose. It happened very quickly, and it was all so . . ." She cleared her throat. "He proposed. He said he was in need of a wife who could be a helpmeet. He begrudged the time he had to spend overseeing the production of his writings and the dissemination of his ideas. If he had someone to whom he could dictate his manuscripts, on whom he could rely to liaise with printers, keep track of social and speaking engagements, and so on, this would liberate time for higher-level thinking. I wanted to be that person. I was enamoured of his ideas. Not just his ideas, if I'm being truthful. I even came to . . ." She'd been going to say that while she hadn't loved Theo—she didn't think—she had held him in great esteem. She had been able to imagine a kind of love growing, over time, alongside their righteous shared purpose.

"You needn't tell us what was in your heart, Miss Morgan," Lord Featherfinch said—again, with a degree of kindness that buoyed her.

"Indeed." Olive squeezed Clementine's hand under the table. "What was—or was not—in your heart is not relevant to how we move forward."

Clementine took the point. The ease with which she'd fallen victim to Theo's honeyed words was mortifying, but not an essential part of the story as far as these gentlemen were concerned. "I had been in receipt of offers previously, two of them, and I'd declined both," she explained, wanting to provide some context.

Archie made a dismissive noise she couldn't quite characterize. Did he not believe she'd had offers? Or was he, as Father had been, upset that she hadn't accepted one of them? When she looked to him for clarification, that quizzical-bordering-on-skeptical demeanor of his remained unchanged, though at least the previously rogue eyebrow remained in line with its mate.

She pressed onward, turning to Lords Featherfinch and Marsden, who, unlike Archie and Olive, didn't know Father. "My father is not the sort of man to force me to accept an offer I find truly objectionable. Or at least he hasn't been historically. But he is *also* not the sort of man to give up when he's set his mind to something. And so our stalemate has ground on, with no apparent end in sight. My plan had been to wait him out, to trudge through however many Seasons it took for him to accept that I was irredeemably on the shelf."

Olive giggled, drawing everyone's attention. "Apologies. I was just thinking that, given how stubborn both my father and sister are, we might be witness, years hence, to a thirty-year-old Miss Clementine Morgan, making the rounds of the Marriage Mart yet adamantly refusing to marry."

Olive had been jesting, but she wasn't wrong, so Clementine didn't chuckle along with the gentlemen. Well, she didn't chuckle along with Lords Marsden and Featherfinch. Archie was unamused, his demeanor transformed from skeptical to stony.

She picked up her story. "I'd begun to fret that I mightn't be able to keep holding off my father indefinitely. He was exceedingly upset when I turned back my most recent suitor. With Mr. Bull, I was suddenly presented with a way to break the stalemate. A different sort of suit. A marriage, yes, but one that would allow me to do some good in the world. This seemed a union worth settling for, all things considered."

She hated the way that sounded. While she hadn't harbored any starry-eyed, missish ideas about making a love match of the sort her parents had—she knew most people were not so lucky—she also did not like to think of herself as someone who could be so calculating, so mercenary, when it came to matrimony. She wasn't Olive. This wasn't how she wanted to be seen by Archie's friends. Or by Archie, whose countenance remained inscrutable. She wasn't accustomed to not knowing what Archie was thinking. But then, she supposed she wasn't accustomed to Archie himself anymore, not to this grown-up, unsmiling, imposing version of him, anyway.

"So you accepted Mr. Bull's hand," Lord Marsden prompted, drawing her attention from Archie.

"Yes, and my father was thrilled."

"Oh, he was *so* happy!" Olive added.

Clementine thought about how to tell the rest—*whether* to tell the rest.

No. As Olive had said, every detail, every sentiment, need not be aired. All that mattered was the outline of the events themselves, the external shape of them. "After I accepted Mr. Bull's suit, I came to understand that his interest in me had been largely financial." She thought back to his questioning about Hill House. "He wanted to know how big our country house was, how many servants we had there, whether it was entailed." And, oh, how ardent his attentions became after she'd answered that last question in the negative. She should have seen what he was doing. It had all been right there in front of her. As Olive would say, he had been showing her who he was, if she had only cared to look.

"It's not that I flattered myself he thought me a great intellect," she went on, trying to explain her actions to herself as much as to the assembled gentlemen, "but it turned out I had vastly overestimated his regard for my ideas, or even merely for my utility as a helpmeet—"

Another of those vague scoffing noises from Archie, but louder this time, so much so that it stopped her mid-sentence and drew everyone's attention.

"Did you have something to add, Harcourt?" Lord Marsden asked.

Archie made no response other than to gesture for her to continue.

"My father had offered quite a sizable dowry, you see, given how desperate he was for me to marry, and while Mr. Bull had enjoyed a period of acceptance in some society households, he was certainly never going to make a match among the highest echelons of the aristocracy. I was, to put it plainly, the best he could do."

"And with a cheery nature and the prettiest hair in Town—not to mention eight hundred pounds and an unentailed house—you are no consolation prize, Clemmie!" Olive cried with a tone of affront.

Olive thought she had pretty hair? Clementine's hand floated up to touch the mass she had tried to tame into a chignon before nuncheon. But that was not the point. Theo hadn't given a fig about her hair. "I should have seen that the money and the house were what he wanted. I'd been utterly daft not to. The maddening part"—the mortifying part—"is that even if I had, even if I'd fully understood that Mr. Bull regarded me a financial means to an end, and not the helpmeet I wanted to be, I still might have reconciled myself to the situation, for it is certainly true that married ladies enjoy a great deal more freedom than their unmarried counterparts. But then, certain . . . matters came to light. Certain . . . realizations were had."

She kept returning to Olive's refrain in her mind. Her audience needn't know everything. The fact that there had been realizations that inspired her to break the engagement was the salient point; the content of said realizations was not.

"I cried off," Clementine concluded, hoping that would be the end of it. In fact, there was a way to make sure that *was* the end of it—or of her part of it anyway, and that was by telling the truth about what happened next. "And the next thing I knew, my sister had run off with him."

As Clementine had hoped, all eyes swung to Olive.

Who promptly burst into tears.

The gentlemen were greatly shocked, Clementine less so. This happened sometimes, with Olive. Everything would be fine, seemingly, then Olive would be overtaken with a dramatic bout of despair. Sometimes these bouts seemed performative, perhaps even manipulative. Other times, as now—and last night, at the inn—they appeared sincere. These episodes, the sincere ones, were puzzling. Why, for example, was Olive so distraught over Theo when this morning she'd been dismissive and had professed relief at being rescued from him?

"Oh, Olive," Archie said sympathetically, offering her his handkerchief and patting her arm.

Why couldn't Archie be kind to Clementine in such a fashion? Why, when it was her turn to speak, was he either stonily silent or else expelling incredulous huffs and skeptical snorts, yet the moment Olive became distraught, he was all chivalry and solicitousness?

"Will you tell me what happened with Mr. Bull when you confronted him?" Clementine asked Archie. "What did you say to him—or do to him?"

Archie turned from Olive and furrowed his brow at Clementine. He was trying to decide how much to tell her, which irked her.

Though her question had been directed at Archie, it was Lord Marsden who answered. "To put it plainly, we assaulted Mr. Bull."

"I see." Clementine appreciated the honest answer. "And are you confident he will not reappear in society?"

"He will not," Archie said firmly. "He's bound for America."

"America!" Olive exclaimed. "I thought he was bound for the Continent."

"Harcourt gave him—"

"He will not reappear on English soil." Archie shot a quelling look at Lord Marsden. "Rest assured."

Clementine tried to tamp down her annoyance. She ought to extend the logic of Olive's maxim to Archie and Lord Marsden. She needn't know exactly what had happened. The salient point was that she and her sister were here, safe—and blessedly unwed. "Thank you," she said quietly, suddenly humbled by the magnitude of these men's loyalty. Archie's to her and Olive, and the others', she supposed, to Archie. "Thank you for everything."

There was a moment of slightly awkward silence, but Lord Featherfinch punctured it by waving a hand dismissively. "Think nothing of it. We haven't had this exciting an Earls Trip since the year we accidentally—"

Archie cleared his throat censoriously, but he did it with a smile. His good humor had returned.

"Indeed," Lord Marsden said. "Featherfinch, are you forgetting the most important rule of Earls Trip?"

There were rules for these trips? How curious.

"Yes, yes." More dismissive waves from Lord Featherfinch. "My point, ladies, is merely that your travails have lent an air of excitement to our holiday that I, for one, have found positively invigorating. Now, what does everyone say to a walk through the haunted woods?"

Olive was perking up at the prospect of a jaunt, but Archie intervened. "I've told the Misses Morgan that they are to stay out of our way as a condition of their continued residence here. This is an *Earls* Trip, after all, and I am disinclined to upend our traditions more than they already have been."

"But only two of you are earls," Olive said, and Clementine shot her a look. "Why do you call it 'Earls Trip'?"

"Yes, I am a mere viscount," Lord Featherfinch said. "I suppose 'Earls Trip' had a ring to it—I believe the name arose after Marsden inherited. We probably thought two out of three was sufficient to inspire the name."

"And, Olive, Lord Featherfinch is heir to an earl."

"Alas," Lord Featherfinch said, which struck Clementine as curious.

"The relevant point," Archie said, "is that this is a *gentlemen's* trip." He turned to the gentlemen in question. "So *we* shall go investigate the woods, which are almost certainly not haunted. Let me just fetch my fowling piece first."

Clementine wanted to object to the prospect of Archie's hunting, but felt she hadn't the right. Happily, her cause was taken up by Archie's friends, who began vociferously objecting to the notion. More was said about rules.

"Well," Archie said as the lot of them bickered their way back inside, "I can hardly think *that* applies anymore. Imagine how differently things might have gone had I not had the weapon at the posting inn yesterday."

Left alone, Clementine and Olive stared at each other. Clementine found herself entirely without speech.

"I say, Olive." Archie popped his head back out. "If you're going to the neighboring estate to inquire about a cook, you can't go alone. Wait until we're back, and one of us shall accompany you." He paused, at attention, as if bracing for objection. Normally, Clementine would have issued one on Olive's behalf. There could be no harm in walking through the countryside to the next house. But as with the hunting, she was feeling uncharacteristically chastened and without the moral standing to defy Archie's wishes.

"It's not a far walk," Olive said. "I'll take Clementine with me."

"I can't allow it. Clearly, your reputations are safe in this house, but we've no idea who resides nearby. What if someone recognizes you?"

"I hardly think that likely," Olive countered, and Clementine had to smile. She hadn't been able to muster the will to stand up to Archie, but it turned out she hadn't had to because Olive was.

"Yes," Archie said, "but we have so far averted disaster, and against great odds. Suddenly the unchaperoned Morgan sisters are going to show up at—"

"I shall take Mrs. MacPuddle with me," Olive said. "I was planning to anyway. I can hardly knock on a stranger's door and demand to be lent a servant. She will provide an introduction. We will call through the servants' entrance and almost certainly not even encounter the family. If an explanation is required, I shall tell a version of the truth: I am visiting Quintrell Castle with my family"—she gestured to Clementine—"there was a bit of a mix-up regarding staffing, and we are in need of a cook."

Archie opened his mouth, but Clementine interceded. "Better to err on the side of caution and wait for the gentlemen to return, Olive." She couldn't believe she was saying it. Neither could Archie, apparently. His eyebrows—both of them—flew up.

Olive acquiesced, but huffily. "All right." She performed a put-upon sigh. "But even if we can secure a cook later, when one of you gentlemen can make yourself available to escort me, it will almost certainly be too late for her to remove from here and prepare dinner for tonight, so perhaps we may also venture into the nearest village to purchase something more edible than these biscuits?" She nodded at the unfinished plate.

"A fine idea," Archie said. He paused as if unsure about taking his leave.

"After today's outing to procure food—and a person to prepare our meals going forward—you shan't see us again the rest of your holiday," Clementine said.

Archie nodded stiffly and departed.

Olive looked as if she were going to say something. Clementine was suddenly so tired of talking. Of people. Of *indoors.* "I'm going on my own walk."

"But Archie said—"

"Not to go to the neighbors' house, and not to go to the village. I shall keep close to the house."

Olive nodded. Clementine supposed, as she rose from the table, that she ought to ask Olive to join her. But she didn't want to. In Clementine's younger years, she had roamed the countryside with Archie without it feeling any different from when she was alone. But with anyone else, the company felt . . . too human. Like a mark of civilization inserting itself between her and the world. It was akin to wearing stays. Even if one managed to avoid being made overtly uncomfortable by them, one always knew they were there.

That was true even of her sister. Perhaps especially of her sister, who had often tried, as younger siblings were wont to do, to follow along after Clementine.

She no longer did that, though. In fact, Clementine had no idea what Olive did with the majority of her time.

Which perhaps did not reflect so well on Clementine as Olive had apparently spent some of her time lately making plans to elope with Theodore Bull.

She *should* ask her sister to accompany her, but she wasn't going to.

By seven o'clock, Archie was hungry and annoyed. Effie had volunteered, earlier, to accompany the Morgan sisters on the necessary outings to secure dinner for the evening and a cook for the rest of their stay. To Archie's surprise, Simon had opted to join them. Archie had been imagining pouring a scotch—the absent Sir Lionel didn't keep much in the larder, but he had quite an enviable scotch collection and had apparently left instructions that they should avail themselves of it—and indulging Simon in an against-the-rules discussion of political matters. It would be Archie's way of thanking him for helping dispatch Mr. Bull yesterday. Simon had never been a fighter—he favored words over fists when it came to settling disputes—but he had planted a facer on Mr. Bull, stunning him sufficiently that Archie had been able to finish the job.

But no, to Archie's shock. Simon apparently preferred venturing out with their gate-crashers to a bracing chat about the gold standard.

Archie would have gone, too, except that would have made it too much a party. He was still annoyed at the Morgans for putting themselves in such danger, and, having insisted so vociferously that they stay out of the men's way, he couldn't quite see his way through to joining the outing. So, with no one around to tell him not to, he'd gone hunting. He'd come home with a pair of pheasants, and Mrs. MacPuddle had assured him the kitchen maid was up to the task of plucking and roasting them. He hoped she was better with fowl than she was with biscuits.

As usual, hunting had calmed Archie's mind. When he was stalking through the grass with the intense focus required to shoot a bird, especially without a dog, there was no room for anything else. Hunting made it feel as though his usually frayed attention was being sewn up. He'd been looking forward to dinner with the boys, who had a similar knitting-up effect on his spirit. He pulled his beads from his pocket and settled in to wait.

His stomach rumbled aggressively. Nuncheon had been both inadequate and ages ago. And tea had been just that—tea. The brown steeped liquid and none of the traditional accompaniments he generally found insufficient anyway. Archie's many athletic pursuits tended to work up quite an appetite. If his friends were any longer, he'd be forced to eat the birds by himself.

"Well, aren't you looking cross."

It was Effie. Finally. He clattered into the drawing room with his cheeks pink—and wet, for it had begun to rain—and his voluminous greatcoat still on.

"Where have you been?"

"In Doveborough."

"For four hours?"

"Capital little village." This was from Simon, who appeared looking as ruddy and high-spirited as Effie but had taken the time to shed his outerwear. "Lots going on."

"Excellent modiste for such a small place," Effie said.

Archie refrained from pointing out that there was "lots going on" in *London* that Simon usually managed not only to avoid but to actively look down upon—not that Archie blamed him. And that surely London's modistes were more excellent than Doveborough's.

What business did Effie have with a modiste, anyway?

"We've returned with steak and kidney pies and a bushel of pears—just before the rain really started, so we were well-timed," Simon said. "Miss Morgan posits that the pears can be transformed into a pudding with very little trouble. She's at it even now."

Archie started to object that Clementine, the daughter of a baronet, should not be toiling in the kitchen—the very point of their outing had been to find someone else to do such toiling, had it not?—but he stopped himself. As already established, this household was no threat to Clementine's reputation. Therefore, it was no concern of his how she chose to fill her days. As long as she filled them far from Archie and his friends.

Which she was apparently doing.

"Well," he said, shaking himself out of his musings, "shall we dine? I, for one, am fair gutfounded. I shot us some pheasants, so we shall be able to cobble together quite a credible, if odd, feast by the sounds of things."

"Went hunting, did you?" Simon raised his eyebrows at Archie.

"If the rules of Earls Trip have been *completely* abandoned," Effie huffed, "I shall insist upon reading my new sonnet at dinner."

Archie smirked, but inside he was smiling most genuinely. The trip was being set to rights. Flagrant breaking of the rules usually waited until the second week, but it always happened, and it was always accompanied by banter and feigned martyrdom.

And honestly, Archie adored listening to Effie's poems. The

man had a genuine talent, and more than that, Archie appreciated how his friend's love of poetry never waned as the years wore on. He'd grown from a boy composing clumsy limericks about exams into a man whose work was published, albeit anonymously, in magazines. Every time one of Effie's poems was accepted for publication, Archie felt it almost as his own victory.

He would also enjoy listening to Simon drone on about whatever outrage the Tories currently had brewing.

He was proud of his friends and their accomplishments, and he was feeling rather smug about his own ability to seek out and keep the best company.

Though to be fair, that sentiment had to be tempered by his egregious lapse when it came to the Morgans these past few years. Perhaps dinner could also be the start of righting that ship. He vowed to ask Clementine and Olive for details regarding their father's condition—and for details about their lives, the horrid Mr. Bull aside.

"Where are the ladies?" he asked twenty minutes later as he and Simon and Effie sat at a table large enough that the entire occupying MacCallum clan could have feasted at it—one that was, he noted, only set for three.

"They're taking their meal in the breakfast room," Simon said as he shook out his serviette.

"Why?"

"I believe because you told them to stay away from us."

"I—" He had done exactly that. But . . . "I did not mean they shouldn't *dine* with us." There was a bell on the table. He wondered if it had been set there by Mrs. MacPuddle. Would ringing it summon anybody? He gave it a go.

While they waited, he tried to explain. "I only meant I didn't want our trip to turn into one long feminine parlor game."

"Was there ever any risk of that?" Simon asked, wearing a puzzled expression.

"One long, feminine parlor game," Effie echoed drawing out the phrase as if tasting it on his tongue. He tilted his head and stared off into space, a stance Archie recognized as one associated with his creative process. "I'm not sure exactly what that means, but it sounds *terribly* compelling."

"Yes, my lords?" Mrs. MacPuddle arrived and dropped a curtsy.

"Will you ask the Misses Morgan to dine with us?" Archie said, and after Mrs. MacPuddle retreated, he surveyed the table. The pheasants had been roasted to a deep golden brown and dressed with mushrooms and sage. The pies were piled onto a large platter that was flanked with bowls of the same grapes and peaches that had been served earlier. There were no inedible biscuits in sight.

"An odd assortment of dishes, but a rather pleasing one, I think," Effie said.

"And served all at once instead of in a series of removes, which is also pleasing for some reason," Simon said. "I suppose it's that it makes one feel that one is enjoying a reprieve from the strictures of society."

Archie's friends had given voice perfectly to his own thoughts. The hearty but simple repast seemed perfectly suited to the occasion; its informality was cheering and its abundance welcome. His mouth watered.

"My lords." Mrs. MacPuddle reappeared. "The ladies send their thanks for your thoughtful invitation but must decline it, as they do not wish to cut up your peace."

"No, no; they misunderstand. Miss Clementine Morgan is taking my earlier words about them giving us a wide swath too literally. Please tell them they are most welcome to sup with us."

"My Heavens, Archie, what did you say to Miss Morgan to scare her away so thoroughly?" Simon asked as Mrs. MacPuddle departed.

"You know, this is like those letters from school," Effie said. "Miss Morgan would write to you, and you would huff and complain about the burden of reciprocity her letters created, but then you'd follow me around entreating me to help you write her back."

Archie remembered. This was part of the reason, he suddenly realized, he had fallen out of touch with Clementine and her family. There was the inescapable fact that the two families were almost never in the same place these days, but Clementine had continued to write to him after he was out of school. Without Effie to help him write back, and with Father endlessly and aggressively filling his head with estate matters, Archie's intentions to answer Clem's letters somehow always got pushed aside in favor of something more immediate.

And at some point, she stopped writing.

He felt the loss, perhaps more now than he had at the time.

"Yes," Simon said, "and remember the time she told him she had gone to a dance at the assembly rooms in Chiddington and had been surprised when she was asked to dance not once but twice, but she hadn't said who either partner was? And then he wrote back and asked her, but an answer to that question was not part of her next letter? He went near mad with the not knowing."

"It was merely that I, too, was surprised Clementine had danced twice that evening. Clementine in those days was not very . . ." *Civilized* was the word he wanted to use, but he feared it would sound unflattering in a way he did not intend. He understood how elementally unsuited Clementine was for balls and musicales and teas, but to say so to others would sound like criticism when it was, in fact, the opposite. Other people, even Simon and Effie, wouldn't understand.

Once again, Mrs. MacPuddle returned. "Miss Clementine Morgan has decided to refrain from the consumption of meat while she is in residence, and Miss Olive Morgan has decided to join her in this endeavor, so they regret that they cannot accept your kind invitation."

Archie blinked. It sometimes took a moment to understand Mrs. MacPuddle's thick brogue, which felt somewhat at odds with the formal way she was speaking to them; it was as if she was playing the role of a housekeeper on stage. "Well, they needn't eat any pies or pheasant." Though he was strangely disappointed at the notion that Clementine wouldn't be tasting the fruits of his labors. His friends always praised the spoils of his hunts. In fact, they would probably do exactly that in a matter of minutes—if they could ever start their meal—even as they simultaneously harangued him for having broken the no-hunting rule. "Tell the ladies to bring whatever it is they're supping on in here. We'll wait." His stomach grumbled fiercely, objecting to the ongoing delay.

It wasn't until a few moments later, when Simon cleared his throat and Effie guffawed, that Archie realized he was staring at the door and drumming his fingers on the table. "I'm *hungry*," he said peevishly. "Too hungry to make small talk."

"Since, as has been well-established, we are not standing on ceremony here, why don't we just start?" Simon said.

"No, no, if the ladies are to join us, we must wait," Archie said. "We're on holiday, but we're not heathens."

Effie and Simon shared a look Archie couldn't make sense of.

"My lords." Mrs. MacPuddle sighed as she appeared again and dropped into a half-hearted curtsy. She had been a remarkably good sport, what with all the back and forth. "The ladies have finished their meal and reiterate their wish not to disturb you." She glanced pointedly at the untouched food, and Archie heard her unarticulated censure.

Oh, for Heaven's sake. He was tempted to suggest they all at least eat the pudding together but feared that to do so would make him look desperate for the ladies' company. Which he absolutely was not. This was an *Earls* Trip, after all. "Very well, then. Gentlemen, shall we?"

The three of them made quick work of pies and pheasants both, and if Archie had been out of sorts by being snubbed by the Morgan sisters, he was put to rights by the praise his friends bestowed on him for the birds, even if it was, as he'd predicted, interlaced with a good deal of griping about the attainment of said birds.

"You can't enjoy the spoils at the same time you criticize the method," Archie insisted with feigned affront, but in truth he could feel his rough edges being smoothed by the company of his friends just as his hunger had been sated by the feast.

And then the pears came.

"Dear Heavens!" Effie exclaimed after his first bite. "What sorcery is this? Honey, but what else?"

"Walnuts," Archie said, eyeing the steaming bowl in front of him. "But I'm not sure what the dark liquid is."

"Apparently Miss Morgan's disapproval of consuming animals does not extend to consuming the fruits of their labor, given that bees make honey," Simon said, his first bite on a fork poised to enter his mouth. Once it did, he moaned. "Sorcery indeed. This is the greatest thing I have eaten in weeks. Months."

"It's a pear!" Archie protested.

"It's *sorcery*," Effie declared again, but it came out sounding more like "It's torture me," since he'd jammed half the fruit into his mouth before speaking. That seemed an apt sentiment. Though Archie couldn't quite articulate why, he did rather feel as if he were being tortured, and he couldn't blame the sensation on hunger any longer.

"Well, it certainly isn't better than the pheasant was," Archie grumbled, peevishly stabbing a pear with his fork as the other two mused about what the mystery ingredient might be.

He took a bite, and flavor exploded on his tongue, an amalgam of familiar—honey and pear—and darkly mysterious.

It was better than the pheasant, blast it.

7

Guess Who's (Still Not) Coming to Dinner

After their strange-but-satisfying dinner, the gentlemen retired to a dusty drawing room that made Simon sneeze repeatedly. The space was studded with buckets collecting rain that was falling *through* the roof, so it took some doing to arrange themselves in such a way that facilitated conversation but discouraged dampness. Once they were settled, Effie read his sonnet about Sally. One would think a sonnet commemorating a dead parrot would be ridiculous. One would be wrong.

That was the thing about Effie. He *was* in some ways ridiculous, with his severe attire and his dreamy demeanor. Though Archie would never countenance anyone besides himself or Simon *calling* Effie ridiculous. More than one boy at school—chief among them Nigel Nettlefell—had made that mistake and had subsequently come to regret it.

What Simon and Archie and perhaps few others understood was that beneath Effie's embroidered silk waistcoat beat the heart of a true artist. He had a way, with his best poems, of using a handful of exquisitely economical phrases to pluck at heartstrings one didn't even know one had.

And this poem, "Lamenter, Be Not Proud," was one of his best. It was about a bird, but not. Effie had a way of writing around a specific, seemingly small subject in such a way that one ended up astonished at the realization that the small subject *wasn't* actually the point as one was blindsided by analogy to one's own experience of the world. It was rather like believing oneself to be on a pleasant punting outing, only for the boat to suddenly overturn and plunge one into a river of astonishing truths and terrible beauties. It seemed like alchemy, this ability of Effie's, and it made Archie proud to call him a friend.

Archie and Simon applauded when Effie finished his recitation. Archie had to swallow a lump in his throat before he could speak, because somehow, this poem about a parrot Effie had loved had put Archie to mind of the death of his own father, whom he had . . . Well, whom he had learned not to love, to be frank. And of his mother, who, while not dead, was sufficiently lost to him he sometimes thought she might as well be. He sometimes wondered, as he sat by her side and attempted to engage her in conversation, if he *would* mourn her. Perhaps a man only had so much mourning in him to attach to any given person, in which case he feared he had spent his allotment for Mother. What he wouldn't give to come home one more time to her wide-open arms that always greeted his arrival home from school. What he wouldn't give for one more of her garden games, or one more hand of whist. She always used to beat him at whist, but she always made him laugh while doing so. He had lost all those things so slowly, in such a piecemeal fashion, that he hadn't known to consider whether any specific experience of them might be the last.

His thoughts were growing mawkish. He cast them away. "You're going to send this sonnet to *Le Monde Joli*, yes?" he asked, naming the magazine that occasionally published Effie's poems.

"Forget *Le Monde Joli*," Simon said. "You ought to aim higher than a mere ladies' magazine with this one. Or never mind that, you've enough good ones now that you could publish a chapbook."

"I've already sent it to my editor at *Le Monde Joli*," Effie said, "and while I am loath to appear overly self-impressed, I am confident it will be accepted." Effie was doggedly loyal to the publication that had accepted his first poem, after years of rejection everywhere else. Amusingly, when he'd first submitted, he hadn't realized the publication was targeted at ladies, but the knowledge hadn't dampened his enthusiasm one jot. To hear it told, his editor was a harsh taskmaster but one who brought out the best in Effie. "And frankly, if I were a lady I would take offense at your use of the word 'mere.'"

"As long as you're happy," Archie said. It all had to be anonymous anyway. It wouldn't do for a viscount, the son of an earl—especially the son of the high stickler Earl of Stonely—to be publishing poems, in a ladies' magazine or any other. Perhaps if Lord Byron were more respectable and therefore provided better precedent, things might be different for Effie, but as it stood, he felt the need for secrecy.

After the poetry, they poured a round of port and a companionable silence settled, the crackling of the fire the only sound. Archie sighed happily, anticipating the slow spread of satisfaction through his bones. This evening, they would drink, they would talk, and they would be together. It would be like old times, at school, in the sense that the responsibilities and pressures of adulthood, and of the earldom, felt very distant. But also not like old times, because they could do whatever the hell they wanted to. There were no teachers or parents or social conventions to stop them. No bloody essays to write—or to beseech Effie to write for him. Nothing but them and the pure pleasure of long-standing friendship.

Archie was aware that to voice such a sentiment would make him seem ridiculous, but this moment was one that he looked forward to all year. If the toast on the way out of Town signaled that an Earls Trip was underway, the first evening they settled in together, after unpacking—or after detouring to a posting inn, getting shot, rescuing some childhood friends, and threatening a criminal sufficiently that he would never return to England—signaled the true start of the retreat. Simon had said earlier that he was sorely in need of respite. Simon was not alone in that sentiment. Earls Trips were about the restoration of Archie to himself. He had always enjoyed these trips, but as the years passed and the situation with Mother deteriorated, he *needed* them.

He sometimes felt as though he was one of those ghosts he didn't believe in, that through the course of a year, some essential essence of his being—his spirit, he supposed—slowly became unmoored from his body. As if there were two versions of him that were meant to nestle together as one, but by the time autumn rolled around, the edges didn't match up at all.

Simon and Effie got his edges matching again.

He rolled his eyes at himself. Was this sentimentality the result of too much drink or not enough? He picked up his glass. Only one way to find out. As he was taking a deep drink, something popped to mind. Another example of this feeling of freedom and camaraderie, one from long ago. "Remember the couple of years we all spent the Christmas holidays at school?"

"Those were grand times," Effie said.

"I was so happy that first year you stayed back, too, Archie, and then when you joined us the next, Effie," Simon said, gracing them with a rare unrestrained smile.

"Yes, why *did* you start staying back?" Effie asked Archie. "Aside from the fact that our school Christmases were so much more enjoyable than those at home, at least in my case."

Simon had always stayed at school over the holidays because he wasn't wanted at home. Effie had usually gone home for Christmas, but that year, and one or two others, his parents had been traveling.

"I'd been home previously that year, during a term break," Archie said, casting his mind back to that disastrous visit. "My mother had undergone a sharp decline in the weeks I'd been away. Her lapses—and outbursts—could no longer be explained away. My father began doubling down on his insistence that I take on more responsibility for the doings of the estate. He sat me down and instructed me to read aloud the latest report from the steward." He paused, hating that the memory still had the power to make his face heat. "You can imagine how that went. I suppose the charitable interpretation is that evidence of Mother's decline was inspiring him to think about the succession."

"There's also the true interpretation," Simon said.

"And what is that?" Archie asked.

"That your father was a right arse."

Archie lifted his glass in acknowledgment of that interpretation.

"The concept of family is a curious one, don't you think?" Effie was staring at the fire as he spoke, looking broodier than usual.

"How do you mean, Ef?" Simon asked, and Archie sighed happily. Even though the ensuing conversation was likely to be gloomy, the fact of it comforted him immensely.

"Do you know that I felt worse when Sally died than when my grandmother died last year?" Effie said.

"Well, to be fair, your grandmother was a terrible person," Simon said, continuing to not mince words.

Effie looked cheered. "She was, wasn't she?"

Archie chuckled, though he did not disagree. The late dowager countess had been known for her casual cruelty. She would think nothing of, for example, "accidentally" spilling tea on a person whose attire she did not approve of and had done so to young Effie on several occasions. He still had a mark on the side of his neck from one incident in which he was burned quite badly.

"My point," Effie said, "is that if you truly consider it, the idea of family is rather odd. You're born into a group of people, and it's as random as throwing salt into the wind. The grains land where they land."

"Who is the salt here?" Simon asked.

"Anyone is. Everyone is. And perhaps you land on something you're well suited to—a leg of lamb, say, that is improved by salting. But perhaps you land on something like a strawberry. What good is salt on a strawberry?"

"Is the strawberry . . . a parent?" Literal-minded Simon was struggling to make sense of Effie's fanciful musings.

"Oh, I don't know. The metaphor is admittedly terrible. Sally's passing has got me thinking about how much I dislike my parents. Which would be one thing if I *loved* them, but I don't think I do. Although to be fair, *they* don't love *me* either, so one could argue that they started it." He considered Simon. "Did you love your father? Do you love your mother?"

Leave it to Effie to get right into it. One of the things Archie loved about Effie was his fearlessness.

"I suppose I did love my father, in a generalized, filial way," Simon said. "Although, like you, I don't believe my father loved me. Mind you, I don't think he *actively* didn't love me; it was more that he didn't think of me at all. I was bound for the Church, and that was as much thought as he ever gave me and my fate. I think my mother loves me, in her way, but that love coexists with a sort of perpetual disappointment. Which I understand, to some degree. I was never meant to be earl. I was never meant to be *born*. Do you know that she still talks about my brothers every day? I miss them, too—I *did* love *them*, in the way a boy loves and idolizes older brothers."

Simon's much older twin brothers had died five years ago in a fire, thrusting Simon from the seminary into the earldom. As the third son, Simon had gone largely ignored by his mother until he suddenly inherited, at which point she threw herself into trying to make him "worthy of the title," which really meant making him over in the image of his late brothers.

"Somehow," Simon went on, "Mother's constant and vociferous missing of the twins feels rather . . ."

"Hurtful?" Archie supplied. "As if her love for them must be subtracted from her love for you, even though that's not at all how love should work?"

"Yes, I think that's right." Simon looked surprised at the revelation. "I know she will always miss them. I will, too. But I wish she wasn't always comparing me to them."

"And you, Archie?" Effie prompted. "I suppose it's less complicated in your case. You clearly love your mother and she you. And your father . . ." He pulled a face to show what he thought of the late earl.

"I did love my father, I think, when I was younger. There were years where our annual hunting trip, just before the start of Michaelmas term, was the highlight of my year."

Archie was seized with a kind of uncharacteristic melancholy, thinking of those trips. They'd always been much anticipated. His chance to be with Father away from the day-to-day workings of the estate. But there had been an edge of tension to those outings, too, like a loaf of bread overbaked and surrounded by a too-hard crust. Archie supposed his desire to excel at hunting and outdoor pursuits had originated in a desire to impress his father. He certainly hadn't been going to do it with his marks.

He also remembered how lovely it had been to return to the comforts of home after their trips, and in those years Mother had been among them. She would tut over the state of him, send him off to bathe, and take tea with him in her sitting room while he rambled about the hunt. Archie had always made the time away seem much more exciting than it had actually been. He'd wanted to impress Mother with how congenial he and Father had been as well as with his own accomplishments. She'd always pulled him close to her on the settee and praised him, telling him what a good son he was and what a good earl he would make someday. Even when he was old enough to know the latter was not true, he always strove to be the former. He still did.

"And now the highlight of your year is *this* trip," Effie said with an exaggerated flourish.

"Yes," Simon agreed jocularly. "No doubt this one is loads more fun than hunting with the late earl. For one thing, the weather is better this time of year. Secondly, one can get foxed with one's mates in a way one can't with one's father. Better company in general, I should think."

"*That's* true." Archie knew what they were doing. They had

somehow intuited that he'd grown morose thinking about his parents. "And I think"—Archie turned to Effie—"that is the answer to your question about family."

"How do you mean?" Effie asked.

"It does feel like happenstance, doesn't it, when it comes to the family one ends up with? The only family I know of that was truly and uncomplicatedly happy, where the love each member had for the others was apparent and easily worn, were the Morgans."

"That's difficult to countenance," Simon said. "Would a happy, tightly knit family result in not one but two daughters swindled by a man like Mr. Bull?"

"I take the point." Archie had never been overly fond of Sir Albert—he was Father's friend, and Archie had learned, by the time he was out of leading strings, to stay out of Father's way as much as possible. Yet he carried a vague memory of the Morgans as just that: a happy, tightly knit clan. "I think perhaps Mrs. Morgan was the glue of the family, and that her death has destabilized things, but I don't think that means they don't love each other."

"Sir Albert did go to extreme measures to retrieve his daughters," Effie pointed out. "His anguish in that letter seemed genuine."

"Yes. Regardless, my point is that for most of us—and to take up your metaphor, Effie—we're salt on strawberries. But that's fine, because that gives us leave—frees us up—to make our own families."

"Last I checked, one had to be married for that kind of activity—or at least for that kind of activity to result in a *respectable* family," Simon joked.

"Not that kind of family. Why must family be defined by blood relations? That's what I'm trying to say. Why can't we make our own families by surrounding ourselves with like-minded people? With people who appreciate us?" Archie was speaking as though he had spent a long time honing this philosophy, but in truth the notion had just popped into his head.

"Why can't we go find a plate of roasted potatoes if we're legs of lamb, or pots of cream if we're strawberries?" Effie asked.

"Precisely."

"Like those years we spent the Christmas holidays at school," Simon said. "And for that matter, that's exactly what we've done here, isn't it?" He waved his hand around in the space between them. "Unknowingly, perhaps. But we're a sort of found family, are we not?"

"A found family. Oh, that's *lovely*, Simon," Effie said. "Yes, we found each other at school, and we made a family."

Both men looked at Archie, who was starting to feel sheepish even though he agreed with the sentiment—and even though he was the one who had introduced the idea to begin with. It was this business with Clem and Olive. It had him thinking of the past and examining his soul or some such nonsense. "Enough sentimentality," he declared. "Time to get foxed."

They often did this, in the evenings during an Earls Trip, talked about serious matters, and when things started to feel *too* serious, moved on to drinking. Though admittedly in most years the serious matter wouldn't have been the nature of their own bonds.

But this was not most years, was it? Somewhere under this leaking roof was Clementine Morgan. Archie wondered what she was doing as he got up to fetch the scotch decanter. Was she already asleep? Was she even inside? He sincerely hoped she was not tromping around the grounds in the rainy dark, but he wouldn't put it past her—and he could hardly go on a mission to find out as he'd told her to stay away. She'd been doing a remarkably fine job of it, if her stubborn refusal to appear for dinner had been anything to go by.

"This is the last round for me," Simon said as Archie sloshed a generous pour of scotch into his glass.

That was also a familiar refrain. As were Effie's exhortations that Simon should stay, that he went to bed too early, that he was on holiday, that he was old before his time.

Archie joined in on pestering Simon, but in truth he was not sad to see him retire early. Part of the sweetness of an Earls Trip was that Effie was a night owl and Simon a lark. Archie would gladly sacrifice sleep for the pleasure of spending time with each man in his own milieu. Archie usually needed a holiday from his holiday when he returned to Mollybrook, the result of sleeping too few hours each night. The exhaustion was worth it, though. It was a fortnight of physical fatigue traded for mental replenishment that would last a year.

With Effie, Archie drank and talked about poetry. Apparently Effie's editor at *Le Monde Joli* had put forth an opinion about Lord Byron that Effie was having difficulty countenancing. "Of course one can read and enjoy and accept the work of an artist even as one disapproves of the artist himself. It isn't as if the art itself is tainted by the distasteful behavior and opinions of the artist. Don't you agree?"

Archie wasn't sure if he did or he didn't. The question brought to mind the year Clem, who had probably been around ten at the time, refused to eat Easter dinner. Her family had been dining with his at Mollybrook, and when it was announced that the ham had come from the nearby Smith farm, she had paled, set down her fork, and pronounced herself not hungry. Archie had been the only one who'd known the source of her lost appetite. The pair of them had gone on a ramble a few days previously. They'd stumbled upon Mr. Smith, loudly and cruelly berating his wife for spilling a bowl of slop she'd been taking out to the pigs. They'd been drawn by the commotion and had watched the scene play out from behind a fence. Archie had been paralyzed by shock. He'd never seen such a display, his own father's cruelties being significantly more subtle. It wasn't until Mr. Smith raised his hand as if to strike his wife that Archie had been galvanized into action, and to his shame, that action had merely been talking loudly to Clem and pretending they were just strolling up. It had been enough to diffuse the confrontation. But as Clem had said later, on their way home, if that was how Mr. Smith behaved outside, where anyone could come upon them, what was he like at home?

And then she had refused to eat his ham.

"It's an interesting conundrum," Archie said to Effie, shaking off the memory. "I suppose one can always err on the side of caution and set aside Byron's works."

"So what you're saying is I have to throw out *The Siege of Corinth* because Byron is a bounder?" Effie protested.

"No, no. I'm merely thinking that there are so many poems in the world, what's the harm in skipping over a few of them?" Just as that Easter, the table had been laden with plenty of other things to eat. Clementine hadn't gone hungry, and neither had he when he had stealthily joined in her abstention, feeding his ham to Olive's lapdog under the table. But perhaps pigs and poetry were not properly compared in this manner. "I am far from an expert. I'm sure you know better than I about these things. Let's have another drink."

It was a lovely evening, all in all, providing a large dose of Effie and his Effie-ness.

And then there was a Simonesque version of the same the next morning in the breakfast room, albeit with tea instead of scotch.

"Perhaps I have judged the Luddites too harshly," Simon announced from behind a book when Archie appeared.

"I hadn't realized you'd judged them at all." Archie knew little about the Luddites, but one didn't need to know what one was talking about to enjoy a conversation with Simon.

"Yes." Simon lowered the book, which upon further examination was a pamphlet. "While I have sympathized with their cause, I used to think the violence they espouse reprehensible. And pointless, too. You can't stop progress. Mechanization is inevitable, is it not?"

"I should think so," said Archie, who honestly had no idea. He contemplated the buffet set up in the corner of the room and happily served himself a large portion of eggs and kippers. The kitchen seemed to have righted itself.

Did Clementine eat kippers? he wondered suddenly. Surely fish did not rate as "animals" in her estimation? What about eggs? No, that would be taking it too far, even for her. What would she eat for breakfast otherwise?

"I am now convinced, however," Simon said, "that the sentences handed down in some of the trials were overly harsh. Machine breaking made a capital crime? Obviously, I wasn't sitting in Lords at the time, but good Heavens!"

"Didn't the Luddites burn mills, though?" That was about all Archie knew of the Luddites.

"Yes, and I can't condone that. Absolutely not."

Archie joined Simon at the table. "Where did you get that pamphlet?"

"I discovered the Misses Morgan outside this morning. Miss Olive Morgan was ritualistically throwing the remnants of her time with Mr. Bull into a stream. It was really rather amusing, given all the mud from yesterday's rain." He shook his pamphlet. "I rescued this. Apparently Mr. Bull has been branching out from his original cause. I was idly curious—I do miss my newspapers— but I really ought to consider the source before finding myself persuaded by these arguments. I'm usually much more circumspect. I begin to see how both sisters . . ."

Simon's monologue continued, but Archie was stuck on the fact that Simon had come upon Clem outside this morning. Archie thought he'd gotten up early, but apparently not early enough.

Though why would he think that? Early enough for what? He had risen early enough to catch Simon at breakfast, which had been his objective. Drinks and poetry with Effie last night; breakfast and politics with Simon this morning.

A perfectly, gratifyingly, wonderfully *ordinary* Earls Trip. Exactly what he'd been aiming for.

The rest of the day was also satisfyingly typical. After Effie rose around noon, the three of them went for a ramble. Later, they settled in to play cards in the drawing room. At seven o'clock, they were informed by Mrs. MacPuddle that dinner was served.

"She's a right charmer, she is," Mrs. MacPuddle said of the new cook, who had indeed been lent them by the neighboring estate. "Do you know she's embraced Miss Morgan's challenge and is dedicated to serving the ladies their own three-course meal in the breakfast room every evening?"

"I fail to see why the ladies should not join us here in the dining room, even if their meal differs from ours," Archie said peevishly as the kitchen maid carried in a platter of trout.

"I believe the ladies have already dined." Effie turned to Mrs. MacPuddle. "Didn't they dine earlier?"

"How do you know that?" Archie asked, a little chagrined by the accusatory tone his question had taken.

"I encountered the elder Miss Morgan on my way here, and she told me she was off to meet her sister in the library where she was submitting to post-dinner embroidery lessons."

"Oh, no. You must have misheard. Miss Morgan does not do embroidery."

Effie shrugged, and Mrs. MacPuddle said, "Yes, the ladies are finished dining, my lord. Cook is happy to accommodate the misses' special request, but prefers to do it before dinner for my lords commences, wanting yours to be her sole focus while you are dining."

"Well," Archie said. "That is most appreciated."

Wasn't it?

This was, after all, an Earls Trip.

Wasn't it?

Embroidery was not so bad, Clementine reflected as she climbed out the window of her bedchamber just as the clock in the hallway outside her room struck midnight. She was starting to feel more like herself, having spent the day tromping around out of doors. It turned out the wilds of Cumbria had the same restorative effect as the wilds at Hill House, though the mechanism was a bit differ-ent. Around Hill House, she knew the joy of familiarity, could put her hand out to touch the papery birch that marked a turn in the path she knew to anticipate. Here in this unfamiliar forest where she was an interloper, she had the eyes of a beginner, an unwilling city girl suddenly confronted with a network of sessile oak roots covered with moss. But only on the one side—the north. So the tree was a compass, as trees always were; that was one thing that could be relied on in this capricious world. This particular tree had been a perfect combination of strong and whimsical: an octopus, half naked and half dressed in its green Sunday best.

Both sights—the comforting familiar birch at home and the bizarrely delightful oak here—aided in the task of sinking Clementine's soul back into her body. And it wasn't only trees restoring her to herself; it was, somewhat surprisingly, people. Generally, she found human company to be quite draining, but she had enjoyed a trip to the nearest village yesterday with Olive and Lords Featherfinch and Marsden. In the process of procuring pies for the gentlemen's dinner, they'd learned that Doveborough was preparing for its annual fall fete, which she gathered was a big to-do that drew crowds from the region and beyond. The three of them had a grand time watching some ladies decorate an outdoor stage with ribbons and fall foliage, and they'd enjoyed warm spiced cider in a tearoom off the village green.

And today, after helping Olive ritualistically dispose of the remnants of her time with Theo—an activity which had turned out to be surprisingly restorative—the sisters settled in the small parlor they'd adopted because it was far from the one the gentlemen seemed to have settled in. Olive was working on a sampler the likes of which Clementine had never seen. The pastoral scene from the road between Hill House and the village of Chiddington was both ambitious and lovely, and Olive was creating it purely from memory. Clementine had never considered that aspect of embroidery: that one could conjure something from nothing, transform a blank canvas into a thing of beauty. "Men are much ballyhooed for their painting," Olive had said. "The old masters were just that—masters. I wager there were plenty of old mistresses who were a good hand with a needle and thread, but we don't talk about them."

Olive, it turned out, had become a veritable font of wisdom while Clementine hadn't been paying attention.

Clementine's dress caught on the window sill, and she had to yank it free, wincing at the ripping sound that resulted. She had only the one dress. She was going to have to borrow another from Olive, for eventually she would need to surrender hers to the housemaid for washing. And now for mending, too, she supposed.

But she was out, ripped dress and all. The window in her room was in a dormer that jutted out from the roofline of this part of the house, and once clear of the window, she could settle herself on the slope of the roof. The slate was cold but not uncomfortable. Being this high up was exhilarating. It reminded her of being perched in a tree, which was a place she used to find herself quite a lot, before being forced to endure London and the Marriage Mart.

The stars were out in force, like buckets of pearls had spilled across the sky. She wondered if it would be possible to embroider the night sky. Could one do a sort of reverse-embroidery where the image itself was blank space, unstitched canvas representing stars, set against a dark, stitched background?

"Success in embroidery is all in your choice of subject," Olive had said. "You must choose a subject that is achievable and to which you feel a connection." Clementine refrained from pointing out that Olive's scene featured a herd of sheep, and Clementine was certain the only time her sister had ever interacted with sheep was while wailing at them when they were in the road preventing her from getting where she wanted to go.

With Olive's guidance, Clementine decided to attempt a simple collection of leaves from the types of trees most common around Hill House—beech, willow, and alder. She had only just finished the first leaf, and while it looked as if it had been made by a girl still in the schoolroom, she didn't think it too awfully terrible for her first attempt at embroidery in more than a decade. In truth, the repetitive nature of the task had turned out to be soothing, and after the events of the past few days, she could do with some soothing.

Embroidery also allowed for conversation. In fact, it somehow made it *easier* to talk to one's companion, she supposed because it occupied one's eyes and hands, making the conversation seem idle, even when it was not. In the two evenings they'd been alone together, Clementine had learned a great deal about her sister. Not what she really wanted to know, which was Olive's mysterious reasons for offering herself to Theo to prevent him from black-mailing Clementine. Olive just wasn't that selfless. But Clementine *had* learned other, smaller things, some of which she found unexpectedly delightful. For example, Olive had fascinating, if fanciful, theories on Napoleon's escape from Elba. And she had, all these years, only been pretending to like their closest neighbors in London.

It was all quite astonishing.

Clementine sighed happily as she pulled a blanket around her shoulders and lay back against the sloped roof. All right: the Pleiades. She probably should have brought a lantern and the star chart she'd been perusing earlier—she'd found the latter in the castle's chaotic library—but she hadn't been sure how steep the roof would be. And though she would admit a tendency toward recklessness, even she could see the utility in getting her bearings unencumbered on her first trip out to the roof.

"Clem?"

"Ahh!" She jerked, startled.

"Oh, hell, Clem! Don't fall!"

Archie. He'd stuck his head out of his own window, which was apparently next to hers. Just as she was registering the presence of his head, he heaved his entire body through the window and was at her side in an instant with one arm extended in front of her—as if his arm would stop her if she were truly falling.

It was a little . . . unsettling to think his bedchamber was just on the other side of the wall from hers. She composed herself. "What are you doing here?"

"Funny," he drawled, "I was about to ask you the same thing."

"I came out to look at the stars."

She expected him to scold her—that seemed to be their chief mode of interacting these days—so she elaborated. "I'd have gone outside—below outside." She waved her arms to indicate the grounds below them. "But this place is so overgrown, you can't see the whole sky from the grounds, and I'm trying to find a constellation that's close to the horizon."

The upbraiding she was anticipating didn't come. Archie merely tipped his head back and said, "Ah, yes. Stunning, isn't it?"

"It is. I've missed the sky during my time in London. The daytime *and* the nighttime versions of it."

"Do you *never* get to Hill House? Or do you just not bother to call on us at Mollybrook when you're there?"

She heard the jesting in his voice and smiled. "I never get there. I wasn't exaggerating earlier. Father has been so desperate I should marry that he's kept me in Town, even in the depths of summer. And Olive does not like the country; she prefers the amusements of the city. You know how among my family I've always been . . ."

"More inclined toward outdoor pursuits?" Archie supplied, as if he knew she'd been going to finish her thought with something more like "an outcast" and preferred his version. And he was right. *Outcast* was putting too fine a point on it. Olive and Father loved Clementine and made pains to include her in their doings, as had Mother. They just didn't *understand* her, or she them. She could not fathom the appeal of a stuffy, overcrowded ballroom, just as they grew restless and bored after too long a sojourn in the country.

She was the changeling child among the Morgans.

It occurred to her that back when she'd actually been a child, she'd had Archie around. Even when he was at school, she wrote him letters, and when he came home on breaks, they'd be off on their rambles.

She realized that she was lonely. That even though she had spent these past years in the jammed ballrooms and bustling streets of Mayfair, she had been, elementally, alone.

"More inclined toward outdoor pursuits," Archie said firmly, his previous question transmuted into a declaration.

"More inclined toward outdoor pursuits," she echoed, because, again, it wasn't as if she didn't love her family or they her. "The last time we were at Hill House was Easter, for a week only, and I believe *you* were in London."

"Yes." He was silent a moment. "There was a new doctor I wanted my mother to see. In fact, she is in London now for a course of treatment."

"Oh, Arch. How is she?" She had been wanting to ask, but since she'd been following his instructions to stay out of his way, she hadn't had an opportunity. "I always include her in my prayers."

The silence stretched on. Just when she was gathering her thoughts to issue an apology for asking in the first place—imagine having to apologize for saying something to *Archie*—he spoke. "She is . . . worse than you remember."

The Dowager Countess of Harcourt was afflicted with a disease of the mind. She was forgetful beyond what seemed usual for a woman her age, and at times it seemed that she conflated present and past. It had started when they were young, had been something the family grappled with even when Archie's father was alive, and it seemed to have gotten worse as the years progressed, and to have been joined by occasional flares of ill temper.

"Perhaps that isn't a fair assessment," Archie said. "In some ways, she's better. Do you recall how angry she used to get at my father?" Clementine nodded. She remembered more than one dinner derailed by Archie's mother's lashing out at his father for some perceived slight—although sometimes the slights were real. Archie's father had not been a particularly kind, or patient man. "With my father's passing, her anger faded." Archie snorted. "Which is understandable. No one could ever live up to his standards, even those of us in our right minds. But in other ways, she *is* worse. She doesn't recognize me anymore, hasn't for months. She held on to her memory of Miss Brown for longer—you remember the companion I engaged after Father died?" Clementine nodded again, not wanting to interrupt Archie with speech. "Very occasionally, she *still* remembers Miss Brown, though those instances of lucidity seem to be fewer and farther between."

How utterly heartbreaking. Clementine missed her own mother a great deal. Though they hadn't been cut from the same cloth, there was something about a mother's hand laid against one's forehead that comforted, no matter one's age. She rather thought that it might be worse to have one's mother physically present but at the same time *not* to have her.

Archie laughed, though there seemed little mirth in it. "Though sometimes Mother thinks Miss Brown is her own mother—my grandmother—which can be darkly amusing. It turns out Grandmother never cared for Father, and Mother seems bent on relitigating that old disagreement with Miss Brown."

Oh, this was sounding worse and worse. Why couldn't Archie's mother reminisce about happy times with Miss Brown standing in for her mother? "How curious," she said carefully, for in her memory, the marriage between Archie's parents had not been a particularly close, or cheerful, one.

"Indeed. I'd always assumed, given my parents' cool attitudes toward each other, that the match had been championed by *their* parents. But according to these reenactments, my mother was the driving force. It was, and remains, surprising."

"Hmm."

"I must say, Miss Brown is wonderful about it," Archie went on. "We're lucky to have her. She plays the role of my grandmother with kindness and patience, gently trying to assure Mother that she grew to love and approve of Father." He paused and cleared his throat. "There was a time when they had that conversation at least weekly."

"Who does your mother think you are when these conversations occur?"

"No one. I'm no one."

Something about the way he said that didn't sit right with her. He'd spoken quickly and his tone had gone alarmingly flat, as if he meant the statement elementally, not just as it related to his mother's affliction. But she thought that was an observation Archie would not appreciate, so she tilted her head back and said, "I am trying to locate the Pleiades."

"The Seven Sisters," he said, his voice restored to its usual timbre.

"It's supposed to be near the horizon."

"Yes, it's that clump of stars there." He pointed. "You see the ones that are very close together?"

"Hmm. That won't do."

"Won't do for what? The heavens not meeting your expectations, Clem?"

She smiled. "Olive and I have struck a bargain in which each agrees to give the other's favorite pursuit a genuine attempt while we're here. I have been learning to embroider."

"Truly? I'd heard something about that, but I didn't believe it."

"Embroidery fills the time in a way I must admit is not entirely unpleasant. Besides, after all the upset of late, I have been endeavoring to take a more concerted interest in Olive's pastimes."

"And what is Olive doing at your behest?"

"I have yet to decide. It is difficult to distill my interests into a single discernable pursuit. 'Be out of doors' is not a pursuit, per se."

"Yes, I see your dilemma."

"And I could hardly say *walking.* That is not specific enough, and it wouldn't be as if I'd be introducing Olive to something novel."

"This is the part where normally I'd suggest hunting."

"You would, wouldn't you?" Honestly, Archie was one of her favorite people, or at least he used to be, back when they were children, so it was difficult to reconcile that with Archie the murderer of animals. But to be fair, he had always loved the hunt, so it wasn't as if he'd changed elementally.

Perhaps *she* had.

That was a disconcerting thought.

Not wanting to get into it—with him or with herself—she said, "I have been leaning toward stargazing, but I'm doing some preliminary investigation in order to make it more interesting."

"These majestic stars on their own are not sufficiently interesting?"

She smiled, something in her warming at his gentle teasing. "You know what I mean! Olive will respond better if I can superimpose a story on what she's seeing."

"Luckily, the ancients did exactly that."

"Precisely. I found a star chart in the library, and I'm endeavoring to match up what's on it with what I can see—and with what I can remember of the myths behind the constellations."

"The Seven Sisters is thematically apt for you and Olive, I suppose."

"That's what I thought. Daughters of Atlas, turned into stars. Alas, though, it doesn't make a picture. It's merely a clump of stars. I thought if they were bright enough, or . . . clumpy enough, it might not matter, but now that I see them . . ." She shrugged.

"You think they will underwhelm Olive."

"I fear so."

"What about the plough? It's part of a great bear, I believe."

"Too common. Everyone knows about the plough, probably even Olive."

"Ah."

They sat in silence, and it felt like old times. The Archie of her youth, when he came home on school breaks, used to slot right back into her life as if he had never been away. He would simply appear, in her favorite spot in the woods, say, and plop down next to her. Or he'd fall in beside her suddenly when she was walking into Chiddington. "Hullo, Clem," he might say, as if it had been a mere day, rather than months, since they'd last seen each other.

A bit like how he had popped his head out of the window just now, and was sitting beside her on a rooftop at midnight as if it were the most ordinary thing in the world.

She'd been fretting that there had been too much time between them, or too much fuss with this Theo business, or too much *something*, to allow things to feel easy between them again. Their reacquaintance certainly hadn't *felt* easy, what with the dramatic escape from the inn and Archie's insistence she not spend time with him and his friends.

But here it was, that ease. Here *he* was. She hadn't realized how much she'd missed this. Missed *him*.

"A pity it's not later in the year," Archie said, "for then you could see the great hunter, with his belt."

"Ah, yes, my favorite activity, immortalized in the heavens for all eternity."

Clementine had meant the remark ironically, but Archie asked, "You don't care for hunting?"

"Have I ever?"

"I . . . don't know." It was too dark to see any detail on his face, but somehow, she could *feel* him furrowing his brow.

Oh, Archie. He could be so attentive but also so very . . . daft. "Well, considering that I eschew the eating of animals, it is safe to conclude that I also do not care for the killing of them for sport."

"I . . ."

She had shocked him. He *did* love hunting. She didn't care to get into a moral discussion just now, or to insult his favorite pastime, so she returned her attention to the sky and said, blithely, "Didn't the hunter follow the great bear into the sky and get stuck there? He is still in pursuit, after all. He must not be a very talented huntsman."

Archie grumbled, but it was a good-natured grumble.

Another companionable silence settled. Clementine was starting to feel as if she could sit here forever on this roof with Archie, neither of them needing to speak. The quiet between them felt almost medicinal—in the same way the trees and the streams and the stars, even the ones that formed a picture of a hunter, always had been.

"Clem?"

"Hmm?"

"Promise me you'll stay away from men like Mr. Bull in the future?"

She thought she could, but at the same time, when she went back over it in her mind and considered what she could have done differently, she didn't come up with much. "Well, if I'd known what kind of man he was, I would have stayed away from the start. But of course I can promise to stay away from men like Mr. Bull because I am resolved to stay away from men in general from now on."

"Present company excepted?" he teased.

"I am resolved to stay away from any man who might want to marry me," she laughingly clarified. "Which in Town, with Father around, is a category that might as well include all men."

"Perhaps it's time for a sojourn at Hill House."

"Oh, how I wish."

"It might allow you to clear your head, provide a respite from the machinations of London life."

"I fear that for Father, the machinations are the point. Though perhaps now that both of his daughters have had to be snatched from the brink of ruination, he will permit a country holiday. A palate refresher of sorts."

He chuckled, and she was gratified that she had the ability to amuse him—and that they could already laugh about their recent harrowing travails.

"But I *will* exhaust him, Arch, even if he doesn't permit an immediate retreat to Hill House. I shall outlast him, and when I'm finally allowed to be the spinster I was born to be, I shall retire to the country, and I shall be glad to have you there for a friend."

She'd been trying for more levity, to gently mock her own situation, but her voice had come out strong and resolute, as if she were making a vow.

"I am sure you will outlast him if you want to," Archie said thoughtfully. Then, more animatedly, he added, "I say, join us for dinner tomorrow, won't you? You and Olive both."

"I thought you didn't want us underfoot." Besides, Clementine was thoroughly enjoying her meatless meals with Olive in the breakfast room. The cook they'd borrowed seemed not only to indulge but to genuinely embrace the challenge Clementine's dietary preferences posed. The sisters had been presented with some ambitious—and often delicious—victuals.

"One meal a day does not constitute 'underfoot,'" Archie said.

It was kind of him to offer, but when she compared the pause before he'd said, "One meal a day does not constitute 'underfoot'" to the intensity with which he'd stared at her that first morning when he'd insisted she and Olive stay away from him and his friends, it was easy to see which of the two sentiments was the truer.

8

Beware the Common Stinkhorn

By the next evening after dinner, Clementine's leaves had advanced quite a bit. Well, they had advanced in the sense that there was a great deal more stitching on the fabric, but they were also advancing into looking . . . significantly less leafy.

"What does this look like to you?" Clementine held her hoop at arm's length. "It looks like a cottage with a wavy roof, does it not?"

Olive squinted at Clementine's paltry efforts. "I think it looks more like green water with sticks beneath the surface."

"Hmm. What should I do?"

"Well, I could tell you how to fix it, but that would be as good as me actually fixing it for you."

"And that would be a bad thing?"

"Well, then it wouldn't be yours, would it?"

"I suppose not, but that didn't stop you with Theo, did it?"

She regretted it the moment it was out. She'd shocked herself, in fact, with the outburst—shocked Olive, too, judging by the little gasp that burst out of her.

Clementine couldn't seem to let go of this whole business with Olive and Theo, even though her feelings didn't make any *sense*. She had spurned Theo *before* Olive ran off with him. How could she be hurt about Olive's stealing something she'd already cast aside? Something she actively didn't want, had come to despise, even?

"I was trying to *help* you," Olive snapped, her shock rapidly papered over with irritation. "At some personal cost, I might add. Perhaps I ought not have bothered."

"I know, I know," Clementine said, chastened. She needed to keep things in perspective. Olive had been attempting to save Clementine from ruination. What she didn't understand, was: "Why, though? *Why* did you do it?"

"He said he was going to ruin you!"

"I know, but that doesn't answer the question!"

Olive's eyes bugged out as they always did when she was frustrated. "I already *told* you: he said you'd given yourself to him." She'd switched to speaking slowly and with an exaggerated air of patience, as if talking to a child, which made Clementine want to scream. "You had changed your mind about the betrothal, and he said he was going to tell everyone he had taken your maidenhood so you would be *forced* to marry him."

"But *you* were forced to marry him!" That was what underlay Clementine's *Why?* She wasn't disputing the facts as told by her sister; she was struggling to understand the motivation behind Olive's actions. Olive was not known for her selflessness.

"I *wasn't* forced to. *I* suggested the switch. *As I already told you.*" Olive sounded miffed, as if having her intelligence underestimated by her sister was a greater affront than being married to a blackmailer.

"Yes, but once again: *Why?*" Clementine was equally miffed. Would Olive just answer the dratted question? "Why would you *do* that? You are being purposefully obtuse! Please just tell me! And don't give me any of this vague nonsense about us not needing to know everything about each other. That may be true in general, but I need to know *this*!"

Olive stared at Clementine for several beats, her azure eyes unblinking. When she eventually spoke, she dropped her gaze and shrugged in a manner that struck Clementine as performative. "I want to see the world. Theo was planning on a grand tour. And I want to marry. So he seemed as good a prospect as any."

That didn't make any sense. Olive was the sort of girl who loved love. Or the idea of it. She was always developing brief but intense tendres for gentlemen, had done so since long before her debut. It hardly even seemed to matter to whom she attached her fancy; the object of her affection was always secondary to the fact of it. The son of visiting friends. A gentleman they'd met in passing at a party. Once, she had even taken a liking to the blacksmith in Chiddington, and she'd gone around and checked every foot of every horse they owned in the hopes of finding one in need of being reshod.

That trend had only intensified this past year, her first out in society. Olive had adored everything about the Season in London. Parties and dresses and outings with friends. Promenades and teas and trips to Gunter's. And though her tendres had come faster and more furious than ever, given the wider availability of gentlemen to inspire them, none ever seemed to stick. "It's a question of timing," she would say. "I don't want to make a match too soon. And I should so adore another Season. But I also don't want to wait until it's too late." She would look at Clementine as she said this last part, as if Clementine were the corporeal manifestation of the concept of *too late*.

Clementine could only wish *Father* would look at her like that, would allow her to be well and truly on the shelf. "So Theo offered you marriage, and you want to travel." Clementine could see that, on paper, Theo might be a sensible match according to those two criteria. "But what about love? You want love, do you not?"

Olive shrugged again, and this one seemed real, and it seemed resigned. "Two out of three isn't bad."

"Oh, Olive, you're still young! Don't—" Clementine cut herself off. She was hardly in a position to deliver an encouraging talk about holding out for a love match.

Olive stared at Clementine for a long while. She looked as if she were trying to come to a decision of some sort. When she finally spoke, she said, briskly, "Come with me. I want to show you something."

Clementine followed Olive to her bedchamber. Inside, things were, as per usual in Olive's domain, in disarray. Clothing was strewn on every surface, an open book lay facedown in such a way that had surely damaged its spine, and a half-drunk cup of tea sat on the bedside table alongside another embroidery hoop. Clementine marveled that Olive had managed to create such chaos in mere days, and even more so that she had managed to fit all this into the portmanteau she'd had on her person when she escaped Theo. Clementine moved to take a look at the sewing. "You're doing another project?" The stitching Olive had been working on at Clem's side, the one of the sheep near Chiddington, was already an ambitious endeavor.

"No, no!" Olive vaulted over the bed, grabbed the hoop and turned it over. "Just experimenting with something that isn't ready to be seen."

Well, that might be the most interesting thing Olive had said in a great while. Clementine's hands itched to grab the hoop, but she kept them by her side.

It was strange, come to think of it, that Olive was stitching such a bucolic scene when she professed to hate the country. It was also strange that Olive did so hate spending time at Hill House. The young Olive of Clementine's memory, while perhaps not as enthusiastic about scrambling up trees and stomping through streams as Clementine, had been quite happy when the family retreated to Hill House. And Olive's beloved dogs were much more content there than in Town.

"Sit." Olive pointed at a chair by the window, and Clementine obeyed, watching as Olive extracted her book of days from her valise—Olive was as attached to the worn leather volume as some children were to a doll or special bauble. She had carried it around for years. She slid out from between its covers an equally worn piece of parchment, which she handed to Clementine.

It was a list written in Olive's familiar loopy hand. It didn't have a title, but it was easy to see, as Clementine scanned it, that it was a list of experiences Olive wished to have.

1. *Travel: the Continent, Egypt, America, Upper Canada.*
2. *Ride in a gas balloon.*
3. *Participate in a high-stakes game of cards of the sort gentlemen play.*
4. *Be the mistress of my own house and decorate it entirely in florals.*
5. *Have as many dogs as I want in my house decorated entirely in florals, and allow those dogs to do whatever they want in that house (after #1–4 completed).*
6. *Have children (also after #1–4 completed).*

Clementine's entire view of her sister abruptly shifted. It was a similar feeling to having drunk that ale on an empty stomach at the inn, as if the ground beneath her feet was not as solid as she had always believed. Who knew Olive was such an adventurer at heart? "This is extraordinary."

"I want to *live*, Clemmie. I want to live a big life. You know as well as I do that women don't usually get to do that. I don't pretend I'll ever get to do most of the things on that list, but with Theo, the travel was guaranteed, and since he's an unconventional sort, I thought perhaps he would not mind having a wife who wanted to do unconventional things."

"There you were mistaken. Theo was very much in want of a conventional wife. A subservient one, even, as I discovered."

"As did I. I hadn't watched him sufficiently. That was my fatal mistake."

"You *are* always saying you have to watch people closely."

"Yes. If you watch people closely and carefully and for long enough, a certain kind of knowledge will result. A kind of truth. I admit that I made an error with Theo. It was because I wasn't able

to watch him for long enough before I had to decide what to do."
She leveled an implacable stare at Clementine. "And that, Sister,
is your fault."

Oh, dear. Clementine had blamed Olive for this mess, but she
was afraid the heavy, uncomfortable feeling in her stomach meant
that at least some of the culpability rested with her.

She was trying to think how to respond, but Olive pressed on,
her countenance gentling. "Surely you can see my logic. I thought
Theo and I would travel, and when we eventually settled down,
I would become the mistress of my own house. Although I do so
want to travel, my home must be in England, close to you and
Father. I am not prepared to bend on that."

Clementine grabbed Olive's hand and squeezed. She was overcome by that last declaration.

"And, yes," Olive continued, "I would've had to endure Theo's
attentions in order to have children, but only for a limited time,
and after that, I thought we could strike an agreement by which he
would ignore me and I him. I have observed that such an arrangement between husbands and wives, one of mutual benign neglect,
generally leads to a content, peaceable union."

"That is . . ." Clementine had no idea what to say. Such an arrangement sounded sad. But also practical. And like nothing her
sister would even think of, much less settle for. It was certainly not
the type of union their parents had.

"After all, our parents' union was not a love match, yet they
were quite happy together."

"I *beg* your pardon!" Clementine cried, and had she not been
so shocked she would have laughed at how her sister had all but
plucked the very thought from her head—but inverted it entirely.
"How can you *say* that?" Father had doted on Mother and she
him. "You are wrong."

"I am not wrong. I heard Mother talking to Aunt Susan once,
saying that the best decision she ever made was to marry Father.
It was back when Susan was trying to decide whether to accept
Uncle Roderick's proposal. 'We are not in love,' Mother said about

Father, 'but we like each other a great deal. He is my dear friend.' She went on to say that she appreciated the fact that if Father undertook any dalliances, he hid them well."

Clementine made a noise of dismay. Truly, she felt as if she might weep.

"Clemmie," Olive said soothingly. "They had a good marriage. A good life. We had a lovely family." She sighed. "Until Mother died, anyway."

When all Clementine could do was nod because she was too overcome to speak, Olive said, "Do not be so distressed. I believe they came to love each other. I asked Mother outright, during the final months of her illness, how she knew she loved Father. It was a trick question, mind you. I wanted to know if she would say anything like she said to Aunt Susan."

That sounded exactly like something Olive would do. "How did she respond?"

"She said, 'One day, we were sitting together after dinner in Town, and your father was answering his correspondence.'" Clementine smiled at the way Olive was mimicking their mother's voice. She would have made an excellent actress. "'He was irritated because there was some problem with the well at Hill House, and he was muttering through his letter to Mr. Hughes about it,'" Olive went on in the role of Mother. "'I said we should return to Kent in the morning, and he absently pointed out that we couldn't because we were attending a ball the next night—I can't even remember which one. I countered that surely a failed well was more important than a ball. He set his letter down, peered at me through his spectacles, and said, "Not to you, it's not; therefore it isn't to me, either. We'll go the day after tomorrow." He said it with such fondness but also such matter-of-factness, as if it were a given. I remember thinking how lucky I was to be so loved, and how much I loved your dear grumbling father.'"

"I wonder when that was," Clementine said. "There were often problems with the well at Hill House." What she was really asking was when Mother had decided she loved Father.

"I know," Olive said. "It could have been anytime in the last decade or so before she died. But the important part is that it happened."

"I suppose. Does *anyone* marry for love, though? From the outset, I mean. Love of the passionate, romantic sort."

"Honestly, the older I get, the more I understand how rare it must be. I think that kind of love is only found in novels. But you would know about that better than I—you were the one always reading novels in trees."

She hadn't realized her sister knew about her reading-in-trees habit, but perhaps this was another example of Olive watching people closely enough to glean the truth. "Olive, I—" Clementine wanted to say that true love must exist somewhere in the world, but did that matter if neither Morgan sister was destined for it?

"I'm sorry, Clemmie. I've upset you. Perhaps I should not have said anything. My point is merely that I know how the world works. I was—am—trying to play the game in such a way that I land on a satisfactory ending. I made a mistake with Theo. A grave enough one that I am chastened and shall return to my corner, regroup, and try again next Season." She smiled. "And who knows, perhaps eventually I'll have enough money saved that if I can't get a husband who meets my criteria, I shall follow you into spinsterhood and hire my own gas balloon and such. You would let me live with you once Father is gone, wouldn't you? I daresay you'd even let me redecorate, since you don't care about that sort of thing."

Clementine was all astonishment. "But . . . where are you getting this money you speak of?"

"From Father. It's very easy to wheedle pin money out of him; have you not noticed?" A self-satisfied smile blossomed on Olive's face. "In fact, I've been able to bleed him very freely since my debut. And once he is gone—not that I am wishing to hasten that, not at *all*—we shall each have our portions."

Clementine remained agog. While she had always understood her sister to be clear-eyed, in possession of a practical-bordering-on-mercenary streak, she had thought it in service of shallow, transitory experiences. A new dress, a party, an evening at the theatre. "Olive, I think you are . . ."

"Yes?"

A great deal smarter than Clementine had understood. But to say that, to admit to her past impressions of Olive, seemed unnecessarily unkind. "While I am sorry your goals remain as out of reach as they ever were, marriage to Theo would never have delivered them to you. He is . . . not a good man."

"I know that now," Olive said sadly. "He is quite different when he isn't actively deploying his charms. And I'm sorry that you . . . Did he hurt you, Clemmie?"

"No. I hurt myself. I *gave* myself to him. What was I *thinking*?"

Clementine had thought she would never speak of this particular shame to anyone. But here she was doing exactly that, and it rather felt as though she were the younger sister and Olive the older, wiser one.

"I expect you were thinking you were going to marry him in a matter of weeks, so what did it matter?" Olive spoke calmly, plainly, without the slightest hint of judgment in her tone.

Clementine had most decidedly not given Olive enough credit. She had seen only the ways they were different. She had dwelled too much on her sister's outward attitudes and not enough on her actions, even though sometimes her actions were more well-meaning than they were effective—witness the entire elopement fiasco. But take the business with the cook. Olive had taken it as given that the cook would need to accommodate Clementine's dietary preferences, had made a point to explain it to her. Olive had a kind of radical acceptance about her that was really rather extraordinary.

It appeared Clementine was in the inner circle after all; she just hadn't realized it.

"Clemmie, I want to say that if my running off with Theo hurt you, I'm sorry for it. I knew you'd broken off the engagement."

Clementine wanted to ask how Olive knew this, but if she'd

learned anything in the past few days, it was how shrewd her sister was.

"I figured you had your reasons for doing so." Olive sniffed. "Now that I know him better, I'm *certain* you had your reasons. But when I hatched this scheme, I *was* doing it at least in part to prevent you from having to marry him. I thought any discomfort I caused you would be short-lived. But if that's not the case, I sincerely apologize."

It was amazing what a genuine apology could do: Clementine felt the last of her unfavorable feelings toward Olive melt away. "He *did* hurt me," she whispered. It was all she could bring herself to say just now.

"I'm sure he did," Olive said gently.

"If I'd known what you were contemplating," Clementine said, "I'd have warned you off Theo. As dear to you as your goals were, they weren't worth the sacrifice."

"Well, even so, *you* were." Olive smiled wryly. "On balance anyway."

"What do you mean?"

"I still would have done it, if I'd had to, even knowing what I now know about him, if it'd meant preserving your good name." Clementine was about to interrupt with yet another *Why?*, but Olive kept talking. "My silly list is never going to come to fruition. I know that in my heart. And since I don't care who I marry, I might as well do some good with my choice of groom. Even if I couldn't have gotten *any* of what I wanted, marrying Theo to save your reputation would have done *some* good. It would have given you a fighting chance to be happy. Bought you some time to try to outlast Father, anyway." She performed another of her insouciant shrugs, as if they were discussing settling for lukewarm tea instead of a wildly deficient husband.

"But—"

"It's a moot point since in the end neither of us had to marry Theo. Thanks to Archie."

Oh, Archie. It had been so wonderful to talk to him, to really *talk* to him, last night. Perhaps it had been their perch on the roof, in the dark, that had allowed such a rapid resumption of their old intimacy. It had reminded her of being in a tree with him, which was a category of place they used to spend a fair amount of time. Regardless, it had felt like having her old friend back, and once back, she realized how terribly she had missed him. She'd missed him all day, in fact, in an oddly visceral way. She wanted to talk to him some more. To know that he was in residence—indeed, that he was in residence in the bedchamber next to hers—triggered a strange yearning for his company.

She wanted to tell him about the extraordinary conversation she'd had with Olive. She wanted to tell him that if the origin of his parents' marriage was not what he'd thought, neither was the origin of hers.

"What do you think of Lord Featherfinch?" Olive asked suddenly.

Clementine blinked, taking a moment to adjust to the question.

"He's so *terribly* handsome." Olive flounced back on her bed and sighed melodramatically. It appeared the old Olive was back, the theatrical girl who could develop sentimental feelings in the blink of an eye.

"He certainly is . . . darkly imposing."

"Isn't he, though? And his apparel is absolutely *exquisite*. Who knew there were so many ways to style black? And his hair." She sighed. "I daresay his hair is prettier than yours, Clemmie." She sat up as suddenly and urgently as she'd fallen back. "Perhaps this has all happened for a reason. Perhaps I ought to set my cap for *him*."

Archie had yet another perfectly typical, perfectly enjoyable day with the boys. Somehow, though, it did not have the usual restorative effect. In fact, he found himself growing increasingly tired and irritable as the day unfolded. By dinner, he was actively yawning, shaking achy legs he couldn't keep still under the table, and he had to bring his beads to the table with him.

His mind kept snagging on the fact that they were nearly half-way through their trip. Only eight days left to . . .

To what?

What exactly was he wanting that he wasn't getting?

He was tired. His mind had reached that point it sometimes did where it was incapable of settling. Better to call it a day and start fresh tomorrow. So he begged off uncharacteristically early, not long after dinner.

Which was fine, but that didn't explain why, if he was so ex-hausted, he didn't go back to his room but rather slipped into the empty one next to Clementine's and stuck his head out the window.

Ah. There she was. She had a lantern with her this time, and she was bathed in its warm glow.

"Hello!" she exclaimed, and the undisguised delight in her tone jolted him awake. As he stuffed himself through the window to join her, he wondered if he had *ever* been this awake. It was in such contrast to his previous mood that it was almost whiplash inducing.

"Hello," he echoed, eyeing her. She was wearing the same plain blue day dress as yesterday. Its skirt was voluminous enough that she was able to sit with her legs crossed, and they were wrapped and tangled in the fabric in such a way, and backlit by the lantern in such a way, that he could see the vague outline of them. Her hair tumbled down her back, almost to her waist. He had never seen her hair like this. As a girl, when they'd been on the loose near Mollybrook, she'd always had it braided. Typically, a great deal of it would come loose from its moorings, but this, this water-fall of untamed hair, was another thing entirely. And of course when Clementine came of age, she'd begun wearing her hair up. Well, she wore it up in company, and sometimes she wore a bon-net over—

"I didn't realize until last night that you were in the bedcham-ber next to mine," she said, interrupting his mental treatise on her hair.

"Yes, well." He cleared his throat. "Nor did I, until I happened to look out the window and see you last night."

That was a lie. The gentlemen's quarters were in an entirely different wing of the house, on a corridor that extended out at a right angle from the main one, where Clementine and her sister were housed. He himself had suggested the separation when Mrs. MacPuddle had been musing over where to put everyone, repeating his desire for the ladies and the gentlemen to holiday separately. Last night, when he'd opened his window to let in the fresh evening air, without which he could never sleep, a flash of movement on the roof of the perpendicular wing had caught his eye.

That movement had turned out to be Clementine, and without thinking it through, he'd set out to find her. He'd poked into quite a few rooms in order to find one that provided a means of egress that would allow him to join her on the roof. It was as if she'd been a magnet and he an iron bauble, mindlessly submitting to her pull.

"And here I thought that if I found you out here tonight, I might find Olive, too," he said. "What became of your quest to show her the stars?"

"I did some research today, and I brought this." She reached behind her and produced a map. "I thought I might find a better constellation than the Seven Sisters."

"And have you?"

"Yes, but the problem is the stories behind them. I only have this chart. I went through the library in search of a book that recounts the stories of the constellations, but I didn't turn anything up. In fact, the library here seems to be comprised entirely of Gothic fiction and Jacobite history. While I admit to being fond of the former, it isn't any help when it comes to my current task."

They did used to spend a lot of time reading novels in trees. Well, Clementine did. He spent a lot of time watching Clementine read novels in trees. He smiled at the memory. "A deficient library. Alas."

"Oh, it matters not in the slightest. I'm having a perfectly lovely time."

"It is rather wonderful here, isn't it, despite the rocky start."

"I'm . . . still so very sorry about that."

"Oh, I didn't mean that. I was referring to the initial lack of food. The aforementioned deficient library. The ravens Effie tells me are roosting in the guardhouse turret, and the clan of squirrels that has moved into the old castle keep. The, ah, interesting topiary."

"Do you know that Olive thinks those are mushrooms?"

He burst out laughing. "Mushrooms!"

"Yes."

He snorted. "What kind of mushroom is so . . . elongated?"

"Well, actually, there is a variety of mushroom called *Phallus impudicus*, better known by its colloquial name: the common stinkhorn."

"Nice try, Clem." Clementine knew a great deal more about the natural world than Archie did, and they both knew he was by no means a scholar, but she was going to have to do better than that to fool him.

"I am entirely in earnest! During Mother's illness, I developed an interest in traditional healing. It was misguided, of course, but in my grief, I thought perhaps I could find a way to restore her to health. Can you imagine the hubris required to believe I could achieve what her doctors could not?"

She scoffed, but he *could* imagine it. He knew the pain of grasping at anything that might cure one's beloved mother, even if what one was grasping at was ultimately an illusion—or a delusion.

"As such, I developed a particular interest in fungi," Clementine went on, "and I can tell you with certainty that the *Phallus impudicus* is long and white and has a menacing-looking black, bulbous head that produces a most unpleasant slimy excretion."

He still was not entirely sure she wasn't mocking him. "Hmm. The *Phallus impudicus*. Is it poisonous?"

"I am not certain, but it reportedly stinks to high Heaven—like rotting flesh, they say—so even if not, I imagine it would be unpleasant to, ah . . . put the *Phallus impudicus* in one's mouth."

Again he burst out laughing. Clementine did not share his amusement. Perhaps he was taking too much for granted. Clementine might still be the sly, witty friend of his youth, but that didn't mean she necessarily knew what she was saying. He didn't have the impression that gently bred young ladies were bequeathed a great deal of information on this particular subject—although in some ways, one could hardly call Clem, she of the wilds and the wind, gently bred.

And, if she *did* know what she was saying, if she *was* making a concerted attempt at humor by bringing up the *Phallus impudicus*, was the bit about putting it in one's mouth purposeful or accidental?

Goodness, being friends with the grown Clementine Morgan was a great deal more complicated than being friends with the girl version of her had been.

He swallowed his mirth. She, however, chose that moment to join in. Her high, lilting laugh soothed his worries. Soothed some hidden, inner part of himself, too. Gave him that same feeling the inaugural Earls Trip toast always did, that sense of haven, of balm, the delicious relief of setting down one's burdens and knowing they would stay surrendered for the next little while.

He tilted his head back to examine the heavens. Clementine's lantern was casting a decent amount of light, so tonight's celestial tableau was not as breathtaking as last night's had been, but that wasn't disappointing in the least, so suffused was he with that feeling of remedy. "How goes the embroidery?"

She huffed a little, frustrated sigh.

"The thrill of the new worn off?" he teased.

"I must admit embroidery is a more challenging pursuit than I always believed."

"Ah. Is it the pain of the embroidery itself that drew forth that sigh, or is it the fact that you didn't award your sister enough credit when it came to the difficulty of her favorite pursuit?"

She grumbled, and he struggled not to find it adorable. "You know me too well, Arch."

He was glad, unaccountably glad, she thought that the case. That all those missing years, all his neglect, hadn't created a chasm between them too deep to bridge.

"I'm sorry I stopped writing you back," he blurted.

"I beg your pardon?"

"You used to write to me at school. I have recently had cause to remember that you continued to do so afterward, but I . . . had difficulty replying." He hadn't phrased that well. He didn't want to make himself seem illiterate. "I found the environment at home less conducive than school for keeping up correspondence, but I regret that I didn't—"

"Oh, Archie, do not give it a moment's thought. Letter-writing is easier when one is young, don't you find? And I think it's entirely usual for people to fall out of touch as they grow up. It doesn't even require distance. Olive and I grew apart, too, and we were right there under each other's noses the whole time."

Her absolution relieved him, but he still felt regret. "Hence the sisterly exchange."

"Hence the sisterly exchange—which isn't really an exchange, at least not yet. I've been embroidering for several days and I have yet to come up with anything for Olive to do."

"Perhaps instead of showing Olive the stars, you ought to charge her with a more active task, something with a degree of difficulty. Just to even the scales, you understand. Stargazing doesn't require any skill. What about climbing a tree? Do you still do that?"

"No," she said wistfully. "It has been years since I've climbed a tree. One can hardly detour from the path in Hyde Park and shimmy up an oak."

He chuckled. "Well, if anyone could, it'd be you. But I take your point."

"Besides, am I not too old to climb trees?"

He didn't like the notion that Clementine would regard herself as too old, or too anything, to engage in an activity she used to enjoy as much as climbing trees. "I don't think of tree climbing as an activity with an age limit."

"Hmm," she said, though she sounded cheered.

Silence settled, and he reflected that as much as he liked Olive, he was *glad* she wasn't here. This was his second rooftop tête-à-tête with Clementine, and he had the most absurd feeling that he would like to do this every night for the foreseeable future without Olive or anyone else joining them.

In fact, he was fairly certain he'd begged off drinking with Effie not to go to bed, as he'd said and perhaps even half believed, but to find Clem. He ought to feel chagrined. This was supposed to be an Earls Trip, after all. Not a Clem-and-Archie trip.

But since he *had* done it, and since he *did* have Clementine all to himself, he was going to ask her another question, an old one, but one that had recently risen to the surface of his mind. "Do you remember the dances in the assembly hall in Chiddington when we were young?"

That, of course, wasn't the real question. It was the prelude to the question. Even though this was Clem, to whom he could say anything, he felt some priming of the pump was called for.

"I do. I hated those dances, but in retrospect, they seem so benign."

"How do you mean?"

"If you were of a mind to flee, you could be outside in under a minute. And Chiddington is not large—the buildings themselves are not tall, and there's only the one high street. So from the assembly rooms you could be on the street in less than a minute, and clear of the village proper in another five. Whereas at some society parties in London, you walk for what feels like miles *inside* someone's house before you even *get* to the ballroom." Clem was talking faster as her theory unspooled. "And if you want to depart, there is usually a complicated leave-taking process involving calling a servant to fetch your outerwear, and another to summon your conveyance. And of course you can't do any of that without a chaperone. And if that chaperone happens to be your *father*, who is bound and determined to see you married off, good luck with your attempted escape."

"Ah, yes, I see." He had never thought of it that way, but he shared her outlook on London parties, except of course he did not require a chaperone to attend or to leave them. And as to the Marriage Mart that had Clem so agitated, he had to admit that one not unwelcome outcome of having a dead father and a mother who had taken leave of her wits was that no one was haranguing him about marrying, preserving the lineage, and so on. The title and its accompanying estates and wealth—the whole damn thing—could pass to Archie's cousin Herbert, who was next in line and quite competent, and not a single person in the world would mind.

The thought, which should have been liberating, was in truth a trifle unsettling. Because the notion of not a single person caring about the fate of the title was, of course, equivalent to not a single person caring about *him*.

Though, of course, he reminded himself, Effie and Simon cared about him.

They just couldn't help him with the whole "fate of the lineage" problem.

Not that it was a problem. As previously established.

"And *then,* even if you *do* manage to get out," Clementine finished with a great flourish, waving her arms as if she were conducting a symphony, "you're still in *London*." She made a melodramatic choking sound.

"Indeed." He laughed at her theatrics, but he could not disagree with any of what she'd said.

"And *then* there's the *company*."

Oh, she wasn't done. He smiled and settled in to listen to the rest of her monologue on the merits of the assembly rooms in Chiddington relative to the ballrooms of London.

"There was a rather lot of talking about horseflesh and crop rotation, which are both topics in which I have some interest—and of which I have some knowledge. And though I wasn't meant to show the latter, in reality no one much minded when a mere girl had something to say about the merits of Cleveland Bays versus Yorkshire Trotters as carriage horses."

"Probably because you knew what you were talking about. I recall a time when you advised Aaron Hastings on the purchase of a pair of matched Cleveland Bays he was quite happy with."

"Yes, he had been planning to buy a pair of Suffolk Punches, and that seemed too much horse for the job. It wasn't as if he needed them to do double duty as workhorses. He merely wanted to swan around in his curricle and impress everyone." She scoffed laughingly. "Honestly, the *bays* may have been too much horse for the job."

"So you aren't able to converse on these topics in company in London?"

"Goodness, no. In London it's all dresses and shopping and the on-dits of the day. What is Lord Byron's latest scandal, for example? Mind you, I would be quite happy to discuss Lord Byron's latest *poem*. He does write so piercingly. But so many people who talk about him seem not to have actually read anything he's written."

"You should read Effie's—" Ah, bollocks. Archie was so comfortable with Clem, he'd been about to let Effie's secret spill as easily as tipping over a teacup in a too-close drawing room. He tried again. "Featherfinch is a devoted student of literature, and I believe he's read every word Byron has ever written. You should speak with him on the topic." She could do just that if he could ever get her to dine with him. "If you'd care to join us for dinner tomorrow, I'm sure we could get him to expound upon Lord Byron for significantly more time than you may have thought you'd like to devote to the topic."

Clementine looked momentarily delighted, then her face shuttered before his eyes. "Oh, no, I heard you before. You may have thought me still addled from my trying journey and all that dreadful business with Mr. Bull, but I heard you. My sister and I shan't be intruding on your gentlemen's holiday. Arch, you really must allow yourself to abandon your good manners. Your mother is not here."

He saw her realize what she had said, watched dismay move across her features like a storm coming in at a good clip. She'd only been invoking his mother as a kind of stand-in for polite society, a proxy for whatever norms or practices dictated that a gentleman should always be accommodating and decorous and so forth. She meant to say that no one was watching him, but the thing was, he wanted to be watched—by *her*.

He wanted her to come to bloody dinner.

She looked increasingly stricken, and he did not know how to tell her that it was fine, that she had not erred or offended him or anything of that sort.

Not knowing how to steer them out of this conversational morass, he returned to the original topic—he did want to get his question answered. "Speaking of Chiddington, you wrote me once, when I was at school, about a dance there. You made mention of having danced with two different partners that evening. I was wondering . . ." He was belatedly hearing how odd it was going to sound for him to be focused on, to have remembered at all, such an inconsequential detail. But now that he'd started, he couldn't see a way to reverse course. "I was wondering who it was you danced with that night?" He rushed to add, "It just popped to mind, what with all the talk of the old days, and the assembly rooms."

Her lantern, the one that was blunting the effect of the heavens above them, was sufficient to illuminate her furrowing brow. "Hmm, no doubt one of them would have been Ralph Scully. Do you remember him? He always danced with Olive straight away. They were great friends. When he returned Olive to us, he generally invited me to dance. It was out of pity, mind you, but I always liked him."

"He was the son of Mr. Smith, the surgeon." Mr. Smith had always been kind to Mother, even when he hadn't been able to offer much by way of assistance.

"Yes. Ralph and Olive struck up a particular friendship. I think it went back to the time I broke my arm falling out of that willow by the pond—do you remember that?"

He did. "I believe I was the one who ran to the village to fetch Mr. Smith."

"That's right! I remember lying on the grass beneath that tree, sure I was going to die! *This is it*, I thought, and I consoled myself that at least I would die shrouded by the branches of the willow, which if you recall were quite magnificent in the way they hung down, almost like a waterfall of foliage." She laughed at herself. "Ralph came with his father to tend to my arm, and he and Olive discovered a shared love for—nay, obsession with—dogs, of all things."

"Terrible news when we learned of his death."

"He died?" Clementine's voice sounded genuinely distressed.

"Yes, in Upper Canada—he'd joined the army and was part of a garrison there. And Mr. Smith died, too, a year or so before Ralph, so poor Mrs. Scully is left all alone."

"How awful. And I hate how out of touch I am with news of home. I wonder that Olive never told me."

A morose silence settled for a few moments before Clementine broke it by saying, "Certainly one of my dance partners that night would have been Ralph, may he rest in peace, if only because he was always one of my dance partners. You may remember that the rules there were relaxed. I'd never be allowed to dance with a surgeon's son in London."

"Mmm. And the other partner?" Archie tried not to sound too interested.

"I can't remember the other, but it may have been Mr. Chapman. He came to be rather fond of me. Perhaps I ought to have considered his suit. That is another experience that seems not so bad with the benefit of hindsight. One comes to understand, as time passes, that one must lower one's expectations."

The small, resigned sigh that accompanied Clementine's statement about lowered expectations should have dismayed Archie, but whatever he might have felt about Clem's settling for less than, well, for less than *everything*, was eclipsed by his inability to get past her previous sentence.

"His *suit*? Are we talking about *Frank* Chapman?" Archie did attempt to keep the shock—and dismay—out of his tone, but he feared he had not succeeded. He checked himself. Was it a shock that men had offered for Clementine? No. She had previously mentioned having rebuffed two suits. Despite her claims to the contrary, Clementine Morgan was a prime catch. Yes, she could be odd, and her obsession with the natural world perhaps went too far in some people's estimations—she did tend to walk around with twigs and leaves in her hair and mud on the hems of her dresses—but she was pretty and lively and just generally so . . . incomparable. But Frank Chapman was a widowed gentleman who had to be older than Clementine's father. And he must be the man to whom she was referring. There were no other Mr. Chapmans, Frank Chapman having fathered only daughters.

He wondered who the other suitor was.

"Yes. You might not remember Mr. Chapman. He rarely came to the dances, but he was a particular friend of my father's—and yours—and when his wife died, he was round to our house for dinner a lot."

Archie cleared his throat and endeavoured to make his next observation with significantly more equanimity, as if he were merely commenting on the weather. "I do remember him. You and Frank Chapman would be very ill-suited."

"I'd thought as much. But had I said yes, I'd be in the country, wouldn't I? And he wasn't cruel or dogmatic or overbearing or simple."

"Not dogmatic, cruel, overbearing, or simple? *That* is the standard?"

"Mr. Chapman's only crime was that he was dull as dirt." She tilted her head. "Duller. Because dirt is, in fact, quite interesting if you look at it closely enough." Her head righted itself as if to signal the end of her digression. "And possibly also that he was still in love with his late wife, though she'd been gone for years by that point. The more I think about Mr. Chapman relative to my experiences with gentlemen in Town, the more I wonder if I made a mistake in rebuffing him. So I would have been subject to some mind-numbingly dull treatises on taxation—he was unaccountably interested in taxation. And can it really be counted as a fault that a man loved his wife? *She* was his wife. I would have been a placeholder. He would have left me alone a great deal of the time. And, as I mentioned, I'd still be in the country. Father would be placated, and I would have gotten at least some of what I wanted."

"Who was the other gentleman?" he blurted.

"I beg your pardon? What do you mean 'the other gentleman'? Although I can't remember the evening we're speaking of, I'm almost certain my two dance partners that night would have been Ralph Scully and Frank Chapman."

"Not that. You, ah, mentioned the other day, when we were on the terrace, that you'd been in receipt of two offers of marriage. Mr. Chapman was one."

He did realize that this was none of his affair. He just . . . needed to know.

"Oh, quite." She snorted, which made him smile. "My other offer was from a man called Alfred Potter."

Archie searched his memory for the man and came up with nothing. Clementine must have known that's what he was doing, for she said, "You wouldn't know him. He's an American, if you can believe it. An industrialist."

The idea that Clem had had an offer of marriage from an American industrialist put Archie back on his heels. Highlighted anew how far he had drifted from the Morgans. Good God, what if she'd said yes? Was Archie the sort of person who could have lost such a dear friend *to America* without even realizing it?

Apparently he was.

"He was the son of a shipbuilding magnate based in New York," Clem went on, oblivious to the dramatic reckoning of the soul underway in her conversation partner. "We met at a ball, hiding from the quadrille, and that provided a certain amount of fellowship of feeling." She smiled fondly, and something rumbled unpleasantly in Archie's chest. "He had recently started a company that ships ice to the American south, if you can imagine that!

"He was a refreshingly forthright sort," Clem went on. "Told me outright that he was hunting for a wife. I suggested that hiding from dances mightn't be the wisest strategy if matrimony was his aim. He replied that if any young ladies saw him attempting the quadrille he might as well go home right then. We had a lovely chat. At the end of it, he shocked me by proposing marriage."

Archie tried to interject, to ask what kind of man would propose marriage after mere minutes of acquaintanceship, but he wasn't fast enough. There was a lag between the astonishing things she was saying and his ability to absorb them.

"I did consider it," she continued blithely. "He was a pleasant enough sort, and his passionate interest in ice was really rather compelling. But his wife would have to go to America with him, where he lived in an apartment in New York. A large apartment, to hear it told, but . . ." She shrugged. "He was to inherit his father's empire and was in want of a wife to be a hostess and . . . Well, that wasn't me."

Of course that wasn't her. For God's sake! Archie opened his mouth to agree with her, but once again, she was too fast for him.

"I told him I'd be as suited to that life as he was to the quadrille, and we parted ways amicably. My mistake was in telling Olive about it. Olive told Father, and he was quite angry with me. Which, in truth, I found hurtful. One likes to think one's father might have at least a minor pang of wistfulness at the idea of sending a daughter across the ocean to marry a stranger."

She brushed her palms together briskly and her tone became equally brisk as she said, "So that's that. One offer from an American industrialist who lived in the most urban of conditions, and one from a boring-but-benign man old enough to be my grandfather. But again, one wonders, in retrospect—especially when one's current vantage point is post–Theodore Bull—if one made the right choice."

"Clem, I—" He had no idea what to say. Words were beyond his grasp. She turned her head toward him, her wild hair backlit by the lantern so that, together with her flowing dress, she looked like a feral blue angel. He became so befuddled that even if he had known what he *wanted* to say, he wasn't sure he knew how to make his mouth form the corresponding words. Usually, Archie's problems with words were in reading or writing them, not speaking them, but he had so many thoughts jumbled up in his head.

That Clem had almost *gone to bloody America!* Left England for good.

That she'd come close to settling for Frank Chapman, or God forbid, for Theodore Bull—or for *anyone*.

She was too good to settle. Even if she married a kind, unexceptional gentleman, and even if that kind, unexceptional gentleman loved her, he wouldn't *understand* her. He wouldn't understand that sometimes she had to leave a party because she would die if she stayed a moment longer. Or that the antidote to a concert that went on too long and made her feel trapped was to take her outside. Or that it was a goddamn tragedy that she hadn't climbed a tree in years.

Clementine Morgan didn't just need love; she needed understanding.

Still, even if he could have made his mouth report these thoughts, he could not give that speech. It was fine for him to have this point of view, but he didn't have to live her life. He was, as she had pointed out, free to live *his* as he chose. He couldn't tell Clem not to settle for anything less than love and understanding, because she might have to. It made him . . . well, it made him positively seethe with indignation over the unfairness of it all. He wondered what he could do about it. Nothing, he concluded, short of changing the very basis around which society was organized, and that was well beyond his capabilities.

Archie had heard Clementine say she didn't want to get married. He had sympathized. But perhaps he hadn't brought the proper depth of understanding to her aversion. He did now. If only there were a way to support Clem in her quest to remain unmarried. That would solve the problem for her, if not for the rest of society, and he cared a great deal more about her than he did about society. Perhaps there was a way he could influence her father. He would think on it.

"Yes?" she said.

"I beg your pardon?"

"I believe you were about to say something, but I fear I've quite lost you to your thoughts," she teased good-naturedly.

"Ah. My apologies. I was going to ask, will you please come to dinner tomorrow?"

9

Lady Pirate

She did not come to dinner. Yet another day passed with no sign of Clementine. It was maddening. Archie did not share Effie's fancy that Quintrell Castle was haunted, but Clem might as well be a ghost for how much she was around. After an early morning walk during which he saw no evidence of her, and a late, leisurely breakfast at which he saw no evidence of either Morgan sister, Archie, Simon, and Effie rode past Doveborough and on to the next settlement, which was a market town of some size. Simon disappeared into a bookshop, and Archie and Effie walked an enormous hedge maze and got well and truly lost in it, so much so that Archie had to boost Effie up so he could attain a prospect of the thing and identify a route for their escape.

He couldn't help but think how much Clem would have enjoyed it—the maze, but the long ride, too, lover of horses that she was.

Once again, though, he saw her at night. Which, come to think of it, rather bolstered the theory that she was a ghost. Had Clementine died without his noticing and now she was haunting him? He wouldn't put it past her.

But no, there she was, the real, corporeal Clem, once again perched on the slanted roof beneath her gabled window. Every time he popped his head out of the window in the neighboring bedchamber and spied her there, he'd been torn between the urge to exhort her to go inside before she fell to her death and the opposite urge to join her.

The opposite impulse always won.

He consoled himself that even though she had not climbed a tree for years, that kind of nimbleness didn't desert a person. It remained baked into one's being, the same way the boxing moves he had practiced his whole life could be summoned by his muscles without his mind needing to be involved at all. Those had come in handy with Mr. Bull.

"Where have you been?" he asked as he squeezed himself through the window.

"What do you mean where have I been? Where *would* I be?"

"I haven't seen you for days."

"That's not true. I saw you here last night, and the night before that."

"That doesn't count. I haven't seen you in company."

"Correct me, but I believe not seeing me was your express wish. *You're* the one who keeps joining *me* out here."

"Yes, but—" But what? Nothing he could say would make any sense. Clementine was doing exactly what he'd asked her to. "I brought you a telescope," he said, suddenly remembering the putative reason for his appearance this evening. He handed over the small instrument. "There's a widow's walk on the guardhouse. Effie wanted to go ghost-hunting, and we found it mounted there. It was in terrible shape, but I've cleaned it up. Perhaps it will aid in your stargazing efforts with Olive, though for the record, I still think you should insist she climb a tree."

It was too dark to properly see Clem's expression—her lantern this evening was casting only the faintest of glows—but somehow, he could feel it. It was equal parts surprise, excitement, and . . . something else he couldn't quite put his finger on.

When he passed her the telescope, their hands brushed, and he started. It was odd: he knew Clementine as well as he knew anyone, yet he could probably count on one hand the number of times they had touched. Their childhood ramblings had been conducted side by side, but Clem had never needed anyone to boost her up a tree or help her jump off a wall. There had been the odd time, in their teens, perhaps, when they'd been in company and their parents had expected a show of manners, and he'd taken her gloved hand and bowed over it, both of them struggling not to laugh at the absurdity of such formality between them. And of course there had been the dramatic ride away from the inn last week, but that had been different, somehow. That had been his body going through the necessary motions to make sure they reached safety.

And all those times there had been clothing between them. Gloves.

He thought it possible that this was the first time he and Clementine had ever touched skin-to-skin.

No, he didn't *think* it possible. He was certain. He would have remembered this feeling. It was remarkably like the thrill of the hunt. Of that moment when, after riding hard and long in the cold, crisp air, one suddenly caught a glimpse of the fox. *There it is.* A thunderbolt of recognition, a jolt of elation.

He had been momentarily afraid he would fall off the roof.

"Are you quite all right, Arch?"

He gathered himself and changed the subject. "You and Olive seem closer than you used to be." Though what did he know? He hadn't seen them for years.

"I think we are. We grew apart after Mother died, but we've recently . . . grown back together."

"Why did you grow apart?"

"I'm not sure. It's something I've been pondering lately. We're quite different in terms of our constitutions and interests, of course, and there is an age gap, but honestly, I don't know. I suppose it's like with us: life pulls you one way, and sometimes it pulls friends and family another."

"Perhaps your mother was the glue that held you together."

"I think you may be right."

"What happened to change things? To make you grow back together?"

"Why, Mr. Bull, I suppose," she said wonderingly.

"Yet from the outside, it would seem that Mr. Bull should have driven the two of you even further apart. She did run off with him, did she not?"

"She did, but I had already broken off my engagement to him— and I did think that would be the end of it, but of course it turned out it was not."

He could not help but feel there was more beneath the surface of what she was saying, of what *both* sisters had said. That there was a piece missing.

"Why?" he asked, softly, carefully, trying not to betray how interested he was in her answer.

"Because I wrote him a letter crying off, and he sent me one in return saying he understood and wished me well. He did not protest or try to talk me out of it. So I naturally concluded that would be the end of it."

"No, I mean why did you break it off?" She didn't answer right away, and he began to think she wouldn't. "You said earlier that you'd had 'certain realizations.' Tell me what they were." He winced. That had come out sounding too commanding. He did realize this was none of his concern.

"My realizations are none of your concern."

He smirked into the night. "Tell me anyway."

Another long silence unspooled. She wasn't going to talk. Which was her prerogative. He lay back on the roof. She did, too. That she was going to stay out here with him caused a kind of warmth to spread through him despite the chilly night. They would watch the stars together for a bit.

Just as he had come to relish the silence, she whispered into it. "Arch, I have anticipated my marriage vows."

He didn't know what to say. He swallowed his first impulse, which was to tell her that it didn't matter. Well, no, his first impulse was shock. But that wouldn't do anyone any good. He swallowed his *second* impulse. It wasn't up to him to decide what mattered to her. He considered reassuring her that no one would have to know, but perhaps the fact that *she* knew was enough to distress her, and, again, he could hardly tell her how to feel.

He hardly knew how *he* felt.

She sat up suddenly, as if she were making to leave, and he realized that by not speaking, he was likely giving the impression that his silence was of the disapproving variety. "Well, I have anticipated my marriage vows, too," he finally said, trying to infuse the remark with some levity.

"It's not the same for you. For you, that phrase is mere shorthand."

"I'm not sure I follow."

"Your saying you've anticipated your marriage vows means you've engaged in certain behaviors. You never intended to marry anyone with whom you were . . . doing your anticipating." He could feel the afterthought rise in her mind. "*Did you?*" she exclaimed.

He chuckled. "No indeed."

"See? It's different for you."

"It's different for me because I am a man? An aristocrat? Wealthy?"

He had been asking which, meaning she should choose one of the three options, but she issued a universal "Yes."

He wanted to add a fourth option, which was that it was different for him because nobody cared. Sir Albert might be oppressing Clementine with his insistence that she marry, but wouldn't it be nice to exist on some middle ground between that and no one caring whatsoever about how one comported oneself?

But they weren't talking about him. His shock was coalescing into something sharper. "Perhaps I should have killed Mr. Bull when I had the chance."

One of the reasons it was so easy to talk to Archie, Clementine realized, as she considered how to respond to his murderous observation, was that he never rushed to fill silences, or pushed her to do so. He let her think. He seemed open to the possibility that sometimes she might not answer. He communicated, somehow, without actually saying anything, that things between them would go on unperturbed if she chose not to answer.

Which, paradoxically, made her *want* to answer. His willingness to be ignored made her *want* to tell him everything. His comfort with there being silence between them made her *want* to fill it.

Add to that the fact that they were perched on the roof together in the near dark, and Clementine was inclined to let all her secrets spill. It would be such a *relief*.

She extinguished the lantern. She didn't want to see him while she spoke, or for him to see her. "Arch, I anticipated my wedding vows *willingly*." That had been difficult to say. But he needed to know that if she was to explain everything. "That's the beginning of the answer to your question about my so-called realizations, the prerequisite knowledge you need to understand the rest."

"All right," he said mildly, and Clementine reflected that Archie was perhaps the only person in her world who would react with mildness to such a confession. *This* was why she had known, somehow, that he was safe to tell.

Though she had to amend that thought: Olive had reacted with similar sanguinity.

"I don't regret it," she added, telling the truth but also perhaps trying to provoke him a little. She wanted to test the boundaries of his tolerance, to find out how safe she was here. He was her dear old friend, but that didn't necessarily mean his equanimity was limitless.

There was a beat before he said the same thing: "All right."

She smiled into the dark and laid back down next to him, returning her gaze to the sky. It was easier to talk lying side by side like this. "I don't regret it, because if I hadn't done it, I would not have discovered Theo's true nature."

"And what was his true nature?"

"Theodore Bull turned out to be a conniving, and, well, violent man." She paused, trying to think how, and how much, to tell, to see how closely she could match up the edges of the truth with how much Archie could stand to hear. But no. Had she not just decided that Archie was safe? And now that she was tasting the beginning of the relief that came with telling someone the whole, unvarnished truth—more than she had told Olive—she found she did not want to stop short. "You heard the beginning of the story, earlier, about his charm, about how I'd hoped to be of use to his work, his cause."

"Mmm."

"I had truly reconciled myself to the idea of marriage to him. Well, no, 'reconciled' is not the right word. I was looking forward to it. Well, not precisely that, either." She huffed a sigh. She was having trouble finding the right words. "You know when there's something you have to do, so you set your mind to it, and once you've done that, you just want to get the thing over with? And perhaps there is even a kind of relief in the doing?"

He gave another murmur of agreement.

"Theo wanted to have the banns called immediately. I agreed, and Father was, of course, thrilled. The first of the three Sundays, we all went to church together. Well, I suppose I should say that Theo went to church with us, as he had not previously been a pious man."

"I don't imagine he was."

"Yes, curious how he found religion just when he was hunting for a bride, isn't it?"

Archie's next "Mmm," was decidedly less placid.

"I found myself at home alone with him after church. My father had lightened up on chaperonage requirements even before Theo came around." She chuckled. "I sometimes thought he *wanted* something scandalous to happen. Very likely he was of the opinion that was the only way to get me married off."

"Or perhaps it was that he trusted you."

"Oh, Arch. You are too good." He really did see the best in people. No wonder his friends were so loyal to him. "I adore you for saying so, but you think too highly of everyone. Father is like Olive: he knows how to scheme. As to Mr. Bull, I found myself at home alone with him, the banns having been called that morning, so I allowed things to . . . progress."

"Did you, ah . . . know what that entailed?"

She paused. Archie was her friend, and she trusted him absolutely, but this was still discomfiting. "I did."

"You'll forgive me for asking, but I am under the impression that young ladies, perhaps especially motherless ones, are not always schooled in such matters."

"I have been an observer of nature for quite some time." He chuckled, though she had not been trying to amuse. "But I take your point. Olive, for example, speaks as if she's worldly, but in some ways, I think she's actually quite innocent about the . . . details."

"I gathered as much from her lack of reaction to the topiary garden and from your later report that she thought Sir Lionel's creations of the . . . fungal variety."

It was Clementine's turn to chuckle. "Olive was *not* the observer of nature I was."

"Indeed."

She considered what to say next. She had recounted the necessary plot. Olive would say there was no need to expound upon motivation. But the more they talked—the more Archie let Clementine talk without rushing to judgment—the more comfortable she felt. "In all honesty, I was interested in trying it. It is the act that underlies the world, is it not? It is the basis for all creation, for all the beauty in the world, for life *itself.*"

"That's a very high-minded way of looking at it," Archie said wryly.

"So I have learned."

Archie let loose a sharp exhale. "Clem, I am endeavoring to remain calm, to remember that this is your story and not mine. But honest to God, if he hurt you, I will go to America myself, find him, and—"

"No. No. The, ah, act itself was . . . well, it was underwhelming if I'm being honest. *He* seemed to enjoy himself immensely, but . . ." He made an indistinct, strangled sort of noise, and she rushed to finish her story before she gave him an apoplexy. "So that was fine. Well, not fine, but, as I said, merely underwhelming." A bit of pain followed by what felt like a purely mechanical act. "It was afterward that . . . gave me pause. He had barely, ah, rolled away when he declared that we would be going to Scotland after the wedding, and henceforth on to the Continent—permanently. I objected. We had not talked about that at all, and unlike my sister I have no wish to tour the great cities of the world."

"Olive wishes to tour the great cities of the world?"

Drat. She should not have said that. Olive had confided in Clementine about her heart's fondest wishes, and Clementine shouldn't be sharing those wishes with anyone else, even Archie. Hoping to deflect, she returned to her story. "Mr. Bull also informed me that we would not be having children, which was also not something we had discussed. He had, ah, removed himself before spilling his seed, saying he did not wish to get me with child." In the moment, she'd thought it an act of consideration on his part—his not wanting to get her with child before the wedding in order to preserve her reputation. "When I asked him about it after we'd dressed, it turned out he had ideas about the surplus population I did not share. This led to the discussion about children, which escalated into an argument. When I expressed my opinion, he grew enraged." She paused and unclenched her fists. Her fists remembered what had happened next. "It was as if he shook off a disguise he'd been wearing, and I saw his true face. He told me all I had, including my person, was his, and that we would be going where he wanted us to go and procreating or not as he chose. He grew wild with anger when I would not stand down. He struck me."

She sensed Archie tensing beside her. "All right, now—"

"Don't worry. I struck him back."

"Good girl."

Just as she had sensed Archie's going rigid a moment ago, she somehow knew he had relaxed, at least enough that he was done interrupting her. "I didn't do much damage, but I shocked him enough that I was able to run out of the room. I locked myself in the library and waited. He must have seen himself out, because when my father and sister arrived home an hour later, there was no trace of him."

"So that's when you called off the engagement."

"Yes. Or tried to. I wrote him a letter, he wrote back accepting my decision, and I thought that was the end of it, but . . ." Part of her wanted to turn over and look at Archie, but she was afraid. Not of him, precisely, but of the prospect that what she had told him might change things between them, just when she had gotten her old friend back. "You know the rest. Father wanted me to go through with it. He wrote to Mr. Bull assuring him that I'd merely had an attack of nerves and would come around."

"Sir Albert wanted you to go through with it even with the bit about not having children? Did you tell him about that?"

"I did, and even then, he was not persuaded to my view of the matter." She felt a stab of pain. "I understand that there are many happy marriages that do not produce children. And I realize it's odd for me to say I want children, when I've also been saying for so long, and am saying again now, that I do not want to marry. It's just that if I *had* to marry, especially if I were reconciling myself to a loveless union, I *would* want children. They would be a sort of . . . compensation. That sounds cold, doesn't it? Trying to make the best of a less than satisfactory situation by bringing innocent children into it?"

"No. I understand. I think it is possible for children, for families, to be that to each other—to be compensation, and ballast, against the trials of the world." He cleared his throat. "That is my impression, anyway."

That is my impression, anyway. That sentence struck Clementine as sad, for it indicated Archie had no firsthand experience of such.

"Did you tell your father that Mr. Bull struck you?" Archie asked.

"I did! I must admit, it hurt me so very much when even *that* would not dislodge Father from his position that the betrothal must be salvaged."

"Of course it did."

"He said he would have a word with Mr. Bull about it. Of course I did not tell Father about the rest, about us having been intimate. I considered it, despite how mortifying it would have been, but concluded it would only harden his resolve that I must marry Mr. Bull."

"I think that was a wise omission on your part. Besides, it isn't his concern."

What a friend Archie was. Was there another man in the world who would take her part so thoroughly?

Once again, she was seized with the desire to turn onto her side, to face him, but she did not. She did keep speaking the truth. The dark and the stars and the Archie-ness kept allowing it. "I don't regret any of it." She wanted him to know that.

He turned onto *his* side then, as if he had heard and was granting her silent wish. But, no, more likely he was turning over because he was going to object. She had finally gone too far in his estimation, and he was not going to allow her defiance to stand.

She could not abide that. She was more than a woman Theodore Bull had hurt. So she turned, too, so they were facing each other on the cold slate roof. It was too dark to make out his features, but she could see the shape of him, and she could sense his nearness. "If I hadn't gotten the true measure of him, I never would have broken it off. And if I hadn't done *that*, I would be married." She shuddered. "Is it not better I discovered his true nature before I married him, even if it means I'm ruined?"

"You're not ruined, Clem," he said quietly.

"Of course I am."

"You're *not*," he insisted.

"Well, I suppose no one knows I'm ruined. It's like that philosophical question about if a tree falls in the forest and there's no one around to hear it, does it make a sound?"

"No. I mean you're *not ruined*. The idea that the act of sexual congress imparts ruination only on unmarried women who partake in it is illogical. What if you *had* married Mr. Bull? Then you're not ruined? And what about him? Why isn't *he* ruined?"

Oh, Archie. "That is an exceedingly enlightened viewpoint. I have to say I agree, though I never expected to find anyone *else* who did. I have watched the coming together of all manner of animals. Birds and weasels and even deer. I'm not missish about it. I cannot truly believe the laws of nature should be so different for humans."

"They aren't." His agreement was gratifying. She tried to make out his features in the dark. "'Tis merely that men have imposed their own laws, their own morality, their own sentiment, on the act."

"That is precisely my point. I've seen how it is with grasshoppers. There *is* no morality or sentiment involved. It is quick and efficient, and it gets the job done. Why should it be any different with people?"

"Oh, but it is. You misunderstand me. It is very different."

That gave her pause. So far, they'd been perfectly aligned in their views on the matter. "How *can* it be different, if one considers the natural purpose of it? It is an act that must occur to further the existence of mankind."

"Yes, it is a necessary precondition for propagating mankind, but think of how often humans take pains to *prevent* such propagation."

"Do they?" She hadn't realized. But it made sense. Why did some families have only one child and others a gaggle of them? She'd always assumed it was chance, but it seemed reasonable that strategy could be involved, too.

"They do indeed."

"The pulling out." Theo had been very theatrical about that bit, groaning as if he were being tortured by the devil himself. She could almost have looked back on it with amusement if what followed hadn't been so wrenching. "That is the method for such prevention."

"It is one among several."

"Hmm." It was hard to imagine what else would achieve that goal.

"My point is that among humans, the act can be about so much more than the propagation of the species."

"What? What can it be about?"

"Pleasure, Clem."

Ah. She understood now. "Yes. For the gentleman."

"For the lady, too."

She snorted. "That sounds like a lie gentlemen tell themselves."

"I see," he said blithely, as if she were a child too obstinate to continue reasoning with.

That tone rankled, especially from him. "And I suppose you have a great deal to say on the matter," she snapped back, trying to incite a quarrel—so perhaps she *was* being childish. It was just that she'd had a taste of Archie's radical understanding, and she could not bear to revert to him thinking her silly, or simple, or both.

He did not rise to the bait, though, only said, a little wistfully, "Only that someday I hope you are proved wrong."

Archie did not know how to extricate himself from this—from this conversation, from the roof, from any of it. The last two nights, he could've sat on the cold slate for hours, talking with Clem until the sun came up. Tonight, abruptly, he was talked out. He had the sense that saying any more, *staying* any more, would be akin to trying to drink from a stream rushing so violently that one couldn't actually manage to swallow any water. He'd had to take in too much information, much of it distressing, and was inwardly reeling. He had been trying to see things from Clem's point of view, to stretch the bounds of his beliefs and swallow his initial, outraged responses in favor of speaking gently. Calmly. So as to be worthy of these secrets she was bestowing upon him, these un-earned confidences.

But in truth he was seething with umbrage toward Mr. Bull. That went without saying. But also toward . . . the world. Well, no, the human world. Clem's grasshoppers had done no wrong. Her amoral birds and weasels were blameless. It was the world of *men* that had mucked everything up, and he wasn't even—or only— thinking about the blackmail or the direct assault upon Clem's person at the hands of Mr. Bull. It was patently unfair that the best Clementine Morgan, an intelligent, vibrant, lovely woman, could hope for was a disappointing-but-not-violent match, *and* that such a match was likely to be devoid of carnal pleasures.

Archie had never given any thought to the concept of ruination, but he believed everything he'd said to Clem on the matter. He was aware that this outlook was out of step with that of society at large, but why *should* what happened ruin her and not Theodore Bull?

The more he considered it, the more it sent him into a silent rage.

But not at her, he reminded himself as she sat up. He watched her relight her lantern and lift the telescope.

"You look like a lady pirate," he observed, attempting to shift the conversation for his sake as much as for hers.

She laughed, and it soothed something inside him. "Do I?"

"Yes, with your long, loose hair"—it was truly glorious—"and your spyglass raised, you look as though you might be trying to evade a band of privateers."

"Why am *I* not a privateer in this scenario?" she queried.

"You're too wild to be a privateer. You're clearly a pirate."

He could sense her amusement, though she did not display it overtly. This was a good note on which to take his leave. A moment of lightness. He sat up. "Will you and Olive join us for dinner tomorrow?" His pride should have prevented him from asking yet again, but somehow it did not.

"I don't think so."

Oh, for Heaven's sake. "Why not?" He was aware that he was being a pest, but once again, awareness was not enough to induce him to stop.

"I'm enjoying dining informally with Olive. And honestly, I'm enjoying the respite from eating meat, and from watching others do so."

"What if we agree to forgo meat for an evening?" Yes, he did hear what he was saying. No, he did not understand why he was saying it.

"There is no reason for you to do so!"

"But—" But what? He just . . . wanted her. Up here on the roof but also inside. As much as the two of them had always felt caged in when they were forced into drawing rooms and such, Archie's own drawing room was different. And he wanted her in it.

What he really wanted, he realized with a start, was for Effie and Simon to know Clementine, and for her to know them. More than just in passing. He wanted to know what she thought about the boys' whimsical theory of family, for example.

"We are halfway done with the holiday," he said, as if this had anything to do with anything. But the days were ticking away in his head like the beating of a drum. *Seven days. Seven days.* And since they'd all had their initial meeting, Archie still had not seen Clementine anywhere except this roof.

"How about Olive and I join you *after* dinner tomorrow?" she asked. "I can sit and work on my embroidery like a proper lady."

He snorted. He would rather have the lady pirate than the proper lady. But that would do. "All right, then. Until tomorrow evening."

It occurred to him that seeing Clementine in the daylight, with other people around, as much as he had lobbied for exactly that, was going to be very strange indeed. Up here on the roof, he and Clem had not only resumed their former friendship, they had exceeded it. Not that they had ever bothered with social niceties, but they also had never spoken this intimately. In three nights, they had discussed his mother and Clementine's experiences with Mr. Bull. Concerns and fears and dashed hopes. The coming together of men and women. He supposed the newfound intimacy that had resulted from their time together was because these were adult concerns. The last time they had spoken meaningfully, they had been children.

"Until tomorrow evening," she echoed, and just as he was about to disappear back into "his" bedchamber she called his name.

"Yes?" He squinted back into the dark to find her staring at him. She held the lantern next to her head, and it threw odd shadows onto her face, making him wonder for an instant if she *wasn't* some kind of supernatural creature.

"Thank you," she whispered.

"'Tis merely a telescope," he said lightly. "And probably not a very good one at that."

"That's not what I'm talking about, and you know it."

He did. What he did *not* know was how to tell her that no thanks were needed. Not because he was a saint who was above wanting gratitude, but because sitting next to her, talking with her, being the person to whom she told her secrets, was his pleasure. His honor. Not being able to vocalize any of that, he simply said, "You're welcome, Clem. You're so welcome."

10

The Gentlemen Are
Resplendent in Silk

She didn't come. There were only six days left of their holiday, and she didn't come.

It was fine, though. In fact, it was for the best, because by nine o'clock, Archie, Simon, and Effie were sitting around in silk dressing gowns talking again about salt and strawberries and how their parents didn't love them.

Apparently, Effie's trip into Doveborough with the ladies that first day had involved a stop at a modiste, and his heretofore unexplained disappearance earlier today had been to pick up *dressing gowns* he'd had commissioned for the three of them.

"Just *try* it," he'd said, over and over, after it had become apparent that the Morgan sisters weren't coming. Effie had disappeared, changed into his, and returned and held out the other two beseechingly. "They cost a right fortune, what with the rush I was in. I promise, the wearing of this gown will confer the most delightful sensation. It will lift your spirits, Archie."

Archie had started to protest that his spirits didn't need lifting, but Simon interrupted, grumbling about how he couldn't listen to any more of Effie's entreaties. He'd grabbed the proffered gown and taken himself off to change.

Once two of the three of them were attired in silk—Simon in

royal blue and Effie, surprisingly, in lilac—Archie began to feel cornered, a fox staring down the barrel of a gun.

"Look what a lovely color yours is, Archie," Simon said laughingly, nodding at the forest-green gown Effie held. It was good to hear Simon say anything laughingly.

"I asked for masculine colors," Effie said archly, "knowing that would be important to you lot." He grew serious. "Yours is green because you love the trees, Archie, and Simon's is blue because he is always looking up, imagining a better world."

Well. Archie's throat tightened. He was discomposed by having had Effie's poet eyes turned on him.

"And yours is lilac because . . . ?" Simon prompted.

"Mine is lilac because the modiste was out of black silk," Effie said blithely. "Alas. My gown really ought to be black like my heart."

Archie found his voice. "Your heart is not black."

Effie raised his eyebrows.

"You see the beauty in the darker side of life, when the rest of us look away. I'm not sure if that kind of seeing is a blessing or a curse. But either way, it doesn't mean your heart is black."

Effie blinked rapidly; apparently it was his turn to be at a loss for words.

Feeling a bit sheepish about his little speech there, Archie said, "Oh, give me that," and stalked off to change.

When he returned, Simon was sliding around on his chair. He was rotating his hips and flapping his bent-at-the-elbow arms in such a way that, together with the blue of the gown, he looked like an enormous peacock trying—and failing—to take flight. "This fabric does create a curious but pleasant sensation."

"A curious but pleasant sensation," Archie echoed.

"Ah, you are in agreement!" Effie cried triumphantly.

"No. Well, yes." He was, but he'd been echoing Simon's words because the phrase itself had plucked a chord within him. The hearing of those words was *itself* a curious but pleasant sensation, though it did leave him with the sense that his mind was trying to settle on something just out of its reach. Not unlike when one wakes from a dream and is still connected to it but only by vanishing tendrils.

It never worked, trying to hold onto those dreams, so he turned his attention to the present, where, he had to admit, he was learning that a silk dressing gown against one's bare skin was indeed an agreeable sensation. He joined Simon in his attempt to take flight, flapping his arms as he squirmed in place. If Simon was a peacock in blue, Archie was a mallard in green.

Archie was the sole occupant of a settee that had been covered in silk. In keeping with everything else in Quintrell Castle, it had seen better days. But though it was stained and the stuffing was coming out near one end, the silk was still smooth. Archie's attempts to mimic Simon while sitting on a silk settee and wearing a silk dressing gown caused him to slide off the damn thing entirely.

Laughing uproariously along with the boys, he got up and made a more controlled attempt at the same feat, sliding from one end of the settee to another. "Do you remember that time at school when it was raining on top of a bit of snow that had already accumulated, and the combination of precipitation made for an ice field all around the grounds?"

"We nicked some wooden trays from the kitchen and went out and slid down that knoll that abutted the cricket pitch," Simon continued, coming over and elbowing Archie out of the way. "Let me try."

They all laughed as Simon aped Archie's sideways slide. There was something extra amusing about the starchy, overserious Simon in this particular setting, and judging by the volume of his own laughter, Simon himself knew it.

"My turn! My turn!" Effie did not bother with the measured approaches adopted by the other two, and hurled himself at the settee in such a way that he slid rapidly down it, bounced off the carved wooden armrest on the far side, and landed in a heap of laughter on the floor.

After their laughter died down, Effie suddenly said, "I lied earlier. The reason my gown is lilac is that lately I've been feeling more . . . colorful."

Archie had no idea what that meant.

"It's impractical, of course, to remake one's entire wardrobe, but I have resolved, going forward, to experiment with cheerier hues."

"Is your newfound interest in brighter hues reflective of an inner shift? A change of outlook?" Simon asked.

"I think so. Lately, I've been seized with . . ." Effie looked around as if to make sure they weren't being overheard, but since they were utterly alone, the effect was comical. "I've been seized with moments of joy." Archie had to hold back laughter, and Effie must have realized how silly he sounded, for he pulled a face and said, "But don't worry, I retain my appreciation for the beauty in the darker side of life."

"What's brought on these moments of joy?" Simon asked.

"I've had some correspondence lately that has made me rethink a few things."

Archie could see Simon getting ready to launch an interrogation. Archie himself was desperately curious. But Effie rose and shoved Archie to the side. "Move over. I want to try that slide again."

A tussle broke out over who would gain ownership of the settee, the three of them braying like donkeys as each attempted to sit and to dislodge the others. It was a bit like a game Mother used to set up outside on long summer days. It had involved a grouping of chairs containing one fewer in number than the assembled players. Everyone processed around the chairs until a neutral observer shouted, "Sit!" at which point a mad scramble ensued. The chairless player was ejected, a chair removed, and the process repeated until the final two players went head-to-head for the last chair. Archie had forgotten about that. He had the notion that the game was meant for children, but Mother loved it and cajoled him and Father to play whenever they had familiar guests over—the Morgans had played this game many a time. Mother had had such a sense of fun in those days. And Father had always grumbled at being pressed into such a silly game, but by the end, he would be laughing along with everyone else. How extraordinary. In all regards: that it had happened to begin with, that Father had been regularly coaxed to participate, and that Archie had so entirely forgotten it.

Tonight wasn't exactly like that game, though. Here, the settee was big enough to accommodate the three lords, if just. No one wanted to give up, so as the tussle wound down, they ended up pressed together, each man sitting on just enough space for his silk-covered arse to slip and slide in place. And as they sat there wiggling, laughter started bubbling up again.

And when Simon said drily, "No wonder our fathers disdained us. We are an utter embarrassment," they exploded in mirth.

Then Clementine and Olive walked in the door, and everyone went silent.

Being caught out like this should have been mortifying. It *was* mortifying.

But somehow it was *also* the most amusing thing that had ever happened to Archie. After so much longing for Clementine to appear, that she would choose this exact, absurd, perfectly imperfect moment to do so, felt both providential and hilarious. He managed to get to his feet. "Well, hello. I thought you weren't coming."

Clementine would freely admit that she was never going to be a paragon of manners and decorum. She never noticed when she had grass stains on her dress. Her hair never stayed where her maid put it—and it was even more of a lost cause here at Quintrell Castle, where she had no maid but Olive, whose hairdressing skills were nowhere near as good as her embroidery skills. But those were errors of execution, not of theory. Clementine's training had been sufficient to educate her on how to conduct herself. The fact that she was constitutionally ill-suited for spending a great deal of time in company didn't mean she didn't know how to do it. Theoretically.

None of her lessons had ever covered what to do when one

walked in on two earls and a viscount wearing silk dressing gowns and doing what could only be described as writhing on a settee whilst laughing like Bedlamites.

"Oh, my Heavens," Olive breathed, and somehow it was enough to draw the gentlemen's attention.

The room went dead silent as three pairs of wide eyes swung toward the sisters. The men ceased their moving as if they'd been at a dance and had been struck by paralysis mid-cotillion.

That comportment training Clementine had been thinking back on, while not having covered this specific scenario, would nevertheless have suggested that it was in poor taste to laugh at peers of the realm. Especially this lot: they had been so kind to her and were being so welcoming to her and her sister. Well, two of them were. Archie was running hot and cold on that front. He wanted her not underfoot. He wanted her to come to dinner. *Which is it?* she sometimes wanted to cry.

But, oh, how she wanted to laugh at this absurd tableau. *Needed* to laugh. She bit the insides of her cheeks. Clenched her fists. Anything to stave off the massing storm clouds of amusement, growing heavier with unshed mirth by the moment.

They were frozen, all of them, suspended in amber like poor ancient insects.

Finally, Archie stood. "Well, hello. I thought you weren't coming."

There was a beat of silence before Clementine said, "I can see that."

The storm clouds let loose then. Olive started it, letting loose a great, girlish peal of laughter. Oddly, it sounded like nothing Clementine had ever heard, and she'd heard Olive laugh any number of times. This laugh was unfamiliar: high and musical and infused with delight.

A baritone thrumming rose up from the bottom of the scale, Marsden and Featherfinch joining Olive. The former had a deep, booming laugh; the viscount's was punctuated with the occasional snort, providing a percussive element to the symphony.

That left Clementine and Archie, alone now in their amber prisons, staring at each other while the other insects buzzed with laughter and liberation.

Archie was the first to succumb. Or perhaps not. Perhaps it was the other way around. Clementine initially thought the first upturn of one corner of Archie's mouth was the tinder that caused an echoing flare inside her. But it might have been the reverse, because Archie looked surprised by the fact that he was laughing. Either way, Clementine felt a cracking, as if something inside her she hadn't even realized was frozen, incarcerated, was coming alive, the amber around it fracturing to let in air and light. And laughter. Gales of it.

Archie never took his eyes off her as the chorus rose, a roomful of happy locusts. The others stopped before she and Archie did, perhaps because they'd had a head start, or perhaps because she and Archie needed it more, to allow themselves the balm of laughter, to let the light shine into the fissures created by the splintering of their amber confinement.

The other two gentlemen rose and exhorted Olive to sit. Eventually, Clementine and Archie's mirth tapered off, but still he looked at her, still he smiled at her. She looked back at him, *smiled* back at him, her dear friend, and marveled that she'd been nervous to join him and his friends this evening. She wasn't sure why, only that her reacquaintance with Archie had heretofore taken place in the dark. On the roof. Under the stars where it was easy to say what she meant—what she felt.

She had told him so *much*, recklessly exposed her foibles and her fears. She had snuffed out her lantern, there on the roof under the Seven Sisters, and she had shown him her *self.*

She was forced to break from the steadfastness of Archie's gaze by Lord Featherfinch, who was suddenly at her side. "Won't you please sit, Miss Morgan?"

She felt as if she were coming out of a trance, and she felt the rousing as a loss. Her nervousness was gone, but in its place, a kind of resigned sadness moved in. Now she would have to act properly, remember to address Archie as "my lord," be decorous in front of his friends. She took Lord Featherfinch's proffered arm and revised that thought. If anyone here ought to be worried about the contravention of social norms, surely it was the gentlemen wearing dressing gowns and, judging by the bare legs sticking out of the bottom of them, not much else?

Clementine had never seen bare male feet before. Though he had undone the fall of his breeches, Theo hadn't removed his stockings when they'd lain together. Clementine examined Archie's lower limbs. His ankles were . . . well, they were lovely. The lines of his long feet were graceful, and his ankle bone protruded in a way that kicked up her heartbeat. She allowed her gaze to migrate up his leg. Oh! She hadn't expected so much hair. And she would never have expected so much hair to be so . . . pleasing to the eye. Pleasing yet simultaneously unsettling—probably only because such a sight was so out of place in a drawing room.

Discomposed, she allowed Lord Featherfinch—she refrained from looking at his legs but only just—to seat her next to Olive on the settee while the gentlemen scattered to various chairs. Well, two of them did. Archie remained where he'd been standing. Perhaps the trancelike state she'd been in earlier had been shared. A kind of dual, temporary madness.

"Hello? Harcourt?" Lord Featherfinch waved a hand in front of Archie, who blinked a few times.

"Right. Yes. I should sit." He paused halfway to a chair. "No. I should go change."

"Don't change on our account, Archie," Olive said, her eyes dancing. She sobered. "Oh, I meant Lord Harcourt. My apologies."

Archie grinned as he took in the room, looking at it as if for the first time. "You may call me whatever you like. No one here will mind."

"I suppose one needn't stand on ceremony in such a . . . setting," Olive agreed.

"I only wish I had procured dressing gowns for you and your

sister, too, Miss Olive," Lord Featherfinch said with great earnestness.

"You'll forgive me for asking," Olive said, "but what on earth are you gentlemen doing?"

"Well," Lord Featherfinch began, and Archie interrupted to say that he was going to change. He was followed by Lord Marsden, leaving Clementine and Olive alone with Lord Featherfinch, who spun an elaborate tale of being accosted by an evil patch of hogweed and finding relief in the wearing of his sister's clothing. It was a very amusing story, mostly because its teller was so charming. Clementine fretted as she watched Olive come to life under Lord Featherfinch's attentions. She had a prickling feeling of dismay about this development, though she wasn't sure why. This behavior could be interpreted as the return of Olive to her normal self. Dangling after someone as charming and handsome as Lord Featherfinch was exactly something Olive would do. She told herself there was no cause for dismay. What harm could it do? On the exceedingly slim chance Lord Featherfinch could be convinced to return Olive's affections, he would be a very good match. He would meet many of Olive's requirements. For example, Clementine thought it likely that he would not object to a house decorated entirely in florals. And he was a long-standing bosom friend of Archie's, which meant that in addition to whatever else he was, he was a good man.

And, as was more likely, if he did *not* return Olive's affections, what harm was a little flirtation if it helped her sister find her feet after a very disconcerting time?

It was more a niggling sense that she was watching her sister put on a disguise, one Clementine had only found out about recently. She felt as if she'd been given a peek at the girl beneath the veil, the sister—the real one, the one with the unfamiliar laugh—and she wanted more than a peek. That was not going to be possible if they went back to the way things had been before.

She put her concerns aside when Archie and Lord Marsden reappeared. "Oh look, the gentlemen are back and they're dressed—" Laughter was still so close, an unfamiliar friend. "I was going to say 'dressed in proper evening attire,' but I realized I could stop the sentence after the word 'dressed.'"

"Well, that's all fine and good for them, but no one is going to shame *me* into getting back into 'proper evening attire.'" Lord Featherfinch performed an exaggeratedly satisfied sigh and leaned back languorously in his chair. "Once one has peeled off the trappings of the day and is cozily ensconced in loose silk, the idea of redonning those trappings, however handsome they may be, is simply too terrible to contemplate."

"It's the same when a lady removes her stays," Olive said, and Clementine swallowed her impulse to scold Olive for talking about ladies' stays in company. It was hardly the least scandalous thing occurring here. "Once they're off, the idea of putting them back on is anathema."

"Oh, yes, I imagine that would be the case," Lord Featherfinch said. He sat up suddenly. "Unless I am making anyone uncomfortable. In that instance, I shall gladly go change. I want you ladies to feel at ease; I do so look forward to spending an evening in your company."

Olive and Clementine assured Lord Featherfinch that they were not uncomfortable and were, in fact, quite happy to pass the evening with him wearing a dressing gown. Clementine even allowed herself to surreptitiously examine Lord Featherfinch's legs. They were hairy, like Archie's, but his ankles did not disturb the regular rhythm of her heart.

Another laugh threatened to burst out of Clementine. Comparative ogling of gentlemen's ankles: Was this really her life?

It was for now, and she felt lucky to have it. Soon enough she'd be back in London, and it would be time to battle with Father.

The sisters allowed themselves to be given glasses of scotch, which was all that was available to drink without calling upon Mrs. MacPuddle. Clementine had never had scotch. She would have said she was certain Olive hadn't either, but then she thought of Olive's list and wondered if she could ever again be certain about anything to do with her sister. She took a tentative sip and fell into a fit of coughing.

Archie rushed to her side. She tried to wave away his concern, but he sat next to her and patted her back. She recovered herself, and the patting slowed. When she stopped coughing, she thought he would take his hand away.

He did not.

"I do apologize for the state in which you found us, Miss Morgan, Miss Olive," Lord Marsden said with an air of seriousness. "And for the state in which you still find Lord Featherfinch. Had we thought you would be joining us, we would, of course, have been respectably attired."

"It is I who must apologize," Clementine said, trying to focus on the conversation and not on the steady pressure of Archie's hand between her shoulder blades. "I'd told Lord Harcourt we would join you after dinner this evening. The reason we are so tardy is that tonight, contrary to the pattern that had been established, our evening meal occurred after yours. So we've only just finished our dinner."

Heat was blooming across her back, radiating from the spot upon which Archie's hand rested.

"The cook has taken to the challenge presented by my sister's dietary preferences," Olive said. "Tonight she made us a mushroom pie that apparently required six hours of preparation, chiefly involving the marination of mushrooms. Mrs. MacPuddle asked if we would mind eating later than usual."

"As you can imagine, we could not say no," Clementine said.

"Of course not," Lord Featherfinch declared. "One does not say no to six-hour mushroom pie."

Clementine wasn't sure if he was teasing or in earnest. "The cook is very ambitious." Her ambition had produced uneven results—though the mushroom pie had been quite good—but Clementine left that part out.

"We brought our embroidery," Olive said. "I've been teaching my sister." Olive sat up straighter and looked . . . well, she looked proud. Interesting. Could something as simple as teaching Clementine to stitch make someone as seemingly sophisticated as Olive proud?

"I have to say," Clementine said, "I am a convert. The act of embroidery turns out to be surprisingly soothing, and when you're done, you have a beautiful object. Theoretically." Chuckling, she turned her hoop around to show the gentlemen her "leaves."

The act dislodged Archie's hand from her back. She wished she had stayed still.

"You must not judge my sister's teaching abilities by the result I have achieved," she said. "Or not achieved."

She could tell the gentlemen were searching for something kind to say. She interceded, saying to Olive, "Show them yours."

Olive obliged, and everyone exclaimed with admiration. Clementine watched her sister closely. Their praise was being taken to heart, though Olive responded humbly. "This is nothing. Merely a way to fill the time."

"Well, then I should like to see what you could produce when you were making an effort," Lord Featherfinch said.

Archie and Lord Marsden murmured their agreement.

"I have always wanted to try embroidery," Lord Featherfinch said. "My sister does not care for it, but I have seen other women make the most remarkable creations, though none so fine as yours, Miss Olive."

Olive was a flower blooming under the viscount's praise. "I would be happy to teach you, if you like." She paused, seeming to think better of her offer. "Perhaps that would not be appropriate."

"Yes, Olive," Archie said wryly. "Clearly, for a creature such as this"—he gestured at the scandalously clad Lord Featherfinch— "an embroidery lesson would be beyond the pale."

Lord Featherfinch mock-snarled at Archie, but when he turned to Olive he was half exuberance, half solicitousness. "Would you, Miss Olive? I would be thrilled to submit to your tutelage. Tomorrow after dinner, perhaps?"

"Olive," Clementine said, "while it was kind of the gentlemen to invite us this evening, we can't make a habit of joining them. This is their trip, after all."

"Nonsense!" Lord Featherfinch exclaimed.

"Yes," Lord Marsden agreed. "We would be happy to have you join us in the evenings for the remainder of our time here."

He seemed genuine in his sentiment, and everyone's attention swung to Archie, who smiled wryly and said, "I am in complete agreement, if for no other reason than if you ladies will join us in the evenings, I am certain I will be less likely to find myself wearing green silk."

"Thank you for the invitation; we happily accept." Clementine felt she *should* argue, but she didn't want to. The spot on her back where Archie had laid his hand was still . . . alive. It felt as if the sun were shining on it, awakening seeds hidden beneath the winter soil. So she didn't argue. She didn't even vocalize an "If you're sure we won't be in your way," perfunctory protest. She picked up her embroidery and said, "What were you . . . discussing before we joined you?" By which she meant: What in Heaven's name were you *doing?*

"We were actually having quite a serious conversation regarding the nature of familial bonds," Lord Marsden said. "Picking up on what's been somewhat of an ongoing discussion of late."

Well. She hadn't expected *that*, given the state they'd been in when she and Olive arrived.

"Marsden is being too judicious," Archie said. "We were discussing how disappointed Father always was in me."

"That's putting it too simplistically, I should think," Lord Featherfinch said.

"It isn't, though," Archie said. "Miss Morgan will know what I mean. He was always trying to get me interested in estate management, pressing books on me about agriculture and animal husbandry that I routinely failed to read."

"Hmm," Clementine said noncommittally. She did remember that. Archie *had* always been disappointing the late earl, but

Archie had never seemed overbothered by it. She had interpreted their standoffs—and she thought he had as well—as being more about his father's overbearing nature than about Archie's failings.

"Were you not tempted to just do what he asked, as unpleasant as the tomes may have been?" Olive asked.

"You misunderstand me," Archie said. "When I say 'failed to read,' I don't mean that I couldn't bring myself to, I mean that I *couldn't*. It is true that I don't care for reading. Never have. But I would have done it if it'd pleased Father, and I did—do—care about the estate. I care very much. But it's equally true that I'm not *good* at reading. After a while, and not a very long while, the words start to swim on the page, and I can't make any sense of them, nor can I remember what I read two sentences ago. The more concertedly I apply myself, the worse it gets, until I may as well be looking at something written in hieroglyphs. It's worse still when I've an audience. Writing is equally challenging." He glanced at Clementine, and she thought back to their discussion about having fallen out of touch. Her heart squeezed.

"I'm not clever," Archie went on, "a fact with which I've made my peace. I've got a steward I'd trust with my life; Mr. Hughes is worth every penny I pay him. But my father could never accept a dimwitted heir. The only thing he respected about me was my skill with a rifle."

Several beats of silence followed. It wasn't a fraught silence, though. These men were clearly even closer than Clementine had realized, given how comfortable they were talking about matters that should by all reasonable standards be *un*comfortable. She rather thought no one wanted to disagree with Archie because to do so would seem as if they didn't respect his opinion. He was, after all, the expert on his own life. But his easy, blanket dismissal of his own intellect didn't sit right with her.

"Lord Harcourt has a different sort of intelligence." She poked at her sewing as she spoke and kept her tone mild, as if she were commenting on a fact of the weather.

"He does, doesn't he?" Lord Marsden said.

"I quite agree," said Lord Featherfinch.

"Excuse me?" Archie waved at them as if he were standing on the shore of a lake signaling a passing boat. "I should like to remind you that I'm right here, and also for you to explain yourselves."

"You aren't good at books, fine," Clementine said. "But you can take the measure of a man in an instant. Or of a difficult situation. You got my sister and me out of what might have been a disaster by pulling off a scheme that by rights should have taken a great deal of advance planning. But you just . . . did it."

"Oh," he said dismissively, "those sorts of situations are like boxing."

"I beg your pardon?"

"In boxing, you've got to react to what's in front of you, to what's coming at you in the moment. You might need to anticipate your opponent's next move, see your way through to how the bout will end, but that's as far ahead as you need think. And there's no recall of past events required whatsoever. It's quite easy."

"It isn't easy for everyone," Lord Featherfinch said. "It feels easy to you because you're good at it. I, on the other hand, could train at Gentleman Jackson's boxing club for a year and still not be a decent fighter."

"Well, that's not a character flaw; that's just your nature."

"That is exactly what we're saying," Lord Marsden said. "Perhaps you aren't naturally academically inclined. That isn't a character flaw, either. It unfortunately happens to be the sort of inclination that is rewarded by the social strata in which we find ourselves, but that is neither here nor there."

Archie looked confused, but he shook his head and his usual easygoing countenance returned. "Why do I feel as if my parents are in conference with the headmaster here? Let us change the subject." He turned to Olive. "What say you, Miss Olive?"

"I think my sister and your friends are correct," she said, quietly but assuredly. "There are many different types of intelligence in this world."

Clementine appreciated that Olive was adding her voice to the chorus, but Archie clearly wanted to move on, so she said, "Oh, I have some news you've yet to hear, Lord Harcourt! I've entered the turtle races in Doveborough."

"I've entered the turtle races in Doveborough"?

Archie was having trouble making sense of that sentence. Still, he'd gotten what he'd wanted: a new topic of conversation. A wildly new one, in fact. "I beg your pardon?"

"Well, *I* haven't entered them. That would be ridiculous," Clementine said.

"One would think," he deadpanned, though he was still confused.

"I've entered *Hermes* in the turtle races."

"Dare I ask who Hermes is?"

"Hermes is a turtle, of course. Don't be daft."

"You have a turtle named Hermes. After the god? The speedy one with wings on his feet?"

"Well, the name is aspirational, *obviously*."

"Doveborough has an annual fall festival," Olive said, taking pity on Archie in his befuddled state. "Apparently there was once an event involving turtledoves, as a nod to the name of the village, but somehow the 'dove' bit got dropped, and the contest evolved into a turtle race. No one could quite explain how or why."

"So Doveborough is host to turtle races of mysterious origin, and Miss Morgan has entered them." Of course she had. Who would expect Clementine Morgan to learn of the existence of turtle races and *not* throw her hat into the ring?

"You told me to entertain myself," Clementine said with just a hint of pique in her tone.

"I believe I also told you not to go to Doveborough by yourself." He did hear the way that sounded, rather disagreeably paternalistic. But he would be damned if anything happened to the Morgans while they were under his care.

"I wasn't by myself. Olive and Lords Featherfinch and Marsden went with me to Doveborough that first day, which was when I found out about the race, and then Olive and Lord Featherfinch accompanied me again today when I entered it."

Archie turned censoriously toward Effie, though he wasn't really sure why. If Clem and Olive were bent on going to the village, he was glad they'd had Effie with them.

"I needed to collect the dressing gowns I'd ordered," Effie, sensing Archie's disapproval, said defensively.

"And you did not think to mention these turtle races to me."

"I didn't think you'd be interested," Effie said with a sniff. He turned to Clementine. "I like your chances, Miss Morgan. Hermes is shockingly swift. I'm not sure the name is merely aspirational."

"You've met Hermes," Archie said.

"I wonder if it's down to his size," Simon said. "He's smaller and therefore more nimble? Is that possible?"

Hold up. "You've met Hermes, too?"

"Yes," Simon said mildly. "Miss Morgan has been training him early in the mornings, and I have to agree that his speed is startling. If I were a betting man, I would put my money on Hermes."

"I *did* put mine on Hermes," Lord Featherfinch said. "While I was at the modiste today, I learned there is a bookmaker running odds on the races. I visited him while you and your sister were in the bookshop."

"You *did*?" Clementine exclaimed. "How lovely of you." She beamed.

"Well, one does like to support one's friends."

"I wonder if I ought to bet on Hermes myself," Clementine said thoughtfully. "I'd been focused on the quid of prize money, but think, if I won and *also* wagered on myself, I'd be positively flush!"

Archie opened his mouth, then closed it. He had so many questions. Where had Clementine found Hermes? Where was Hermes now? When were the races? Was he invited to watch them?

Why was he obsessed with a turtle whose existence he had only learned about moments ago?

But he realized that to ask any of these questions would suggest a degree of investment in the matter that would not reflect flatteringly on him.

He had one more question: Was Clementine going to be on the roof tonight?

That last question he actually got answered, a little later when they all parted ways for the evening. Clementine slipped a note into his hand as they made their good nights. His pulse kicked up in a mixture of thrill that she wanted to secretly communicate with him and anticipation over what the content of that communication would be.

I've invited Olive to join me stargazing this evening, so if you were of a mind to join me on the roof, I hope you won't mind making other plans. I suppose this is a disinvitation! How gauche of me. But we are friends, and I know you will understand.

Well. So much for that. He pulled out his time piece. Eleven o'clock. Even if the ladies joined them immediately after dinner tomorrow, it would be at least another twenty hours until he met Clementine again.

11

A Proposition (Not That Kind)

And so it went for the next two days. In the evenings, Clementine and Olive joined Archie and Effie and Simon after dinner. It was great fun. The five of them had wide-ranging conversations, often uproarious, sometimes serious. It was akin to being with Simon and Effie alone, yet not. Which was a completely daft thing to say, Archie supposed—it either was or it wasn't. He only meant that the addition of the Morgan sisters did not change the tenor of their evenings, even if it did change the content of them. As an example of the latter, Effie was learning to embroider. He and Olive would sit together on the settee with their heads together, half participating in the group conversation, half in their own world.

Archie's two sets of friends were becoming one. It was very satisfactory.

Yet he was simultaneously *dis*satisfied. Clementine hadn't been back on the roof. He had steered clear the one night as per her instructions. But the next, when he'd stuck his head out the window of the bedchamber next to hers, she hadn't been there.

Seeing Clementine only in the group setting meant there were so many things he wanted to ask her but could not. How had the stargazing gone, for one?

He began to wonder if the three nights they'd spent on the roof had actually happened.

"What did you have for dinner?" Effie asked the sisters, once they'd all assembled that evening.

"A tomato aspic followed by stewed brussels sprouts," Clementine said primly, inching her chair to one side to remove herself from beneath a leak in the ceiling.

"Tomato aspic!" Effie, incapable as ever of masking his true emotions, made a face of dismay as he placed a bucket under the leak—an afternoon storm had seen the buckets pressed back into service.

"What did *you* have?" Olive asked.

"Roast guinea fowl," Effie said, "dressed with parsley and mushrooms and bacon."

Olive sighed plaintively.

"Miss Olive," Archie said, "do I sense that your devotion to your sister's diet is faltering?"

"No!" she said, a touch too vehemently.

"Olive," said Clementine, "you know you needn't dine with me."

"Oh, but I want to."

"Perhaps we could swap places for a day, Miss Olive," Simon said. "I confess that even though a permanent meat-free diet, especially if the alternative is tomato aspic, does not appeal to my stomach, it is, from an intellectual standpoint, an interesting proposition." He turned to Clementine. "You will correct me if you'd prefer I not bring him up, but I read Mr. Bull's pamphlet, and several of his points resonated with me in terms of their potential to improve the lives of the poor. Certainly it is less expensive to feed people grain than meat. It just had never occurred to me that a person could live on grain alone."

"Well, not grain alone," Clementine said, and they were off, discussing advances in agriculture and potential food distribution systems with great gusto. Olive and Effie had given up any pretense of participating in the conversation and were bent over their embroidery.

"And you know," Clementine said, "Mr. Bull is not the only

one who has written on the topic. The poet Shelley has an essay called *A Vindication of Natural Diet*. And he was influenced by a man called John Frank Newton, who advocated a diet of vegetables and distilled water only, which I personally think is taking it too far. And Newton was influenced by another man before him." Clementine's eyes twinkled. "I take comfort in the fact that these ideas have an intellectual history, so I needn't throw them out along with my erstwhile fiancé."

Simon chuckled, and it did Archie's heart good to hear two of his favorite people enjoying a shared amusement. "In some ways," Simon said, "the arguments aren't dissimilar from those in favor of temperance."

"Indeed, and as a former student of divinity, you would know that many of those ideas overlap with theological matters."

With that, they were off, talking about whether the plight of the poor was more important than any suffering an animal might endure to feed a hungry person. Archie liked the notion that on one side of the room, Effie and Olive were sewing, and on the other, Clementine and Simon were engaged in a lively moral discussion.

"But surely," Archie said when he was able to get a word in with the latter pair, "you must distinguish between animals who meet their fate in slaughterhouses and those who fall prey to hobbyists such as myself. My hunting has no bearing one way or the other on the plight of the poor."

"I think you're missing the point," Simon said after a beat of silence.

"How am I missing the point?"

"What you're saying is you—you personally—don't need to hunt to live, I think?" Clementine asked.

"That's exactly what I'm saying. It's a pastime."

"Then why do it?" She was speaking in a clipped, almost annoyed-sounding tone. He had never heard that tone from Clem before. He didn't like it.

He thought back to the awkward turn their conversation had

taken the other night regarding the constellation Orion, and considered dissembling. But this was Clementine. He couldn't lie to her. "I hunt because I enjoy it." And that was understating it.

A look of dismay passed over her features, though she quickly pasted it over with a kind of haughtiness he had never seen on her. "Killing animals when you don't need them to subsist is enjoyable?" Now she sounded like one of his teachers back at school, mockingly reading aloud to the class from one of his essays. Archie had always been able to hear how stupid his attempts at writing were in a way he couldn't see when he was putting pen to paper.

He wasn't that boy any longer, though. He didn't have to stand for this treatment.

But also . . . Clementine was not his teacher. She was his friend. His friend with whom he was having a disagreement.

That was new, and distressing. He and Clem had never disagreed, about anything. Their youthful friendship had been full of enjoyment and accord. He reminded himself that he hadn't seen Clementine for five years, and that many more still since they had truly talked. Perhaps he had been romanticizing their recent time spent on the roof. Perhaps the darkness that had allowed an unusual exchange of confidences had lulled him, made him forget that they weren't the children they used to be.

"Anyway, Archie is not allowed to hunt on our trips anymore," said Effie, who apparently hadn't completely abandoned the conversation in favor of his sewing. Bless him, he was trying to diffuse the tension—by steering them back onto easier territory: needling Archie for his illegal weapon. Archie welcomed the diversion.

"So I gather," Clementine said. "I've heard you speaking about rules?"

"Yes," Effie said. "I am not allowed to write poetry, Simon is not allowed to talk about Parliament, and Archie is not allowed to hunt."

"Why ever not?" Olive asked. "An annual holiday where you disallow your favorite activities would seem not to make a great deal of sense."

"Hmm," Effie said. "That is an excellent point."

"Though perhaps we might consider that hunting is categorically different from writing poetry and talking politics," Simon said with a smirk. He turned to Archie. "Tell the ladies why hunting in particular is banned."

Bollocks. Archie mumbled his response. "Three years ago there was a bit of an unfortunate mishap."

"What does that mean?" Clementine asked.

"He almost shot Effie," Simon said smugly.

Clementine swung to face Simon. "Tell me more."

"I thought I was alone in the woods," Archie said quickly. If this story had to be trotted out, he was going to be the one doing the trotting. Simon would only embellish it in a manner that would be unflattering. "A flash of white caught my attention. I thought it a deer . . ." He winced, still remembering the close call. "It was Featherfinch's cravat."

"So what you are saying is that while I accidentally shot you in what could reasonably be considered self-defense—you have to admit there was no way I could have known it was *you* entering that room and not Mr. Bull—you accidentally shot Lord Featherfinch due to pure carelessness."

"That is not at all what I'm saying!" he protested, though Clem was only teasing him. He thought—he hoped. This business of hunting was the only thing between them he couldn't quite parse. "It was overcast, and Featherfinch's black attire blended into the tree trunks!"

"Now, now," Effie said soothingly. "If anything, it was my fault. Archie could never have expected me to appear in the woods. Simon sometimes hunts with him, but I never do. And I never rise from bed that early. But that day I'd had the most extraordinary dream, and I'd gone in search of Archie to tell him about it." He paused. "And then I found him, and he almost shot me. It was all terribly exciting."

Archie did not remember that day as "terribly exciting." He'd felt awful—he still did—though Effie ought to have known better. Archie had accepted his hunting ban the next year with good cheer. As much as he loved hunting, had he to choose, he would much rather be the kind of person Effie sought out to discuss his dreams than be a huntsman. But last year—and this—the uproar having faded somewhat from memory, he smuggled a firearm along on their holiday.

Olive, who had been watching the conversation silently but with great apparent interest, said, "I wish I had friends like you gentlemen."

"You do," Effie said. "We are your friends, are we not?"

Olive smiled, widely at first, but it turned wistful. "That is not precisely what I mean."

"What do you mean, then?" Archie asked, thankful for the redirection.

"Oh, I don't know." Olive shook her head and picked up her embroidery. "I'm speaking nonsense."

Archie thought he knew what she meant even if she didn't. It was the whole salt-and-strawberries business. Olive had a loving family, though, even if that love was sometimes frayed by the pressure exerted on it. Still, what she was talking about was the unconditional support—if leavened with good-humored insults—and camaraderie that came with having long-standing friends one trusted and could rely on absolutely. Found family, Simon had called it.

The conversation moved on, but something had been lost. Archie thought about that first evening Olive and Clementine had joined them. They had all laughed so uproariously, what with the dressing-gown business. But after the laughter had faded, a kind of understanding had flowed between Clementine and Archie as they stared at each other. A recognition. It had felt as if they were alone, though they most definitely had not been. And there had been flashes of that silent understanding from time to time since. A joke someone made that hit them both the same way and caused them to look at each other. A memory recounted that turned out to be shared.

That feeling, that sense of being seen, was gone. Archie still felt Clementine's attention from time to time, knew when she was glancing at him. He always met her gaze. But there was none of that previous sense that they were alone together in a crowd, allied somehow. He almost had the sense that she was disappointed in him.

Why was that? Was it just about the hunting? Or was it more . . . elemental?

He was being ridiculous. She wasn't disappointed in him. And even if she was, what did he care?

He cared.

For some damn reason, Archie couldn't bear the thought of Clem thinking ill of him. It had to be the hunting.

Because if it wasn't the hunting, it was him.

And if it *was* the hunting, she was misunderstanding. Hunting wasn't murder. It was the natural way of things. He didn't do it to satisfy a bloodlust. The only bloodlust he could recall having felt in recent memory had been aimed at Theodore Bull. Hunting was altogether different. It put Archie into a meditative state. Calmed his mind the way nothing else did. Other pursuits worked a little bit. Boxing, riding, his beads.

Just not as much as hunting did.

Restless, he rolled over and punched the lumpen mass that passed for a pillow in Quintrell Castle.

Hunting took Archie's oft-fragmented attention and honed it into a perfect, smooth tunnel where he was at one end and his prey at the other. One got to the edge of that tunnel by paying close attention to the forest and the trees and the air, by sensing the minute currents that moved through them. Clementine sensed those currents, too, he just knew it. He had *seen* her doing so.

He would admit, though, that in addition to being calming and clarifying, hunting was also bloody. But so was life.

He threw back his covers and padded to his window to peer out through the misty night, though he knew he wouldn't see her.

There had been no sign of her yesterday, leaving him to conclude that, having given her stargazing lesson the previous night, she was done with nocturnal roof-sitting. Even if she hadn't been, it was wet out there. She was still awake, though: her room glowed dimly.

He should go back to bed.

He should apologize.

The two sentiments were at odds with each other. And since he didn't even know what he should be apologizing for, "go back to bed" was the more sensible option.

Which was why he could not explain why he dressed, hurried along silent corridors, entered the room next to Clementine's, heaved himself out the window onto the roof, inched over wet, slippery slate to her window, and tapped on the glass. He held his breath as if he were a Montague about to be beset upon by a band of hostile Capulets.

It only took a moment for her to appear, holding a candle. He watched surprise make way for recognition on her face. Her hair was down. He wanted to put his fingers in it. She unlatched the window. "Archie?"

"I wanted to speak with you." He paused, realizing how odd that sounded. She was probably wondering why he couldn't speak with her tomorrow like a normal, reasonable person. "It's urgent." Or it had felt so. He hadn't been able to sleep fretting that things were not right between them.

"Why did you not just come to my door?"

That . . . was a good question. He didn't have a good answer for it. "It seemed a little improper?" He considered the exceedingly relaxed evenings the group had passed together. While Effie had refrained from wearing his dressing gown beyond that first night, no one was clinging to any pretense of formality. In fact, when the group had disbanded for the evening a few hours ago, Effie had taken Olive to the guardhouse to show her the ravens, and no one had had anything to say about that except Archie's warning them to be careful on the widow's walk in the dark and Clementine's instruction that her sister should not oversleep breakfast, as the cook was planning an experimental porridge that included locally foraged ingredients Clementine had collected herself.

"A little improper," Clementine echoed.

He ignored the incredulity in her tone. "I've a proposition for you."

"All right. Shall I come out?" She pushed the window open wider.

"No, no. It's slippery out here. It's raining more than I'd realized. I'll come in."

She lifted her candle, illuminating a skeptical face—she was doing that signature nose-scrunch of hers. "Through the door?"

"Just back up and make room, Clem."

He proceeded to make a very ungraceful entrance through her window, landing on the carpet with a thud and shedding water droplets like one of Olive's spaniels. He looked around as Clementine used the candle she'd been holding to light two more. He'd been in this room before, of course, that first night, but it hadn't been *hers* at that point. Now, with the bed mussed and an open book on the bedside table, the space felt occupied. Intimate. As if he were seeing something he shouldn't.

He turned from the tableau, but that put Clementine herself in his sights. She was wearing a white cotton shift and a shawl. She was covered from neck to toe, but seeing her attired thusly added to the sense of transgressive intimacy.

She pointed at the only chair in the room, climbed onto her bed, and reclined against the ornate, carved headboard.

Clementine in bed: the wild, forest girl of his youth all cozily tucked in. The contrast was . . . something. She'd set her candle on the bedside table, so she was barely illuminated, but he could still see the contrast between her dark hair and pale skin. Dark hair and pale skin: Effie would be disappointed by such meager descriptive efforts. Raven hair and alabaster skin? That wasn't much better.

"Well?" she said impatiently, puncturing his pathetic poetic admiration.

Right. "You and I ought to enter into an agreement akin to the one you and Olive had."

"How do you mean?"

"We've been arguing about hunting, about the eating of meat, et cetera. So I propose that I spend a day your way, and you spend a day my way."

"You're going to need to be more specific."

"I abstain from eating animal flesh for an entire day, and—"

"I venture out into the woods and kill animals? No, thank you."

"No. You venture out into the woods with me while *I* kill animals."

"You make it sound so appealing."

"I'll be doing it anyway, so your presence or absence won't have any bearing on the death toll."

"You're macabre."

"Think of it as a day spent in your beloved outdoors, but with a purpose." He truly believed her imagination was running away from her, and that if she accompanied him on a hunt, she would gain a better understanding. This was the same woman who'd been expounding on the natural way of things when it came to the mating of grasshoppers, for Heaven's sake. Surely she could be made to see that birth and death were part of this same rhythm of life. And perhaps he could show her what hunting meant to him in a way he hadn't heretofore managed.

She was silent a while. Just when he was about to admit this had been a daft idea and heave himself back out the window, she said, "All right."

"Really?"

"But we do your day first. I want time to prepare the cook before I feed you."

"Who is this cook, by the way? She looms large in the mythology of this trip. I know from experience that she's very good at what she does, at least on the gentlemen's side of the table, but reportedly she is also capable of delivering such atrocities as tomato aspic."

"Her name is Susannah, and she's wonderful. Her mother is the cook at Winslow House, which is just this side of Doveborough. She is possessed of quite the culinary imagination, and as I'm sure your Lord Featherfinch knows, the first drafts of artistic endeavors do not always enter the world exactly the way one had perhaps imagined."

"Point taken."

"I wish to consult with her, to make sure there is nothing like the aforementioned aspic—which I will admit was rather unfortunate—on the menu. Will the other gentlemen be joining you?"

"I should think not, but let's discuss it tomorrow at breakfast. Perhaps we can make a swap for Olive in the manner jestingly suggested by Simon."

Clementine's demeanour softened. "That would be a good idea. While I appreciate Olive's steadfastness, I know she would give her favorite dress right now for a plate of ham."

"We are agreed, then. We shall make the arrangements tomorrow morning, then set out for the woods." He was unaccountably excited. One of his favorite people in one of his favorite places. It had been too long. "And the next day, I will join you at all your meals." Oddly, he was equally excited about that day.

He wanted to ask one more thing, but he feared that to do so would strengthen her hand in this hunting dispute they seemed to be having. But he couldn't help himself. "Clem, may I make a request?"

"Certainly."

"Can we have those roasted pears again the day after tomorrow?" He couldn't stop thinking about them.

"Pardon me? Was that you *requesting* a dish that does not involve dead animals? I must have misheard." There was laughter, and triumph, in her tone.

He decided to compound her sense of victory, though he had no idea why he would do that. "You heard correctly. Those pears were wonderful."

"Of course we shall have the pears again, if you like." Her voice had gone soft and, he dared say, fond. It was a great relief to know that whatever discord had arisen between them earlier this evening had been smoothed over. He yawned. He would be able to sleep now.

Clementine got up and went to the window. "The rain has picked up. I should hate to have to miss my inaugural hunting trip because you fell to your death off this pile of rocks. Might I suggest you leave through the door? You're only in the next room, after all. Who is going to see you? And if they did, what would it matter? Neither Olive nor their lordships would ever suspect there was anything besides friendship between us."

"Of course they wouldn't." There *was* nothing besides friendship between them. Unless one considered this persistent need, beating like a drum in his veins, that she should understand him, and think well of him.

He didn't have that with Effie and Simon.

While he was pondering the nature of friendship, she made her way to the door. He followed, and just as he opened it and was preparing to bid her good night, the door across the hall began to open, too. Instinctively, he moved to close Clementine's door. He hadn't quite gotten it all the way shut when he heard Effie speak.

His first thought was, what the hell was Effie doing in Olive's room in the middle of the night? His second, that there was no way anything untoward could be happening between Effie and Olive. Archie had never heard Effie express any carnal or romantic feelings. Part of him wouldn't be surprised to learn that Effie reserved all such sentiment for his poetry. Regardless, he was too good a man to take advantage of Olive.

And after all, one might ask the same question of Archie: What the hell was he doing in Clementine's room in the middle of the night?

He was asking her to go hunting with him, and no doubt there was an equally bizarre-yet-innocent explanation for whatever was happening across the hall.

"Thank you for showing me your work, Miss Olive."

There it was. While Archie's faith in Effie was ratified, he was now wildly curious as to what "work" Olive was doing, and why she would be showing it to Effie at such a late hour.

"Thank you for appreciating it," Olive said.

"It would take an imbecile not to. It really is extraordinary."

Archie sent an inquiring look at Clementine, who used the hand that wasn't holding the candle to turn her palm up to signal that she had no special sisterly insight. Unsure what to do, he took another step backward, deeper into Clementine's room, but she must have had the opposite impulse. They collided, her front to his back, and he hissed involuntarily, almost as if she'd shot him again. It was the same sensation he'd had the other night on the roof, when she'd touched his hand, but . . . more. It was as if he'd been violently shaken to life after a decade of slumber.

She pushed him out of the way, which wasn't hard as he was still reeling, set down her candle, and put her ear to the cracked door.

Well, if she was going to eavesdrop, so was he. He went to stand behind her, his height sufficient to allow him to slot his head in above hers. That this put them in contact again, this time in a reverse position—her back to his front—did not help with his discombobulation. This contact was less of a shock since he had initiated it, but it was still unsettling. Her nightdress was thin. He could feel the pointiness of her shoulder blades, and the softness of her arse. She was sharp and soft at the same time, and if that didn't perfectly sum up Clementine Morgan, he didn't know what did.

She shifted against him, making him realize he was half hard. How mortifying. Hoping she had been too distracted by the conversation in the hallway to notice, he took a step back, severing the contact between them, and ordered himself to concentrate on the espionage at hand.

He didn't have to try very hard because Olive's next words were blurted with vehemence. She wasn't yelling exactly, but her urgently whispered cry of "Lord Featherfinch, I beg you, hold up a moment!" pierced the silence of the night. As did the clicking sound that followed. Effie was in a phase of wearing elaborate, old-fashioned court shoes. The clicking drew nearer until it stopped. After a beat, Olive said, "There is something I've been wanting to tell you, but I haven't known how to say it. Or, in fact, *whether* to say it."

"Ofttimes in these situations it's best to simply speak, don't you find? It's usually such an enormous relief. If you—"

"I have developed a tendre for you!"

Olive had spoken so quickly, it took a moment for Archie to register her words. In fact, he sensed Clementine, who had always been smarter than he was, stiffen before Olive's declaration fully penetrated his mind. He lifted a hand to Clementine's shoulder, and she batted it away—batted him away from the door entirely, as if she thought he was going to go charging out into the corridor. He'd only meant to soothe, to offer his presence as a kind of ballast. It was all he knew to do.

Keeping one palm facing him, she returned her ear to the small crack in the door. Once again, he joined her, though he took pains that there should be no contact between their lower bodies. Clementine did not object as Archie arrived again behind her, but she held a finger to her lips to signal quiet. He nodded.

The corridor was silent. Archie could imagine Effie cycling through confusion, comprehension, shock, dismay. He was marshaling his words to deliver a response that would let Olive down gently. He would do a good job. If one had to have one's heart broken, Effie was the man to do it.

"Well, say something!" Olive cried.

"Miss Olive, I'm flattered by your interest. Positively flattened by it, actually."

"Do I sense a 'but' coming?"

"You do. I am sorry."

Archie admired Effie. People tended to look at him and think him flippant, given his disinterest in social conventions. And he could be flippant—sometimes he even leaned into that interpretation of his character for reasons Archie didn't fully understand—but at his core, he was sensitive, kind, and profoundly good. He would never lie to get out of a situation like this. He would tell the truth, but he would do it with exquisite gentleness and probably a good dose of self-deprecation.

"I don't know why I ever thought it might be otherwise." Olive huffed a short, resigned sigh. "I know I'm quite far beneath you."

"No! It's not that at all."

"It's all right. I'm clear-eyed about my position. I am a gentleman's daughter, yes, but you are a viscount and heir to an earl."

"It's *not* that. Miss Olive, please believe me when I say that any man with good taste and eyes in his head would be thrilled beyond belief to be the object of your affection. You will forgive me for speaking so openly, I think, since you have been brave enough to do so yourself?"

"Of course. And you flatter me." She paused. "Or else you are saying you are not in possession of good taste? Or that you do not have eyes in your head?"

"I most certainly have eyes in my head, and honestly, can anyone question my taste? Good Heavens! Look at me!" Olive laughed a little, which had no doubt been Effie's aim. Archie smiled, too, imagining Effie, who had come to dinner wearing a black velvet jacket over a pink silk waistcoat embroidered with black flowers, his snow-white cravat tied in an excessively elaborate waterfall knot, striking an intentionally haughty pose punctuated by his beribboned pumps. His tone had changed, though, when he spoke again. "No, there is an entirely different reason I cannot entertain your proposition." He paused. "My heart belongs to someone else. She owns it. She always has and always will."

What the *hell*?

Also: *she*?

Archie had wondered if the reason Effie's proclivities remained mysterious was because those proclivities did not tend toward ladies the way Archie's and Simon's did. Not that they ever discussed the matter. It was more a . . . feeling. And since it didn't matter to Archie—Effie was Effie and that was all that mattered—he had never pressed the issue.

That aside, Archie knew everything there was to know about Effie's life. He knew about his social engagements, his frustrations with his family, and his secret poetic ambitions. Just now, he had predicted perfectly how Effie would handle Olive's declaration. Archie *knew* Effie.

He'd thought. But come to find out that not only was Effie in love, he had been for a very long time? It boggled the mind.

Archie was distracted from trying to make sense of Effie's astonishing statement by the fact that Olive, instead of answering Effie, burst into tears.

Clementine gasped and made to open the door, but Archie stopped her, tugging her hand off the knob and pulling her body into his, his careful attempts to avoid contact be damned. He bent his head and spoke into her ear. "Leave them for a moment. Effie is the person she needs now." He didn't know how he knew that, but he did. "Trust me."

He expected her to fight him. She'd batted his hand away before when he tried to comfort her. He would let her go if that was what she wished, but to his surprise, she relaxed in his arms. She did more than that: she sagged against him. His body throbbed with awareness, but it was a different sort from before. Thankfully, his prick remained docile. Now, he wanted to use his body to protect Clementine from whatever was about to occur but also, he observed with some wonderment, from anything and anyone who might wish her the slightest ill.

He shoved that last thought aside and held her up as they listened.

"Oh, Miss Olive," Effie said, "I am so sorry."

"It isn't you," Olive managed through sobs. "It's that my heart, too, belongs to another—always has and always will, as you say."

Clementine gasped, loudly enough Archie feared they would be discovered. She must have thought so, too, because she turned in his arms and pressed her face into his shoulder, as if to forestall any further involuntary outbursts. He kept holding her up. It was all he knew to do. But he *also* knew that he knew *how* to do it, how to hold Clementine Morgan upright when the world would fell her. He wasn't good at many things, but he was good at this.

"This was what your embroidery was about, wasn't it? His was the name depicted?"

"Yes," Olive whispered.

"Does anyone else know about your lost love?" Olive must have shaken her head *no*, for Effie said, "Mine either." After a pause, he added, "I wonder if perhaps you *don't* carry a tendre for me. Perhaps it is that something in you can sense something in me that is the same. I myself have grown so fond of you these recent days, and I wonder now if we are meant to be each other's confidants."

"I've never had one of those."

Clementine stiffened again, not as severely as she had before, but enough to tell Archie that she'd been hurt by Olive's words.

"Shall we go for a stroll tomorrow?" Effie said. "You can tell me about your love—just as much or as little as you like—and I will do the same."

"Yes. I would like that. And do you think . . . ?"

"Do I think what?" Effie asked gently.

"Might I write to you, later, after we've all gone home? I have always wanted a regular correspondent. And since I have never had a confidant *or* a regular correspondent, how wonderful it would be to have both in the same person."

"I can think of nothing I would like more than to receive letters from you, except possibly to write you back. I do enjoy writing and receiving letters."

Archie thought back to Effie's speech the other night about embracing color, and finding moments of joy. He'd made vague reference to correspondence. Hmm.

The pair said their goodbyes, Effie clicking away down the hall until all was silent.

Whereas before Archie had felt strong and assured in his ability to hold up Clementine, he didn't know what he was meant to do

now that the holding-up part was over. This would be the analyz-
ing part. He felt very ill-equipped for that. So he just kept standing
there, kept holding up Clementine.

She surprised him by whispering, into his shoulder, "Who is
Lord Featherfinch's long-lost love?"

"I haven't the faintest idea," he said into her hair. He still wanted
to put his hands in it. To tangle his fingers in it and let them rest
in the mahogany nest like baby sparrows in need of shelter. He
settled for turning his face and resting his cheek on her head. Her
hair smelled like the sea, which should have been impossible as
they were nowhere near it. "I am all astonishment."

"It has been a day of astonishment," she said, and when she
pulled away, he let her go, though he very much did not want to.
"A week of astonishment. Nay, a month. Astonishment can be so
very exhausting."

Here he thought she would want to dissect Olive's revelation.
He'd felt unequal to the task, but the idea that she was going to say
nothing about it left him oddly bereft. Because that would mean it
was time for him to go back to his room.

But what could he say? "Effie will be good to her," was all he
could think of.

"Yes," she agreed.

"If you are exhausted, you should sleep."

"Yes."

Clementine had never been this agreeable. He wasn't sure he
cared for it. He led her to the mussed bed and pulled back the
covers. She slipped in, and he smoothed them over her.

Then there was nothing left to do but leave.

"Arch?" she said into the quiet dimness, just as he had reached
the door.

Feeling the reprieve of that word, the shortened version of his
name he used to think he disliked, he turned and caught the end
of her readjusting her posture. "Yes?" He couldn't be sure, but he
thought she'd been holding out her arms, like a child asking for an
embrace. But no. He must have imagined it.

She looked at him for a long moment, and he would have sworn he saw her swallow a sentence, a thought she'd been going to vocalize but decided not to. "Good night."

"Good night." He consoled himself that he would see her in the morning. They were to spend the day together outside, and he could think of nothing better.

12

A Proposition (That Kind)

"Miss Morgan said to tell you she awaits you on the terrace," Mrs. MacPuddle said when Archie appeared in the breakfast room the next morning, "and that she has made the necessary arrangements with the cook for your meals tomorrow."

This caused Simon to lower his book. "Effie and I have opted to join you in your culinary experiment tomorrow."

Archie would rather they hadn't. He preferred the idea of sending Olive to eat ham with the boys while he had Clem to himself. But he told himself not to be greedy.

"And here is the meal you asked for," Mrs. MacPuddle said. "Bread, cheese, fruit, nuts. No meats." She handed him a basket, and Simon cleared his throat as if trying to attract Archie's attention.

"Thank you." Archie took the basket and made a point of not looking at Simon as he grabbed a handful of bacon from the buffet. Once he'd stuffed it in his mouth, conveniently, he could not answer Simon's inquiry about where he was going, so he merely made an indistinct grunt and opened the door to the terrace.

She wasn't there. Which was just as well: his cheeks were bulging with bacon as if he were some sort of carnivorous man-vole. He surveyed the ramshackle grounds. Ah, there she was, standing at the edge of the overgrown gardens, facing the forest. Clementine, at home at the edge of the wilds.

His breath caught.

Which, given the mouthful of bacon, brought on a coughing fit.

The noise carried across the gardens, such as they were, and drew Clementine's attention.

She turned, looked up at him, and smiled. Except time seemed to slow as she did so. Or perhaps it was his brain, incapable of taking in such a sight all at once.

Or perhaps it was the bacon. Perhaps he had choked and was dying.

But, no, his legs were moving, carrying him toward her. As he descended the crumbling stairs from the terrace, he suddenly understood what had been wrong with him all these days, why he had been so restless and unsettled.

It had to do with there being two versions of Clementine. He had thought, earlier, about the difference between the girl he remembered and the woman he'd met on this trip. That difference had been disconcerting. But he saw now that the real, more fundamental difference was between Indoor Clementine and Outdoor Clementine. He had been interacting only with Indoor Clementine. Mostly, anyway. He supposed there was also Rooftop Clementine. Perhaps the roof was a liminal locale, a place where they had been suspended, literally, between the staid trappings of society and the green wilderness where Clementine truly belonged.

This Clementine, this woman before him, *wasn't* a distinct creature from the childhood version of her. She *was* that same wild, happy girl of his youth. That girl had had both qualities in excess: happiness and wildness. He understood now in a way he had not when he was a boy that for Clementine, one quality depended on the other. She had to be wild to be happy. The girl had grown into the woman, yes, but that part, the essential inner core of her had not changed.

He had missed her so.

And having her here, under the same roof, but not having *her*, had been maddening.

"Arch!" she called, moving toward him as he moved toward her.

He was seized with the notion that he ought to spit out the bacon. He looked around almost frantically, a kind of panic rising through him. There was a decaying stone pot, overgrown with weeds, that he could detour past for the purposes of expelling the now unwanted pork.

Why, though? What would that accomplish? He swallowed guiltily.

But, again: Why? There was no call for guilt. Their meatless day was tomorrow. Still, the bacon was overly dry and caught in his throat, and it was an effort to get it down.

Clementine's cheeks were pink, her smile was wide, and she was hatless. The freckles dusted across her nose popped in the sunshine. Her hair was braided, but, as was typical for Clem, there was more of it out of the plait than in it. It was a windy morning, and loose hanks whipped around her head like airborne serpents. Perhaps she was Medusa. Perhaps she was about to turn him to stone.

That didn't feel right, though. If anything, the reverse was true. He felt as if something inside him had been slowly ossifying, without his consent or even his awareness, and the sight of Clementine in her natural habitat was softening him, making him supple where he had been hard, allowing for breath where there had previously been only restriction.

As they approached each other, both grinning, he felt alive, reprieved, an insect unexpectedly freed from a spider's web, testing wings he'd thought irreversibly immobilized.

He had no idea what had come over him. What he had been thinking. He *hadn't* been thinking, clearly. If he had, surely his mind would have stopped his arms from grabbing Clem, picking her up clear off her feet, pulling her into an embrace, and twirling her around.

But it was all right: she laughed.

He did, too, relishing that sweet herbal smell of her.

She slid down his body as he released her, and his prick was back to betraying him. He had to push her away.

A sudden, impossible thought entered his mind like a bolt of lightning on an otherwise sunny day: Clementine should marry *him*. He might even have impulsively suggested it, had she not been, on several occasions, so vehement in her objection to the institution itself. While he felt no pressure to marry, from his perspective, marriage to Clementine would be convenient. She was his dear friend. One of his favorite people. And apparently he could no longer deny that he found her attractive.

He shook his head. He was being ridiculous. Even if Clementine *had* wanted to marry, the idea of her groom being *him* was preposterous. He knew where this flight of fancy had come from. Clementine—and Olive—had just come back into his life, and he wanted to hold onto them this time. Make sure she—they—didn't slip away.

But he was being daft. She was *right here*, with her copper eyes and her unkempt hair and a brilliant yellow shawl draped haphazardly over her blue-muslin-encased shoulders. Effie ought to write a poem about her.

"You're up early," he said, noting the telltale muddy hem that suggested she'd been out and about already.

"Yes. I've been putting Hermes through his paces. Now that I know your friends have wagered on the outcome of the race, I feel some pressure to perform."

"Where are you keeping Hermes?"

"He lives in an enclosure I've fashioned and submerged in the pond in such a way that he can choose to be in the water or on land." She pointed at a pond that abutted one side of the ramshackle garden. "I feel poorly about it, though. I grew overexcited when I learned of the races in the village and signed up without thinking about how I would have to keep my contestant confined until after the race. I might have had a mind to let him go and bow out, but now everyone is so invested, sentimentally *and* monetarily."

"Well, you can free him the day after tomorrow." It was sobering to think that the races would happen that soon. After that, they would have to go home. At least he and Clem were finally outside together, roaming as they used to. As they were meant to, it felt like. He cleared his throat. "Perhaps you can use some of your prize money to buy Hermes a . . . large portion of whatever it is turtles like to eat."

"Oh, I'm giving my prize money to . . . I have plans for my prize money, should I be lucky enough to win any," she finished almost primly, and he intuited that she did not want to speak on the matter. A companionable silence settled as they set out across the garden toward the forest. It was a beautiful day, and it was spread out before them like a feast.

There was a bright quality of watchfulness Clementine always had while out for a ramble. He recognized it because he had it, too. It was the same nimble attention required for a successful hunt. One had to be alert but at ease, watching the path ahead and the trees around while remaining firmly aware of one's more immediate surroundings. It was a kind of split attention, where one watched even as one watched oneself watching. At the best of times, it felt almost reverent, mystical. Akin to the way one was meant to feel at church, he gathered, though he never did, church requiring too much of the kind of singular concentration that had made his school days such a struggle.

It was such a respite from the way his mind usually operated, all jumpy and fragmented.

When Clementine slowed, he knew what had drawn her attention because it had drawn his, too. A grass snake, wriggling at the side of the path. She moved closer. He followed. It was actually three grass snakes, one large and two tiny.

"Is it a mother and her babies?" she whispered.

"It must be."

They watched for a long time. This was one of the things he

loved about Clementine. She never tired of doing things like staring at snakes. Effie and Simon could be counted on for a ramble, but after a while they grew bored, or cold, or started talking so much and at such volume that they scared away everything alive.

"I miss my mother," Clementine said suddenly, quietly, still watching the snakes. "Even though I believe I was something of a mystery to her, she loved me, and I miss that. I miss the fact of her love."

Something in Archie's chest folded over, crumpled beneath the force of a powerful fondness that was almost painful. Clementine Morgan was the only lady in the world—nay, the only *person* in the world—who could attach such a sentiment to snakes.

"I miss my mother, too," he said, as a gesture of unity but also because it was true, and because Clementine Morgan was the only person in the world to whom he could say that.

To his shock, she grabbed his hand. He thought it would be a quick squeeze, her way of sending some understanding back to him. She kept it, though, and straightened, done with the snakes.

"What would you tell her, if you could?" she asked, as if that were an ordinary sort of query. As if it were unremarkable to ask such a question while holding his hand.

It *felt* unremarkable, was the thing.

And it was a *good* question. Most people who asked after his mother, even Effie and Simon, who did so with true care and interest, asked how she was faring, or sometimes how Archie was faring with respect to her. They never asked anything specific, though, anything that would require him to respond unambiguously. "Well," he said, considering, wanting to do Clementine's question justice, "if I had known our last conversation was going to *be* our last, I would have handled it differently. I'd've said things."

"What things?"

The answer that rose through him was, initially, surprising. Yet he recognized it. It was rather like hearing one of Effie's poems, and thinking, *Oh, yes, that's how it is, isn't it?*

"Love," he said decisively. "So not *things*, plural. Just one thing. Love."

"The only thing, in the end."

"Yes." He had never thought of it like that, but she was right.

"You have to believe that she knew you loved her."

"Do I? Do people know things we don't tell them?"

"Mmm." She looked off to the horizon. Had she forgotten they were holding hands? "What would you tell yours?" he asked, because he knew that was what she was thinking about.

"I would tell her not to issue that blasted deathbed order to my father to see me married!" she exclaimed, though it was a good-natured outburst. It was also forceful enough for her to yank her hand from his and do a little dance of frustration down the path ahead of him.

Well, she had to let go sometime, and the dance made him smile. Outdoor Clem, Wild Clem, dancing among the trees.

"It seems odd," he said, "that your mother would consign you to such an unhappy fate." His memory of Mrs. Morgan was of a kind woman who was liberal with her affection, even if she and her daughter were very different sorts of people.

"I've wondered if she said that because she wanted me to be happy, and she couldn't imagine a woman being happy without a husband and children." Her brow furrowed, as if she were trying to make sense of something very puzzling. "Something Olive said recently has made me reevaluate much of what I thought I knew about my parents' marriage. Apparently it was never the love match I'd always believed it to be. But I do think—I hope—that my mother was happy with her life, in the end."

"For what my observation is worth, your mother seemed to be made very happy by her husband."

"And yet your mother was not made such by hers."

He sucked in a breath. It wasn't that he disagreed, or that she was telling him anything he didn't already know. Still, he was set back on his heels by the simple statement of truth. He wasn't accustomed to people knowing about Mother. But of course Archie himself had told Clem all about her, had split open his heart if that were something he did.

"That is true," he ventured once he'd got hold of himself. "Though it is difficult to parse. I have come to believe she did love my father, at least initially. If I am to believe her conversations with Miss Brown playing the part of her own mother, she went against her parents' wishes to marry him. So I am not sure why, by the time I came along, she and my father had grown so chilly with one another. I am left to ponder whether it was *motherhood* that did not agree with her. I have always wondered why she never had another child after me—she had the heir but no spare. Perhaps *that* is the question I would ask her if I could."

"Oh, Arch, it was always apparent to me that your mother adored you. The pair of you always seemed to have a special bond."

It cheered him to hear her say that. He'd been wondering, these recent years, if he'd been imagining the degree of his mother's regard, or even the fact of it. "We did, didn't we?"

"You did. And I didn't mean to cause distress. I merely meant to point out that each person is different."

"I know, and I am not distressed. It is curious, though, isn't it, that your parents apparently did not marry for love but ended up, so far as we can tell, loving each other? Whereas mine, it seems, started out with love, but it faded."

"But *did* they start with love? Or was it merely something else masquerading as love?"

"Such as?"

"Infatuation, perhaps. I . . . Well, I was going to say akin to what I've observed in Olive, but perhaps that isn't correct. A day ago I would have said that Olive was fickle, bestowing and withdrawing her affections at whim, and that all of those affections were shallow. But now?" She shrugged. "Now I have to wonder if I know my sister at all."

And Archie had to wonder if he knew Effie at all. "I take your point. Perhaps my parents mistook infatuation, or passion, or some other transitory sentiment, for love, and when that sentiment faded, there was nothing left."

"We'll never know, I suppose, but I do know that your mother loved you. It was plain as day on her face."

"Do you remember a game we used to play in the garden, where we would process around chairs and compete to sit on them when prompted? There was always one fewer chair than the number of players, so one person always lost out?"

"I do! That is a prime example of what I mean when I say it was obvious your mother loved you. She was always organizing games like that. She would take such delight in them, but mostly in *you* enjoying them. She would embrace you and tease you no matter if you won or lost."

He had always thought so, but, again, recent months had been testing his certainty. It was profoundly relieving to hear Clementine's assessment of the situation.

"And my mother loved me," Clementine went on. "Even if she didn't understand me, she loved me. I do not doubt that. Which is why I have to believe that if she were alive, she would see how miserable London, and the Marriage Mart, is making me and would allow me to retreat to the country."

"But what about your wish to have children?"

"It isn't a wish so much as something that would be . . . nice. A compensation of sorts, as I said, that might help cushion the blow of an unwanted marriage. But in truth, such an outcome wouldn't be fair to the children. I would make a perfectly terrible mother."

He disagreed. Clem was curious, warm, and profoundly nonjudgmental—a rare combination of qualities any child would be fortunate to have in a mother. "I don't know. I seem to recall you nursing more than one abandoned baby bird back to health. And are you forgetting that time you rescued those tadpoles from a puddle and raised them in a soup tureen in the garden?"

"Oh, I remember that. It was one of the worst months of my life."

"Whatever makes you say that? I would have thought you'd be in your element, saving defenseless animals, if one can even consider tadpoles animals."

"You are forgetting that I had to mince earthworms to feed those tadpoles."

"Oh, I am, aren't I?" It was coming back. The knife she'd nicked from the kitchen at Hill House. She'd had him sharpen it for her halfway through the month, as it turned out hacking earthworms to bits with a paring knife blunted it faster than one might think.

"Yes. It was excruciating. I felt as if I were plunging the knife into my own flesh. I used to cry after each feeding, but only after you'd left because I didn't want you to see me."

He was taken aback. "Why did you do it then, if it pained you so?"

"A tadpole can *only* eat earthworms. It can't eat, say, a leaf— believe me, I tried that. I am not immune to your arguments, you know, about the natural order of things. It's just that I don't believe *we* need to eat animals. We can exist perfectly well without them on our plates. You probably don't see the distinction."

"I do see it." He just thought she was taking it too far. "Is it possible that neither of us is purely wrong, or purely right?"

She looked as though she was going to agree, but then her eyes glinted mischievously, and he was glad the mood had shifted. "No. I am right. I always am."

His laughter echoed across the forest.

Clementine forgot they were out for the purpose of hunting. *Forgot.*

She'd been simultaneously excited for and dreading this outing. She'd been so looking forward to a long ramble. Trees and fresh air and . . . Archie. He was so *interesting*. He always had been, but he seemed even more so now than when they were younger. And with his long limbs and his gentle ways, he had a kind of ease about him. A freedom.

But on the other hand: hunting.

Why had she agreed to this?

But on the other hand—the third hand?—was there any "this" involved? Though Archie had his weapon slung over his shoulder, he had given no indication he planned to use it—and he was carrying a picnic basket, so she wasn't even sure he could if he wanted to.

They'd been walking, just walking, for an hour, and talking. About weighty topics sometimes, like mothers and marriage, but at other times about silly things like whether the common stinkhorn would taste worse or better than it smelled and whether the senses of taste and smell were dependent on one another.

And sometimes they didn't talk at all, which was one of the best things about Archie. With Archie, one didn't have to *talk* all the time. One could stop and listen to the staccato percussion of woodpeckers in the distance without having to remark on it. He never hurried her and was just generally so *accommodating*. Her mind could meander the way it did when she was alone. But when it was done meandering, there he was, having stood sentry but happy to hear from her again.

Oh, *Archie*. He was so . . . Archielike. So very much himself, and that was such a good thing to be. They found a spot to eat, and as they feasted on the contents of his picnic basket, he told her tales of his school days with Lords Marsden and Featherfinch. She liked his friends a great deal, and it made her smile to think of the boy versions of them having adventures.

"All right," he said after they'd finished their repast and he'd laid down and stared at the sky for a bit. "I'd better get up or I'll fall asleep when I'm meant to be hunting." He sat up and brushed breadcrumbs off his coat.

"Yes, why hasn't that happened yet?"

"I suppose because we've been talking too much."

Her first impulse was to apologize. Of course one couldn't sneak up on defenseless animals if one was making a racket.

Her second impulse was to keep talking, to say more things and to say them louder.

But that would violate the spirit of their agreement, and he was already packing up.

"But also," he continued, "because we're in the wrong spot entirely for hunting. We'll leave our things here and circle back to get them before returning to the castle." He was tidying as they spoke, folding the square of muslin on which they'd reposed.

He got up. She reluctantly followed.

"The first rule of hunting is safety. I want you to stay behind me once we're out of the woods. Be mindful of where my weapon is and in which direction it's pointing."

"What do you mean once we're out of the woods? Where are we going?"

"Back the way we came. To that old pastureland we traversed earlier."

It was true that they had passed over a scrubby, relatively open patch of land punctuated with the odd grouping of trees, but many fewer and much younger than in the forest proper. It seemed as if it had been cleared at some point in the past and subsequently abandoned. "Whatever for?"

"Because we're hunting birds. Pheasant. Perhaps grouse. One finds birds in scrubby bush, not so much in mature forests such as this."

"But then why did we come into the forest at all?"

"Because you love it so, and I—" He looked abruptly stricken, as if he'd thought through to the end of what he'd meant to say and found it lacking. "I remember how much fun we used to have in the woods around Mollybrook," he finished weakly.

That was true, though she still had the sense that was not what he'd initially meant to say.

"I wasn't supposed to be hunting on this trip, you understand, so I only brought this fowling piece. Too bad, as I saw a stag in these woods yesterday. What a kill that would be." He waved dismissively. "Much too big a kill, though. We wouldn't be able to take it home. And although I'm sure Sir Lionel wouldn't mind my hunting a few birds—technically one requires the permission of the landowner to hunt—anything else seems an overreach without his express permission."

Clementine started to feel ill as she trudged along. A stag was such a majestic creature. Antlers; big, liquid eyes; legs vibrating with leashed power. While she was, of course, glad they weren't out here stalking one, it was dismaying to think that in Archie's mind, the only barriers to doing so were logistical ones such as not having permission.

To think of such a creature versus a man. In a fair fight, the stag would gore the man. But the gun would make all the difference, its shot tearing through the stag's rippling musculature, allowing it to be cut down from a great distance, its life snuffed out in an instant.

Her lunch was sitting like a pile of buckshot in her stomach. "Why was there no meat in our lunch basket?" she asked suddenly.

"Because you don't want to eat any," Archie said, as if the answer should have been obvious.

"But you do."

"But I'm dining with you."

"But our meatless day isn't until tomorrow. I have no jurisdiction over what you do or do not eat until then."

"I was under the impression that not only did you not want to eat meat, you didn't want to *witness* the eating of meat."

That was true, in an ideal world, but she was well aware that the world was far from ideal. She would never have expected Archie to be so accommodating, especially on "his" day of their agreement. He could be so very thoughtful, and also . . .

"Part of the art of the hunt is to match your weapon and any other tools with your target," Archie said, adopting a lecture-like tone.

. . . so very maddening.

"We've a fowling piece, so we're hunting birds," he continued. "And happily, we have a habitat in which we're likely to find birds. We marry our knowledge of local fauna and terrain with the proper tools."

"The proper tools being the gun."

"Yes, though perhaps not exclusively. In this instance, for example, we could do with a bird dog."

"The dog would run ahead and flush out the birds?"

"Precisely, and find them after we've shot them."

"After *you've* shot them, you mean."

Ignoring her correction, he said, "Without a dog, it can be difficult to find felled birds." He was speaking with enthusiasm; this was clearly a topic close to his heart. "Do you remember Baron? What a birder he was."

She did remember Baron, but she was still focused on the logistics of what Archie was saying about the hunt. "So you might end up killing a bird but be unable to find it?"

"Yes, unfortunately."

To kill animals purely for sport seemed infinitely worse than killing them to eat, but she held her tongue. Though she'd sparred with Archie about hunting before, seeing him here, witnessing his almost boyish excitement, the way he all but blossomed as he held forth on the topic, made her reluctant to be so overtly dismissive. They proceeded in silence. The trees thinned as they approached the meadow.

He stopped suddenly, pointed—with his finger, not his weapon. There was a bird standing on the ground not ten feet off. It was fat, patterned with gray and brown markings. It was a grouse, and it had no idea what was coming.

She squeezed her eyes shut and braced, willing herself not to cry.

Nothing happened. When she found the courage to open her eyes, Archie was quite a way ahead of her. She hurried to catch up, but, heeding his warning, stayed behind him. "Why did you not shoot that bird back there?"

"I prefer to shoot them on the wing." He kept walking and was scanning the skies as he spoke.

"What does that mean? You aim for their wings?" How barbaric.

"No, it means to shoot them while they are in flight. If you're quiet enough and careful enough, it's possible to come upon a bird while it's on the ground, as we just did. Of course, neither pheasants nor grouse fly much, but still; it doesn't seem fair to shoot them where they stand."

"As opposed to shooting them as they flee."

He abandoned his survey of the sky and turned to her, a bit taken aback, she thought. "I beg your pardon?"

"I think the problem is in trying to frame any of this as fair. How can a man with a gun versus an animal ever be so?"

"They do get away a good fraction of the time," he said, as if that was at all a reasonable argument.

"You speak of the natural order of things, but is a gun part of the natural order? Animals are meant to kill and eat each other? All right; some of them are, yes. But are they meant to do it with man-made tools of death, with iron and lead and gunpowder?"

"You're misunderstanding." He frowned. "And if there are any birds around, you've scared them away."

She winced. Yes, her voice had gone shrill. She'd agreed to this outing; it wasn't fair to sabotage it.

"May we carry on?" There was just the tiniest hint of rebuke in Archie's tone, detectible only in a tightness that seemed to have papered over his usual affability, but to Clementine it felt like being given the cut direct.

She pressed her lips together and nodded, some of that same tightness spreading across her throat.

For several minutes, Archie stood stock-still, so she did, too. Eventually, she closed her eyes again, to help blunt the blow she knew was coming. In her experience, the disabling of one sense heightened the others, and here, now, she could use that fact to her advantage. There was a slight breeze, and if she concentrated, she could hear the grasses rustling. So, grasses in the wind. What else? The air was warmer here than it had been under the cover of the trees, and the sun heated her cheek. She tilted her head slightly, playing with the angle, feeling the warm spot move along her jawline.

Archie shifted, just slightly, but she could sense it. She opened her eyes but kept the rest of her body still. He hadn't moved, but he had raised his rifle. She could almost tell herself he was a mere statue, more marble than man. The scene consequently began to take on an air of unreality as she stared at Archie the statue. Perhaps she was a statue, too. She rather felt like one, or at least she felt less than human. Cold, removed from her surroundings.

But then she was thrust back into the world, its wonder and terror slowly converging on her. It was a subtle swishing sound at first, like pond rushes in the wind. The sound grew louder, more agitated, an angel crash-landing, its wings flapping wildly. Then a short, sharp, two-note call, like a rooster whose morning song had been cut short. She gasped when the animal appeared. Pheasants, especially the males, had such lovely markings, but their bodies were so heavy-looking, lopsided almost, and seemed so unsuited for flight, which she supposed was why they didn't do it very often. Yet here was one climbing almost straight up, its red feathered head majestic against the clear blue sky, a small, everyday miracle of flight, nature triumphing in that relentless way it always did. She felt as if her heart were tethered to this bird, rising from its burdensome, corporeal constraints up into the sky, up, up—

Bang!

There was the blow. The coiled fist she had sensed, just out of range of her senses, coming down. Her body wanted to scream, and indeed, it started to. The bellows of her lungs prepared to discharge her anguish, like poison being expelled, but she stopped herself with her lungs stuffed full of air. Screaming wouldn't help anything, or anyone: not that bird; not her.

"Damn!"

That was Archie. He had missed.

He had missed!

She didn't know much about hunting, but she had the vague

idea that gentlemen usually traveled with servants to carry and pass along additional weapons when the first was spent. He would have to reload.

She would leave while he did so. She would simply turn and run. It wouldn't change anything, she understood. It was an impulse rather like that of a child covering her eyes and assuming that meant no one could see her. But the fist had struck, and Clementine had bruises to tend.

Bang!

Somehow, the gun discharged again. She turned abject eyes to the sky, and the creature plummeted straight down to earth, all its majesty and wildness snuffed out in an instant. That fall, so fast and vertical and undeviating, felt to her a desecration, a final indignity visited upon one of God's creatures—visited upon this whole forest, it felt like—by a force more brutishly powerful yet so very, very much weaker than it.

And, just like Olive, Clementine burst into tears, which surprised her as much as Archie, for she'd thought it a scream, not a sob, that had been queuing in her throat.

Archie wasn't merely surprised; he was panicked. He whirled, dropped the gun, and began interrogating her. What was wrong? Had she been injured? Where did it hurt? When all she could do was shake her head and weep, he began examining her body, holding out one arm at a time to inspect it, then running his hands up and down both arms as if trying to warm her. He then clasped her shoulders, held her at arm's length, and searched her face. Apparently finding no answers there, his hands landed on her throat, his long fingers sliding around to pluck at the skin on the nape of her neck.

She kept shaking her head. He would not find what he was looking for, which was a visible wound—blood or a bruise on the surface of her skin. It was all inside. Her tears were abating. She whispered, "I am well."

Archie returned to holding her shoulders. He searched her face. "You'll forgive me for saying so, but you don't look well."

"I believe I am . . . having hysterics." She felt as though she might faint. How lowering. Last week she had informed Archie she wasn't the kind of person who swooned. Apparently she *was* the kind of person who swooned. "I . . . wasn't expecting that second shot," which was true but also not at all an adequate explanation for what had happened. "I thought you would have to stop and reload," she finished weakly.

Archie looked at the ground behind him, where he'd dropped his gun, then back at her with an expression that was part worry, part puzzlement. "It is a double-barreled rifle. Two barrels; two triggers. It lets you get off two shots before you have to reload. It's . . . good for hunting that way."

He leaned in, putting his face close to hers, as if he were examining an unfamiliar specimen under a looking glass. He was so near, she could feel the warmth of his breath on her skin. "But it's bad for you, I think? This whole business is bad for you, isn't it?"

Archie was trying to listen to what Clementine was saying. He had, after all, asked her a question. Generally, when you asked a person a question, you listened to the answer. The problem was, she was saying things like, "I know you think me a very sensible girl. Stoic even. Ruled by my intellect . . ." He was *trying* to listen— he *wanted* to listen—but the voice inside his head was louder. It was saying *What the bloody hell were you doing taking Clementine Morgan hunting? Clementine Morgan! Hunting!*

The voice was right. He had been so focused on making her understand, making her see what hunting did for him, that he'd completely disregarded what it did *to* her. He had proposed a swap: a hunting outing for a day of eating vegetables, as if these two things were symmetrical. For him, they were. For her, they were not. He should have *seen* that. What a bloody idiot he was.

There would be time for self-reproach later. He forced himself to attend to what Clementine was saying. "I'm sorry, Archie. I've ruined the day. I'll tell the cook—"

"No."

He had spoken more harshly than he'd intended, although the vehemence of the single syllable *was* proportional to the level of alarm he was feeling. He didn't want this, a Clem who called him "Archie" instead of "Arch" and was all brusqueness and efficiency as she papered over what had occurred and began making plans to release him from their agreement.

He wanted her to talk to him. As she had on the roof. He didn't want a speech on how she had ruined his holiday; he wanted to know what was in her heart.

"Come with me," he interrupted, turning back for the forest. He'd seen a tree not too far in that would do nicely. When after a few steps he realized she wasn't following, he doubled back, grabbed her hand, and said, firmly, "Come along."

When they reached the tree, which was a gnarled oak with a large, long bough that met the trunk six or so feet from the ground and then sloped gently upward, he dropped her hand. He laced his fingers together, turned up his palms, and held them out at the level of her knees. "Up you go."

He expected her to object, and he was prepared to override those objections. She did not protest, though, merely raised her eyebrows, stared at him in wonderment for several moments— moments that seemed like hours, for he felt as if he were being judged by God himself—and, as if having come to some sort of silent conclusion, nodded. She set her foot in his hand and said, "I should like to say that I don't need help, but alas, I probably do."

"You probably don't, but take it anyway."

She was slightly less nimble than she'd been as a girl, but she was still strong, and her arms did more work than his as she hauled herself into the tree.

He followed. He'd thought they would sit side by side on the wide, welcoming limb, swinging their legs and talking, but by the time he reached it, she'd begun climbing higher. He craned his neck and watched her ascent. When she stopped, presumably because she had found a perch that met with her approval, she settled herself, smoothing her skirts over her legs. She leaned forward, met his eye, and cracked a grin.

That grin was like the scotch they'd been drinking in the evenings—sharp but soothing. It told him that things were right between them, or at least that they could be made so. That his error of judgment had not been fatal. That he had not lost his friend, his . . . Clem.

A thought arose, one he'd been having more and more lately for reasons that escaped him: contrary to her self-assessment on the matter, she would make a wonderful mother. He could see it, her tromping through the wilds with her children. Their father lifting them over stiles as she ran on ahead to exclaim over the beauty of a stream or to aid an injured animal. Or perhaps it was nighttime—she would let her children stay up scandalously late over their summer holidays—and she was laughingly telling them the stories of the stars, of the ineffectual hunter who spent centuries not catching the bear. Their father would carry the sleepy youngest back to Hill House, and the entire family would go to bed smelling of pine resin and damp earth.

He found himself irritated at Sir Albert for not seeing this vision. For pushing Clem toward Theodore Bull, who not only would not join the family stargazing outings, but whose only interest in Hill House was to own it, to possess it. Worse than that even, Bull had aimed to possess *Clem*, a wild woman to whom domestication would be a fate worse than death.

When he swung himself up to Clementine's branch with a grunt—he had not retained the same degree of grace she had in matters of tree climbing—she started apologizing again.

He refrained from roaring *no* at her as he had earlier, but he was doing it in his head. "Please stop, Clem. If anyone ought to apologize, it's me, but can we just talk about this? Talk openly and without guile or fear of judgment? Can you tell me what happened back there? Help me understand?"

Though he did understand, didn't he? Hadn't his understanding been the source of his frustration over how Sir Albert *didn't* understand?

"I'm not sure I understand it myself." She sighed and stared up into the leafy canopy, and he smiled to himself. Sir Albert didn't understand her; she didn't understand herself. For Archie to claim that *he* did was the height of presumption, yet he continued to feel as if a perfect grasp of the situation had been conferred on him, albeit too late to have spared Clem significant upset. "I know only that the thought of an animal suffering needlessly genuinely pains me. I am not affecting a stance to cross you."

"I didn't think you were."

"Perhaps it is that I reserve my true affection, my true devotion, for the animal kingdom. I hear you saying that what you love about hunting is the chase, the joy of being outdoors, the taking of fresh air and sunshine. I don't understand why you can't do all those things without the killing."

"The killing is the point."

"Do you *hear* yourself?"

He . . . did. "That was poorly phrased." He sighed, considering how to convey to her the *feeling* of hunting. "It's not the killing so much as the thrill of the hunt, the slow honing of attention that is required until all that exists is oneself and one's prey and the air humming all around."

He thought back to a recent after-dinner discussion, in which the boys made him tell the story of how the Earls Trip hunting ban came to be. He had at the time cheerfully accepted the barring of his favorite pastime because he had thought how much he would rather be the kind of person Effie sought out to discuss his dreams than be a hunter.

He felt the same way here. He felt *more* of the same way here. He would give up hunting forever rather than cause Clem any distress.

"I understand," Clementine said. "Well, I *don't*, but I can see how what you are saying is true for you. Regardless, I'm afraid I shan't be able to continue with our agreement."

"Oh, that goes without saying."

"It does?"

"Of course!" Did she think he was going to march her down this tree, thrust a rifle in her hands, and compel her to shoot?

The affront must have come through in his tone. She said, quietly, "I am not accustomed to men listening to me when I say what I want, much less allowing me to have it."

Ah, the knowledge that he had been, even briefly, one of those men made him ashamed. "I'm sorry I didn't listen, Clem."

"You did, though. You *are*."

"Now, perhaps," he scoffed. "Took me a while. Though we have discussed what a poor student I was. That's what you get for having an idiot for a friend."

"No, that's what I get for having a mortal man as a friend. It is rather amazing, isn't it, how we can rub along with other people and somehow not hear them? Not see them?"

"Mmm."

"I'm not talking about you," she rushed to say. "In fact, you're more highly skilled in this regard than anyone I know."

"Were you talking about you and Olive?"

"I was indeed."

"Have you spoken to Olive about what we overheard?"

"I have not. She was still abed when we left this morning, though in truth that is somewhat of an excuse. I'm nervous about the prospect of bringing it up. How does one broach a conversation like that?"

"Yes, I see the dilemma."

"That wasn't a rhetorical question. I'm actually asking you. You are uniquely good at this sort of thing, at having conversations that are . . . sticky."

He grinned like a boy at her praise, but he didn't have much of an answer. "I suppose you can't take her up a tree and simply ask her who her long-lost love is?"

"How could my sister have had such a love—and have lost it—right under my nose?"

He was fairly certain that *was* a rhetorical question, so he didn't answer. "I was jesting, but only somewhat. If you think I'm uniquely good at having 'sticky' conversations, it may only be because I blunder ahead and just . . . have them."

"You do, don't you?"

"One feels so much better having done so, don't you find? Even if the doing makes one feel somewhat inelegant? And if the outcome isn't what one would have wished, at least there *is* an outcome."

"I think I agree." She looked back up at their green ceiling and said, "Hmm."

"Though this case is complicated by the fact that you are in possession of knowledge you weren't meant to have. Blundering ahead and having a conversation with Olive about a secret she's keeping isn't the same as doing so regarding a secret *you're* keeping."

"You are saying that perhaps it isn't my place to initiate such a conversation."

"I'm not necessarily saying that, but it is a consideration."

"Are you going to ask Lord Featherfinch about *his* long-lost love?"

Archie had asked himself that same question last night. "I think not. I believe if he wanted to tell me about it, he would have."

"Hmm," Clementine said again. "You've given me a great deal to think about."

"Shall we go back to the house?"

"What about that bird? Shouldn't we go find it?"

Ah. Yes. Speaking of sticky conversations. "We should not. *I* shall, but later."

"Will you eat it tonight?"

"Yes. I'll give it to Mrs. MacPuddle to give to the cook." That seemed to satisfy her, or at least to not visibly distress her. "We'll dine separately tonight as usual, which reminds me that I gather you've spoken to the cook about tomorrow? Apparently Effie and

Simon plan to join us for dinner, so I fear Olive's plate of ham is to remain as elusive as ever."

"Oh, no." She waved dismissively. "The happy outcome—for you—of my little outburst this afternoon is that you are released from our bargain as well."

"I don't care to be."

"Arch. Come now. We had an agreement, and my conduct has nullified it."

He was unaccountably glad he was back to being *Arch* in her estimation. "That is of no consequence. I shall be joining you for meals tomorrow. The only question is how many additional place settings there will be at our table. I am merely trying to confirm that we can't figure out a way for Olive to have her ham, and perhaps to persuade Effie to join her for it." And Simon, too. Archie wanted more time alone with Clem, though he knew he was reaching for the impossible. And he was aware that to wish for time away from Effie and Simon on an *Earls* Trip was perhaps ill-done of him.

It was just that they had so little time left. He would see the boys again, but when would he next see Clem? Even if he made good on his pledge to see more of the Morgan family, when would he next see Clem *alone*?

"Oh, Arch." Clem was looking at him like he was . . . well, like he was one of those snakes she'd been admiring so intently earlier. "You are too good to me."

"Hush now. We had a misunderstanding. It's been sorted."

"I wish more people were like you. You *listen*. And not just now, but always. You listen, and you try to make things better. That's rare."

Unwilling to hear any more praise, given how ill-thought-out this whole outing had been, he swung himself down to the lower, larger limb below them. Standing on it, his head just about reached the limb he'd vacated, putting his eyes level with Clem's dangling legs. He could quite clearly see a slice of bare skin on one leg where her stocking had fallen down and was bunched around her ankle.

Damn it all, his prick was taking notice. He tried to tell his prick that this was not the time, but of course it didn't listen, just observed with interest the fine smattering of hair on her calf. He tore his gaze away. "Shall we go? I'll walk you back to the house, then come back for our things." And the dead bird. Yes. *Think about dead birds.*

"Arch?"

"Hmm?" He had to tilt his head back to see her, and he steadied himself with one hand against the tree's trunk.

She was leaning over, looking down at him and wearing a small, impish smile. "I should like to ask you a question."

"I am all ears."

"It is of the sticky variety."

"You know you can say anything to me, Clem."

"It's more of a favor, really," she said, and was she *turning pink*? He must be imagining that, because Clementine Morgan was not the sort of lady who blushed, and aside from the rosiness of her skin, her expression was quite stern.

"As long as it doesn't involve getting shot, I shall happily grant you any favor you ask."

He was trying to be amusing, but her countenance remained implacable. "Do you recall the conversation we had about the anticipation of marital vows?"

As if he could forget it. "I do." Though that was not exactly what he wanted to be remembering at this moment given that he was trying to get his prick to calm down.

"You implied there was pleasure to be had in the act—for the female."

Dear God. Archie was not the sort of person who blushed either, yet he'd be damned if he couldn't feel himself doing exactly that. "Ah . . . yes."

"I should like to experience that, and I wonder if you will help me. I propose that you and I engage in the anticipation of marital vows, except without the marital vows part."

He fell out of the tree.

13

Clem Shoots Her Shot (Not Literally, This Time)

Clementine did not expect Archie to agree to her admittedly outlandish proposition. He would almost certainly decline, and she'd only asked because she was at least confident that her *having* asked wouldn't change his opinion of her. He would almost certainly say no, but he wouldn't mock her or express outrage or incredulity—at least not any more than he did over anything else. Her having shot him, for instance. She was never going to live that down. Oddly, though, she found she didn't want to. Now that the urgency of the circumstances surrounding the business with Mr. Bull had faded, she rather enjoyed being teased. Well, she enjoyed being teased by *Archie*. That was the difference between teasing and mocking, she supposed. To tease someone, you had to truly know her: to know what she would find amusing, to know where the line was between far enough and too far.

Archie might be the only person in her life qualified to tease her.

As upsetting as the hunting had been, Clementine felt as if they'd come through a storm together and achieved an even greater understanding of one another. Their friendship had emerged from turmoil stronger than ever, akin to the way that, under certain conditions, time can turn wood into fossilized stone.

So when Archie responded to her question by hopping down from the tree—she'd thought at first he'd lost his balance and fallen, but he landed more or less on his feet—and merely said, "Yes, all right," with the same mildness of tone as if she'd asked him to post a letter for her, she was astonished. Perhaps the shock she'd expected him to exhibit had bounced off him and refracted back to her.

"Are you coming?" He held out a hand as if making to help her down from a carriage instead of a tree—though since she was two boughs above him, the gesture was purely symbolic. "We ought to be getting back. Effie and Simon are expecting me for dinner, before which I've got to venture back out and find that bird, and who knows what the cook is preparing to suspend in aspic for *your* evening meal?"

Attempting to disguise her discombobulation, Clementine swung herself down to the large limb below and paused. Archie's hand was still extended, and now she could reach it. The prospect of taking it made her feel odd, as if the musculature of her legs had been replaced by the aforementioned aspic.

She was being ridiculous. They had just made an agreement to lie with each other intimately, and she could not even see her way through to putting her hand in his? She brushed her palm against her skirts to dry it off—for it was suddenly damp—and took his hand. She didn't need his help: he had been correct in his earlier assessment that she did not require assistance in matters of tree climbing. And in fact, accepting Archie's help was incapacitating as it effectively lost her the use of the one arm. But he made up for it by catching her as she leapt.

"Oof." She exhaled involuntarily as she landed forcefully in his arms. He brought her to his side and held her there, her feet dangling a few inches above the forest floor. She thought he would lower her the rest of the way, but he didn't. She was a hummingbird, hovering in place. Archie's face was inches from hers, and she was unaccustomed to looking at him at such close range, not to mention in the full light of day. He was studying her with an expression she could not parse, something harder than kindness and softer than ire.

There was something about the intensity of his regard that made the aspic feeling intensify. It wasn't just her legs that felt wobbly now, but her stomach, too. And her chest. She thought initially that Archie was holding her too tight: her breaths were short and shallow, and it was difficult to fully fill her lungs. But no. He was holding her fast against the firmness of his body, but his arm was around her waist; her chest, though very near his, was unconfined.

On he stared. Just as she began to fret that something was truly wrong, he said, "Your eyes are the color of a thruppence. Not a shiny new one, but one that has been worn by time."

The comparison delighted her. Her eyes *were* the color of a thruppence, so it had the advantage of being true, but beyond that, hearing such an observation made her heart twist for reasons she could not articulate.

"*Your* eyes are . . ." She leaned in even closer, studying his irises. Archie's eyes contained many different colors—green, brown, and a kind of yellow-gold. She had always known that. She'd never tried to describe those colors, though. She looked, and he let her take her time. Did not press her to speak. "Your eyes are the color of the moss that grows on that big beech tree we used to climb, the road to Hill House just after it's rained, and the straw in the fields outside Mollybrook after it's been bailed." Yes, that was exactly right. "Your eyes are the color of home."

Those eyes lit, as if he appreciated her inept attempts at poetry more than was warranted. But only for a moment, before, astonishingly, they grew . . . shy? That did not seem right. He ducked his head and lowered her to the ground, though the hummingbird found she did not particularly want to be set free.

"Let's go." He turned for the castle and she followed, reasoning that surely now he would begin raising objections to her proposal, or at least questions and/or points for discussion. After all, *she* had questions and points for discussion despite the fact that the whole thing had been her idea.

Question: When were they going to engage in the act?

Point for discussion: They would have to agree not to tell anyone. Even their closest confidants couldn't know.

Question: Would he remove himself from her and spill his seed outside her body as Theo had?

Point for discussion: She would have to ask him to, or, alternatively, to enlighten her as to one of the other methods he'd alluded to that prevented the conception of a child.

But Archie said nothing. Everything was the same as ever as they walked.

When the castle came into view, she was almost out of time. "I must extract one promise from you," she blurted.

He shot her a quizzical look.

"You must promise me one thing if we are to . . . enact the plan I proposed earlier." Had he *forgotten*?

"All right. What is it?"

She drew a fortifying breath. If they weren't going to talk about the rest of it, that was one thing, but this was an essential condition. "You mustn't get any ideas about marrying me as a result of our lying together. You've got to leave your overdeveloped sense of honor at the bedroom door."

"Overdeveloped!"

He had stopped in his tracks, but it had taken her a moment to realize it, so she halted a few feet ahead of him and turned. "Indeed."

"Need I remind you," he said, a note of pique entering his tone, "that it's thanks to my 'overdeveloped' sense of honor that neither you nor your sister are currently Mrs. Theodore Bull?"

"Need *I* remind *you* about the time you broke a vase at Hill House and instead of hiding the pieces as any sensible child would have, you sought out my mother and confessed? Or the time you fed Mr. Smith's Easter ham to Olive's dog under the table?" His jaw dropped, and she smirked. He had thought he was being so subtle that day. "Or," she cried, overcome by the momentum of her own argument, "that time you went way out of your way to rescue Olive and me from an unscrupulous knave, *were* prepared to marry one of us if need be, and didn't even get angry when I *shot* you?"

She thought they were going to have an argument then, but he laughed. Threw his head back and cackled. When he was done, he righted his head, looked her in the eye, and said, "All right, Clem. I promise not to get any ideas about marrying you. You've made your aversion to the institution quite clear."

She was tempted to point out that just because a woman had aversions—or preferences, for that matter—it didn't mean that a man need heed them. In fact, most men found the aversions and preferences of women completely irrelevant. But better, of course, to retain the advantage here. "All right, then."

"All right, then," he echoed, and she was about to resign herself to the fact that none of her other questions or points of discussion were going to be dealt with, at least not right now. He was about to turn, and they would make the final approach to the castle. He would, as before, conduct himself as if everything were the same as ever. She wasn't sure why that annoyed her so.

He did turn, but to her shock, everything wasn't the same. He offered her his arm.

He had never done that before. Well, there may have been the odd time when the Morgans were dining at Mollybrook and one or both sets of parents had insisted on a show of formality. But he had never done anything so courtly as offering her his arm when they were alone. Being themselves.

But there it was, his wool-encased forearm, bent at forty-five degrees, the elbow making a point that pierced like a knife through her aspic heart.

She laid her fingers on his arm, and walked with him.

As they approached the castle, Archie had been intending to suggest they meet on the roof again after dark. On the roof, he would talk Clem out of her ridiculous proposition. He needed the time *between* then and now to rehearse his speech. He wasn't good with words at the best of times. And even though in some ways Clem offering herself to him *was* the best of times, her doing so had him completely and utterly befuddled. That feeling he got when he tried to read something important? Where the words started to look wrong and the letters began to slide out of place and his head felt as if it would burst from the pressure?

He usually got that feeling from books, but for a moment back there, the entire world had done that to him. So much so that he'd *fallen out of a tree.* He couldn't think straight, so he'd known he'd never be able to talk straight. So he'd landed as best he could from that fall, dusted himself off, and allowed himself to pretend, just for a while, that he was in agreement with Clementine. That he *could* have her.

They would sort it out later, in the dark, where it was easier to talk.

He wasn't able to whisper an instruction to meet him on the roof, though, because they were met in the gardens by Effie, Simon, and Olive, who were running around like Bedlamites.

"Clemmie!" Olive shrieked when she caught sight of her sister. "I've lost Hermes!"

"Pardon?" Clem took her hand off his arm, and even though Archie had a sense that the laws of nature didn't work this way at all, he felt the removal of her hand as the slamming of a door. She was releasing his arm, but he felt the opposite: a sort of imprisonment.

Olive launched into a story about how she had decided to sketch a picture for Clementine to memorialize their time at Quintrell Castle. "I asked the gentlemen to pose for me, and I thought we ought to include Hermes." She sniffed loudly, seeming to Archie more distraught at losing her sister's turtle than she had been at stealing her sister's fiancé. "So I got him out of his enclosure, and I *lost* him!"

"Miss Olive," Effie said, "I cannot allow you to take the blame for this unfortunate turn of events. Miss Morgan, it was I who suggested the introduction of Hermes to our tableau. I am truly sorry."

"Oh, don't be so dramatic," Simon called from where he was on his hands and knees beneath a cracked stone bench surrounded by overgrown grasses. "Hermes can't have gotten far, and if you lot would spend as much time helping me look as you have in hysterics, we might actually get somewhere." He paused and twisted his head over his shoulder. "Hello, Harcourt. Hello, Miss Morgan."

And so Archie found himself not whispering instructions to Clementine for a clandestine rendezvous but scrabbling around the overgrown estate looking for her turtle.

"It is all right, everyone," Clementine kept saying. "It's unfortunate we'll have to skip the races, but it isn't as if Hermes can't survive in the wild. He'll be fine. In fact, he'll be better off. I've been feeling increasingly guilty about confining him. Captivity, no matter how comfortable, is still captivity, after all."

She was roundly ignored. Well, she was ignored by everyone else. Archie heard her as if she'd been speaking into his ear, nay, into his very soul, as absurd as that was. *Captivity, no matter how comfortable, is still captivity.*

The phrase brought to mind her instance that he not take a marriage-minded approach to their liaison—not that there was going to be a liaison. It had never seemed out of character for Clementine to be opposed to marriage, but he hadn't thought about it in the context of the word *captivity*. No wonder she hated the idea. Wild Clementine could never thrive in captivity.

"I found him!" Olive screeched a few minutes later, sounding for all the world like a banshee foretelling death rather than a girl proclaiming victory. She strode up from the banks of the pond, holding poor Hermes over her head like a trophy. Her hem was dirty and wet—she resembled her sister that way.

"Oh, Olive, you've ruined your dress," said Clementine, whom Archie knew had never spared a care for her owned ruined dresses.

It was, perhaps, only in captivity that people minded ruined dresses.

"And so I have!" Olive exclaimed. "I don't know how you bear it, Clemmie. Wet feet are the absolute worst. Come, let's change before we dine. Happily, I overpacked for my botched elopement, so I've plenty of dresses where this came from."

It occurred to Archie that he'd noted—several times—the blue day dress that Clem had been wearing. When the light was right, you could see the outline of her legs beneath it. She'd worn it nearly every day except for twice when a pink dress trimmed with ribbons had taken its place—almost certainly a loaner from Olive. Yet he could not recall one thing about Olive's appearance since they arrived, until now when he'd noticed her Clemlike muddy hem.

Olive took her sister's arm, and chattered at her as they departed. Clem looked over her shoulder at Archie, just briefly as they mounted the stairs to the terrace. He could not read her expression.

As Archie sat alone in the drawing room waiting for Simon and Effie, he thought about what a wonderful day it had been, in the end. The worst part had been the bacon. Which made no sense, because what about the Clem-abjectly-weeping part? While he never wanted to cause Clementine pain, her distress had led to a forthright conversation he was very glad they'd had. And then she'd made her ridiculous proposition. He would, of course, be nipping that in the bud, but nothing had ever—*ever*—flattered him more. So, on balance: a wonderful day.

But the bacon. Having to swallow it guiltily while he made eye contact with her. Something about it was still bothering him. He reminded himself of Clementine's own words on the matter. She had no jurisdiction over what Archie did or did not eat today.

Still, that bacon weighed heavily, almost as if it remained undigested in his gullet.

All at once and fully formed, a memory surfaced. Mother used to have a bedtime ritual she would perform with Archie when he was small. She had called it "Rose, Thorn, Bud." She would lie next to him in his bed, and they would look back over the day and name their roses and their thorns, the rose being the best part of the day and the thorn being the worst. Then, the bud: a hope for the next day.

So, thorn: the bacon. Rose . . . He could hardly choose. The moment after he'd swallowed the bacon and caught sight of Clem and suddenly understood her in a way he hadn't been able to articulate previously? No, not quite. Perhaps watching her stare so intently at the family of snakes? No, not that either.

It was, in fact, the moment he'd fallen out of the tree, as nonsensical as that seemed. Clem's offering herself to him. It wasn't a matter of lust, though. No, that moment wasn't his rose because of *what* she'd offered; it was the *fact* of the offer. To be trusted with such a delicate thing. To be recognized as a person Clem could confide in, as a person who tried to help where he could.

To be known.

By God, she had known all along that he hadn't eaten that ham all those years ago? And more to the point, she'd known *why*. Then she'd looked into his eyes and described them so perfectly he'd felt almost as if she were describing more than his eyes. He rather thought he had never been so thoroughly *seen* before.

Except perhaps by Mother. A great while ago.

Yet that had felt different from this, somehow. With Mother, it had been a . . . calmer sort of seeing. Clementine saw him in a way that both comforted him and agitated him.

He let his mind wander forward to tomorrow, searching for the bud that might bloom. Of course, Archie was not a saint. He was honored by Clem's trust in him, and he was inordinately flattered by her proposition. And he had to admit—to himself—that he was attracted to her. A man's prick did not lie, and on several occasions recently while in proximity to Clem, Archie's had . . . not lied.

Such attraction was logical, he told himself. Clementine Morgan was a very pretty woman. She was kind and clever, too.

It was also irrelevant.

Time to put Clementine and her extraordinary proposal out of his mind, an endeavor that was made easier when the boys clattered in, professing hunger and pouring drinks and asking him what he'd shot today.

"A pheasant," he said with a mildness he hoped wasn't too studied. "I gave it to Mrs. MacPuddle for her own dinner." After he'd gone to retrieve it, he couldn't bear the thought of eating it, probably because he associated it with Clementine's anguish. He could see the boys gearing up to ask him more about the day. "Shall we go into dinner? Mrs. MacPuddle came while you two were changing and said we may eat anytime. I, for one, am famished and would happily forgo an aperitif."

Archie's hunger pangs turned to another kind of pang entirely when they entered the dining room. Cook had outdone herself. At the center of the table sat a suckling pig roasted to perfection, its skin crispy and deep brown, and . . . its mouth opened unnaturally wide to hold an apple and its empty eye sockets appearing almost demonic.

He thought yet again of that encounter with Mr. Smith, the farmer, all those years ago. Too bad Olive didn't have any of her dogs with her here.

Seating himself at the rear of the unfortunate creature where at least he did not have a prospect on that uncanny, eyeless face, Archie surveyed the rest of the table. Having enjoyed the informality of their inaugural dinner at the castle, the men had asked for their subsequent meals to be served all at once, rather than in a series of removes. They'd been enjoying helping themselves willy-nilly to whatever they liked, their conversation undisturbed by the presence of servants, who were too thin on the ground at Quintrell Castle anyway to serve a proper meal.

That their dining tradition had been established thusly was a boon to Archie this evening. It meant Effie and Simon did not notice he didn't take any of the pig. He filled up instead on potatoes, stewed apples, and some kind of wilted green he didn't care for but shoveled into his mouth all the same. He followed it all with an enormous helping of sticky toffee pudding. Tomorrow was his meatless day with Clementine, but after that, he would find himself some meat that didn't bring to mind Mr. Smith berating his wife or Clementine screaming as he shot a bird. Perhaps some mutton.

"I've been thinking." Archie angled his chair to face Simon as they pushed their plates away and Effie went to the sideboard to fetch the brandy decanter. He had done so to better see Simon, who was seated next to him, but the adjustment had the happy consequence of putting the ravaged pig outside his field of vision. "Perhaps I ought to take my responsibilities in Lords more seriously. Turn up for more than just the most essential votes."

"I beg your pardon?" Simon asked, even as Effie exclaimed, "Why in God's name would you do that?"

He should not have said anything. It was merely a half-formed idea. Not even that. It was an absurd notion that had suddenly popped into his head and just as rapidly out of his mouth. "I've been thinking about how I don't really . . . do anything."

"You do plenty," Effie said, inserting himself between Archie and Simon to fill their glasses. "You're the most accomplished hunter I know, for all that we harangue you about it. You're a master of so many pursuits: boxing, archery, riding. You, Archie, are a true Corinthian."

"Yes, but those are *idle* pursuits. They don't do anyone any good."

"But do you really want to become a parliamentarian?" Simon asked, squinting at Archie as if he didn't quite recognize him.

"I *beg* you, *please* don't," Effie said dramatically as he reseated himself. "I can't have the both of you squawking at me about excise taxes, what Howick is or isn't doing right, and God knows what else."

"Shall we return to the drawing room rather than linger here?" Archie asked. Effie had retaken his seat across the table, and Archie preferred not to have to stare at the wreckage of their dinner.

Simon and Effie shared a look Archie could not parse but agreed. Once reinstalled in their drawing room, Simon, still studying Archie as if he were a specimen under a quizzing glass, said, "Archie, where is this all coming from?"

"Mr. Hughes runs the estate with minimal help from me. I almost never show up in Lords. I'm depressingly ordinary. I don't do anything of worth."

"That's *ridiculous*," Effie proclaimed. "*I* don't do anything of worth."

"That's not true," Archie said. "You are a poet."

"One might say that poems are *less* than no use. Lord knows, my father does."

"He is wrong. You bring people beauty, and understanding." Archie turned to Simon. "And you strive to make the world a better place. I, by contrast, do nothing of use."

"That is entirely false," Simon said quietly, his muted but firm objection the tonal opposite of Effie's earlier outburst.

"Oh, come now." Archie was starting to grow impatient. He did not wish to be coddled. "Even if you do not share Miss Morgan's moral objection, hunting, while enjoyable, isn't important, not in any elemental way. At least not if one doesn't need to hunt to live."

"He's not talking about that," Effie said dismissively. "What you do is love people."

Archie blinked, taken aback. "I beg your pardon?"

"You love people, openly and without reserve. That is entirely rare."

Archie looked to Simon, who merely gestured at Effie as if ceding him the floor.

"Consider your mother," Effie went on. "I don't know another son in England who would take such devoted care of his mother. That's why you're never in Lords. You're taking care of your mother."

"Yes, but Miss Brown is there, and honestly, I could hire any number of nursemaids. It needn't be *me* taking care of Mother."

"But it *is* you. That you have taken up that burden so willingly and with such kindness . . . well, that's exactly the kind of thing you do. And forget the countess. What about *us*?"

"What do you mean?" Archie was confused.

"You find people, and you love them," Effie declared. He was on a roll now, gesticulating dramatically into space. "I, for one, wouldn't have anyone else who did if you hadn't adopted me. Can you imagine the lonely state I'd be in if I didn't have you around? If you didn't drag me around England for a fortnight every autumn?"

"If you didn't make these trips a priority, they wouldn't happen," Simon said. "If I'd stayed home, you know I'd've spent the past fortnight reading newspapers, but what would that have accomplished? Parliament isn't in session. I'd merely be reading, sending my mind on a fruitless whirl. It is only here that I gain a sense of remove from the troubles of the day."

"Indeed," Effie declared. "This is my favorite fortnight of the year."

"Mine too," Simon said.

Well. Archie hardly knew what to say. Between this, and Clementine's trust in him, he feared he was about to get a big head. He didn't hate it, though.

14

The Lady's Delight

Clementine waited for Archie until well past midnight with her window open. She had hoped—assumed—he would pay her a visit. She sat near her door, listening for any sign of his return to his own room. He had been so very quiet next door. She never heard him moving around. The walls must be very thick.

When the clock struck one, she decided to take matters into her own hands. After all, she'd done the difficult part already, making her bold proposition.

Perhaps not, though. Perhaps the difficult part was still to come. Her stomach flipped when she thought back to her initial kisses with Theo. Well, no, her stomach flipped when she substituted Archie for Theo in that memory. Even though Archie had assured her there was pleasure to be had in the act, and even though she trusted Archie more than anyone else in the world, she was exceedingly nervous about their planned assignation.

Before she could think overmuch about it, she took up a candle, crept into the corridor, and knocked softly on Archie's door.

There was no answer. But, she reasoned, that did not necessarily mean he wasn't in there. He might be asleep.

How could he be *asleep*, though, given what was meant to happen between them? She had barely made it through dinner, what with the nerves and the anticipation, and she'd spent three hours—three hours!—pacing her room.

With one more, slightly louder warning knock, she pushed open the door.

And found a completely empty room.

The space contained nothing but cobwebs. They hung from the corners and trailed down the walls so thickly as to be visible even by the light of her single flame.

"But where is he?" She sent the fruitless question into the air. Befuddled, she forgot the need for stealth as she went back out into the corridor . . . and encountered Lord Featherfinch on his way out of Olive's bedchamber.

Judging by his horrified expression, he was more surprised to see her than she him. He didn't know that she knew he was no threat to Olive. So she decided to disarm him and simply asked, "Lord Featherfinch, would you be so kind as to point me in the direction of Lord Harcourt's room? I have an urgent matter to discuss with him." She smiled brightly, as if they were meeting by happenstance mid-promenade in Hyde Park.

His mouth opened and closed a few times. He looked like a fish out of water. A very fine, exotic fish. She giggled. Which she was aware was likely to undercut her prior assertion that she had weighty matters in need of Archie's attention. Lord Featherfinch's countenance changed, appearing less fishlike and more as if a realization were dawning, and he *did* surprise her then by following her giggle with one of his own. "I would be delighted to assist you, Miss Morgan. The room you seek is that way. At the end of the corridor"—he pointed—"make a right. Archie's door is the second on your right after the turn. It has a great big gouge in it."

"A gouge?" She smiled, overcome with a fondness for this curious man who was such a good friend to Archie, and, it would seem, to Olive. "Perhaps dating from when the invading MacCallums tried to break it down? Or, better, perhaps it is a mark left by the *ghosts* of the invading MacCallums!"

"Ah, Miss Morgan!" Lord Featherfinch exclaimed, apparently thrilled by her conjecture. "You will do quite nicely indeed."

She had no idea what that meant, but she wasn't inclined to press him. She had an assignation to get to. She bobbed an abbreviated curtsy as if she and Lord Featherfinch *were* parting ways after that Hyde Park encounter instead of outside Olive's bedchamber at one o'clock in the morning.

At Archie's door, she traced the edge of the gouge, thinking about how old it likely was, regardless of whether its origins were spectral. It had no jagged edges, and her fingers encountered no splinters. This castle had stood for centuries. The fact buoyed her. Usually she felt that way about the outdoors. A river, for example, kept flowing no matter what men did or said next to it. If the blood they shed flowed down its banks, the current carried it away with indifference. She had always thought of the natural world and the world of man as opposites. People were unreliable. They misunderstood each other. They caused each other pain. They died. But here was a place that had been home to Sir Lionel for his entire life, and to his ancestors before that. Here was a door that had stood the test of time. Perhaps *some* things men built lasted. She leaned all her weight on the solid bulwark. It would take more than her meager efforts—more than phantasmal marauders, even—to move such a door. Sometimes, it seemed, you could trust something besides yourself to hold your weight.

Clementine had been remarkably successful in putting the details of the task before her out of her mind. But now that she was here, looking at Archie's door—touching it, leaning on it—she could no longer save such thinking for later. She was going to have to go in there and—

"Oh!" The door swung open abruptly, and she pitched forward. She was falling. She was going to—

"Clem?"

Archie's chest interrupted her descent. His chest was not as solid as the door. She knew that with her intellect. Yet it was solid enough to keep her from falling. To bolster her. She knew that with some *other* part of her, some part that was at once larger and smaller than her intellect, the part that usually only came alive when she was outside.

Archie's arms came around her, just as she'd regained her balance and might have thought he'd step away.

"Clem," he repeated, quietly, gruffly, and she felt his cheek against the top of her head.

Her hair was down. She was wearing her shift and a shawl, not having packed a proper night rail or dressing gown. She'd forgotten the state she was in. What a picture she must have made conversing with Lord Featherfinch in her makeshift nightclothes!

And how extraordinary that she could trust Lord Featherfinch to not remark upon it to anyone.

Archie began to pull away from her. She wanted him . . . not to do that. "I–" Oh. He pressed his fingers against her temples, letting the pads of his fingers slide along her scalp as he tangled his fingers in her hair. "Oh," she breathed. Who knew having someone's fingers dragging along one's scalp could feel so *good*?

He took a step back, and she went too, a cat following the pressure of a human hand with its head. He led her into the room like that, step by step. Only when they'd stopped moving did she realize her eyes had been half closed, so surrendered had she been to the divine sensations starting in her scalp and shimmering down her neck and arms. She opened her eyes fully to find Archie studying her with that same unreadable expression from earlier, from when they'd been describing each other's eyes.

"I was coming to find you," he said. He did not take his hands out of her hair.

"*I* was coming to find *you*."

"And so you have."

"I'd been going to suggest that we make a plan to begin our . . ." She needed to be able to say the words if she was actually going to do this. "I'd been going to suggest we lie together tomorrow."

"Tomorrow? Why tomorrow?"

"Because it is late, and I'd imagined this happening out of doors."

He cocked his head. "Had you?"

"Yes, isn't that always where we had our fun?"

"I suppose you are right."

"Why were you coming to find me?"

"What do you always smell like?" he asked, the abrupt segue confusing her.

"I beg your pardon?"

"Is it your perfume? Something sweet but also herbal, almost medicinal?"

"Oh, it's chamomile."

"It is, isn't it?"

"I make my own eau de toilette."

He looked at her exceedingly fondly, which was a bit confusing. She repeated her previous question. "Why were you coming to find me?"

"I was going to tell you I could not in good conscience agree to your proposal."

No! That was not what she expected, or wanted, him to say. "Why not?" she demanded, not liking the way her voice rose and her tone went shrill.

His implacable expression cracked then, made room for something that appeared part fondness, part resignation. "All the usual reasons, I suppose. Your reputation, for one."

"We discussed this. I'm already ruined."

"We did discuss this, and no, you are not." He spoke in an uncharacteristically sharp way. His hands remained in her hair, though, and that was something. She never wanted them to *not* be there.

"Yes, I am. And if I'm to be judged wanting because I've given my virtue to one man, what difference does it make if I give it to another?" When he didn't answer, she tried a different tack. "What if I told you I would find another man to help me if you won't?"

"You won't."

"I will," she lied. "So it might as well be you."

He laughed, the beastly man. Not unkindly, but as if what she said was so absurd it merited only laughter. She lifted her chin—but not too much, as she didn't want him to take his hands off her head.

"Who else would you ask?" he asked in a way that clearly communicated he was humoring her.

Who else, indeed. He had her there. That had been the point of her proposal: Archie was uniquely suited for the job.

"See?" he pressed when she did not answer. "That was an empty threat, Clem."

She could feel the beginning of a retreat as his hands started to reverse their way back toward her temples. No. She was losing control of the situation. She tried to muster another argument, but as those fingers slid over her temples, she considered that perhaps now was not the time for more words.

So she kissed him. Well, she kissed what she could reach, which even on her tiptoes, was only his neck, but pressing her lips against the scratchy whiskers there seemed to have a paralytic effect on him. He stood frozen, his hands still bracketing her head and his body stock-still with the exception of his chest, which rose and fell as his breath grew labored. Encouraged, she applied herself more decidedly to the task, dragging her lips across his Adam's apple. And, look: his chest was positively heaving now, as surely as that of the heroine of a Gothic novel. She almost wanted to laugh in triumph but found, to her consternation, that her own breath was not coming sufficiently reliable to allow for laughter. How curious that a man standing stock-still could have such an effect on her. He needn't know it, though. She was enjoying having struck him dumb and rendered him immobile. It was a curious kind of power, one she'd never thought to want but also, now that she had it, was loath to surrender.

"See, Arch?" she whispered, moving her lips against his skin as she spoke. Her lips were chapped from too much time out of doors today, and his evening whiskers abraded them in a way that was slightly painful yet altogether agreeable. Two sensations that shouldn't have coexisted. "What's a little more ruination?"

He came to life then, reanimated, a butterfly freed from a net. His arms banded around her, and though Clementine had never liked being confined, she found this particular brand of imprisonment rather thrilling. He pulled her to him and leaned over to speak into her ear. She almost didn't recognize his voice as he rasped, "Do this because you want to, not because you're already ruined. You're not ruined now, and you're not going to be ruined afterward if we decide to do this."

She had to concentrate on what he was saying, to not lose herself in a curious warm sensation that seemed to be spreading inside her body. "Because you won't tell anyone."

He sighed, and his hands came to her shoulders. He took a large step back so he was holding her at arm's length. He looked her right in the eyes and said, "Of course I wouldn't tell anyone, but no, that's not why. You wouldn't be ruined because you wouldn't be ruined. I reject the premise."

The warmth continued to spread even as she shook her head at him. "You reject the premise. I adore you for saying that, for *believing* that, but you, my dear Arch, are but one man. You are not the world."

She wanted him to be, though. She wanted everyone to think like him, or, failing that, she wanted *her* world to shrink such that he was the only person in it. How could she make that happen?

Perhaps the trick was merely to agree with him? It was worth a try. "All right. I'm not ruined now, and I'm not ruined afterward. I still want to lie with you."

He was kissing her then, and she could see where she'd gone wrong. She was going to be ruined, but not in the usual sense of the word. She was going to be ruined for any other man—not that she was planning on having any other man. But she could see where she'd gone wrong with Theo, with the idea of settling.

Archie, gentle Archie, kissed her as if the world were ending. His lips were strong yet soft. Another pair of words that should mean the opposite of each other yet somehow, with Archie, did not. He was intent on his task, intent on *her*, and as his mouth moved over hers, and his fingers dug into her scalp anew, heat marshaled between her legs. Different from the slow, spreading warmth of before, it was a sharp, disconcerting sensation that would have alarmed her had she been kissing anyone else. With Archie, she could let it happen, she could follow the unfamiliar like a newly discovered stream that led to parts unknown, and know that she would not lose her way.

She sighed into his mouth, which summoned an answering groan from him. She'd thought he was so in control. He'd been kissing her so firmly, so carefully. But that was another thing she must have gotten wrong, for everything that was happening—the movement and pressure of his mouth, and his fingers—grew more intense, almost frantic.

Until he let loose another groan and left her all at once, taking his fingers and his lips and his whole self away in one giant step back. He was stunned, eyes wild and chest back to heaving. The *Gothic* part of her earlier description might have been correct, but she could see now that *heroine* had not been. He was tall and imposing, and though he looked like he might have just come inside from being lost on the moors, she was suddenly so very aware of him as a *man*.

She tested her voice. "We are agreed, then? You will lie with me?" Enough with his misplaced moral objections.

He sighed and began to look less like an untamed Highlander and more like her old Archie. "Not precisely. But close enough, for your purposes."

"What does that mean?"

"It means"—a slow smile blossomed—"I will show you the pleasure of which we spoke."

"The pleasure that Theo did not show me."

The smile slid off his face. "That is correct."

"Was he withholding it, do you think? Or did he not know how?"

"I would prefer not to speak of Mr. Bull just now."

"I take your point. Let us speak in generalities, then. Let us speak of the average gentleman. Does the average gentleman know how to show a lady this pleasure of which you speak?"

"I should think so. It isn't magic. Nearly every man I can think of is equipped with the necessary tools."

"And what are those?" she asked, startled by his choice of word: *tools*.

He let go of her with one hand, lifted it, and wiggled his fingers. She could not imagine what he meant. In her admittedly limited experience, fingers hadn't been involved at all.

Still, something inside her, that part she'd been thinking of as not-intellect, flared. She had a knowing inside her, a creature who moved by instinct rather than by senses. She looked around the room. Archie's bed was mussed—very mussed, as if he'd been tossing violently. She went over and sat on it. "I don't want to wait until tomorrow."

"All right."

His easy agreement was unexpected, and welcome. Instead of coming to her, though, he turned to a table by the door that was littered with his personal effects.

"What are you doing?"

He struck a match and lit a small lantern. "Lighting this place up." He moved to a bureau where there was a branch of candles.

"Why?"

"Because I want to see you." He paused. "Because I want you to see me."

Yes.

While she waited, while the room glowed up, she began loosening the drawstring at the neckline of her shift. When Archie finished, he came to the edge of the bed and watched. It was the same attention he always paid her, so it was in one sense familiar.

But the watching turned the sharp heat between her legs higher, just like the flame in the lamp, and that was new.

Instead of being embarrassed by this heat, she was emboldened by it, as if it were the sun summoning to life the buds of spring. She lifted her hips enough to get her shift over them and pulled it over her head. Or tried to—she got herself tangled in it. Struck by the absurdity of the whole circumstance, she laughed.

He was there, then, laughing, too. Untangling her.

Wasn't that what Archie always did? Untangled her? From ill-made matches and poorly thought-out rescue missions, and more crucially, from the barbs and brambles of her own mind.

Together, they got the garment off, and the mood shifted.

"Your skin is glowing," he whispered, and that was exactly how she felt, as if the light and heat from the lamps were inside her somehow.

Archie, by contrast, was fully dressed. The gentlemen often dispensed with the formality of coats here, but he was still attired in a waistcoat, shirt, and breeches. "Will you undress, too? I want to see you."

Wordlessly, he stepped back and shrugged out of his blue silk waistcoat. He let it fall to the floor. Archie had never been a dandy, but he was always carefully dressed, and to see him treat such a fine garment with such a lack of care was strangely thrilling.

For his boots, he had to sit, but he held her gaze as he backed onto a chair near the bed. He struggled with the Hessians, breaking her gaze only as necessary to get the job done.

The breeches followed. "I'm afraid watching a gentleman divest himself of boots and breeches, especially without the assistance of a valet, isn't a very enticing sight," he said as he lifted his hips and tugged the tightly fitting breeches over them.

On the contrary. She did not verbalize the thought because she didn't know if she was supposed to be finding Archie enticing. Perhaps that was not the done thing in a situation like this, an assignation out of wedlock.

He came to her with his shirt still on. His legs were magnificently sculped things, the muscles in them so plainly apparent under his skin. There was a kind of leashed power in them, she realized, just as a horse at rest has within its body the potential to gallop away. He pulled the shirt over his head, revealing a chest covered in hair, more than she would have expected, though she had to remind herself that Archie's was only the second male chest she had ever seen. He stopped just shy of the edge of the bed and let the shirt join the rest of his clothes on the floor—the carpet behind him was dotted with islands of fabric and leather.

His shirt had hung low, and now it was gone, and he was all there was. In her line of sight, in her world. Earlier, she had wished the world would shrink so that it contained only Archie. Clementine was not accustomed to getting what she wanted. It was a heady feeling.

Not as heady, though, as when, before her eyes, his male appendage . . . well, it twitched.

He came closer, close enough for her to touch him, so she did. She raised a shaking hand and touched his chest, but she didn't—couldn't—lift her eyes.

He inhaled sharply when she let her hand trail across his chest to a shoulder, and the appendage grew.

She laughed, delighted. "Did I do that?"

He took himself in hand. The sight was utterly thrilling. It made her mouth go completely dry. "You did indeed."

"What do you call that appendage?" Her mouth was so parched, her voice sounded odd to her own ears.

"I suppose there are many names for it, none of them suitable for polite company."

"Well, good thing we aren't in polite company just now."

He laughed.

"Tell me," she insisted.

"Prick. Cock. Less commonly, the silent flute. The gaying instrument." He smiled wryly. "I've heard it called the middle leg." She smiled, too. "Or even the lady's delight."

"The lady's delight!" she echoed. How . . . well, how *delightful*.

"Yes, but enough talking, I think?" He crawled onto the bed, slowly, calling to mind the way a fox might stalk a fawn. Perhaps this was a sort of hunting she could endorse. She laid back as he advanced over her, trying to keep her wits about her. She wanted to remember every detail.

"Enough talking," she agreed just before he lowered his mouth over hers. This time, though, he touched her body while he kissed her, let his hands, so rough but so gentle, slide down her neck and trace her collarbones. She hardly knew where to focus her attention as sensations from both fronts assailed her. But then, "Oh!" A finger grazed a nipple, and she jerked involuntarily.

He pulled back, studied her face.

She responded by reaching for his hand. "Come back."

As he grazed her again—and again and again—she had an almost violent reaction. It was just so . . . much. But also so wonderful. But also so much.

Just when she felt she couldn't take it anymore, his hand came down more firmly, kneading the flesh of her bosoms. "Clem. I want to put my mouth here. Is that all right?"

"Goodness, yes!" It wasn't something she would have thought to want; it wasn't something she would have thought of at all. But as soon as he'd mentioned it as a possibility the nipple in question grew taut, painful almost, and she somehow knew that his mouth would soothe it.

They both groaned when his lips made contact. The pressure wasn't soothing, it turned out. It was, in fact, discomposing, but it was providing a focus for her agitation. As if she were walking along a road with many branches but now the road was narrowing into a single pathway as she approached her destination.

And it was a good kind of agitation, though *good* seemed too anemic a word to describe what was happening. It occurred to her that racking her mind for words with which to characterize this experience was probably detracting from the enjoyment of it. She ought to treat it, she thought, like being in the woods. She ought to just *be*.

In doing so, she began to feel a kind of heartbeat, but not one that was emanating from her heart itself. It was akin to waves rhythmically hitting the shore, but the waves were *inside* her.

She let herself ride those waves. After a few minutes, Archie lifted his head from her breast. His hair was disheveled and his face was damp, and he was *beautiful*. "Clem," he rasped, his voice having gone as scratchy as his whiskers, "I want to touch you here." His fingers fluttered gently over the area between her legs. "This"—his fluttering fingers seemed to be searching out a particular spot, and when he found it, she gasped—"is the source of much potential pleasure. May I touch you here?"

"Yes." As she'd done with her head chasing his touch before, she now felt the most powerful instinct to lift her hips to meet his hand.

"That's right," he murmured, so she did it again, and soon they *became* the waves, she and Archie, his hand and her hips. They were working in unison, undulating together. The waves inside her were getting stronger, and somehow she knew Archie could feel them, too.

"Oh," she breathed, when, at the top of one wave, something happened. Something caught, snagged inside her so that she lost the rhythm.

"That's right," he said soothingly, so perhaps the rhythm was meant to be lost. She wasn't sure—

"Oh! Oh!"

Oh.

Archie was going to hell. There was no way around it.

But wasn't the descent going to be fun?

He lay next to Clem, both of them panting and staring at the ceiling. His prick was hard as a rock, but he didn't mind. It would calm down. Eventually. Or, Clementine would go back to her room soon and he could take care of matters then. Though he found he would rather suffer if that was the price of keeping her here.

"I had no idea," Clem said a few moments later when she got her breath back. "Why didn't anyone tell me about this?"

He chuckled. "You can do it yourself, too, you know."

"*What?*" she shrieked.

He took her hand and guided it between her legs. "You're probably too spent now, but you can do for yourself what I just did." He fit his fingers atop hers and maneuvered them so the pads of hers were in roughly the correct spot. "It may take a little time to accustom yourself to the finer details of what works most expediently, but I have observed that you enjoy a moderately firm pressure." He pressed, and she gasped. It made him want to gloat. Not in a prideful way, but he was glad to finally have done something decisively useful. Too bad he couldn't tell the boys about it. Here was something, something practical, he *was* good at.

Clem moved her hand experimentally. "I am all astonishment. And I repeat my earlier question: Why didn't anyone *tell* me about this?"

"That I do not know. I suppose, as we discussed earlier, that a young lady generally learns about these matters from her mother, perhaps in advance of her wedding night?"

"So a motherless girl is out of luck."

"Mmm. I do get the impression that these sorts of matters may be discreetly discussed among women." Some women of the ton gave an impression of such worldliness—worldliness bordering on world-weariness—and Archie had even heard of books being circulated among young ladies, manuals of a sort.

"Hmm." She rolled onto her side and considered him. He considered her back. The light of all the candles made the room look cozy, domestic. Yet Clem looked as wild as ever, her hair as unkempt as he'd ever seen it. That was, he was certain, due in large part to him. He had *finally* been able to indulge that ever-present desire to tangle his fingers in it. He hadn't *satisfied* the urge, though. He wondered if he ever could. "Perhaps in Town," she said. "Or perhaps even in the country, but for that I suppose one has to go to tea parties and such. There are no discreet discussions of that sort in the forest."

"Yet you claimed being an observer of nature prepared you," he teased.

"Clearly I was mistaken. I was not at all prepared for that."

"Perhaps you gleaned the mechanics of things from your observations in the outdoors but, paradoxically, spending so much time running wild means you also missed the nuance that might have been covertly imparted by women in society."

"I think you may be right." She grinned.

He grinned back. He wanted to put his hand back in her hair, or perhaps rest a palm on her cheek, but that might be an overstep. He'd been charged with a task, and he had carried out that task. Clementine was so very dear to him, though, in this moment. In this moment and always.

"I have so many questions."

"Well, let's hear them."

"The most important one is, when are we going to do that again?"

15

Three Square Meals

"Why no kippers, though?" Archie asked Clementine the next morning at breakfast, the first meal of their meatless day.

"Why would there be kippers here if we are not eating animals today?" Clementine asked from the table where she was seated with Olive and Simon—Effie never ate breakfast on account of his habit of sleeping in.

Archie paused at the buffet where he was filling his plate with pastries and . . . pastries. So many pastries. "A fish is not an animal."

"It isn't? What is it, then?"

He made his way to the table. "It's not an *animal*-animal. You don't shoot it."

"No, you merely yank it from its peaceful, watery home and slowly suffocate it."

Simon snickered.

"All right, you two, that's enough." Olive lowered the magazine she was reading, and Archie was amused to see that it was *Le Monde Joli*, the one that sometimes published Effie's poems. He wondered if that was a coincidence or if Effie had told Olive *all* his secrets.

To Clementine, Olive said, "I do believe his questions are in earnest, so perhaps a less barbed response is in order." She turned to Archie. "And *you*." She sniffed. "If you're going to do things Clementine's way for the day, may I suggest you use your eyes and ears more and your mouth less? You're meant to observe and learn, are you not? Rather than opine?"

Simon snickered again, and Archie shot him a look, but he smiled to himself, thinking of their first full day here, when he and Clem had been coming to terms for the visit. She'd said everyone knew that Archie was like a brother to the Morgan girls. That felt decidedly true in the case of Olive. She was like a younger sister needling him.

Clementine, though . . .

His gaze found Clem's lips.

Clem, of course, did not feel like a sister to him anymore. He wasn't sure now that she ever had.

His face heated. Nay, his entire body heated as he thought of her flushed, writhing on his bed, his ministrations sending her over the edge, her—

"Ahem." Olive was still looking at him with her eyebrows raised.

"Yes, quite," he said. "I understand. More listening, less talking." He made a show of shutting his mouth.

Simon snickered yet again.

It was going to be a very long day.

Clementine had taken Olive's admonishment to heart, and she was afraid Archie had, too. "You know, you *are* allowed to speak despite what my sister says," she said to him when they'd passed the first ten minutes of afternoon tea almost entirely in silence.

They were alone for the first time today, and there were important matters to discuss, so she needed him to snap out of his uncharacteristically pliable quietude.

"I notice you have eaten eleven sandwiches," he said.

"I beg your pardon?" That was not what they needed to discuss.

"I have been following Olive's directive to watch and listen, and I have noted that you eat rather a large volume of food."

She was not sure if she ought to be offended by the observation. If it were anyone other than Archie making it she would have thought herself being accused of gluttony.

"It's just that I always thought you had a small appetite," he added, his brow knitting ever so slightly.

Dear Archie. He *was* watching and listening. He was trying to understand. "No, I always pretended not to be hungry so I didn't have to eat what was being served. It turns out that now that I'm in charge of what I eat, and don't have to come face-to-face with a dead animal on my plate, I have rather a *large* appetite." She pinched a bit of flesh on her arm to show him. "I am not the skinny girl of yore."

"Yes." He looked as if he was trying to suppress a smile. "I have recently had occasion to notice that, too." The smile escaped its confines, and they grinned at each other as if they had a shared secret. They *did* have a shared secret. "But that can't have happened in the short time you have been resident here." His smile turned upside down. "So may I assume you are getting enough to eat under your father's roof?"

"Yes. I became mistress of the house after Mother died, so I get to oversee the menus. I've given the cook a book called *A New System of Vegetable Cookery* that Theo recommended—so perhaps he was good for one thing. I simply order up plenty of dishes I can eat and no one pays any attention to what I do or don't consume at the table."

"Good."

"Father never pays attention to me anyway, not really. He never has."

"That is . . . less good."

Enough discussion about her diet. "Archie, I have wanted to get you alone all day, and it has proven more difficult than I'd anticipated." Olive had spent most of the day with Clementine, and had only just accepted an invitation from Lord Featherfinch to take a ramble.

"Yes, I know the feeling."

She was starting to get that sensation again, the one she'd come to think of as the aspic feeling. A significant proportion of her body felt wobbly, and she was overtaken with a kind of . . . not shyness exactly. Not trepidation. More akin to . . . Oh, she was frustrating herself. What did it matter how she felt? She needn't struggle over naming the unfamiliar sentiment inside her. She knew what she wanted, and for once, she was in the presence of a man who listened to her. So she blundered onward. "Archie, may I come to you again this evening?" She hoped they would not have to relitigate the matter. They hadn't, last night, discussed the specifics of a second assignation.

"You may," Archie said carefully. "I shall tap lightly on your door on my way to my room. When you hear that tap, wait ten minutes and come to me—carefully. Check the corridor." Clementine refrained from telling Archie about her meeting with Lord Featherfinch in that same corridor yesternight. "And for Heaven's sake, do not come in your nightclothes. If someone should discover you, you'll be better able to make a credible excuse if you are properly attired."

She waited for more, but there was none. The aspic feeling intensified. "The evening is going to feel very long, I fear. It is going to be a struggle to act as if everything is the same as ever."

"Well, you must," he said. "We are among friends, but if word of our . . . activities should reach my friends or your sister, I am afraid I shan't be able to suppress my 'overdeveloped' sense of honor any longer." He paused. "And I know how fervently you wish to avoid marriage."

Yes, she . . . did desire to avoid marriage. And, as previously established, Archie paid attention to what she said. "Indeed. So we must act as we always do."

"Yes."

"Well, let us practice right now."

"How do you mean?"

"Stop being so agreeable about today's meals. Stop inquiring so earnestly about whether I'm getting enough to eat. Start telling me again that fish aren't animals!"

"What about eggs?"

She smiled. "What about them?"

"Do you eat them?"

"I do not."

"You say you don't want to come face-to-face with an animal on your plate. Eggs do not have faces." He grinned. "Therefore, eggs are not animals." He sat back and turned his palms to the sky, triumphant.

Dinner was perhaps the greatest experience of Archie's life to date, and it didn't have anything to do with the food. The meal had been delicious, he had to admit. The cook's now famous six-hour mushroom pie had been the centerpiece. Its pastry had been divinely flaky, its filling rich, and he dared say, meaty. It had been accompanied by various vegetable dishes as well as a savory cheesecake that was both odd and delightful.

And now they were enjoying some of those pears everyone loved. The boys were interrogating Clementine about their preparation.

"It's vinegar!" she exclaimed when pressed about the mystery ingredient.

"Vinegar!" Simon exclaimed right back. "Never in a million years would I have thought of putting vinegar on pears."

"Nor would I. The cook suggested it. It's a locally made fig vinegar, so perhaps that makes a difference."

"One hears the adage about catching more flies with honey than with vinegar, but perhaps that is not the case here," Olive said laughingly, "for I do believe these pears would attract more than their share of flies were we to leave them unattended outside."

"Oh, but there *is* honey in them, too," Clementine said.

"I knew it!" Effie said.

"So to test the theory," Simon said, putting on his serious face, "we would need to prepare two batches of pears: one with just vinegar and one with just honey. Put them both outside and observe their respective insect visitors."

"You know, I think I might paint those pears," Effie said suddenly. He turned to the Morgans. "I dabble in painting. I'm not very good at it, but I persist in trying."

Archie was attending to the conversation but not participating in it. He sat back and let it wash over him. Here were all his people: Effie, Simon, Clementine, and Olive. Everyone together, yet each person so very much him- or herself.

He remembered that first dinner, when he'd sent poor Mrs. MacPuddle on a goose chase—a Morgan sister chase—trying to lure the ladies to the dinner table. He thought then that he wanted the Morgans to know his friends and his friends to know the Morgans.

Now they did. It felt right. It felt right in the way that few things in his life did, or ever had.

And oddly, it felt different from the other times they'd all been together, the evenings spent in the drawing room after dinner. Perhaps the act of sharing a meal created an even more convivial atmosphere than usual. Or perhaps time spent in close quarters far from home had knit them more closely together, created a kind of easy familiarity. He couldn't imagine what else it would be. Nothing else had changed.

Well, that was not precisely true. He glanced at Clementine. She must have felt his regard, for she swung her gaze around to meet his and smiled—unreservedly. He had to duck his head to hide an answering grin and settled back into his happy repose, letting the voices of his beloved friends weave a cozy cocoon around him. The only barb in his satisfaction was that sense of an ever-ticking clock. Of the end of their holiday growing near. It was day twelve.

"What do you think, Archie?" Simon asked.

Archie looked up. He had no idea what the question had been. "I beg your pardon. I was woolgathering."

"We were discussing the coronation," Simon said.

"Particularly the queen's exclusion from it," Olive said archly. "Did you know they met her with armed guards?"

"That seems extreme," said Archie, who hadn't known that.

"She was never in any danger," Simon said.

"Still," Archie said.

"Archie's a very pacifistic sort," Effie said.

"Except when it comes to killing animals," Clementine said tartly, and everyone laughed, including Archie, though to be honest, his mirth was somewhat spurious. He didn't like Clementine thinking of him as a *killer*.

"Or defending people he loves," Effie added. "I can't tell you how many times he made a boy named Nigel Nettlefell pay for being cruel to me when we were in school."

"Oh, yes," Simon agreed. "He did that quite a few times. Archie can be quite combative in defense of his loved ones."

"Come now," Archie said, wanting to get back to listening to them talk idly about things other than their overinflated impressions of his character.

He got his wish, but not for long. It wasn't twenty minutes before Clementine suddenly announced that she was going to bed early. "The turtle races are tomorrow, and I need to get a good night's sleep."

"Yes, but Clemmie, all you need do is place Hermes at the starting line and cross your fingers," Olive said.

"Nevertheless, I find myself quite tired." Clementine yawned in a way Archie recognized as false. He hoped the others were not paying such close attention.

Clementine bobbed a curtsy to the assembled, a formality that was patently out of character, and took her leave. He could only consider himself fortunate that she did not shoot him a look as she departed.

16

The Lady's (Continued) Delight

When Archie opened his door to Clementine's knock around ten o'clock—he, too, had begged off early, though not as early as she had; someone had to be responsible for keeping up appearances—she began talking the moment she entered the room.

"I may not have a great deal of practical experience, but as we have discussed, I have always been a great observer of nature."

"And a good evening to you, too." Her hair was down, and she wore the same yellow shawl he'd seen on her several times. She looked exceedingly . . . relaxed. She wasn't wearing her shift, though, so that was something.

"I know for a fact that what we are doing is meant to involve the both of us."

"What are you talking about?"

"Perhaps I should speak plainly."

"Please do."

"I want you to lie with me."

"I did."

"You did not."

He sighed fondly. "Must you be so literal-minded?"

"Must you be so obtuse?"

He wasn't trying to be. "Did you not enjoy yourself? Wasn't pleasure the relevant point?"

"I did, and it was, but I want you to enjoy yourself, too."

"I did!" That was understating the matter entirely.

"You know what I mean!" She huffed a sigh and tilted her head back as if seeking divine patience. He knew the feeling. "Archie, you are not a virgin, are you?"

He laughed, but quickly sobered as he didn't want her to think he was mocking her. "No—alas."

"Why 'alas'?"

Why indeed? He had no idea why he'd said that. "Perhaps you would care to sit down rather than stand arguing just inside the doorway?"

He considered her question as he led her to a sitting area at the far end of the room, under the window. His tongue, without the approval of his brain, had added that *alas* qualification because some absurd part of Archie, some soft inner core, wanted Clementine to be the first. The only. He shoved the thought aside. It would only muddle his thinking, and the sight of Clem in her yellow shawl with her hair down, as if she were rattling around her own house—with him, so it must be his house, too, in this flight of fancy—late at night was already distracting enough.

"Well, I'm glad you're not," she declared, and he realized she hadn't followed him all the way across the room but had, in fact, stopped near the bed. "That way we're not both clueless."

He chuckled, which he was fairly certain had been her aim. "All right, Clem, but we shan't be lying together in the sense you mean. There is too much risk of getting you with child."

"But what about the methods to which you alluded? Did you not say there were ways to prevent that?"

"They require an intimate knowledge of your, ah, womanly cycles. They have to do with timing and are suited for a couple that is settled together for some time. And they are never entirely foolproof." Though he supposed there were French letters, though he didn't have any. God, though, the thought of getting to be inside her body, of being engulfed by her.

Archie generally thought of himself as an easygoing sort, but his imaginings were making him rather agitated. He cleared his throat. "However, I think I can offer a compromise."

"How so?"

This kind of talk should have been embarrassing. With her, somehow, it was not. "We can pleasure each other. You can experience the release you did last night, and I can spend, too."

"Yes, I want you to spend."

Dear Heavens. She was only stating her desires, and doing so in a moderate, matter-of-fact fashion, but there was something about it that was making him lose hold of himself.

"But, tell me, how will that work?" she asked.

"I wonder if it is better to show you than to discuss it theoretically."

"Yes." She let the shawl fall, and although she wasn't wearing her shift, she also was far from properly dressed. The back of her blue dress had been unbuttoned, so when the shawl fell, so did the entire front of the dress.

"Lord above." She had perfect breasts. Perfect small handfuls of flesh dotted with the prettiest pink rosebuds. One of them had three freckles on it. He could stare at them forever.

He hadn't realized he was standing there, frozen like a simpleton, until she, letting the dress slide down her legs, said, "May I suggest that you also disrobe?"

"Yes!" Because why stare at Clem's breasts when he was allowed to *touch* them? He made quick work of his clothing, and was gratified when, as he rose, he realized she was staring at him with her mouth hanging slightly open.

Smiling, he walked toward her, his prick at attention, and because they'd already established what was going to happen, he let it make contact with her stomach. That prodded her out of her trance, and she sucked a loud inhalation at the contact. "What do I do?" she said, wonder in her voice.

He bent his head to kiss her, smiling against her lips. "All in good time," he whispered, walking backward toward the bed, pulling her along with him. She wound her arms around his neck and pasted herself against him as he laid back on it, and, God's teeth, it felt so *good* to have the friction of her skin against him.

She was impatient, and wriggled away from him, sat up, and, Heaven help him, took hold of his cock and said, "All in *now* time. Show me."

So he did, showing her how to grasp him, and stroke, how to retract his foreskin and let her hand trail over his cockhead the way he liked. He heard a moan rip from his throat as he allowed his eyes to close and his body to go still. He allowed himself to surrender to Clementine Morgan.

But only for a minute. He needed this not to be over just as it was beginning. So he pushed her gently off him and guided her down so she was on her back, swallowing her protests with his mouth, stroking deeply into her mouth with his tongue, letting the throbbing of his prick be like a drumbeat exhorting him to kiss her ever more deeply. Soon, she was moaning, and he loved to hear it. He would never get tired of hearing it. He had to push away the thought. His feelings on the matter were not relevant because he wasn't going to hear the sound of Clementine moaning anymore, not beyond this trip.

He had been so careful, up till now, not to involve his lower body in their coming together. He'd meant what he said about not wanting to risk getting her with child, not wanting to trap her. He had heard what she said about not wanting to marry. He wasn't going to be the one to force her into it.

But he also wanted this to be about her. He'd wanted to show her pleasure and care and affection—all the things he feared Clementine Morgan had not had enough of lately, or possibly ever. But now that he had permission to involve his body and not just his mind, he let himself lower his body over hers as they kissed. He let himself rut against her, and, God, it was so *good*. He felt like he might explode. He *wanted* to explode, yet at the same time, he wanted this torture to go on forever. When she suddenly wrapped her legs around his waist, he had to bite back a curse. He allowed, for one brief, blindingly glorious moment, the tip of his cock to enter her, just an inch, just for a moment. He did curse then, at the soft heat of her. Making himself pull back, he took himself in hand and slid his cockhead over the pink bud between her legs, used it, along with his thumb, to rub and press until she was panting. "Archie," she muttered, "Archie."

"Yes. I'm here." He kept going, maintaining a steady pace and pressure.

"Archie, it's more than it was before. I don't know if I can—" She wailed, but it was a good wail. She began shuddering, and it caused a surge of pressure in his bollocks.

He wanted to wait for her to come down, but he couldn't, not if he wanted to come with her hand on him. Which he did. He would have given up his title for it. He would be selfish, just this once. "Can you touch me again?" he panted, trying harder than he'd ever tried not to spend.

"Yes!" she exclaimed breathily. "Yes, of course."

And she did, grasping him like he'd shown her before, squeezing and pumping him.

"Harder," he exhorted. "Faster."

She did as he asked, and for a moment, he was afraid he was going to pass out as light exploded in his field of vision.

He did not pass out. Eventually the sparks of light faded and what was left in their place was Clementine. Smiling down at him with her hair wild and her face pink and her eyes dancing.

"That," she said with a grin, "was most satisfactory."

One thing Mother had always told Clementine was to live in the present day. It wasn't wise, she said, to look too forward to something, because one often ended up disappointed when one actually arrived at the thing one had been so keenly anticipating. Conversely, it was not advised to dread something because that only robbed one of the present day's joys, flooding one's day with fears of a future that might or might not come to pass.

It was good advice.

It was also good to remember that though Clementine and her mother were very different, that didn't mean her mother hadn't taught her things. Hadn't loved her.

Oh, she missed Mother so much sometimes.

Still, she couldn't help it when she said to Archie as she was lying half atop him, half next to him, their legs entangled, "If I found a way to stay at Hill House, we could keep doing this."

"I suppose we could."

"You dazzle me with your enthusiasm."

"It's nothing personal, Clem. You can tell by the way I am unable to move any of my limbs that I enjoyed myself immensely last night. And this morning." She smirked. They had napped, but had largely spent hours giving each other pleasure. "But carrying on in this manner, on an indefinite timeline, would be an unconventional arrangement."

"Would it, though? Don't men take mistresses all the time?"

"Men might, but I won't. I would not do that to a wife."

Of course he wouldn't. What was this but another example of his robust sense of honor? "Ah. You plan on taking a wife."

He paused before saying, "It is customary for a man in my position."

She was taken aback, though she did not know why. Archie had never seemed overly concerned about marrying, but he did have the title to consider, the succession. If he wanted an heir, he would need a wife. Her stomach began to hurt.

Who on earth would Archie marry?

Most likely someone he did not know yet, else he would have already wed. She tried to picture this woman, this ghost-wife. She would be the Countess of Harcourt.

"Well," she finally said, "we could carry on until that time."

"No, Clem, we can't." Archie sighed, and even as he absently stroked her arm, said, "We should not have done this."

"You regret it?" She managed to keep the question mild, though his statement shook her. How could she have enjoyed herself so thoroughly, so profoundly, yet his reaction to the same experience was regret?

"Not exactly. I regret . . ." She hadn't been able to stifle a hurt intake of breath, and he turned his head sharply. Studied her face. "No. No regrets, Clem."

"We have one more day."

"Yes." He sounded sad. She wasn't sure why that should be a surprise. *She* suddenly felt rather melancholy.

She knew the solution to that. "I know I'm meant to get up and sneak back to my room. But what if we both get up and sneak outside?" Who needed sleep? She had the rest of her life to sleep. "We could have a ramble before we need to leave for Doveborough. Just a quick one?"

A slow smile blossomed on his impossibly dear face. "Yes." The smile grew wicked. She wondered what he was thinking about. "Let us ramble."

What Archie regretted, what he hadn't told Clem, was that now he was going to know what he was missing. Cutting things off after this holiday was going to be hard enough. Doing so after her proposed time-limited affair would be impossible. He felt strongly that he wasn't going to offer Clem a carte blanche. Even if he did, even if he could see his way past the revulsion the notion inspired, it would only be a matter of time until they were caught, or she accidentally fell pregnant. She would be forced to marry him. And the one thing Archie knew with certainty was that he was *never* going to be the man to force Clementine Morgan to do what she despised: hunting, marrying, any of it.

As they strode out through the gardens just as the sun was coming up, he considered trying to explain. But his speech would be inelegant, and she would only argue with him. He told himself not to think overmuch on the matter. They had today. And tonight.

As soon as they cleared the gardens and entered the forest, he took her hand. Spun her around as if they were performing a Scottish reel among the trees. She laughed, and as their spin wound down, he walked her backward and pressed her gently up against the trunk of a large oak.

"We don't have time!" she laughingly protested as he tugged down her bodice and bent his head to kiss the small mounds of breasts exposed by his adjustment.

"We do, though!"

"But it took ever so long this morning. Last night. Whenever."

"That was by design. It needn't take long." He was fairly confident he had her measure and could deliver a most expedient release.

"Elaborate."

He dropped to his knees.

"What are you *doing?*"

"Applying myself to the task at hand." He lifted her skirts and handed them to her. "Hold these."

He moved aside her small clothes and kissed between her legs.

"Archie!" she exclaimed.

"Shh." They *didn't* have much time, so, with regret, he dispensed with further teasing, and spread her inner lips with one hand. Let his mouth come down on the pink bud he found there.

"Archie," she said, her voice a low warning, a bit uncertain.

He paused. "Trust me?"

"Of course."

The speed and vehemence with which she answered shot a bolt of lust down his spine. He lowered his mouth again, and licked. When she gasped, he did it again. And again, with a bit more pressure each time. Dear Lord. She was soft and vulnerable and somehow also like a gale-force wind, whipping his entire body, his entire *being*, into a frenzy.

It wasn't long before she was moaning, and, judging by what he'd observed about the sounds she made when she was close to release, he calibrated his ministrations so he began sucking as her moans deepened.

It only took another few moments until she was fluttering beneath him. Like a foolish, unschooled boy, he ripped open his

breeches, took himself in hand, stroked, and soon he was joining her.

Mindful of the time, he forced himself to stand, took her skirts
back from her, smoothed them, and adjusted her bodice. "There.
No sign whatsoever of what has just occurred."

He was tucking himself back into his breeches, when she
stopped him. Her hand came to rest on his prick gently, but her
tone contained a distinct note of pique when she said, "I wanted
to do that."

He laughed. "My apologies. Time was of the essence."

She pouted, looking for a moment very like her sister. "Well,
what I really wanted was for you to lie with me. In the true way.
Right here against this tree. Is that scandalous?"

Oh, how he wanted to lie her down on a blanket of pine needles
and push into her. Or to do so against the tree, like she'd said.
To pretend for a moment that he was a country boy, without the
weight of title and society and marriage and the like. Without a
mother who didn't know him. Clem could be a country lass, always and forever free to roam the land—and perhaps inclined to
allow him to roam alongside her from time to time.

"Not scandalous," he said. "But also not practical. I will not
risk getting you with child." He almost added, "Because then
you'd have to marry me," just to see what her reaction would be.

But he didn't. Because he already knew. She'd told him half
a dozen times in no uncertain terms that she was opposed to
marrying—she'd likened it to captivity. And she'd told him men
never listened to her.

He did. It was the one thing he knew how to give her. "Not that
I didn't enjoy what *did* just occur," Clem said. "I rather think that
was scandalous."

"Depends whom you ask, I suppose."

"Let me see your shoulder," she said suddenly, reaching for the
loosened neck of his shirt. He was in his shirtsleeves, not having
bothered donning a waistcoat or coat for their ramble. His exer-
tions beneath her skirts had discomposed him, and the edge of the

wound from her shot at the inn nearly a fortnight ago—a lifetime ago—was visible in a way it probably had not been in the dim candlelight of his bedchamber.

He pulled his shirt back into place. "No."

"Let me see it."

"No." He wasn't sure why he was being so obstinate. Part of it, he supposed, was that although he had teased her for being the cause of the injury, he didn't want her to truly feel bad. He was fine. "You merely grazed me. It is well on its way to healing. There very likely won't even be a scar."

Absurdly, he wished there *would* be. It could serve as a memento of sorts of Earls Trip 1821, which he was quite confident would stand the test of time as the most extraordinary Earls Trip ever.

If he was lucky enough to scar, he would run his fingers over the mark in the months and years to come and think of Clementine Morgan.

The notion was disconcerting. He shoved the image down, took a step—a large one—away from Clementine, and put his attire to rights. He had a turtle race to attend.

17

Lord Help the Mister

Even though Clementine preferred the wide-open country to civilization, she had to admit there was something exceedingly satisfying about walking in the sunshine with a group of cherished friends, taking in the sights and sounds and smells of a village fete. Perhaps her dislike of London was at least in part that she lacked true, bosom friends with whom to sample its enjoyments.

And she did feel that these people *were* her true, bosom friends. How remarkable. She'd only known Lords Featherfinch and Marsden for a fortnight, yet they felt like brothers. And in that same span, Olive had gone from being mere sister to treasured companion.

And Archie. Oh, Archie. He was the only one of the lot Clementine could say had been her friend before. He had been a lifelong friend, even if their paths hadn't crossed in recent years.

"Miss Morgan," Lord Marsden said as they sat at an outdoor table enjoying a light repast, "I hope you won't think me beastly when I say that this pâté is divine."

"Of course I won't think you beastly!"

"But you do have me wondering—"

"I *beg* you all," Lord Featherfinch said dramatically, "*please* may we not revisit this topic?" He turned to Clementine. "Let us instead exhort you to make sure Hermes wins this afternoon."

"I'm not sure there is much I can do but point him in the right direction." Clementine had attempted to train Hermes, but she had to admit that Olive had been correct earlier: there wasn't anything for a turtle wrangler to do beyond cross her fingers.

"Need I remind you that I have placed a not-insignificant wager on young Hermes?" Lord Featherfinch said with a wink.

"I shall be quite alarmed if you viewed that wager as a sound investment, my lord!" Clementine protested, though she knew he was jesting. "I was under the impression you made that hazard as a gesture of friendship."

"And so I did." He lifted his teacup, and the rest of them followed. "Here's to you, Miss Morgan, whether you emerge victorious or no."

Something twisted in Clementine's chest. She had never been the subject of a toast before. She hadn't thought to want such a thing.

"I, however, never confuse investments with gestures of friendship." Lord Marsden set down his teacup and turned to Clementine with a serious expression. "And since I've put three quid on Hermes, I believe you ought to take this race more seriously."

Oh, dear. Clementine, taken aback, did not know what to say. It was only when Olive started giggling, which in turn caused Lord Marsden to crack a smile, that Clementine realized he was in jest, too. "You lot are terrible," she said, though she meant the opposite. How wonderful to have a group of friends like this, friends to tease one and to . . . wager on one's turtle.

Archie pulled out a pocket watch. "Well, investments and gestures of friendship aside, we ought to go. It's nearly two o'clock."

"I declare," Olive said as they stood, "part of me doesn't want the race to start, because it means our time here has almost come to a close. I don't want to go home! I wish we could stay forever in our falling-down castle in the wilds of Cumbria!"

At the starting line, Clementine made polite conversation with the other turtle wranglers. As far as she could tell, her stiffest competition was going to be a girl of about twelve named Miss

Franklin. Last year's winner, a Mr. Hurt, was, in Clementine's opinion, overconfident.

The master of ceremonies, a portly, ruddy-faced man who owned the pub underwriting the race, made an energetic speech to the large crowd assembled, making sure to insert the name of his establishment at every opportunity. To the (human) competitors, he said, "Take your marks . . ."

A pistol fired, which Clementine hadn't been expecting, and she jumped. Her startlement lost her precious seconds; she was late in lowering Hermes to the lawn of the village square, which had been closely trimmed for the event.

Oh well. Her friends would simply have to lose their wagers. They were rich enough that it wouldn't sting. Though she was sorry she wouldn't be able to hand her prize money over to Olive as she'd planned. She hadn't been able to shake the notion of Olive's wheedling pin money from Father not to waste on fripperies but to advance—someday—her extraordinary list. Perhaps Olive ought to apply to her new friend Lord Featherfinch for a loan. Clementine had yet to talk to Olive about what she'd overheard in the corridor. She did not know how to broach the subject—or even whether to. Archie may have been correct in his assessment: perhaps since her knowledge of the situation was ill-gotten, it wasn't hers to do with as she pleased.

"Hermes!"

Speaking of Olive, her shriek broke through Clementine's reverie. Clementine had been woolgathering, but the other handlers had kept pace with their turtles and were a few yards down the green. She hurried to catch up and discovered that Hermes had made up for his slow start. He was firmly in the middle of the pack now.

"Look at him!" Olive's voice carried from the finish line, where she and the gentlemen had positioned themselves. "Make haste, Hermes!"

The reptilian contestants were approaching a barrier—a row of wine barrels—that was meant to inspire them to make a ninety-degree turn. Only about half of them did, but Hermes was among them.

"Huzzah!"

"Hermes!"

"I say, I think Hermes is going to overtake the leader!"

Clementine kept her attention on Hermes, but she could hear the exhortations of her friends and sister rising above the din. Clementine thought she had the largest—or at least the most vociferous—cheering contingent. She ordered herself not to get too swept away. Hermes was still a good shell-length behind the leader, a smaller turtle named Temperance who belonged to Miss Franklin.

Something happened inside Clementine then, something that had nothing to do with turtles even though it was catalyzed by turtles. It felt as if Hermes was *inside* her, which she realized was ridiculous. It was as if, in the style of his namesake, he *did* have invisible wings on his little legs, which pumped furiously. He was trundling toward the finish line, toward a happy, victorious ending, even if he couldn't see it just yet.

"Hermes!" Clementine cried. "You can do it!" He could! He was!

To her utter astonishment, and slight chagrin, when Hermes came up even with Temperance, he *butted her out of the way.* Crashed into her on purpose, and, as Temperance reeled, made a break for it.

As Clementine approached the finish line, she was vaguely aware of the *huzzahs* of Lords Marsden and Featherfinch, and of Olive exclaiming with delight, but she only had eyes for Archie.

"Clem!" he exclaimed, and in two giant strides he was by her side. He picked her up and twirled her around. He had done the same thing this morning, and the other day, and it was beginning to feel usual. As if it was simply the way he greeted her. But of course that wouldn't do. People would talk.

She wished *they* had wings on *their* heels, that they could kick their legs and fly away from here.

But that was pure folly, she reminded herself as he set her down and cleared his throat.

The others caught up, and there was a slight moment of awkwardness, as if she and Archie were children again and had been caught misbehaving. But it faded into the joyous hubbub of the awards ceremony. The burly pub owner called Clementine up onto a makeshift stage and made quite the production of awarding her a ribbon and the pound of prize money.

When all was concluded, she was surrounded by her friends.

"I think we ought to celebrate," said a grinning Archie.

"Yes, after we collect our winnings, we should have quite the pot of blunt," Lord Featherfinch said. "Together with your prize, I should think we could buy out this whole village. Or at least order up a fine celebratory feast."

"I have my prize money earmarked for something else," Clementine said.

"Oh, for what, Clemmie?" Olive asked.

Clementine hesitated. Perhaps she ought not say anything. Excitement won out, and she held out the golden sovereign. "For you, Olive." Olive was struck dumb, which was both novel and amusing, and Clementine took the opportunity to explain her largesse to the gentlemen. "My sister is saving for something important."

"You can't give me your money, Clemmie!" Olive protested. "You earned it!"

"Hermes earned it, and I can do whatever I want. I don't have need of it anyway." It was true. She and Olive were fortunate in that they never wanted for anything—for anything material anyway. There were of course other things they wanted, things one couldn't put a price on. Clementine's version of that—to retire to a quiet life at Hill House—was free. It required persuasion rather than pounds. Olive's version, by contrast, was not. Her list was going to be expensive.

"Then I shall give you my winnings, too, Miss Olive," Lord Featherfinch said. "I've merely to go collect them."

"Mine, too," Lord Marsden said, talking over Olive's objections.

Olive, of course, burst into tears.

"Would you take Hermes?" Clementine said to Archie, handing him the box into which her prizefighter had retired. "Olive and I are going to take a little stroll." She looked around. "We shall meet you back where we had the tea." In case Archie was planning to object, to argue as he'd done before that they couldn't go about unchaperoned lest someone recognize them, she added, "No one here knows us, and we shan't be gone long."

Archie nodded and turned away. Rethinking her directive, Clementine called him back. "You may as well set Hermes loose. He's more than earned his freedom." She'd been going to do it herself, but what was the point in keeping Hermes in that box any longer than necessary?

Olive let herself be taken by the arm, but when they were sufficiently away from the festivities and Clementine tried to press the coin on her again, she recoiled. "You don't even know what I want it for."

"I do, though. You showed me your list."

Olive sighed.

"Was your list not in earnest?" Clementine hated to think, after all they'd come through, that the list had been a lie. The list had allowed her to see Olive in a new light, and Clementine didn't want to let go of that version of her sister. The one with secrets and ambitions.

"The list was in earnest," Olive said carefully. "But I am not truly saving for any of that."

"What do you mean? What about your travels?"

"When am I going to travel, Clemmie? Realistically?"

"When you are married to a rich older man you esteem but ignore and who esteems but ignores you in return? And also funds the travels you undertake with an interesting yet respectable older companion?"

Olive smiled fondly. "Oh, how I wish. But in that case, I shan't need my own money, shall I?"

Clementine chuckled. "I suppose not."

"I am going to tell you something, Clemmie."

"All right." Was she finally going to find out about her sister's long-lost love?

"I have been saving my pin money, yes, but not for frivolities. Not even for the items on my list. I've been giving it to Mrs. Scully from Chiddington."

It took Clementine a moment to catch up. "Mrs. Scully the widow of the surgeon?" It took another moment for Clementine to *truly* catch up. "*Oh*. Mrs. Scully, Ralph's mother."

"Yes."

"Why would you do that?" Clementine kept her tone mild.

"Because her husband and son are dead, and she has nothing."

"That is very generous of you."

"It doesn't feel like generosity," Olive said quietly. "It feels like . . ." She sighed. "It feels like an imperative."

"You and Ralph were very good friends," Clementine said carefully, still moderating her tone. She didn't want to scare Olive away, not when it felt as if they were on the threshold of something.

"Yes," Olive said.

"I'm sorry I hadn't realized he died."

"You didn't realize because I never told you."

Clementine wanted desperately to coax out more, but she didn't know how.

Or perhaps she did. "When we get back to London, I'm going to convince Father to let us spend some time at Hill House. A good, long stretch." Even if it would be torturous to be so close to Archie and to not . . . have him.

"I don't want to go," Olive said sharply.

"You were just saying you wished we could stay here longer."

"Here, yes. Hill House, no."

"What is wrong with Hill House?" Perhaps Clementine was pressing too hard, but she could not shake the feeling that they were on the precipice of revelation. That everything was about to make sense.

"Nothing!"

"Then why don't you want to go?" she pressed gently.

"Because I'm tired of country life!" Olive cried. "Because I want to go back to London where I belong!"

A month ago, Clementine would have heard the words her sister said, and observed the petulant tone in which they were delivered, and dismissed the outburst as childish. She would have silently judged Olive for yearning for the shallow trappings of society.

She had not understood that sometimes self-protection can look like ill humor.

She laid her hand on her sister's back. One more try, then she would leave it alone. "Olive, love, won't you tell me what is troubling you?"

Olive didn't look at Clementine. She didn't look anywhere, just bowed her head and closed her eyes. "I don't like being at Hill House because Ralph is dead."

"You and Ralph were very good friends." Clementine repeated her earlier assessment, hoping this time Olive would hear the meaning behind it.

"No. Yes. We were . . ." Olive exhaled shakily.

"You were more than friends? Is that it? You loved him, and now he's gone and you can't mourn him because no one knew what he was to you?"

Olive did meet Clementine's gaze then, her eyes devastated and leaking tears.

"Oh, my sister, my love. I am sorry. So very sorry." She opened her arms, and Olive stepped into them. They stood there for a long time while Olive cried. Clementine didn't try to shush her. She didn't say anything; any words she could think of would only sound hollow.

Eventually, Olive spoke, but she did not move out of Clementine's embrace, so her words were muffled. "I was going to marry him when he came home from Canada. He'd asked me before, but I said no. I was afraid."

"Of what?" Clementine asked gently.

"I don't know!" Olive cried, wrenching free from Clementine's arms as if she'd been confined there against her will. "Of Father, I suppose. Of society. It was fine for Ralph and I to be friends when we were young, when we were at the country house where the usual rules were relaxed. But can you imagine if I'd announced I was marrying the surgeon's son?"

"Yes. I see." Clementine wondered if perhaps there would have been a way to make Father come around. While Mr. Scully hadn't been a physician, which would have meant he was received in society, he'd been respected in Chiddington, where there *was* no physician. Clementine remembered one occasion when Father had been thrown from a horse and Mr. Smith had been out to tend to him. He'd been invited to dine with the family instead of the servants.

She didn't say anything on the topic, though, for she suspected Olive knew all that. Olive had probably been flagellating herself for some time. Clementine reached for words of comfort. "If you'd married him before he joined the army, it wouldn't have changed anything. He would still be dead."

"You're wrong. It would have changed everything." Olive swiped her tears away almost angrily. "I would have claimed him. He would have *known* I'd claimed him." Clementine had never heard Olive speaking so passionately before. "Instead"—Olive's voice rose—"Ralph went to his death thinking he wasn't good enough for me, when really it's the reverse."

"Oh, Olive. Ralph loved you."

"Ralph was such a comfort to me when Mother died. I want to be that for his mother now that he's dead. I want to be able to comfort her, and for her to comfort me. But it can never be."

"I see." Clementine didn't know what to say that wouldn't sound like she was being dismissive. So she didn't say anything. Just looked into her sister's devasted blue eyes and tried to witness her pain and regret. To *see* her. Archie had taught her that sometimes, having someone to witness your pain, even if they couldn't do anything about it, was a kind of balm.

"I want to show you something when we get back to the castle," Olive said.

"Of course. Anything you want to show me, I want to see."

"Good God, man, will you just let the damn thing go?"

"I'm afraid I have to concur with Simon," Effie said, clomping through the scrub that lined the shores of a small river that ran through Doveborough. "The ladies are bound to be back soon, if they aren't already, and they will wonder what happened to us."

"Right, yes." Archie turned to see Simon approaching, too. The boys had been waiting for him on a bridge that spanned the river but were now headed determinedly toward him as if they were parents come to collect a wayward child. He wondered how long he'd been standing lost in thought. "It's just that I was trying to find the ideal place in which to set Hermes on his way," he explained as they arrived at his side. "Do you think Hermes will like it here?" He had chosen this spot because the river sloshed gently over its banks, and Archie reasoned that if he set Hermes loose where water met land, he could decide for himself where he wanted to be.

"I think," Simon said archly, "that Hermes is a turtle."

"Yes, but he's a *prizewinning* turtle," Archie said. "He's earned a happy retirement."

"Perhaps you should secret him home and have the cook make him into turtle soup," Simon said. "I had some at the last Lord Mayor's Day banquet, and it was surprisingly delicious."

"Dear God!" Archie cried, hugging Hermes's box tight to his chest. "What a monstrous thing to say!" He gathered from Simon's raised brows and Effie's guffaw that he was being mocked, but honestly, he couldn't find the humor in any of this.

He wanted Hermes to be . . . what? Free?

Yes, but he also didn't want to say goodbye.

He had to, though, didn't he?

Captivity, no matter how comfortable, is still captivity.

He shook his head. How had Archie gotten to the point where he was seeing meaning—metaphors—in a turtle? It *was* just a turtle! An uncommonly swift one, but still. And he took Effie's earlier point: he didn't want to leave the Morgan sisters waiting. It was one thing for them to take a quick stroll unchaperoned, another for them to loiter in the village green without a maid.

So he squatted at the edge of the water and gently upended Hermes's box. The creature crawled out but didn't go any farther than that. Archie sat back on his heels and regarded the little turtle. The little turtle regarded him back.

"Well, go on, then." Archie made a shooing motion, but Hermes stayed put. "You're free, you daft reptile. Go!"

Why wasn't he going?

"Ahem." Simon cleared his throat, and Archie stood. He spoke to the boys behind him but kept his attention on Hermes. "You know Miss Morgan will require a thorough accounting of Hermes's release, and I can hardly tell her that he refused to go."

"Perhaps if you walk away first?" Effie suggested.

It might work. He just . . . didn't want to.

A turtle, he reminded himself. *Hermes is a turtle.*

So he turned and trudged back up the embankment, gesturing for the boys to follow him to the bridge. He leaned his elbows on it, and Simon and Effie did likewise, one on each side. "I just want to make sure he goes," Archie said.

He took their silence for agreement, and they stood there for a few minutes watching Hermes watch them.

"Tonight's our last night," Simon said. "Back to Town tomorrow."

"The fortnight's gone so quickly," Effie said. "Though I suppose it always does."

"I need to remind you, Archie," Simon said quietly, all jesting excised from his tone, "that when we're back to civilization, you can't act the way you've been acting with Miss Morgan."

That was enough to jolt Archie from his herpetological vigil. He straightened. "I know that, you dolt."

"Do you?"

Archie bristled at the question. He might not be clever, and he might dislike London, but he did know how to comport himself when he had to. "Do you think I'm going to swan around in green silk calling her by her Christian name?"

"No, but I think you are unaware of the little familiarities that pass between the two of you."

"What do you mean?" Surely Simon was being his usual over-cautious self. He turned to Effie. "What does he mean?"

"The way you embraced after the turtle races, for one," Effie said.

"I know enough not to embrace Clementine in company. Give me a little credit."

"Not the embrace itself, or not only that," Simon said. "It was more the way each of you immediately turned to the other. You were, for a moment, transported to a place the rest of us were not welcome."

"That's—"

True. It was very possibly true.

Damn it all to hell.

"All right," Archie said carefully. "I see that perhaps the in-formality of life at Quintrell Castle, the high emotion associated with our rescue of the ladies, and a history of friendship with Miss Morgan going back to childhood have perhaps combined to create a kind of familiarity that is ripe for misinterpretation. So I thank you for the warning." He made eye contact with each of them in turn and gave a little nod. "For if the two of you misinterpreted it, so might those who know us less well."

"We misinterpreted it, did we?" Simon asked mildly.

"Yes," Archie said, "you did."

He turned to check on Hermes. He was gone. Wandered off while Archie wasn't paying attention. Archie *hoped* he'd wandered off. Dear God, what if he'd been preyed upon, plucked off the ground by a stealthy goshawk?

What was he going to tell Clementine?

It turned out he didn't have to tell her anything. Something was wrong with Clementine when she and Olive turned up. She didn't ask about Hermes, and the smiling, victorious countenance of before was gone.

She held her sister's hand all the way back to the horses, and the pair of them rode side by side at the head of the pack all the way back to the castle.

"I think," Archie said, once they'd dismounted, "we ought all to dine together again. It is our last night, after all. We will join you ladies for your meal." The boys murmured their agreement.

"Oh, you can't," Olive said. "Mrs. MacPuddle told me this morning that the cook was hard at work on a final feast for you gentlemen. You can hardly put all that food—and all her efforts—to waste."

"Right." They could not. Could they? He wanted to.

"We should be delighted to join you after we dine, though, shouldn't we, Clemmie?"

Clementine concurred with a smile, but something still was not right with her. He could hardly ask what it was, though, especially given the warning he had just received from his friends.

Clementine and Olive took their leave and retreated. They were still holding hands.

Archie wanted, more than anything, to fix whatever was wrong. He didn't know how to.

And by next week at this time, he wouldn't even be around to make such observations.

He got out his beads and wondered where Hermes was.

"You know my book of days?" Olive asked, crossing over to her bedside table.

"Of course." The worn, leather-covered volume Olive pulled from a drawer was familiar to Clementine. She had seen it just last week, when Olive had extracted her list from it.

Olive sat on the edge of her bed. "Ralph gave it to me."

Of course he had. Everything made sense now. Clementine sat on the other side of the bed.

"He gave it to me the day before he left. It was meant to count down the days until we could be together." Olive rubbed her fingertips over the cover in a pattern Clementine suddenly recognized as a habit. "I told him not to write to me, because I didn't want Father finding out about us." She stopped rubbing abruptly and dropped the book on the counterpane. "I told him not to write to me, Clemmie! If I hadn't done that, at least I'd have letters from him! But I never thought he would die! He went to a place called Fort Henry in Upper Canada, not off to Waterloo!"

"How did he die?" Clementine asked gently.

"I don't know. I haven't been able to find out. I only know he's dead to begin with because I overheard someone talking about it in a shop in Chiddington. The garrison there was supposed to help prevent another American invasion of Canada. There was no active fighting!" Her voice rose as she said, again, "I told him not to write to me!"

Clementine clambered across the bed and put her own hand on the book. She wanted to touch it, to show her sister that she understood now what she hadn't before. "Olive, you were a child. A girl. You were overwhelmed."

"I told him that while he was gone, I'd think of a way for us to marry. What was I going to do?" Olive's voice took on a brittle, almost sneering tone. "Suddenly grow brave and tell Father when I'd spent years *not* doing that? Ralph went to serve our country, and I couldn't tell a simple truth."

"But it *wasn't* a simple truth," Clementine said quietly, searching her sister's face. Olive wasn't looking at her; she only had eyes for her book. "It never is, for women. It may not have been life-and-death. I'm not making an analogy to joining a military campaign. But it *wasn't* simple. I think you ought to acknowledge that."

"I want to show you something else."

Clementine wasn't sure if her heart could take anymore, but she murmured her agreement.

Olive opened the next drawer down in the bedside table and pulled out the embroidery hoop she had taken pains to hide before. It depicted a gravestone. A large one, imposing gray against a late autumn forest.

Ralph Albert Scully
1801 – 1819
Son, soldier, beloved

This was what she had shown Lord Featherfinch that night.

"Is . . . Ralph lying to rest in Chiddington?" Clementine asked.

"I don't know."

"You could ask his mother." For that matter, Olive could ask Mrs. Scully about the circumstances of Ralph's death.

"But how would I do that?"

"Well, what do you say to her when you give her money?"

"Nothing. I send it to her anonymously."

Clementine had to swallow a gasp. She felt as though she were being cut down as surely as any soldier. How thoroughly she had misunderstood her sister, and for so long. For *years*. What a waste. But such a lament was not what Olive needed now. And more to the point, there was no sense in crying over wasted years. They had a lifetime ahead of them. She hoped. "You could look for the stone while you're there." There were only two cemeteries in the village.

Clementine regretted the suggestion immediately. Olive . . . Well, she crumpled.

Clementine felt terrible. Olive had *just* told Clementine she could not bear to be in Chiddington, and Clementine was suggesting she wander through its cemeteries in search of the grave of her lost love?

"No," Clementine said quietly but firmly. "I see that you can't do that. It was an ill-thought suggestion." Seeing her sister so upset, knowing she'd hidden such grief—and such love—for so long, continued to make her head spin. "What about the list?"

"You still think I was lying about that?"

"No! I was merely hoping it might provide some comfort in your grief, or at least some distraction. Though I admit it is somewhat difficult to reconcile all that you have told me, all that I've seen just now of how losing Ralph has shaped you, with that list."

Olive lifted one shoulder, and let it fall. The gesture seemed to return some of her former veneer to her, the face she showed the world. "If I can't have Ralph, I don't care who I marry."

"I'm not sure I follow. You don't care who you marry, yet you seem at least somewhat invested in the list."

"Well, life is short, is it not? But also long."

Clementine thought she understood. "You are biding your time."

"Yes. I will settle for someone, at some point, but I will try to wring as much as I can out of the doing. At least that is what I tell myself in London. I can distract myself there, with parties and dresses and such." She performed another shrug. "If you have to be in pain, you might as well be surrounded by pretty things and delicious food. If your spirit must suffer, why not coddle your body?"

Astonishing. And logical, in its way. Clementine rued all the days she'd spent thinking her sister shallow, when she was actually burying her pain in pretty things.

Olive shot Clementine a wry smile. "These revelations shouldn't raise your opinion of me too much, Sister. It isn't all performance. I *do* love a party—and a hair ribbon, and when a gentleman prostrates himself at my feet and proclaims his undying love." Clementine smiled as Olive sobered. "It only works in London, though."

Clementine wished there was something she could do to ease her sister's sorrow. "I wonder if there is a way you could return to Chiddington and see it as the site of all your good memories with Ralph, rather than a source of torment."

"No. Perhaps someday, but not yet. I know the dogs much prefer the country, and I feel guilty keeping them from it, but I can't bear it there. At Easter, I was miserable."

Clementine remembered that. She had thought at the time that Olive's antisocial behavior was snobbishness, that she was being petulant and self-absorbed. How gravely she had misunderstood.

Olive stood suddenly, briskly returning her needlework and book to their drawers. "You will go home, though, to Hill House. I will help you convince Father to allow it. I am very good at manipulating him."

"And you will stay in London?" Clementine asked, though she knew the answer. Knew there could be no other answer.

"Yes."

"I don't like the idea that our home is not the same." Especially now that she felt, for the first time in years, that she truly saw Olive, and that Olive truly saw her.

"I don't, either."

Clementine thought her heart might break. To have gained a sister, then lost her.

But then Olive slid her hand across the bed, the knotted cotton of the counterpane making for a bumpy journey. She grabbed Clementine's hand. "But we still have tonight."

"Yes!" Clementine leapt at the consolatory notion like it was an eligible bachelor and she a scheming miss.

"Clemmie, will you sleep with me tonight?" Olive pulled Clementine's hand to her mouth and kissed it. Clementine was a little startled by the request but also flattered. "After our time with the gentlemen, we can come back here and whisper into the night."

Clementine pulled their joined hands to her mouth and kissed Olive's knuckles. "Yes, I will sleep with you tonight." She would come back here with Olive and hold hands across the bed and whisper late into the night, even though that would mean giving up her last chance to be with Archie.

Gentlemen would come and go. Sisters were forever.

Now that she had Olive back, Lord help the mister who came between her and her sister.

Even if the mister was Archie.

* * *

Archie told himself he wasn't taking any of the lamb the cook had prepared for their final meal because he wanted to honor Hermes.

But then when he tried to actually articulate—in his mind; he would never have tried to do so out loud—the connection between Hermes and the dead lamb at the center of the table, he lost the plot.

Turtle freed . . . dead lamb . . . and then there was that bacon from the other day. Why had he not just spit it out rather than swallowed it in such a hurry?

And Clem in a tree.

And Clem shattering under his mouth.

He shook his head. It was all so confusing.

He spent the first few minutes of the meal doing as he had done last night, trying to hide from the boys that he wasn't eating any meat, trying to arrange things on his plate so they wouldn't notice, trying to take enough of the accompanying dishes to fill his belly. Trying, trying, trying. All in the name of subterfuge.

Bollocks! he thought.

And then he said it: "Bollocks!"

There was no reason to be hiding this from Simon and Effie. When you loved people, you told them the truth, or at least as much of the truth as was yours to tell.

"Are you quite all right?" Simon inquired in a maddeningly mild tone.

"I am *not* all right! I can't eat any lamb!"

Effie threw his head back and cackled.

"What are you laughing at?" Archie was affronted. You told the people you loved the truth, and they *laughed* at you? It wasn't as if he deluded himself into thinking the world was a just place, but wasn't the whole point of found families, of salt and strawberries and all that nonsense, that those people took you *seriously*?

"I *am* laughing at you," Effie said merrily. "I am laughing at how it is possible for someone to be so utterly un-self-aware. Were we not just talking, mere days ago, about how attuned you are to the emotional undercurrents of any situation?"

This coming from the man who'd been writing a sonnet and sitting in a house he'd had outfitted in mourning *for his parrot* while he had entirely forgotten Earls Trip 1821.

Archie huffed.

"Perhaps," Simon said placatingly, "you have been persuaded by Miss Morgan's arguments." He pursed his lips as if he too were laughing, but on the inside. "Or by Mr. Bull's, but for the sake of your reputation, let's just say you have been persuaded by Miss Morgan."

Archie nodded. *Yes. Let's just say.*

"So you cannot eat the lamb," Simon went on. "On the one hand, that is unfortunate, for the lamb"—he took a bite—"is delectable. But on the other, it is not the end of the world, is it? So you have joined Miss Morgan in her renunciation of meat."

"But what about hunting?" Even as Archie asked the question, the old sentiment, the thrill of the hunt, seemed very far away.

Effie tilted his head, looking intently at Archie, and Archie wasn't sure he didn't prefer being laughed at. "I hardly think you can hunt if you have given up eating meat."

"Well, you *could*," Simon said, "but it doesn't seem very morally consistent."

"Right," Archie said, nodding decisively. "I cannot." And that was . . . fine. Surprisingly so.

He thought back to Earls Trip 1818, the year of the hunting mishap. Archie had considered the ban that resulted from the near-miss a fair trade. Decided he would rather be the kind of man sought out by a friend who wanted urgently to tell him about his dreams than the sort of man who hunted.

He substituted Clementine for Effie in this mental exercise. Her tears when he shot that bird. The way she'd opened up to him later, explained how it affected her. It felt like *more* than a fair trade. It felt like . . . everything.

"Although," he posited, thinking ahead to the coming days and weeks, "perhaps all this will . . . wear off once Miss Morgan is back in London, and I am back at Mollybrook."

The thought was more than a little discomposing.

When Clementine arrived with Olive after dinner, he was stricken by a longing-in-advance. To watch her talking and smiling, and to know that tomorrow everything would be different. To know that the effect of her might indeed wear off. The bittersweet nature of it all was enough to make him maudlin.

He consoled himself that at least they had tonight. One more night.

The evening was tinged with melancholy, and Archie was fairly certain he wasn't the only one feeling it. They were chatting and laughing as usual, and everyone was recounting the moment when Hermes had overtaken the leader of the pack back at the race. But the evening was overlain with a kind of unspoken, anticipatory wistfulness.

Well, unspoken until Olive spoke it. "I don't want this holiday to end!"

The boys heartily agreed, and though it was coming on midnight, Effie proposed a game of whist, and everyone got up to move chairs and settle themselves in the new formation. Archie took drink orders. Clementine joined him at the sideboard. His heart thudded when she brushed close, and he spilled some of the ratafia he was pouring for Olive. And it sank when he registered what Clementine had whispered to him. "I am staying in Olive's room this evening, so I cannot come to you."

"What? Why?"

"Shh!" She looked around and, once content no one was paying them any mind, said, "She needs me."

She floated away, drink in hand as if she'd been visiting the sideboard for mere refreshment, rather than to crush Archie, to absolutely level him.

What an ignoble way for this extraordinary fortnight to end.

18

Girls Just Want to Have Fun

"That was not nearly as horrible as I was expecting," Olive whispered to Clementine. They were in the parlor in London, and Father was seeing Archie out. Their return had been anticlimactic—at least so far; Clementine had no doubt there was more to come. Archie's leave-taking had been anticlimactic, too. Archie had merely bowed to Clementine—and to Olive, as if Olive and Clementine were interchangeable in his estimation—and taken his leave as if it were an ordinary day. As if they were ordinary friends.

Which, she supposed, they were.

He had given no indication, on the journey from Cumbria, that he thought of her as anything else. Of course, he could not have done otherwise. They'd all been on top of each other, both in the coach and in the inns they stayed in along the way. But Archie's indifference, which had been so dismayingly convincing, left her wondering: Had all that occurred between them been a mere fever dream?

"All in all," Olive continued, "it could have been much worse."

"Oh, it will get worse," Clementine said. "Mark my words."

"You think so?"

"Once we are alone, yes." Clementine leaned forward to try to see her way out into the foyer where Archie and Father were still talking in low tones.

"Hmm," Olive said. "I wouldn't have thought Father would censor himself around Archie, given all that Archie has done for us, but I suppose you are correct."

"I am correct." Clementine gave up her attempt at eavesdropping and slumped back on the settee. "Alas."

Indeed, she was proven so not a minute later when Father reappeared, the graciousness and gratitude he had directed at Archie no longer in evidence. She braced herself as he sat across from them. She started to take Olive's hand but stopped. They'd been holding hands so much lately, but was that another thing that was now only a fever dream? That last night at Quintrell Castle, when she'd given up Archie in favor of lying in Olive's bed, holding her hand, and listening to her talk about Ralph—what was going to happen to all that had been said that night? Would it change things permanently between the sisters, or would they slip back into their old ways, pretending Olive's confessions had not occurred?

When Father did not speak, when he merely pondered them—and not even grumpily—Clementine entertained the notion that perhaps she had been wrong. Perhaps the drama of Clementine's botched engagement and Olive's botched elopement had finally made Father see. He *had* embraced both girls—one arm for each—in an uncharacteristically sentimental display the moment they arrived. Perhaps that meant something. Perhaps things *were* going to change.

Clementine had been plotting how to roll out her plan, but she decided it was better to merely ask. To strike while the iron was hot, so to speak, and not dissemble. "Father, I should like to go to Hill House, spend some time there." When he didn't say anything, and in the name of not dissembling, she added, "A great deal of time. In fact, I should like to retire there."

He regarded her for a beat, his face unchanged, before he

said, "No. I forbid it." He spoke with a calmness that unnerved Clementine. The anger she had expected had not materialized. He was just . . . blank.

"You shall both be under my thumb," he said with more of that unnerving equanimity. "You shall be here in the house at all times, unless I am with you. You shan't go out without me. Not with each other, not with a maid, not with any chaperone other than me. I shan't let you out of my sight until I give you to your future husbands in front of the vicar. You, Clementine, may return to Chiddington for your wedding and not a day before."

Stunned, Clementine considered voicing a challenge. Not so much to the content of what Father had said—not to the confinement he was imposing—but to the idea that her future would contain a wedding. She tried to reach back for some of the certainty she'd felt at Quintrell Castle, and even before that, on her flight after Olive and Theo. She had been so resolved, possessed of a quiet but firmly entrenched confidence that she would finally have it out with Father on the topic of matrimony, that she would *make* him see.

She was so tired. The journey had been long. Her body was sore. Her heart was sore.

"Wash up," Father stood, and he was speaking in that same unnervingly flat tone. "Confer with Mrs. Henning about this evening's menu, for Lord Harcourt and his friends are returning to dine with us."

"They *are?*" Olive exclaimed, and Clementine wanted to cry. The excitement in Olive's tone was unwarranted. This would not be a dinner like any they'd had this past fortnight. It was to be merely a performance: of Father thanking Archie, and of Father shutting the door on Clementine's cage. She consoled herself that at least she now knew about Olive's motives in accumulating pin money. If Clementine had no other reason to live, at least she could help Olive in that quest.

"Yes, before they all scatter to the winds, I must thank them."

Father pursed his lips, confirming Clementine's previous assessment. "For averting your ruination, Olive." He turned to Clementine. "And yours."

The last thing Archie wanted to do was to dine with the Morgans, but he hadn't been able to see his way through to declining Sir Albert's invitation.

Well, he wanted to dine with one Morgan. Or perhaps two. He *was* fond of Olive.

Or perhaps even three, for he was . . . well, he wasn't sure if he was fond of Sir Albert, but he did respect him.

Didn't he?

Sir Albert *was* Father's oldest friend.

He thought back to Mother's games with the chairs. Sir Albert had been quite the enthusiastic player, if Archie recalled correctly.

All right, he was overthinking. What was this but a convivial dinner with the Morgans, and Effie and Simon?

It was not convivial.

The conversation before dinner was tense, and dinner itself was no less so. He watched Clementine, and he wasn't sure if it was because she had just gotten home and had had no jurisdiction over the meal in the way she had previously described to him, but there was very little for her to eat. She picked at a few potatoes, and he watched Olive surreptitiously spear a slice of beef from Clementine's plate that Clementine had not managed to turn down.

It was all very excruciating, and he thought it would never end.

He was shocked to life, though, when Simon said, "I thought I might pay a visit to Vauxhall Gardens tomorrow evening. Will any of you join me?"

Simon wanted to go to Vauxhall Gardens? Had the world turned upside down?

"No, I am for Highworth first thing tomorrow," Effie said, confirming Archie's thesis that the world *had* turned upside down. Effie's refined tastes and his love of art had historically made him a devoted city dweller, though come to think of it, he had spent an awful lot of time at his family's estate in Cornwall this past year. Still, Effie had never been one to eschew the fantastical fancies of Vauxhall.

"I am expecting a very important letter at Highworth," Effie added defensively, almost haughtily. His tone did not go unnoticed by Simon, who turned a raised eyebrow to Archie. Perhaps Effie's uncharacteristic geographic preferences of late had to do with his long-lost love. Archie so wished he could press him about that, but he had decided not to. He hadn't been meant to hear that, and all he could only hope was that someday Effie would confide in him.

All he could do in the meantime was be Effie's friend, his brother by all but blood. Be the salt to his lamb or . . . what have you. Hope that time, and loyalty, would yield the dividends that needed yielding.

He had been woolgathering long enough. "I'd been planning to return with Mother to Mollybrook in the morning, but Vauxhall sounds like a pleasant way to spend an evening, so perhaps we shall delay our departure a day."

"Will Miss Brown join you?" Simon asked.

"Perhaps," Archie said, wondering what it was to Simon. "If Mother wants to, and is in a state to go." He turned to the Morgans. "Will you join us? May I collect you in my carriage?"

"Oh Father, yes, let's!" Olive exclaimed.

"The last thing I want to do is drag these old aching bones through Vauxhall," Sir Albert said.

"Mrs. Abernathy can chaperone," Olive said, and to Archie she explained, "Mrs. Abernathy lives two houses down and was a dear friend of Mother's. She often accompanies us to events when Father is indisposed."

It was amusing—sadly amusing—to think that after all that had passed these recent weeks, the Morgan sisters needed a chaperone to be seen in public with Archie and his friends. This was the world that so chafed Clementine, and he couldn't blame her.

"Of course you may not go, Olive," Sir Albert said matter-of-factly.

"But, Father!" Clementine laid a hand on Olive's arm and sent her a quelling look.

"They're not to go outside at all," Sir Albert said.

"I beg your pardon?" Archie asked.

"After the near-misses of the past fortnight, my daughters will remain at home unless they are going somewhere with me, somewhere I deem worthy of our time."

Archie couldn't have heard that right. "What about the park?" The park was not the forest, but it was better than nothing.

"The park is not worthy of our time." Sir Albert paused with a bite of roast beef halfway to his mouth, and appearing to reconsider, added, "Unless, of course, one of the girls is invited to promenade by an eligible gentleman." He smiled, as if pleased by the notion he'd conjured. The beef resumed its journey, and as Sir Albert chomped down on it with more gusto than necessary, Archie didn't miss Clementine's wince.

"Sir Albert." Archie paused, gathering his thoughts. He needed to proceed delicately. "With all due respect, I must object. That is no way for . . ."

Clementine to live.

". . . anyone to live. What you are describing sounds akin to incarceration."

"It isn't akin to incarceration," Sir Albert said mildly. "It *is* incarceration."

Well. Archie cleared his throat, buying time, trying to think how to proceed. "Surely we can chalk up recent events to a surfeit of youthful indiscretion. Mr. Bull is no longer on English soil; everyone's reputations remain unblemished."

"My boy, what exactly are you arguing for here?"

"I . . ." He wasn't sure. He didn't have the right to argue at all, did he?

"The last thing I would wish is for you to think me ungrateful. You and your friends"—Sir Albert gestured toward Simon and

Effie—"have gone to extraordinary lengths to help my family. But it's my family, and I must do as I see fit. I have grown too permissive, and—"

"No." Archie surprised himself by pushing back his chair and standing. The act shocked Sir Albert into silence, a silence that Archie filled. "Perhaps I haven't any jurisdiction here, at least not of the legal sort, but I believe I do have a sort of moral jurisdiction. Miss Morgan is my friend. You can't lock her up as if she were a common criminal with no allowance made for her wishes!" His voice had taken on a wild tone, and he paused to clear his throat. "And Miss Olive, too," he added, regretting his initial omission of Olive.

He didn't know what to say next. Debating wasn't fraught for him in the same way reading was, but it was still far from his natural milieu. He had probably gone too far, but he couldn't find it in himself to care. He blundered on.

"Clementine needs access to . . ." He'd been going to say *Clementine needs access to the wilds. She needs to be free.* But he would be better off reframing his argument. And of course he had erred by using her Christian name. "Miss Morgan needs access to fresh air. As does Miss Olive. All young ladies do. Fresh air is beneficial to the constitution."

His delivery was as weak as his argument. It was difficult to explain in a way that would not expose him as having too much knowledge of Clementine.

What Sir Albert failed to understand, what seemingly everyone failed to understand, was that Clementine's aversion to marriage was just that—an aversion. It was not a mere disinclination that would wear off with time and persistence. It was—

"My daughters will thank me later," Sir Albert said, looking up at the still-standing Archie. A hint of pique had come into the older man's tone, a contrast from all the smooth gratitude he had previously expressed. "When they are mothers, when they have their own children, they will understand."

When they are mothers.

Clem wasn't going to be a mother. Archie seemed to be the only person in the world who understood that. His fanciful image of Clementine setting out on a ramble with her children, was just that: a fancy. His mind had invented a pretty picture of her hopping over a stile and turning around to help a child, a child lucky enough to be hers, make the descent. It was hard to let go of that vision, though he wasn't sure why, because he had heard Clem's thoughts on the matter, and he respected them. He was—

He gasped, as it hit him. "Oh, dear God."

Why hadn't he seen this before? It was one thing to be less than clever, but he wasn't completely daft. Or so he liked to think.

"Is everything all right, Lord Harcourt?"

That was from Olive, who was regarding him with concern. Everyone was regarding him with concern, suddenly.

There had been a man in these imaginings, a vague outline of a husband, a father. The man lifting Clementine's child over the stile, handing him to her. The man listening to Clementine tell the story of the hunter made of stars who never caught up with the bear. The man carrying sleepy, dirt-mussed children upstairs to the nursery and smiling as their sticky fingers patted his face.

The man in his imaginings was him.

Or it could be. Those children could be his.

Could he . . . have that?

He fell into his chair with a thud.

"*Archie*," Clementine said, a low urgency apparent in her tone. "What's the matter?"

What's the matter is that I'm in love with you.

He couldn't speak. He was looking at Clem, dear Clem whom *he loved*, but she was growing fuzzy around the edges. She was not the kind of lady who swooned, she'd said, but apparently he was the sort of gentleman who did.

This was why he had been so intent on taking her hunting with him, on getting her to understand what it meant to him. He had wanted her to love the thing he loved because hc loved *her*.

And conversely, this was why it had been so easy, in the end, for him to give up hunting, for him to give up the eating of meat—both of which he realized were already done.

He loved her. He laughed out loud.

Why had he not realized it? All he could come up with was that he hadn't allowed the possibility to penetrate his mind, given how continually and vociferously she went around objecting to marriage.

"Are you all right?" Clem pressed.

"I'm fine," he managed, shaking his head to clear it. The edges of her face sharpened. "In fact, I am excellent. I am—"

No. That wasn't right. He wasn't excellent. He'd had a revelation, but he had been wrong about what it meant. The image he had, of what his life could be, was lovely. It was exquisite, almost painful, in its perfection. But the fact remained that Clementine did not want to wed. She *did* continually and vociferously object to the institution of marriage.

He needed to talk to the boys. He stood again, the astonished faces of all assembled telling him that he was behaving very erratically indeed. "I just remembered." He looked daggers at Simon, willing him to understand. "We were meant to be at that parliamentary . . . thing this evening."

"That parliamentary *thing*?" Simon echoed, bewildered.

"Yes, of course," Effie said. "That committee or what have you. You talked about it all morning."

"Yes." Archie turned to their host and deliberately did not look at Clem. He couldn't. He needed to sort himself out first. "Sir Albert, I was so pleased to be invited to join you this evening that I quite forgot my responsibilities."

Simon jumped in to embellish the clumsy lie, and they managed to extricate themselves. Inelegantly, but it hardly mattered. As Sir Albert had said many times today, he was in their debt. Clementine and Olive would rightly sniff out "parliamentary responsibilities" as the lie it was, but Archie couldn't care right now.

"I'm not sure when we'll see you again, my boy," Sir Albert said, and Archie wished Sir Albert wouldn't call him that. It reminded him of the way Father sometimes used to affect a kind of exaggerated jocularity that made Archie feel bad for reasons he couldn't articulate. "You'll return to Mollybrook, and we're here in Town for the foreseeable future."

Archie wanted to say that he would postpone his return to Mollybrook if need be. As much as he hated London, it was where Clementine—*whom he loved*—was stuck, therefore he felt he ought to endure the incarceration with her. But . . . how would he go about doing that? Would she even want him to? And what about Mother?

He needed to talk to the boys. That was what he kept coming back to. That was step one, and they'd help him sort the rest.

"I believe I am in love with Clementine," he blurted once the three of them were back in his carriage.

"Of course you are," Effie said.

Simon, for his part, merely laughed.

"Well, thank you very much," Archie said.

"I'm sorry. We are being too glib," Effie said, trying, Archie thought, to be soothing, but mucking it up by joining in Simon's laughter.

"What am I going to do?" Archie all but wailed.

"Archie," said Effie with sudden seriousness. "Do you remember our recent discussion when you came to us musing about taking your parliamentary role more seriously?"

"Well, it was less a discussion and more a monologue," Simon, still snickering, interjected before Archie could answer.

"I remember," Archie said warily.

"What did you say to us?"

He searched his mind. "I think I said I was ordinary."

"You are an earl, man!" Simon objected.

"Yes, but I didn't do anything to earn that title, or the benefits that come with it."

"I, for one, believe you are anything but ordinary," Effie said, "and I would believe that no matter your title or lack thereof. As previously discussed, you are among my favorite people on this earth."

"So it is proximity to you that makes me not ordinary." Archie smirked. If they were going to mock him, he was going to dish it back.

"No," Effie said, "it is, also as previously discussed, your astonishing capacity for love and loyalty that makes you extraordinary."

Archie felt his face heat.

"You were moaning about how you didn't do anything of use," Effie went on, "and we corrected you, establishing that you find people, and you love them. And if there's anyone in this world who could use some of that love right now, it's those Morgan girls."

"I think what Archie is saying," Simon said wryly to Effie, "is that his feelings for Clementine Morgan are quite a bit different from his feelings for Olive Morgan."

"I know that, you dolt." Effie turned to Archie, who was still bewildered—by this conversation and by his recent realization. "My point is merely that this is not the catastrophe you seem to think, Archie. In fact, what we have here is a situation where your exact skills are called for."

"I . . . What am I going to do?" The question came out quietly this time, rather than wailingly, but he was no closer to answering it. *Having* a realization was one thing, knowing what, if anything, to do about it was quite another.

Effie raised his eyebrows. "Well, you'll have to talk to her, I'd imagine."

"I don't suppose you'd write to her for me?"

"Oh, for Heaven's sake." Effie threw up his hands.

"I am in jest, Effie." Archie was trying to lighten the mood, to give himself—all of them—a respite from the weight of revelation, a breath between unanswerable questions. "Even I know such a declaration must be original."

"What sort of declaration are we speaking of?" Simon asked.

"What sort do you think, Simon?" Effie said irritably, swatting

Simon's shoulder. "Honestly, have you been paying attention at all?"

Simon deflected Effie's continued swatting. "Yes, of course I have. I just want to hear him say it. I want to make sure *he* has been paying attention."

"We are speaking of a declaration of love," Archie said quietly, "and not the fraternal kind we've been talking about this past fortnight. *Love*." As the carriage rumbled to a halt in front of his house, a kind of muted but righteous certainty began flowing through his veins. He was sure about this path, but also terrified. "What if she doesn't feel the same?" He paused as the answer to his own question rose in his mind. "I can't control that, can I? All I can do is tell her how I feel and try not to make a muddle of it. I've got to leave the rest to her. Her answer will be her answer, but to get it, I must first ask the question."

"There's a good man," Simon said, at the same time that Effie said, "See? You're very good at this sort of thing."

"The problem is *how?*" The certainty Archie had felt a moment ago was starting to fray at the edges. "I'm liable to make a hash of such a declaration at the best of times, and this is not the best of times. And I feel as if the declaration requires a certain degree of panache. I wish Sir Albert would allow the girls to travel to Hill House, where I might have some hope of speaking to Clementine outside, where we can both breathe." He was going to have to approach her in London, on account of her imprisonment, and thinking about trying to talk to Clem, to really *talk* to her, in that small, closed drawing room, made his breath go shallow.

"What am I going to *do?*" There was no more certainty now; it had been crowded out by panic. "Show up in Sir Albert's drawing room and make a stumbling speech in front of both Clementine and him? I suppose the logical answer is to ask his permission first in order to secure a few minutes alone with Clem, but I can't do *that*, because he is certain to give it."

"And that would be bad because . . . ?" Simon asked, his brow knit.

"Because if Clementine doesn't want me, then I'll have effectively forced her hand. It would be as good as abducting her!"

"I think it highly unlikely that Miss Morgan won't want you," Effie said.

"She doesn't want to get married!" He should have led with that. "She has said as much, frequently and forcefully."

She had suggested an illicit arrangement, one he'd rejected out of hand, but if that was all he could get, he would take it. But how was he to secure that type of arrangement if he couldn't speak to her alone? How were they meant to . . . execute that type of arrangement?

Was he ever going to see her again outside the watchful eye of her father?

He let loose a very unmanly whimper and bonked his head back against the squabs.

"Poor Archie." Effie patted his arm. "What a trying evening you've had. I almost want to write a poem about your doomed love."

"It isn't doomed," Simon said firmly.

"Quite right. Perhaps we should call it a love at the edge of doom," Effie said with a flourish. "A love flirting with doom."

"You needn't solve it forthwith," Simon said. "Take your mother home. Get her situated with Miss Brown, and come back to Town. When you're back, we can invite Sir Albert and his daughters somewhere he can't reasonably refuse to attend, and come up with some kind of distraction that will allow you to speak to Miss Morgan alone." He turned to Effie. "Can your very important letter at Highworth wait? A journey there and back would take so long I fear Archie might expire in the interim."

Effie nodded. "I daresay things are about to take a turn for the dramatic here, and I shouldn't want to miss that."

Archie sighed. A turn for the dramatic sounded like a terrible idea to him. But what choice did he have? "All right. I'll go home tomorrow, settle Mother, and aim to be back by the end of next week."

"All right, then," Simon said. "For now, let us part ways. Having been on holiday, I have mountains of work to attend to."

"And I am going to work on an epic poem to be read at your wedding to Miss Morgan," Effie said.

"She's not going to—"

Effie talked right over Archie. "And as for this nonsense about being ordinary, I can think of many ways to be *extra*ordinary, but none so much as to marry a vegetarian."

That night, in bed, Clementine was reading—well, no, she was brooding whilst holding a book—when Olive appeared. She crossed the room silently, pulled back the covers, and settled herself next to Clementine as if this was something they did.

Perhaps it was. They'd shared a bed of necessity in the posting inns on the way home from Cumbria, but they'd also shared one at Olive's request that last night at Quintrell Castle.

The night Clementine had given up Archie in favor of Olive.

She would do it again, but not seeing Archie that night, together with the odd way he'd left them in the middle of dinner earlier, had her fretting.

"Did you think it odd that Archie suddenly had parliamentary responsibilities this evening?" Clementine asked Olive. "Responsibilities so apparently urgent that he had to leave that very moment?"

Olive waved a hand dismissively. "Oh, that was surely a lie."

"It was?"

Of course it was. Clementine just wanted it . . . not to be.

"Yes. He couldn't get out of here hastily enough."

"That's . . ." Devastating.

"He was very stiff, didn't you find?" Olive asked, stealing one of the pillows propping up Clementine and punching it into her preferred shape. "Not at all his usual easygoing self."

That was certainly true. He had been awkward, and at times, downright agitated. "He couldn't even look at me when he left."

"Yes. I noticed that." The punching continued. If Olive was so particular about her pillows, Clementine didn't know why she hadn't brought her own. "He avoided you much of the evening, in fact, and when he finally took his leave, he bowed over my hand and smiled very prettily at me, whereas with you he was standoffish and looked at the floor."

Well. Clementine felt positively deflated. She hadn't thought her entanglement with Archie would end like this. If anything, given the ardency of their encounters those last few days in Cumbria, she'd have thought they might have trouble saying goodbye. She'd never imagined a scenario in which her old friend couldn't even stand to look at her.

"I've come to plot." Olive stole another pillow—or tried to. Clementine grabbed one end in an attempt to prevent its abduction.

"To plot?" she echoed as she stood her ground with the pillow.

"Yes." Olive stood hers, so they were apparently having a tug-of-war. "I've rethought my aversion to Hill House. We must make Father take us. We need to spend a good long stretch there, the both of us."

Clementine was so shocked she let go of the pillow. "What? Why?" Why was everything so *confusing*?

"Yes." Olive smirked and began punching pillow number two. "I will admit that the prospect of repairing to the country is terrifying. But is it going to be any less so next week? Next month? Now that I've told you my sordid secrets, it feels as if they have a less firm hold on me. I think I should like to look for Ralph's grave. Well, not *like*. That's the wrong word entirely. But I think I ought to." She finished her pillow arranging and leveled a plaintive look at Clementine. "Will you help me?"

"Oh, Olive, of course."

"But that's not the main reason we've got to go."

"What's the main reason?" Clementine started to reach for one of her pillows back.

Olive swatted her hands away. "The main reason is Archie, silly. You've got to tell Archie you're in love with him."

"It doesn't matter if I'm in love with Archie, because we're never going to marry," Clementine said unthinkingly.

"I notice you didn't dispute the fact of the matter."

"I . . ." Clementine *hadn't* noticed that. Oh. Oh *dear*.

She burst into tears.

How mortifying. That was supposed to be *Olive's* signature maneuver.

"Oh, Clemmie." Olive tugged one of Clementine's hands into her own. "It's going to be all right."

"I'm not in love with Archie," Clementine tried. "I'm just confused." She ordered herself to stop crying.

"We need to get the two of you together in one place, and I definitely think that place should be Mollybrook or Hill House, or more specifically, *outside* Mollybrook or Hill House."

"It's been a very trying few weeks, and my mind is muddled."

"I've hatched a plan. I shall pretend an interest in a gentleman in Chiddington," Olive said. "If Father thinks I'm genuine, he will allow us to remove to Hill House. The question is, who?"

"And we were observing country rules at Quintrell Castle," Clementine said. "Things were exceedingly relaxed. So if I gave you the impression that——"

"The question is, who?" Olive repeated. "Help me think of someone plausible. He must be——"

"Are you even listening to me, Olive?"

"No, I am not, because you're speaking nonsense."

"I am not in love with Archie?"

"Is that a question?"

"No."

"Say it as if you mean it, then."

"I am not in love with Archie?" Dash it. That second attempt hadn't come out sounding any different from the first.

"Do you want to go to Hill House or not, Clemmie?" Olive

huffed a frustrated sigh, but she handed back one of the pillows. "Here."

"I do want to go." She did, regardless of this whole accidentally falling in love with Archie business.

"Then help me think of someone I can pretend to fancy!"

Watching Olive manipulate Father now that Clementine knew what was going on beneath the surface was amusing. It provided a temporary respite from the reeling of her fevered mind.

In love! With Archie!

She still was not sure how that had happened.

Well, no, that was not true. It was, she supposed, the natural outcome of spending time with someone so kind and handsome. Someone who listened to her and respected her. Someone who *saw* her.

What she didn't know was *when* it had happened. In novels, heroines were often struck by love as if it were lightning. Love seemed to be something that happened to one, suddenly and sometimes violently. It was never a thing that was just . . . there. There quietly but so decidedly that one wondered if it always had been.

And in novels, the heroines always *knew* when they'd fallen in love. They did not require a sister to point it out.

"So you see, Father," Olive said as she poured tea, "it isn't only Clementine who wants to go to Hill House." She leaned in as she handed him his cup and said, *sotto voce*, "I realize she is the elder and, let's be frank, the more desperate case." She turned to Clementine. "Now, Clemmie, don't make that face. Don't object, for you know it is true." Contrary to her words, Olive seemed to be telegraphing a silent message to Clementine that she *should* make "that" face, that she *should* object, and so on.

"I say," Clementine tried, attempting to play her assigned role. She was, after all, a mere puppet in the presence of a master. "That was rather hurtful, Olive."

"I know, Clemmie, but we must face facts, mustn't we? The

stink of the broken engagement, even though it will be accepted that you're the one who cried off, will take a while to fade." She turned back to Father. "However, if *I* were to wed first, that would only help Clementine's cause, do you not agree?"

"Hmm." Father took a sip of his tea. "Tell me this chap's name again?"

"Mr. Ozymandias Macduff," Olive said with a smoothness and confidence that Clementine would never have been able to muster given that Mr. Ozymandias Macduff was entirely fictitious. After going through the eligible gentlemen of their acquaintance last night, the sisters had decided to invent a suitor for Olive. The only flesh-and-blood men in Chiddington who were of a suitable age and situation to seem credible were sufficiently known to Father that the sisters couldn't be certain their ruse wouldn't end in an actual engagement. And Olive had had quite enough actual engagements of late.

Hence was born Ozymandias Macduff, Ozymandias after the eponymous poem by Shelley that apparently Olive was fond of thanks to Lord Featherfinch's having introduced her to it, and Macduff because inventing a Scotsman brought to mind Macbeth, and as Olive pointed out, *"Macduff is one of the few left standing at the end, and he gets to brandish Macbeth's severed head. I imagine marrying someone like that would at the very least be not-dull."*

The name made Clementine want to giggle. She forced herself to remain implacable as she said, "Apparently Mr. Macduff inherited that big old house near Croftly Lane."

"I thought that house belonged to an absent duke. Which one?" Father sipped his tea and stared out the window as if the missing duke was due to appear. "Devonshire? No."

"I think that's a myth," Olive said. "You know how the house has taken on an almost legendary status."

That part was true. There was a great old abandoned house not too far outside Chiddington, and it was the source of much fascination and speculation. Clementine thought the rumor about it belonging to a duke was entirely plausible. If anyone was going to lose track of an entire house, it would be a duke. But for their purposes, the mystery house belonged to one Mr. Macduff. It was even surrounded by a rusting iron fence with spikes that would do nicely for displaying the severed heads of one's enemies.

"Lord Harcourt told us he heard that Mr. Macduff is from a landed family near Glasgow," Olive said, daintily stirring sugar into her tea.

"Why hasn't anyone been to claim the house in generations?" Father asked.

"I can't imagine," Olive said. "But I'm sure I would like to find out."

The sisters had, in fact, invented an entire backstory for Mr. Macduff, but they'd agreed not to trot it out unless they absolutely had to. It would be better for Mr. Macduff to remain a vague figure. That way, when he disappeared again, it wouldn't seem too suspicious. All they had to do was get Archie to corroborate the rumor they were claiming he'd heard.

"And"—Olive lowered her voice—"I have heard it told that Mr. Macduff is descended from Robert the Bruce." One final stir of her tea and she lifted her cup and sipped, triumphant.

Clementine coughed to cover a laugh. They had not discussed that embellishment.

"Autumn at Hill House *is* pleasant," Father said, "and I suppose we could all do with a bit of country air."

Olive squealed and jumped up and embraced Father, who looked almost his old self as he patted her shoulder fondly.

"I don't suppose there is anyone there for your sister," Father said, "if we all put our minds to it?"

Olive winked at Clementine over Father's shoulder. Whatever else happened, how lovely it was to be in cahoots with Olive. "Oh, no," Olive said breezily. "Clementine is a lost cause until next Season. You may as well let her loose in the woods when we get there. The outdoors always has a restorative effect on her. Then we can regroup on that front next Season. And when I am a respectable married lady, I can sponsor her."

Father grumbled something that sounded like assent, and Clementine's heart soared. Not because of Archie, but because she was going home. Well, all right. Perhaps a little because of Archie. Perhaps a lot because of Archie.

She resolved to think on it all later, when she was let loose in the woods as Olive had said.

"Now, Father," Olive said briskly as she pulled away and sat back down next to Clementine. "I have almost everything I need in my quest for Mr. Macduff, but I badly damaged my most fashionable hat in the midst of all the . . . unpleasantness of late."

"Did I not give you funds for the milliner not a month ago?"

"You did, but this hat had the most *remarkable* bird sewn on it, and I don't know what's happened to it. It's simply *gone*." Olive kicked Clementine under the table, and Clementine finally lost the battle with the laughter that had been threatening. No one noticed, though, as Olive kept talking. "It was my *favorite* hat, and I can't *begin* to tell you how many compliments I received because of it." Olive's voice had risen several octaves, and begun wavering, too. "I suppose I must count it as part of the wreckage of this unfortunate business with Mr. Bull." She suddenly gasped, and Clementine was startled even though she understood this was all pretense. "Oh! I've just had the most marvelous idea! What if I were to commission one just like it, but ensure that the bird perched on it is *native to Scotland*? La, that would give me something to converse with Mr. Macduff about, would it not?"

"I must admit that's a clever idea." Father got up and went to his desk, and after rummaging around, came back with a handful of coins for Olive, who practically had a fit of the vapors as she expressed her thanks.

"Now, now, there's a good girl," Father said, peeling Olive off him.

"Clementine must come with me to see the milliner," Olive declared, once she'd "recovered." "She knows all kinds of things about birds and the like and can help me explain my vision."

"Yes, quite," said Father. "I shall leave you girls to make the arrangements for our journey." Father had a tendency to remove himself abruptly after an outburst of emotion from Olive, but since they were in his study, he was, effectively, dismissing them.

With a final flurry of effusive thanks from Olive, the girls found themselves in the corridor. Olive sniffed, smoothed her hair, raised her eyebrows at Clementine, and made a show of pocketing the money she'd extorted from Father.

Clementine raised her eyebrows back and clapped her hands in a silent gesture of applause.

They didn't speak until they were safely around the corner. The laughter came then, from both of them.

"That was impressive," Clementine said.

Olive shrugged with false modesty. "Now we're off to Hill House, and you can speak to Archie."

"I don't know about that part. I don't think there's anything to say. But I do appreciate your having sprung us from Town."

"There is plenty to say, Clemmie. And you're going to have to go first, because he won't. He's too upstanding for that."

"What do you mean?" She was bewildered.

"He's only heard you say a thousand times that you refuse to marry, that marriage would kill your soul or some such nonsense. Archie isn't the man to kill anyone's soul, least of all yours. So you shall have to start the conversation. You must tell him what is in your heart."

"Why would I do that? Assuming there is anything in my heart"—there was, but she wasn't ready to admit it, even to Olive—"what does it matter if there isn't anything in his?"

"Do you remember our evening conversations at Quintrell Castle?" Olive said as she mounted the stairs.

"Of course," Clementine said, following, as confused as ever.

"One night we were talking about Archie, and you said he was a pacifist."

"Yes," Clementine said, struggling to see Olive's point.

They had come to Olive's room. Olive put her hand on the latch and said, "Lords Marsden and Featherfinch disagreed with your characterization. They said Archie could be quite combative when defending the people he loves."

"Yes. It was gratifying to think of him sticking up for his friends so loyally back when they were children. That's Archie for you, though, isn't it? I still fail to understand what you're on about with him not wanting to kill my soul?"

Olive sighed theatrically. "Clementine. Think back to dinner last night. Before Archie was lying his way out of our house, before he was not looking at you, what was he doing?"

"I . . . don't know."

"He was *defending* you."

Clementine gasped. "No!"

"Yes! He was defending you, and quite forcefully, too. He kept making these impassioned speeches in support of you, and as they wound down, he'd append my name to them, as if he'd only just remembered his logic ought to apply to me, too."

Clementine's skin felt tight, as if she'd fallen asleep in the sun and awakened to find it burnt. She had to force herself to mind Olive, who was still talking.

"Now, Clemmie, I'm going to work on my embroidery for a while, but I'm coming to your room to sleep tonight, for once we're at Hill House, I suppose I must give up having you as a bedfellow." Olive waggled her eyebrows at Clementine and shut the door in her face.

Clementine was left standing in the hallway gaping like the poor sun-addled creature that she was.

People that he loves.

Could she possibly be so lucky?

Could she possibly be so brave?

19

The End

Four days later, Clementine called at Mollybrook, hoping having come alone wouldn't cause a stir. She could have brought a maid, but she had a mission, and she trusted that the friendship the two families used to enjoy would make her solo visit unremarkable.

"Miss Morgan, hello!" Miss Brown swept into the sitting room Clementine had been installed in and greeted her warmly, dipping a curtsy and smiling widely. "How wonderful to see you! I daresay it has been years. Is your family at Hill House for a while now?"

"Yes, I think so. I hope so. I was—"

She was coming to declare her love to Archie. But she could hardly say that. She hadn't thought this through. She'd spent the last several days of planning and packing and traveling focused only on moving her body through space. Toward Archie.

She tried again. "I was hoping to pay the dowager countess a visit." Archie aside, she found it was not untrue. She had fond memories of the countess, and it had been too long. She was ashamed, in fact, at how much the family had been suffering without her knowledge.

"That is very kind of you. I would be happy to take you to her. I wonder, though, if you are aware that she is not herself these days."

"I . . . have heard something of that," Clementine said carefully.

"Perhaps my wanting to see her is ill-advised." Perhaps it was selfish. Would her presence confuse the older woman? Upset her?

"Not at all. She enjoys visitors, for the most part. I merely wanted to prepare you for the fact that she will not recognize you. She doesn't recognize anyone these days, not even her son."

Clementine, of course, could not tell Miss Brown that she knew that. The knowing didn't matter anyway; it didn't make the hearing any less sad. "I understand."

And so she was ushered through the house and into the garden. Lady Harcourt was seated at a small wrought iron table beneath the wide green canopy of a majestic beech. Clementine remembered this tree. Although she and Archie had spent more time in the wilds around Mollybrook than in its manicured gardens, she had nevertheless passed many an afternoon perched in this tree's branches. And she remembered Lady Harcourt under this tree: this was where she had generally set up her lawn games.

"My lady, you have a visitor," Miss Brown called as they approached.

The older woman turned in her chair, and in so doing, revealed her son, who had been seated across from her.

He gasped, and lurched to his feet.

Oh, Archie. Archie. She wanted to tell him to sit. That it was just her. That she was here. That she was home.

She loved him so very much. It was fantastical to think that mere days ago she had been protesting to her sister that she didn't.

They were insects in amber again, staring at each other across the expanse of lawn. She watched surprise give way to something else, something like delight, but darker. He smiled, but there was something else yet again there, a kind of knowing that was new, that was—

"Well, Clementine Morgan, as I live and breathe!" Archie's mother exclaimed.

Archie gasped again, but he wasn't alone this time. So did Miss Brown. So, albeit on a bit of a delay, did Clementine. The shock of being recognized by Archie's mother shattered her amber trance.

"Yes," she said carefully, giving her attention to the old woman, who looked so much like Archie—Clementine hadn't noticed when they were all younger, but she had Archie's kind, multicolored eyes. "My lady." Clementine dipped into a curtsy.

"Oh, none of that, my girl. You think you and my son can steal all the tarts from my kitchen one day and come in here the next with your curtsies and your *my ladys* and be forgiven?"

Clementine had no idea what to say. There had been a day, when Clementine was about eleven, when she and Archie had stumbled upon an empty kitchen featuring half a dozen lemon tarts left to cool, and . . .

Well, why not try for the truth?

"Your cook remains legend in my mind, my lady. I know I ought to rue my actions that day, but if I am truthful, I find I cannot."

To her shock, Lady Harcourt laughed and gestured for her to sit. Clementine glanced at the still-standing Archie, for the chair she was being directed to had been his a moment ago. He gestured animatedly for her to sit, and retreated to stand a few feet away, next to the tree trunk. Clementine surmised that he wanted her to continue conversing with his mother, to try to extend this rare stretch of lucidity.

"How is your mother, my dear? I haven't seen her for so long."

Clementine didn't know what to say. She used the excuse of settling herself on the proffered chair to gather her thoughts. Something inside her rebelled at the notion of lying outright. Deciding to fall back again on the truth—though this was a more melancholy truth—she took one of Lady Harcourt's hands in hers. The skin at the back of it seemed impossibly thin, like a bird's newly laid egg held up to the light. "I am so sorry to have to tell you that my mother died."

"Oh!" Tears gathered in the corners of eyes bracketed by fine lines. "I'm so sorry. What happened?"

"She contracted an infection of the lungs that lingered. She never fully recovered—she languished for years—and then one day she took a turn for the worse and she died about a fortnight later." Clementine left out that Lady Harcourt had been to visit her mother's bedside in those final days.

"Sometimes I am befogged about time," Lady Harcourt said quietly, picking up what looked like a tattered blanket that had been resting on the chair beside her.

"It is all right, my lady. What does Shakespeare say? 'We are all time's subjects'?"

Clementine thought for a moment that she had lost Lady Harcourt, for the older woman's eyes grew distant, as if she were turning inward, to a world Clementine couldn't see. But then she surprised them again with another question. "Do you remember the time we all went to Lydd-on-Sea?"

"I do!" She hadn't, until that moment, but sure enough the memory was there, waiting to be uncovered. Both families had made a trip to the seaside town. Traveling together wasn't something they'd been in the habit of doing, and to Clementine's memory, they'd never done it again. She had no sooner wondered why when Lady Harcourt supplied the answer. "We only went the one time because my husband doesn't care for traveling with your family."

"Oh!" Clementine pressed her lips together to suppress the laughter that was threatening and sought out Archie's gaze. He was already looking at her, and though he clearly shared her amusement, he made that same urgent gesture that seemed to mean he wanted her to keep the conversation going.

She turned back to the mother, feeling the son's gaze upon her. "I remember Archie and Olive and I nearly had our ears boxed on that trip because we wandered off and you and my mother feared we had drowned."

"Yes." Lady Harcourt tilted her head back and gazed at the leafy canopy above them. "How long ago was that?"

"Hmm. I was perhaps six or seven years of age, so that would have made it seventeen or eighteen years ago."

"My goodness, you're older than I thought! Time's subjects indeed! Did you marry Archibald?"

"Did I *marry* Archie?" Clementine was tempted, so tempted, to look at Archie then, but she was afraid the web they seemed to be spinning might break if she withdrew her attention from the countess, even for a moment. "No."

"Did you marry anyone else?"

She was struck again with twin urges: to laugh, and to look at Archie. She resisted both. "No, I remain unmarried."

"Oh, good. Then you can still marry Archibald."

Her face heated, despite the cool shade. Lady Harcourt had been insensible for who knew how long, but she had apparently chosen this moment to see with uncanny clarity. To see into Clementine's very soul, even. "I beg your pardon?"

"Give me one good reason why you should not." Lady Harcourt rotated her shoulders as she spoke, her tone peevish. She was growing agitated.

"I wonder if perhaps you ought to have this conversation with Archibald himself."

"I would if he was here."

"It happens he is."

"He is? Where?" She looked around.

Clementine made eye contact with Archie and gave him a little nod. It seemed worth a try.

After a moment of indecision that probably no one but Clementine recognized as such, he stepped forward. He had no chair, having given up his to Clementine, but he squatted near his mother's side.

"I'm here, Mother," he said, his voice raspy.

Clementine waited on bated breath, feeling like a mother bird must when she pushes her baby out of the nest.

"Archibald, I've been waiting for years for you to marry Clementine Morgan."

"Have you?" There were so many unshed tears in those two words.

"What on earth is taking you so long?"

Archie cleared his throat. "Well, I haven't asked her, for one thing."

"Oh, honestly. Well, that's easily remedied."

Archie's hand floated, shaking like a leaf caught in an eddy, an inch or so above his mother's arm. He was afraid to touch her. Clementine understood. It was the visual manifestation of that feeling she'd had earlier, of not wanting to break the delicate web connecting them—to each other and to this time and this place.

"And if you're worried about your father, you needn't be." Lady Harcourt rolled her eyes. "I can handle him."

"I have come to understand," Archie started slowly, "that trying to gain Father's approval has always been a futile endeavor." He let the hand float down and rest on her arm. "I'm more concerned about you. That you approve. For I love you so tremendously, Mother."

"And I love you, my boy. You have always been my greatest joy."

Archie made a kind of indistinct noise then and let his head fall to his mother's lap. Lady Harcourt's eyes grew startled, then confused. They were losing her. Clementine had to get her back.

"I think your mother is right, Archie. She always is. We should marry."

Archie's head whipped up.

"I can't imagine why we've waited so long, what with . . ."

Clementine had been trying to recapture the light, almost glib tone she'd used before, the one that seemed to have amused Lady Harcourt—to have reached her—but she found she could not continue in that vein. A lump rose in her throat, and she finished her sentence in a whisper, ". . . all that has passed between us."

He was studying her so intensely, it almost felt as if they were back in his bedchamber at Quintrell Castle.

"Young man," Lady Harcourt said sharply, drawing both their attention, "I believe this young lady is about to propose to you! How extraordinary." She narrowed her eyes at Archie. "What is your name, young man?"

Clementine's heart sank.

"Archie," Archie said.

"What is your surname? Who are your people?"

"I'm Archibald Fielding-Burton, Earl of Harcourt." He waited for recognition. There was none.

"Well, Archibald Fielding-Burton, Earl of Harcourt," Lady Harcourt said, "in my day . . ." She trailed off and looked around, the agitation from before reappearing. "In my day, we . . ." She picked up her teacup, looked at it in dismay, and let it clatter to its saucer. Tears gathered in the corners of her eyes. "I think I need to repose." She looked around, as the tears began to fall. "Is my mother here?"

Miss Brown, about whom Clementine had entirely forgotten, appeared out of nowhere, murmuring soothing words and giving Lady Harcourt her arm. Archie leapt to his feet and made to escort the women back to the house, but Miss Brown shook her head at him—not unkindly, but firmly. "You've had quite an exciting afternoon, Lady Harcourt, perhaps you would care to lie down?" She spoke resolutely, articulating the question as if it were not a question at all but a foregone conclusion. Lady Harcourt seemed to accept it as such, and allowed herself to be led away. When the women were halfway back to the house, Miss Brown called over her shoulder, "I find myself rather tired, my lord, and if you will excuse me, I think I shall rest in a chair by your mother while she sleeps."

And suddenly Clementine had what she had wanted for so long: a private audience with Archie.

Too bad she had no earthly idea what to say.

Archie was not the kind of person who believed in fate. He had not, after all, done anything to deserve the good fortune of being born heir to an earldom. Neither had he done anything to deserve the ill fortune of being born to a father who didn't respect him, or even love him, probably. It was all an accident, the result of a roll of the dice of the fates. If Archie believed in anything, it was honest work and good friends. Loyalty.

But at this moment, it did not feel like an accident that Clementine Morgan was standing before him in his garden, that they were alone together at last. That she had, for one brief, glorious moment, reached his mother.

He burst out laughing.

Which was entirely the wrong thing to do, judging by the war that broke out between confusion and hurt on Clementine's face.

He grabbed her hand and started towing her out of the garden. "I'm laughing because you're here."

No, that wasn't right, either.

"I'm laughing because if you knew the inane plot I'd cooked up to try to get you alone in London so I could talk to you, you would laugh, too. At the plot, and at how absurdly simple my goal turned out to be in the end. You simply appeared in my garden."

Her lovely, high laughter rang out across the blue afternoon. "It wasn't that simple. There was, in fact, a great deal of inane plotting required on *my* end."

"Well, then I should thank you." They had reached the edge of the manicured gardens. He kept going, steering them onto a gravel path that would shortly give way to dirt as it entered the forest. "For your plotting, and for what you did back there. For giving me my mother back."

"I think she gave herself back."

"Whatever the source of that interlude of lucidity, it was a gift."

They were under the cover of the trees now. This was, therefore, as good a place as any.

He brought her round to face him and took her other hand in his, his heart thudding. He hadn't practiced this, so focused had he been on the aforementioned inane planning. He'd written Effie and Simon with their roles in it—he'd been going to throw a party himself, at the London house, which he reasoned Sir Albert would not be able to refuse to attend, and Simon and Effie were to mount a distraction involving a broken heirloom soup tureen that they were meant to spill over Sir Albert, while Archie stole away with Clementine.

But here she was.

Here *he* was, tongue-tied.

Well, what course did he have but to come out with it? "I think we *should* marry."

There was an echo. He hadn't noticed that about this spot in the trees before.

Oh. Wait. That wasn't an echo; that was Clementine, saying the exact same thing: "I think we *should* marry."

Was it to be that easy? "All right," he agreed, as his heart soared. "Wait."

Ah. Apparently it wasn't to be that easy. Clementine's brow furrowed—deeply. "What is the matter, my dearest?"

"I won't be tamed. I can't be. I tried that. It didn't work out."

"I don't want to tame you. I want to love you."

Clementine burst into tears, suddenly and utterly, like Olive tended to do.

"I *do* love you," Archie clarified. "That is an unchangeable fact. What I want, I suppose, is to be able to do it publicly." He grinned. "And privately, too. Repeatedly."

She cried harder.

So he tried harder. "Not only do I not want to tame you, I want to be wild with you."

More tears. Well, in for a pound . . .

"I want to have wild children with you. I want them to be christened in the pond at Mollybrook and for them to grow up in the forest. I want to feed them nuts and berries and walk through mud puddles with them, and I want them to know every day how much they are loved.

"They will have an aunt, a loving grandfather, and two honorary uncles. They'll take their grandmother on picnics by the pond, and perhaps she will feel their love. Even if she doesn't know them, perhaps she will know, somehow, that they are *hers*.

"At night, we will look at the stars together and make up our own stories about them. We'll fall asleep outside, and I'll carry the children into the house and kiss their foreheads. And that . . ."

Those were all the words he had. The contents of his heart, articulated as best he could. "That is all I have to give you." He paused. "Well, there is the earldom, I suppose. You'd be a countess. But I rather fear that is not a mark in my favor."

She laughed.

That was a good sign—he hoped. It seemed better than tears, anyway.

"What do you say, Clem?"

"I say yes," she said quietly.

"Truly? You have abandoned your opposition to the notion of marrying?"

"I seem to have done," she said in wonderment. "I think perhaps I wasn't able to imagine being happily wed because I'd never considered marrying *you*." She shook her head as wonderment turned to bewilderment. "Though now I can't imagine why. It seems, in retrospect, obvious that we are well suited."

"We have both been rather dimwitted on the subject."

"Indeed."

"Of course, dimwitted goes without saying for me, but honestly, I expected better from you, Clem," he teased.

She tried to pull a face, but she was laughing—that high, lilting laughter he so loved winding around him like a warm quilt. "We're getting married!" he exclaimed.

"We're getting married!" she agreed, and he whooped and picked her up and twirled her around. As he set her down, he said, "Do you remember when you used to read novels in trees?"

"I do indeed. In fact, I've been thinking a great deal lately about those novels."

"In what way?"

"Well, I'd been thinking how real life is generally very unlike novels, but now I may have to revise that opinion."

"How so?"

"Well, I don't want to seem overconfident, but I believe I am about to marry an earl and live happily ever after?"

"You are indeed."

"Not that I care about the earl part, so perhaps it's better said that I am about to marry the person I love and admire most in the world and live happily ever after."

Oh, his heart. It was possible he wasn't going to survive this day. Well, at least he would die perfectly happy, sure of the love of both his mother and his . . . Clem.

He swallowed a lump in his throat. "I think we ought to go find a tree and climb up it. What do you say?"

She smiled, but very wickedly. "I say yes, but only if we may anticipate our marriage vows at the base of it first."

20

After the End

In novels, the happily ever after was generally the wedding. The heroine married the hero, and that was that.

Clementine had never cared much for the idea of a wedding, and that was understating it entirely.

Which wasn't to say she hadn't enjoyed hers. Allowing Olive to coo and fuss over her, to adorn her and generally treat her like a beloved doll had been rather enjoyable, once she surrendered to it.

And standing at the front of the chapel in Chiddington three weeks and two days after her visit to Mollybrook—Archie had spoken to her father and they'd had the banns called immediately after their reunion—had been surprisingly sentimental. There had been a moment, when she looked out into the pews to see the small but beloved crowd of guests, when she almost wept.

Father *did* weep.

Which, ironically, was what saved her from having to. In fact, it made her want to *laugh*. It did Olive, too, judging from the merry look her sister shot her at the sound of her father's first sob. Olive was wearing that ridiculous hat they'd had made to entrap the fictional Mr. Ozymandias Macduff. It featured not one but two Scottish crossbills, handsome black-and-red birds the milliner had managed to make almost alarmingly lifelike, and as Olive shook her head to stave off laughter, Clementine could almost believe one or both of them might take flight.

The wedding breakfast had been pleasant. Archie had seen to it that there was plenty she could eat. In fact, she could eat everything except a ham that he had made sure was placed at the far end of the table from her—and she noticed he didn't eat any of it, either. Archie's mother wasn't lucid during the meal, but she was calm and content, and Lord Marsden and Miss Brown took especial care of her.

But for Clementine, the real happy ending came that evening. She changed out of her wedding finery, donned her favorite blue dress and yellow shawl, and made her way outside.

"Lady Harcourt!" Lord Featherfinch called. "Huzzah!" She tried to tell him and Lord Marsden, who were scrambling to their feet, not to get up on her account.

Archie, by contrast, did not get up. He merely laid on the carpet they'd spread out under the big beech tree and gazed up at her with love that was so plain, and looked so long-standing, that she marveled again that she hadn't seen it before. They really had been daft, the pair of them.

"May I make you a plate?" Lord Marsden asked. Archie had ordered up a vegetarian picnic dinner for them and their friends, complete with the pears everyone loved.

"I still can't believe you're spending your wedding night with us!" Olive exclaimed.

"Come now," Archie, finally coming to seated, said. "It's just dinner." He shot Clementine an alarmed look. "It *is* just dinner, yes?"

"Yes," she said laughingly. And to Olive, she added, "I couldn't imagine anything I wanted to do more this evening than to dine al fresco at Mollybrook with my sister and my friends."

Everyone made murmurs of appreciation and agreement.

"Olive," said Archie, "we do have some post-wedding travel plans. We're leaving next month for Italy."

"Oh, are you?" Olive grasped her hands together beneath her chin. "How wonderful!"

"We should like you to come with us," Archie added. "For neither your sister nor I speak Italian. We'll enjoy ourselves ever so much more with someone who's fluent."

Olive burst into tears, and as Lord Featherfinch comforted her, Archie met Clementine's gaze. Clementine had no particular interest in a honeymoon, but when Archie proposed a trip—and that Olive join them on said trip—she could not refuse.

"Yes," Archie said. "We'll go to Rome, of course, and Venice and such. But you shall also have to endure long detours through Lombardy, I'm afraid, for my wife . . ." He paused and shot Clementine a wink as if the phrase "my wife" were a private jest. "My wife is determined to get her feet wet in Lake Como." He smiled. "And I am determined that my wife shall have whatever she wants."

That stopped Olive's tears, and she rolled her eyes, albeit affectionately. "Clementine, you are so lucky. I would almost hate you if I didn't love you so."

Clementine winked at her sister and said, "Oh, but you have Mr. Macduff, remember." The sisters had continued to spin the tale of Mr. Ozymandias Macduff. It was a diversion that seemed to amuse Olive, and Olive, who had indeed found Ralph Scully's grave with Clementine by her side, needed all the diversion she could get. "I'm sure you'll be able to bring him up to scratch . . . if he ever shows up." The sisters burst into laughter and waved away the gentlemen's puzzled inquiries.

"Where will you gentlemen go for Earls Trip next year?" Olive asked. "And may I gate-crash again?"

"No, you may not, Olive," Clementine said, just as Lord Featherfinch said, "Oh, *would* you?" Clementine had never told Olive about her eavesdropping in the corridor that night, but it seemed that her sister and Lord Featherfinch had indeed become bosom friends.

"I am in jest," Olive said smilingly to the gentlemen. "I'd been meaning to propose to my sister that she and I take up our own tradition during that fortnight in September." She made a silly face. "For I know that the year the sacred masculine tradition of Earls Trip was disrupted was but an aberration."

"We could go on our own trip, now that I am a respectable married lady," Clementine suggested.

"We could, but remember you are already—apparently—taking me to Italy! I suggest we hole up here at Mollybrook and tromp around in the woods while the gentlemen are gone." Clementine started to protest. Happily, her entire life was henceforth going to be holing up at Mollybrook and tromping around in the woods. She needn't impose such on her sister, who had gently told Clementine this morning that she planned to return to London after the wedding. But Olive cut off her objection. "I'm sure we can think of a mutually agreeable plan, Clemmie. I was merely teasing the gentlemen." She turned to them. "But I do wish to know where you're going next year."

"We haven't talked about it," Archie said. "The next trip is Marsden's to plan."

"I'd been thinking I'd like to see the Royal Pavilion in Brighton," Lord Marsden said. "I don't know that it will be finished, but I understand it's already quite the feat of engineering by Mr. Nash."

"A fine idea," Archie said.

"Ah, yes, staring at an unfinished building," Lord Featherfinch said wryly. "At least we can go sea bathing."

Clementine smiled and let the good-natured bickering of her friends wash over her. After they'd eaten and Archie, being none-too-subtle about it, had hinted that their guests should retire for the evening, she lay on her back on the carpet and looked at the sky. It was a deep, inky blue, navy fingers between the branches of the tree she lay under.

The tree *they* lay under.

Archie rolled over and started undoing her chignon. She had

noticed, in the weeks they'd spent anticipating their marriage vows, that he liked to tangle his fingers in her hair.

She liked having them there, so she assisted with the removal of the pins keeping her elaborate wedding coiffure in place. When they were done, he laid her back down and loomed over her, adding his dark silhouette to that of the branches above him, which were now difficult to discern from the blackening blue of the sky. "Clem," he said seriously, "we're home now, you and I, aren't we?"

"Yes," she said, for they were.

A fortnight later

"My lord." The new footman entered a parlor at Highworth where Effie was attempting to paint a gravestone.

Effie had been inspired by Olive Morgan's embroidery and had a mind to send her the finished painting. Though unlike her creation, his did not depict a particular gravestone—it wasn't her Ralph's. That was why he'd thought he could paint from his imagination. But as the interruption prompted him to ponder his progress, he realized his efforts might have been improved had he taken his easel outside and found a model.

"What does this look like to you?" he asked the footman.

"It is a gravestone, is it not?"

"It is!" Effie was cheered. Perhaps his efforts were not as feeble as he'd feared.

"A gravestone against a chartreuse sky," the footman added.

It was. Drat. Effie had intended for the painting to be somber. It was of a cemetery, after all. But then he'd decided perhaps a gravestone at twilight might feel a tad less oppressive. So he'd added some cobalt, intending to lighten the background ever so slightly.

And now, somehow, he had a chartreuse sky.

He sighed. He wasn't sure what was wrong with him lately. It was almost as if he was . . . happy?

"My lord," the footman said, "I am told that letters arriving addressed to a Miss Euphemia Turner are to be delivered to you."

"Yes!" Effie stood so abruptly that he disturbed his easel, and the footman had to lunge to save the ridiculous painting. He cleared his throat and tried again. "Yes, thank you. That will be all."

A letter from her. *Finally.*

He waited an eternity as the footman righted the easel, crossed the room, and bowed.

The moment the door shut behind the servant, Effie tore open the letter's seal with hands gone inexplicably clumsy.

Miss Euphemia Turner
Highworth, Cornwall

From the desk of
Miss Julianna Evans, editrix
Le Monde Joli

October 20, 1821
London

Dear Euphemia,
  You know I am economical with praise. (What did you call me? A "notoriously picksome nit-picker"? I still maintain that is an oxymoron beneath someone with literary capabilities such as yours.) So you will appreciate that when I say that your latest sonnet is very good, what I truly mean is that I was <u>transported</u> by it. While I'm ever so sorry it was inspired by the loss of your dear Sally, may I be so bold as to suggest that Sally's demise has not been in vain? You have performed a kind of alchemy here: a transmutation of grief into beauty.
  I am rather vexed, though, that I didn't save your letter for the evening. The reading of your verse—and reading of it and reading of it and reading of it—positively ruined me for productive labor today. In fact, I canceled all the meetings I was meant to take—I even pushed off a visit to the printer to inspect the

*proofs for next month's issue—except for my weekly tea with
Mr. Glanvil, which of course I could not duck.*

*Which brings me to a tangent. (I shall return to the matter of
the astonishing "Lamenter, Be Not Proud" momentarily.) You
are aware that Mr. Glanvil is a source of endless frustration for
me. And that since he is also the source of my wages, I must
handle him with a delicate touch. You are not aware, because I
have not cared to burden our correspondence with such fripperies, that he has cooked up a scheme by which the magazine is to
print a regular column entitled "Advice for Married Ladies." I
have so far fended him off, reminding him that we are not the
Lady's Monthly Museum, but I fear he is insistent. And as he
likes to point out, he is the publisher. Alas.*

*I was having trouble paying attention to him—well, more
trouble than usual—because of that dratted poem of yours. It
would not loosen its grasp on my mind. But then it receded just
long enough for me to be struck with the most brilliant idea. I
told Mr. Glanvil that upon reflection, I agreed with him, that
a column providing advice to married ladies on manners of de-
cor, household management, and the achievement of marital
harmony would, in fact, be just the thing—and that I knew
the ideal lady to dispense this advice. Who is she? he asked.
Oh, I responded, a married lady of some years, a gentlewoman
with a spotless reputation, mother of six, overseer of a refined
and happy household, et cetera, et cetera. He thought that
sounded fine. Of course, I added, the lady would need to remain anonymous—her own marital harmony depended upon
it. I expected him to object, but he was delighted by this twist.
While Mr. Glanvil is intent upon stuffing my magazine with
the most mawkish drivel, I must admit he does sometimes have
an eye for the dramatic in a way that sells magazines.*

*So what say you, dearest? If I have to subject myself—and
my readers—to a monthly dose of "Advice for Married Ladies,"
how grand would it be for you to be at its helm? My motivation
for asking you is twofold. First, I would be endlessly amused by*

the secret knowledge that my advice-giver is not at all who is advertised. Well, you are a lady, of course, but not a married one. Second, and all jesting aside, you have a clear-eyed yet compassionate outlook I truly believe will benefit our readers. It would benefit anyone; I know it has me. The job would pay two shillings a column, payable quarterly by bank note.

If you accept, I will of course continue to print your poems. (And to reject them; I do note your acceptance rate has been creeping up of late, and in case you were worried that our friendship has influenced matters, let me assure you it is quite the reverse. If anything, as the years slip by and my regard for you increases, my editorial standards sharpen, if only to avoid any occurrence of favoritism.)

Now, on to the matter at hand. You, my dear lady, my dear Effie, have a way of seeing the world that is at once buoying and devastating in its truth. I would be honored to print this poem as is, but I would not be myself if I did not have a few minor suggestions, which I enclose herewith.

Yours,
Julianna

P.S. I do hope you have fully recovered from your bout with that unfortunate patch of hogweed. I must confess, though, your account of such was amusing enough that I spat out my tea whilst reading it.

Effie set the letter down and smiled. He wasn't remotely qualified to dispense advice for married ladies, but oh, what fun this was going to be.

He picked up his paintbrush. Who said the sky couldn't be chartreuse?

Acknowledgments

I want to thank my sister, Erin. If you know my books, you know that I'm usually a minimalist when it comes to acknowledgments. Not today! I want to start by saying that my sister and I are not Clem and Olive. People often ask me if my books are autobiographical, and the answer is always *No.* But the truth is that sometimes autobiographical bits do make their way in. These are not bits of fact, but tendrils of feeling. My sister and I have known what it is like to be constitutionally different but to be sisters. To be different but the same. To have the same points of reference, the same inputs, even if they have led to different outputs. The older one gets, the less these divergent outputs seem to matter. The last few years have shown me what a gift it is to have a sister, to have *my* sister. That gift, *her*, has been the silver lining of all that has befallen us, and the world, these recent years. So, Josie: thank you for being there, for being you. I feel like I should end on an inside joke here. I hardly know where to start; we are lucky we have so many. Perhaps I will just say, *See you on the roller coaster.*

Everyone else matters, too! First and foremost, Courtney Miller-Callihan, who rolled with the punches, as she always does. When I was like, *Hey, what about we interrupt this program with a Regency that has nothing to do with anything?* she was like, *YES.*

Kelly Bowen, who talked to me about this idea when it was an ill-formed mess, and who read about it when it was only slightly more formed.

Sandra Owens, who read an early draft, as she always does, but also was in receipt of approximately one million texts about this book and the circumstances surrounding its writing and somehow did not divorce me.

Emma Barry, who also read an early draft and came back with the clear-eyed but encouraging feedback that is her hallmark.

Rose Lerner, who helped with an eleventh-hour research question, shared her considerable expertise with me on matters parliamentary (though of course, any errors are mine), and soothed my anxieties with her thoughtful take on historical romance.

Finally, to everyone at Kensington, particularly Elizabeth May. You guys *got* this book from the start, and I'm so lucky to be working with you all.

Look for Effie's story in MANIC PIXIE DREAM EARL,
coming in Spring 2025!

Visit our website at
KensingtonBooks.com
to sign up for our newsletters, read
more from your favorite authors, see
books by series, view reading group
guides, and more!

Become a Part of Our
Between the Chapters Book Club
Community and Join the Conversation

Submit your book review for a chance to win exclusive
Between the Chapters swag you can't get anywhere else!
https://www.kensingtonbooks.com/pages/review/